VALOR OF THE NORSEMEN

JERRY AUTIERI

1

Orange flames twisted into the sky, streaming off thatched roofs. Wind fed the blaze and smeared black smoke across the pale morning. Yngvar coughed, his throat roughened both from bitter smoke and from shouting orders. He frowned and leaned on his shield. His crew had spread out through the Danish village to handle the tedium of chasing down stragglers and herding prisoners.

The prisoners, he noted, were the typical hopeless and poverty-stricken families that dared resettle a village only burned out two summers ago. Anyone with better choices would have gone else-where. The haggard women and their bony children staggered between Yngvar's warriors, who loomed over them as war gods dressed in mail and carrying colorful round shields across their backs.

None of the captives made any protest. They went like sheep to shearing. A pathetic lot forgotten by the gods and noticed by the Fates long enough to have the threads of their lives tangled with suffering.

Yngvar spit in the grass, trying to expel a bitter taste that would never be scraped from his tongue.

Bjorn and Gyna picked over the corpses of the few warriors that had faced them this morning. They were bold men, these Danes. Yngvar had raised enough noise in his approach to be heard in Valhalla. The fools had chosen to defend their homes. How could they have loved this place enough to die for it when they could not have lived here longer than two years? The last time he had burned these hovels everyone had been slain or enslaved. Perhaps they had nothing left to live for.

Gyna fell back as she wrested off a boot from one of the pale corpses. Bjorn held a sword up to the light, appraising it with his single eye as if it might be worth a kingdom of gold.

He then flung the weapon into the field behind him.

Distant shouts echoed from the surrounding woods. No doubt his men had run down those who had fled. Yngvar had no desire to chase these fools, but his men needed both the exertion and the belief they pursued someone of great wealth.

Otherwise they would get nothing on this raid.

"Lord, I believe this village is no longer capable of sheltering a Dane invasion force."

Alasdair stood to Yngvar's left, his own shield still strapped to his arm. Yngvar imagined the frown on his bright, smooth face matched his own. The youngest and smallest of the Wolves, Alasdair had proven himself as formidable as a man twice his size. Moreover, he was smart and swift.

"Nor could it have done so two years ago when we first burned it to the ground. But King Hakon fears the Danes will one day launch their ships from this point. So we watch this coast and sweep away whatever grows back."

Thorfast stood to Yngvar's right, but his sword was still in its sheath and shield on his back. He flipped his long, pale hair over his shoulder as he snorted at Yngvar's comment.

"Yes, we scrape this coast like we scrape barnacles from our hulls. And it's about as entertaining."

Yngvar chewed on his mustache as he watched his men pile their booty in the field. Thus far he noted junk someone hoped might be worth a bit of silver, but he did see several cooking pots. At least cooking pots could be traded without trouble. Livestock came next, spindly-legged goats and chickens. He had hoped for a cow, but such a luxury was beyond the means of these people.

Slaves formed the largest part of his reward for today's service. The women might fetch a decent price, but children were always questionable. Some paid well for healthy children, but those looking for strong backs to row ships or haul goods saw them as worthless in the short-term. Buyers paid for what they thought a slave could do in the coming months. Too often, they did not live much longer than that.

He had more children than women today, and the remaining men were the old and ill. Anyone strong enough to be a worthy slave had died defending this burning trash heap.

"I expect less than five pounds of silver from this," Yngvar said. "And that is if the children sell for more than they are worth."

"Lord, perhaps King Hakon will take them?" Alasdair asked.

Yngvar smiled. "You think he will be a good master because he is a Christian? Think harder on that point, my friend. I can't count all the Christians who buy slaves and return for more at the next market because they accidentally beat the last one to death."

Alasdair shrugged. "King Hakon is a just man. He would not beat a slave unless he deserved it."

"Nice of you to think of these wretches' welfare," Thorfast said. "But you might have noticed we've a crew to pay? They expect a reward for risking their lives, and a few cooking pots and Uncle Harold's favorite drinking horn won't be enough. If King Hakon took these captives, he'd pay a lot less than we can get at market."

"You've never been a slave," Alasdair said. "It is a hard thing to see done to children."

"Let's not argue," Yngvar said, rubbing his face. "We are done here. Thorfast is right. And this is not the first time we've taken prisoners, Alasdair. Your trip home seems to have softened your heart."

Alasdair lowered his head and touched the silver cross that now hung always about his neck. He claimed it had saved his life, though as of yet Yngvar had not learned the full tale of Alasdair's journey home. His cousin, Calum, had been found enslaved. Perhaps the fresh reminder that Fate could be cruel to anyone left its mark on Alasdair's heart.

He shrugged his shield back over his shoulder, then patted Alasdair's arm.

"Fate rules all," he said, his voice soft and nearly lost behind the crackling flames of the burning village. "If it is not us to enslave them this day, then others would tomorrow. A man cannot slip his doom, no matter how he wishes it otherwise."

They joined Bjorn and Gyna, who had decided nothing interested them and now idled with a dozen of the crewmen. Gyna was already prodding some of the women prisoners like they were calves to be slaughtered. Yngvar thought it cruel, but even Gyna needed to have her fun. Otherwise, she would vent her frustrations elsewhere and likely to Yngvar's loss.

"What a shitty raid," Bjorn said. "A bunch of shriveled cunts and their runts for a prize."

"My, you're poetic this morning," Thorfast said.

"If it ain't the truth. What did I risk my life for?"

"You didn't risk anything," Thorfast said. "Your stink alone killed half these men."

Their laughter jarred the prisoners, who flinched as if they had been lashed.

Yngvar and the rest fell to companionable silence as they watched warriors returning empty handed from the surrounding woods. The village was set inland from the coast, but sat a short distance from a large shingle where a score of ships could beach. That was the attraction for this place and the reason for Hakon's fears. Yngvar wished he had a way to destroy that shingle and its tranquil harbor rather than have to kill and enslave those who settled too close to it.

Wind blew the black smoke flat to the roofs. The grass sighed and a goat bleated.

Then he heard shouting.

His Wolves—Thorfast, Bjorn, Alasdair, and Gyna—recognized

the threat the same moment he did. The rest of the crew were too absorbed in their own concerns, thinking the danger long done.

"That's not our crew," Yngvar said.

"And not our numbers," Thorfast added.

"To the ship!" Yngvar shouted. He sloughed his shield onto his arm and drew his sword. The crew closest to him stared up at his shining blade. The prisoners did as well. But Yngvar read their dreadful expressions.

They glowed with hope.

"Hurry!" He grabbed a man by his mail sleeve and pulled him. "Are you deaf?"

The distant roar of approaching enemies answered for him. The fire and smoke had deadened the noise of their approach as well as guided them atop Yngvar's position.

He ran down the line, pulling men away and setting them running. With every heavy footfall he cursed his own hubris. Never count an enemy finished on his own land. He had indulged his crew rather than follow his good sense. Now they would all pay.

The Danes emerged screaming from the tree line. Scores of men in leather and furs with axes and spears raised for battle. Their faded and beaten shields spoke to hard use. Even from this distance, their eyes were white with hatred.

"Don't fight!" Yngvar shouted at a line of men preparing to shield wall. "We're outnumbered!"

Unlike the Danes, Yngvar and his warriors were hampered with heavy chain and thick shields. They were unmovable in a shield wall. But in flight, they plodded like oxen in a muddy field.

Thorfast sounded the warning horn, three long blasts. He looked as if he were guzzling ale as he leaned back. The handful of guards left by the ship would hear, or so Yngvar hoped, and have it launched and ready for escape.

Some of his men would die, those who had ventured after their prizes unworthy of their cost. If they hadn't been run down yet, they would soon be.

The slaves scattered, women and children adding their horrified

5

shrieks to the demonic song of a burning village and battle-hungry warriors. A woman in a pale green dress fled in front of Yngvar, and he trampled her like a withered stalk as he fled for the ship. His feet caught up in her, and Alasdair caught him before he fell.

"Lord, they are coming fast. Hurry!"

At least fifty Danes were at their back, enough to outnumber his full crew which he no longer had. His men had broken up and melted away the moment the enemy arrived in force. But even with his delay, Yngvar was ahead of his enemies.

He ran a dozen more paces to the slope that led to the beach, and his stomach clenched.

A score or more Danish spearmen had gotten behind him. They had killed the ship guards, leaving the vessels leaning placidly in the gentle surf.

"Thor, send your hammer down on their heads!" Yngvar shouted. "Hurry, break them before a shield wall is set."

Bjorn went screaming past Yngvar. His ax raised overhead like the mast of some great longship cruising into battle. Gyna was shrieking right behind him, her shield and short sword drawn. She was as crazed as his cousin, Yngvar thought.

"Follow them!" he shouted at his warriors appearing over the slope. "Kill everyone on the beach!"

The Danes formed a rough shield wall, having only just dispatched the men guarding the ship. Flaming torches whirled through the air and landed on the deck.

"Shit!" Yngvar cursed, realizing this was not an opportunistic attack but a Danish trap. They were going to burn his ship and surround him onshore. They knew he would be here.

Bjorn hurtled into the line, heedless of the spears that turned to him. The gods loved Bjorn more than they loved any man. He sent them headless heroes to fill the benches of Valhalla. These went on to Odin's hall by the dozens whenever Bjorn let his madness consume him. In return, the gods turned aside spears and arrows, broke shields and bent swords wherever he fought.

For he shattered through the thin Danish line as if he had merely kicked a rotted door out of its frame. A head spun through the air, spraying gore over his former spear-brothers. The body reeled back along with another that left its arm where the rest of the body had once stood.

Now Yngvar, Thorfast, and the others fell upon the shield wall. Their work was harder, for the gods favored but did not depend upon them as they did Bjorn. The Danes shoved back with their shields. A spear blade skittered across Yngvar's shoulder, deflected by his mail armor.

He did not strike high like an untrained fool. Instead his blade sought thighs and knees. Put a man on the ground and he would soon be dead. No sense wasting strength attempting to take a head when a strong jab to the top of the knee would suffice.

Cursing and screaming mingled with the hiss of waves lapping the shore. The foam soon turned pink as men on both sides of the clash collapsed into the sea's edge.

Yngvar leapt for the ship, stepping atop a face-down corpse to drive himself forward. The Danes had broken and now fled along the water's edge. No one chased but for Bjorn.

"Get that fool back here," Yngvar shouted at Gyna. She was sprayed with blood, leaning over a man rolling in the waves. "We need his strength."

More of his crewmen poured over the crest. They flowed down toward the ship, screaming.

"Alasdair, get to the tiller. Thorfast, give me your shoulder here." Yngvar splashed through the cold seawater and put his shoulder against the rough hull. Thorfast joined him along with three other men.

The longship was new and sturdy. King Hakon had gifted it to him after he had lost his own ship in Ireland. This one was light but sturdy. It skipped the waves and seemed to float above the beach. It slid into the water, righting itself as it raised on the waves.

Crewmen were already crashing knee-deep into the water and lunging over the ship rails.

With a glance, Yngvar saw Bjorn running with Gyna hauling him by the arm. In another circumstance, he might have laughed at this vision of a hen-pecked husband. He allowed a smile, then pulled himself aboard.

Men scrabbled aboard as the Danes drove them into the sea. Adventurous enemies followed, but Yngvar's crew cast spears at the first Danes to close. Only a handful needed to spear an enemy to dissuade the rest from closing.

Alasdair surrendered the tiller to Hamar, the traditional steersman. He reversed the ship easily, having moved the rudder from one end to the other. Other crewmen struck the sails and the wind filled it.

Yngvar shouted his challenge to the Danes gathered on the shore. The enemy lined up behind round shields painted red, green or white. They were a poor band, but had enough numbers to keep Yngvar pinned. Had he taken up their challenge, heavier troops were likely behind these skirmishers.

He staggered to the side as the ship lurched over a steep wave. The rest of his crew raised their weapons in defiance. The Danes did the same.

"Both sides too stupid to bring bows to the fight," Thorfast said, grabbing the rail to steady himself. "Look at them lined up. We could've feathered them good, and they could've kept us from fleeing if they had brains enough to shoot."

"Let's count this a boon from the gods," Yngvar said. "For I think they were sent to hold us down for the real warriors yet to arrive. This was a trap. One we barely slipped."

Yngvar scanned his crew. All of them wore fresh blood like stolen jewels. Whether it was their own or a foeman's, they took to the oars with fresh strength and shot the ship toward the open sea. Despite the chaos, he guessed five of his thirty men had died or otherwise not made it to the ship.

The narrow bay was like a miniature fjord. Land spread out on both sides like hands cupping the water into a gentle current. It was deep water, making a fine home for ships. No doubt next time he had to visit this shore, Gorm the Old, king of the Danes, would have built a fortress here. Only the rocky, high sides of the land masses flanking the bay made a seaside fort impossible without a major excavation.

Yngvar let a sigh escape and turned away from the ever-diminishing enemy still watching from the shore.

"Lord," Alasdair said. "Why are they trying to follow us?"

"What?" Yngvar turned, squinting back to where columns of smoke marked the morning's carnage. Alasdair's eyes were sharper, and now Yngvar marked what he had. Men were climbing into the rocks and scrabbling over the rough ground to keep pace with Yngvar's ship.

"They have no chance to catch us," Thorfast said. "They're probably just battle-crazed boys too stupid to know they're beat. They want to impress their elders with their spirit."

But Yngvar noted more of the Danes following the first few. He turned to the edge of the bay. The prow of his ship slashed through the waves as it sped toward the open sea. The rocks and trees to his left were blurs of green and brown.

"It's an ambush," Yngvar said so calmly that no one roused to the warning. Instead of convincing anyone, he rushed to the tiller and bowled Hamar aside.

He grabbed the handle and hauled hard to the starboard side. The light and responsive ship turned as if it glided on ice. But the sudden shift sent standing men grasping for a hold.

"What are you doing?" Hamar shouted, more from shock than anger.

The answer came as a Danish longship launched from behind the tip of the rocks that marked the end of the bay.

Its deck was crowded with warriors cursing and shouting, screaming their ship forward with the strength of their wrath.

No one had a moment to react. Men who had just racked their shields now reached for them again.

The Danish ship flew like an arrow. Had Yngvar not pulled his own ship aside, the enemy would have hit them broadside.

Still, the Danes flew with such force that their ship clipped Yngvar's hull, shattering oars that had not been withdrawn in time.

"Shields up!" Yngvar shouted.

Archers were ready in the Danish ship. Their own collision had decked some of them, but enough remained upright to loose their arrows.

Shafts clattered into Yngvar's deck, slamming into the rails and mast. Others thumped shields and others bore into flesh. Men screamed and cursed.

Alasdair fell back, a white streak of an arrow driving into him.

Yngvar spared a moment to consider his friend. Boarding hooks were already biting into the fresh wood of his rails.

"Cut us free!" Yngvar ordered. "They'll never catch us on the open sea!"

Danes leapt across the short gap. But Yngvar's own crew used oars and spears to shove away the enemy vessel. The next Dane to leap found the gap widened, and splashed into the dark sea.

Yngvar hacked away the rope from another hook. He looked up in time to see the arrow pointed at his head.

"There he is! Yngvar Hakonsson!"

He ducked behind the rails, feeling the air rip over his head. The mangled words of the Danish language grated on his ears. But he heard the enemy calling for him.

"Face us, coward! Get your due, Yngvar!"

He hugged to the gunwales and crawled across to where Bjorn stood with legs wide. He held a Danish boarder by the throat so that his feet dangled as he struggled for life.

"We're free!" Hamar shouted.

"Get to the oars," Yngvar ordered. He stood, expecting another arrow. But the gap had widened enough for his ship to speed away. The Danes were cursing him, spinning new hooks for a final attempt to stop their ship.

Bjorn roared, shaking the hapless Dane in both hands. Then he flung his victim to the deck. He rode him down, slamming the Dane's head onto the hard deck boards until his skull broke.

"We're away," Thorfast said, breathless.

"That was a near thing, lord."

Alasdair stood, holding a broken arrow shaft in his hand. He held it up with a boyish smile.

"Your god protects you," Yngvar said.

"It snapped when it hit my cloak. A thumb-width to the left and it would've taken me in the guts."

The ship rocked as it clipped over the waves. Bleeding men, red-faced and shimmering with sweat, pulled the oars with all their strength. The Danes behind him shouted as their prey escaped.

"You'll not escape, Yngvar Hakonsson! We will find you!"

2

The fjords of Norway's southeastern coast were a comforting sight to Yngvar and his crew. The dark green trees and rocky hills were shrouded in mist. Birds darted through the milky distance, their calls lost to the water sloshing along the hull of the ship. The coolness of the trees seemed to reach out to Yngvar across the waves. He allowed himself a moment to sit on his sea chest and let the cool spray relax him.

Rowing had been hard across the North Sea. The Danes had pursued a brief distance, and were now long lost beyond the horizon. No matter how much they had wanted Yngvar's head, he doubted the Danes would be willing to approach Norway's coast without far more than a single warship.

They bumped along the coast north into shipping traffic. Their ship traveled in peace. With their shields racked, everyone knew them for a friend. At last they turned into the fjord that would lead them to Hauger where King Hakon built his feasting hall. In recent years he had been more inclined to spend his days in the western and southern coasts. But his great mead hall sat atop the highest point of Hauger as a reminder to everyone that his authority remained over this town and the countryside around it.

Once docked and assembled on the shore, Yngvar and his crew

shuffled back to their meager hall. Alasdair went with two men to announce their arrival to Hakon's chiefs. Hakon himself might not even be present. Hauger was alive with traders and farmers both. Their haggling shook walls. A dozen scents from the rancid to the sweet filled the air.

"Well, a fucking waste," Bjorn said as he walked into their mead hall.

"The king will reward us," Yngvar said. "And we have fulfilled another task of his."

Thorfast entered behind Bjorn and rolled his eyes at Yngvar. "This hall is a wreck. I say we return directly to Grenner and spend our summer nights by Brandr's hearth. There is no joy here anymore."

The majority of Yngvar's crewmen sheltered with him, while others had family or lovers to offer them other beds. After long days at sea, everyone went elsewhere to get a break from the same faces. Only Yngvar and his Wolves returned to the hall. Even their small number felt crowded under this dark roof.

"Enough complaints," Yngvar said, settling his sword and pack against a wall. He then pulled up the closest bench, too tired to bother walking to the high table. He rubbed his temples and closed his eyes, letting the throbbing in his head settle.

The raid had been successful by King Hakon's standards. By Yngvar's own, it had been a disaster. They would take nothing back from this raid besides Hakon's thanks and a measure of generosity meted out in the least amount of silver he could pay. The crew would have enough to waste on drink and women, and some might be set aglow by the king's praise. Yet Yngvar and those who hoped for more would have to wait for a new raid.

Gyna fetched them all stale beer. Yngvar was grateful for anything in his current mood, and slurped the mug dry in one go. Mag, the witch-woman who watched the hall and its servants while they were away, had returned. She only had words for Gyna, and Yngvar ignored their chatter as he stared at the gray wood wall.

The long day passed, and Alasdair reported King Hakon was due back in two days. At that time they could present themselves. In the meantime, they were to come to his hall and avail themselves of his better food and drink.

"We were betrayed," Yngvar said to Alasdair, who now sat beside him. "The Danes knew we were coming and laid a trap."

"Not a clever one, lord. It smelled of something done in haste."

"Right," Bjorn said. He slapped the table, sitting across from Yngvar with Gyna pressed to his side. He fixed Yngvar with his single eye. "I say Loki whispered news of our raid, just before we arrived."

"As much as the gods meddle with us," Yngvar said, "I think a more human culprit is at work."

"Someone in Hakon's hall?" Thorfast sat at the head of the table, as if he expected to command their attention.

"Where else?" Yngvar shrugged. "Our own men would not pass on such news, unless they spoke unawares to a spy."

They fell silent. Yngvar remained as he had all afternoon, resting his chin on the palm of his hands. None of his thoughts turned to anything good.

"Still, we succeeded, and our deeds will be praised," he said at last. "It was a shame to have left our riches on the beach, meager as they were. We carried nothing back of any worth."

The rest grumbled and nodded. Only Gyna lowered her head and folded her hands in her lap. Her dark eyes fluttered and refused to look at anyone. Her high cheek-bones reddened.

"Actually," she said, her voice only audible for the complete silence of the others. "It wasn't a total failure."

She pulled her hand out from beneath the table. She set gold cross as large as her palm on the table. Ruby chips decorated it. The gold was deep orange and the rubies lusterless. Still, against the worn gray wood of the table it seemed like priceless treasure.

Yngvar's eyes widened and Thorfast gasped. Bjorn shifted on his bench to give her a skeptical look with his single eye.

"Now where'd you pluck that from, woman?"

Gyna gave a weak smile. "One of the Danes had it hidden in his boot, wrapped in dirty cloth. He must've stole it."

"And you weren't going to share it?" Bjorn asked. "Don't make my only eye fill with tears."

"I'm sharing it now," she said, then clicked her tongue. "I just wanted to hold on to it for a bit. If the others saw it, they'd all want it cut up and divided."

Yngvar collected it off the board, giving Gyna a brief nod. He struggled to keep the smile off his mouth and not gush with relief.

"You did well," Yngvar said.

"I did?" Gyna asked, eyes widening.

"She did?" Bjorn asked, shifting back around on his bench. "Looks like she was thinking of keeping it herself."

"I was not!" Gyna punched Bjorn's shoulder, though her face reddened.

Yngvar weighed the gold in his palm. It was warm from Gyna's flesh. He believed as Bjorn did, but it only mattered that she surrendered the gold. Everyone shared the spoils of battle equally, but the leader took the best portion. A good leader, as Yngvar considered himself, would return his part to the pool of loot. Gold and silver could be retaken or mined from the earth. The loyalty and goodwill of men, however, were treasures both scarce and hard-won.

"We can sell this for more gold than it's worth cut up," Yngvar said. "Our master trader, Thorfast, can talk someone into spending more than the weight of the gold alone."

Yngvar handed the cross to Thorfast, who raised it to his appraising gaze.

"Shine those stones," Yngvar said. "Burnish that gold. Then weave a story of how we carried this from some Irish bishop who cried holy tears over it every night while praying in the golden light of heaven. Someone will open his purse for that."

"Lord, that's blasphemy," Alasdair said, touching his own silver cross.

"It's good business," Thorfast said. He clacked the cross onto the table. "If your heart ails you, then give your share of the sale to your church. King Hakon is building enough of them now that you'll have a choice."

Now Alasdair's face turned red, and he turned aside. Yngvar and the rest laughed, but when it seemed the jibe cut deeper than intended, he waved the group to silence.

"However it is done, we need to show our men some gain greater than what King Hakon awards us. Else the men might be more inclined to follow him rather than us."

The majority of his crew were new men come to share in the glory of the name he had made for himself by raiding the Danish coast. For many this was their first raid, and to have it end with a narrow escape would cause many to doubt their choices. Even if men held to their oaths, if their belief wavered even by a shadow's width, they would collapse in a close battle. Yngvar needed loyal men who believed gold and glory waited for them just across the waves.

They spent the following days as guests in King Hakon's hall. They regaled his hirdmen with exaggerated stories of bravery and valor. Even his newest men took heroic roles in the retelling of their raid. Yet they might have done nothing more than row across the sea to bang their swords upon their shields. The Danes had not offered a heroic fight, only slaughter.

The night before King Hakon returned, Thorfast had found his buyer and invited him along with six of the buyer's guards to their hall. Yngvar had found other duties for his crew, and now only the Wolves remained. All men were seated around the high table, wooden mugs foaming with warm beer.

"This is truly a holy relic?" The buyer weighed the cross on a scale that sat at the center of the table. His name was Dagby and he had cool eyes and a constant expression of distaste. He placed weights until the cross balanced and raised his eyes.

"You want more for it than its weight in gold," Dagby said, folding blue-veined hands atop the table. "The stones are mere chips, hardly worth the extra cost."

"I swear it on my name," Thorfast said. "That we carried this from the tomb of a Christian saint. He was an Irish bishop as well. Seems he made dogs speak and snakes dance on their tails. It's all Christian magic, you see. More than I can explain. But he was laid in a coffin of stone, and when we opened it his flesh was as whole as if he only lived the day before."

The six guards sat back and hissed, but Dagby only smiled. He looked between Thorfast and Yngvar, who both sat across from him.

Yngvar, unsure of what to say, kept his beer to his lips. He was hardly the liar Thorfast was, and if pressed he might reveal their deceit. Yet from Dagby's arched brows it seemed he did not believe Thorfast.

"Now there's a magical tale," Dagby said. "And while I have it on my own information that you were in Ireland recently, how do I know what you say is not a lie?"

"Because all five of us will swear to the same story," Thorfast said, his smile never slipping. "And if you take each of us outside in turn, we will all tell the same tale."

"And you did not present this Christian relic to your king because?" Dagby spread his hands wide.

"Because he's a Christian!" Thorfast raised both his hands in frustration. "Do you think he'd be pleased that we robbed the coffin of one of his god's saints? Worse still, he'd take it from us and we'd be unable to sell it for it's true worth."

Dagby seemed to consider the explanation, turning his head from side to side. At last, he rapped the table with his knuckles.

"You might be a liar, but it is a good story. If you would swear to it, then I will pay a price. But not the foolish price you set."

"We will all swear to it," Thorfast said. "And if anyone should question your word, then you can send them to us. This is Yngvar Hakonsson, as you know. His word alone should guarantee anything."

Dagby gave a weak smile, his watery eyes settling over Yngvar. "Yes, the scourge of the Danes and Erik Blood-Axe's sworn enemy. You have made a name for yourself, Master Yngvar."

"That this cross comes from my hall should double its value." Yngvar sat up straighter and slapped the table with his palm. Dagby's guards wavered between laughing and closing up to their master. Dagby just laughed, removing his weights from the scale to let the gold cross clank artlessly to the table.

"Let us make a deal," he said.

Thorfast and Dagby haggled. Yngvar sat with Bjorn and Alasdair, unsure of when to add his voice. In the end, he had nothing to say. For in a series of verbal jabs and parries, Dagby and Thorfast shook on a price. It was more than the weight of the gold, but less than what Yngvar had hoped.

Dagby collected his cross, a frown of disbelief creasing his face. Yngvar could not imagine why he would make a bad deal.

His guards pulled together a sack which they threw on the table. The chime of gold and silver was unmistakable. Thorfast, who had his own scale, weighed the payment and pronounced the deal completed.

"Now more drink!" He looked to Yngvar, who was gladdened for something to do in this exchange.

They all refilled their mugs, toasted success, praised Dagby's acumen, and chugged mug after mug. When Yngvar felt his face warming, he pulled open the sack of coins to admire them. He dug into the cold, orange metal and withdrew a fistful of coins.

"You got a fair price," Yngvar said. "The cross will bring you good luck."

Dagby shrugged. "We will do business again. You will collect other treasures and perhaps you will consider me when needing to dispose of them without the king's knowing."

Yngvar smiled. So that had been Thorfast's story. Dagby was one of those traders who worked in the shadows, buying and selling goods away from the public eye. He likely accepted this sale as a loss so that Yngvar would return to him in the future. Dagby would drive a harder deal then. Such men were useful to know.

He looked at the coins spread out in his palm. They were thin and nicked, but the gold was all that mattered. His sight was blurry but the lettering on these coins was strange to him. He was not literate, but he recognized the shapes of his own language and the stranger shapes of the Latin words found in churches. But this was a hypnotic, twisting language. It was like a spell to bind his sight. He flipped the coin to reveal more circles within circles of strange writing.

"No crosses?" he asked to no one. He spread the coins out, and all the gold bore the same writing. His brow furrowed as he sorted the coins. None were different from the other. "This is strange. Where are the crosses, kings, and gods?"

Dagby gave self-satisfied nod. "You've a sharp eye, Master Yngvar. These coins have made a long journey to your hands."

Alasdair leaned in and sucked his breath. "These are heathen coins. I cannot read this, lord, but that is the writing of the dark men of the south. Same ones as bought my cousin Calum for a slave."

"Really?" Bjorn leaned in, turning his eye to the pile of coins. He shouldered Yngvar aside to run his thick fingers through the pile. "What's a heathen? Is their gold worth less?"

"Heathens have heard Christ's word, but do not believe," Alasdair explained patiently. His bright face took on a pedantic expression. "Those men of the south, Serklanders, all believe in a god they call Allah. They are heathens. This is their writing. You are a pagan, which is different."

Bjorn stared with his mouth open. Gyna laughed at him, then jabbed her finger between his teeth causing him to jump. She pulled her hand back, laughing.

"Why so many of their coins?" Yngvar asked. "It is more common to see coins of many times and places, but never a sack of new coins of the same kind."

"I deal with men from every part of the world," Dagby said, dusting his shirt with the back of his hand. "I have met these Serklanders before. But this gold came to me by way of Norsemen just returned from adventures in Langbardaland."

"I don't know this place," Thorfast said, joining the rest to examine the coins.

"It is a long stretch of land where the ancient Romans once ruled. The old people may have perished long ago, but gold and riches remain after them. I've heard tell of palaces of white and black rock, all polished as smooth as ice on a still pond. The halls there are filled with gold and treasures beyond anyone's dreams."

"Could such a place be real?" Yngvar asked. He let the coins run through his fingers and chime on the table.

"Its wealth is passing through your fingers now," Dagby said. "It is there for the taking, if a man is bold. But the gold of Langbardaland is guarded by the spirits of the old people. And more practically, by their living descendants. It is a strange place of strange men, and not an easy road for our people."

"Yet our people have gone to this place," Yngvar said. "And they've brought back gold like this."

Dagby nodded. "Great wealth, but at a great price. The men I treated with will be mighty jarls wherever they settle themselves. They plucked a kingdom's worth of gold from those strange lands. I admire their bravery. I would never dare such a thing myself."

Yngvar's eyes no longer saw the table before him. Instead, he saw a pathetic stack of cooking pots that faded to a scene of palaces of silver and gold.

3

King Hakon sat at the high table, smiling down on Yngvar like a painting of a Christian saint. Sharp light from a crackling hearth filled the spacious hall and sent hard-edged shadows dancing at the rafters. The sweetness of its smoke masked the sweat from the gangs of hirdmen that had gathered behind Yngvar. He felt the heat of their presence as they leaned into his recounting of the raid.

Yngvar shared all the facts of his latest adventure, including the ambush. With so many unfamiliar faces present, he dared not imply any sort of betrayal. Hakon was a young king, perhaps a handful of years younger than Yngvar. He depended on veterans for advice, but was maturing into his power. He would realize the same conclusion as Yngvar.

They could discuss possible spies in private, if Hakon thought Yngvar's opinion mattered. Since failing to avenge Hakon's half-brother in Ireland, despite having executed exact orders against gargantuan setbacks, Yngvar had fallen in Hakon's estimation.

"You have served me admirably," King Hakon said. A slight nod accompanied his placid smile. "The Danes must never be allowed to build up strength on their northern coast."

"My crew and I are pleased to serve you, lord." Yngvar dipped his head toward the king.

"Take this as reward for your service." Hakon accepted a small sack from a hirdman standing behind him. He held it out to Yngvar to accept with both hands. Silver bits chimed together as he stepped back with the weighty bag. Hakon then twisted a thin gold band off his finger and held it out.

"'This is for you alone, for your loyalty and bravery. You are a model for all my warriors."

Yngvar again bowed and took the ring, warm gold from Hakon's finger to his own. "Thank you, lord. I am flattered by your words."

"Though you bring no spoils to share with me?" Hakon asked, a wry smile on his face. He looked less like a king and more like a boy who had caught his father in the wrong.

"We barely escaped with our heads, lord. We were forced to abandon all we had collected, including the slaves." He bowed lower to hide his face. He thought of the strange gold coins now secreted in his hall.

Hakon waved the air as if dismissing the entire thought of riches. "You will of course remain for the feast tonight. Bring all your men. They have earned a place in my hall."

"They will be pleased, lord."

It was the same ceremony every time they returned from a raid. A feast would be held—any reason to eat and drink until every man became walrus-bellied. Yngvar could have defeated a colony of feral cats and still been regaled with meat and ale. Feasting kept men in high spirits. While he dared not insult his king by checking the contents of the sack while in the hall, he knew from the sparkling jingle of the metal that it was silver rather than gold. Once the reward was spread among thirty men, no one would be richer for having crossed the sea to face the Danes on their own shore.

To think, he had slipped death to collect a worn-down ring and a bag of silver bits.

During the feast he, his Wolves, and crew sat at a long table of their own. They drank toasts to each other and to King Hakon. Bjorn attacked feasts like he did enemy shield walls. All around him the bones and scraps of his meal were scattered like slain foemen. Gyna was no less wanton, joining her lover in drunken carelessness. She cursed and boasted with the best of his men. Yngvar could only smile at the pair. The gods had inexplicably set them together, though none understood why. Least of all himself.

"You are thinking," Thorfast said, sitting at Yngvar's left. "When you should be drunk."

"I am simply tired. Too much drink will put me to sleep."

"No, lord, you have drunk nothing of your usual measure. A gloom is over you. Some of the crew have noticed this."

"That's not true," Yngvar said. He sat up straighter, as if he had just been called to task by his own father. Yet he noted King Hakon's stolen glances and how his own crewmen noted his sudden shift.

"Perhaps I am thinking too much." He drained his mug, then held it up for a refill.

"Get that filled now!" Bjorn shouted. He stood, sweaty and red-faced, his hair and beard like a frizzy halo. "He shouldn't have to wait."

"Sorry, lord." A young woman with golden hair and a sharp nose rushed with a jug to refill his mug.

"Well, you are beauty," Yngvar said as she poured his beer. "The king brightens his hall with you, doesn't he?"

She smiled and ducked away without a word. Though she was beautiful, she was the king's servant and only the most beer-addled fool would dare more than tease her.

"She made you smile," Thorfast said. "First time this night. Remember yourself, will you. If you don't believe we had a victory, will the rest of the crew?"

"She's probably the Danish spy," Yngvar said bitterly, yet it made both Alasdair and Thorfast laugh.

The celebration continued and Yngvar pretended what he could of joy. But as men began to succumb to their drinks, he returned to his gloomy mood. The king, now fully surrounded with his hirdmen, no longer paid him any mind.

"There are lands filled with gold and treasure," Yngvar said. "Waiting to be plucked by brave men. Yet we break our backs rowing the frigid sea to fight bony men and their scrawny wives to steal their cooking pots. Is this what we left Frankia to do?"

"Well, it's what our fathers did before us," Thorfast said. The beer had found its way into his words, turning them soft and thick.

"Our fathers stood beside Hrolf the Strider and won a kingdom with him. Our fathers sailed the wide sea and found danger and adventure along with gold and fame. This is what we swore to do, years ago. But what have we done? What lord do we stand beside? What kingdom do we win?"

"Lord, your voice," Alasdair said. He grabbed Yngvar's sleeve.

King Hakon did not glance at him. Bjorn and Gyna had collapsed together on the table, arms around each other's shoulders. But some of his men looked askance at him.

"Well, have you no answer?" Yngvar lowered his voice, leaning into Thorfast for his question.

"We fight the Danes for the king. So we win this kingdom."

"You are clearly drunk," Yngvar said, leaning back. "That argument is as soft as boiled leeks. This—kingdom—used to belong to our families until King Hakon's father stole it from us. Now he deems to grant a sliver of it back to us while he gambles our lives to defend the rest of it for himself."

"Well, what are you saying?" Thorfast's drunkenness seemed to pass into alert concern. "We swore an oath."

"And we will not break it," Yngvar said. "Have no fear. But I am frustrated. We risk everything for so little. Think on it, man. What if we had all been caught by the Danes? They would've hanged us then fed our bodies to dogs. After our deaths, Hakon might have paused to think of us. He might have ordered a priest to pray to his god for us. Then we would be forgotten. No mark left on this world. Our names soon forgotten because all our deeds have been to bring glory to another man."

"History only remembers kings, lord." Alasdair said.

"And heroes." Yngvar slapped the table. "The men Dagby spoke of. They are heroes. And the gold they have carried back from Langbardaland will buy them a kingdom. Why are they free to sail where they will, and we must forever scour Denmark's poor coast?"

"Because they are lawless raiders," Thorfast said. "They know no honor and honor no oaths."

Yngvar wiped his face in frustration. "You are not seeing the point. We have demanded nothing of Hakon for our service. Now's the time to change it. We will go to Langbardaland ourselves and take our fortune home. We will become kings of our own countries."

Though Thorfast was the drunkest between the two, he sat back with an expression of horror. "You're serious?"

"Never more."

Yngvar stood from his bench and nearly fell again. Perhaps he had drank too much. It did not change what he knew must be done. The gods had shown him a place of great treasure. The raiders Dagby dealt with could teach him the way. He had a ship and crew ready for a great challenge.

Ready for an adventure to make them all immortal heroes.

"My king," Yngvar said, bowing low before Hakon's table. "I beg a moment alone."

Despite being the ostensible guest of honor, Hakon's hirdmen regarded him as if he had just drawn a sword. But the young king, whose raptor-like face was so much like his brother Erik Blood-Axe, again gave an indulgent smile and stood.

"Some fresh air would be welcomed." He gestured to the door.

Thorfast and Alasdair watched Yngvar in awe as he passed through the hall.

Outside, the summer night was bracing compared to the hot and odorous hall. Hauger was dark but for the pinpoints of orange torch-light from patrolling guards. Being alone with King Hakon meant he was accompanied by two of his strongest warriors. They remained back a polite distance, but guarded their lord even against his allies. Kings could not know too much caution, it seemed to Yngvar.

"You have been bothered," Hakon said. "It's plain on your face and thick in your words. But your men rejoice and have no cares. Look at how Bjorn celebrated. Can you not find the same peace?"

That Hakon unmasked his mood with ease sent a cold jolt through Yngvar's gut. Despite his irritation, he wanted to present a cooler demeanor to his king. Heat came to his cheeks.

"Forgive me. I do not mean to insult your hospitality, lord. But I am troubled and I must ask a favor of you."

Hakon raised his brow but said nothing.

"Lord, these raids on Denmark, as important as they are, bring me less gold and less glory each time. It is my honor to serve you, lord. In that, there is glory. But skalds do not sing of service well done."

"Though they should," Hakon said. "Few know how to serve selflessly and with intelligence."

"True, lord," Yngvar said. He wondered if that was a compliment or observation. Since Hakon did nothing more than continue to stare, he took it for praise. "I'll come to my point, lord. There is a place called Langbardaland. Do you know of it?"

Hakon smiled and stroked his thin beard. "It is where the Lombards make their kingdom on the rocks and bones of the old people. A land of ancient treasures, I hear."

"Yes," Yngvar said, his voice rising. His heart lifted with Hakon's recognition. "There are palaces there of magical rock, their chambers filled with gold and treasure. I would go and win these treasures, to the glory of both of us."

Despite his age, Hakon's smile was fatherly and indulgent. "It would be a glorious deed. But have you given no thought to why more men have not succeeded in the same attempt?"

"Because their minds are filled with small thoughts, and they dare only what they are certain they can win. Because the gods do not favor them, and Fate scorns them."

"Of course," Hakon said, continuing to run his hand along his young beard. "It is a long and dangerous journey. This land of gold and treasure you imagine does not sit with its palaces open to any wanderer. The descendants of the old people still dwell there, and though their empires have crumbled to piles of stone, they are still mighty foemen. Between the perils of the sea and the people of those lands, a single longship might never expect to return home."

"The sea is perilous everywhere, my lord. And I do not mean to instruct you in the dangers of raiding, but even starving Danish villagers could bring down a single crew. We undertake the same risks wherever we raid, only the rewards have become scant."

"You seek my leave to travel to Langbardaland."

"I do, lord." Yngvar's heart began to pound. "The Danes have marked me well. They know when and where I will strike. I was nearly captured this time. Next time the gods might tire of protecting me. If I were to spend a season away and let another take my place raiding Denmark, we might confuse our enemies."

Hakon nodded, now clasping his hands behind his back as if lost in thought. He focused on a distant point in the darkness of Hauger. While his face was as predatory as his brother Erik's, there was humanity there as well. Something Erik Blood-Axe and his son Gamle lacked.

"There are many holy relics in those lands," Hakon said, turning his gaze back to Yngvar. "If you were to bring a real one to me—not pig knuckles wrapped in old cloth that are supposed to be holy remains—then it might do much to aid me in spreading Christ's teachings."

"Of course, my lord," Yngvar said. Hakon had learned Christianity from his fosterage in Wessex. He struggled to import it into Norway, where people balked at a religion that turned their heroic ancestors into damned souls rotting in the underworld.

"And what you say is true. The Danes have marked you too well. They take pains to know where you are and when you will strike. They have grown accustomed to your tactics, and prepare for you."

They spy on your court, Yngvar thought. But he was unconcerned with convincing Hakon. He seemed ready to grant his leave. So Yngvar held his breath rather than answer.

"You will share a full quarter of whatever you bring back, and any holy relic must be handled with reverence and given to me."

Hakon straightened his back and squared his eyes to Yngvar's. He might be younger than Yngvar, but he was as bold and confident. As yet untried in battle, Yngvar did not doubt his king would acquit himself well.

"A full quarter is a steep share, my lord."

"I have paid for your ship and will provision your crew. Further, I must now find another to take your place and cover that expense as well. This will be a risky use of my wealth, and so the reward must match it."

Yngvar bent his mouth in agreement. He could not argue with the king on this point. Besides, if he truly earned a windfall from this raid, he could hide a portion of this treasure before returning to Hakon. It would be twisting the terms of his oath, but he agreed to releasing a quarter share of what he returned with to Norway—not what he took from Langbardaland.

"Then it is agreed, my king." Yngvar extended his arm to Hakon, who grasped it. The king's grip was firm and warm, and he shook Yngvar's arm with vigor.

"The journey will be long, but I will outfit you with such gear as I can to aid the early leg of it." Hakon released his grip. "I admit, this scheme of yours excites me. I wish I could go with you."

"It would make a song worthy of a king," Yngvar said. He begged the gods to steer Hakon away from such thoughts. Hakon would not only claim all the wealth of the raid, but also all the glory.

Hakon shook his head and laughed. "My songs must be written about other things. I have a country in need of law and protection. Such problems my brother wrought in such a short time as king. It is shocking."

"Fate will see to him one day," Yngvar said.

Hakon's smile was weak. "He means to be king again, if not here then elsewhere. I hear he has designs on Yorvik. That will raise his power and keep him too close to me. Perhaps when you return, I will have a new task for you."

Yngvar could not resist his smile. "My back is thick with lash scars that I would dearly love to give to Erik Blood-Axe. Bjorn owes him an eye as well. You will always find me ready to deal with your brother, my king."

"I know it too well. But for now, you go to find gold and glory."

"I will return great wealth to you, lord. I swear it."

Hakon nodded. "Of course you will. To be certain, I will keep a hostage to your word. The young man in your crew, the good Christian lad, Alasdair. He will do."

4

B randr's hall was as dark as the mood that enveloped it. The front doors hung open to allow a cool evening breeze to enter along with the feeble golden light of sunset. Despite the iron pot's simmering stew wafting savory notes into the hall, Yngvar had no appetite. A rotund woman clanked a spoon against its side as she stirred. The tables and benches beneath the high table sat empty, though wood bowls and mugs were set for the men yet to arrive.

Yngvar sat beside his cousin, Brandr, at the high table. Bjorn, Gyna, and Thorfast sat across from him. The open doors at the far end framed them like a painting of solemn faces.

Brandr's age showed more with every season. His beard was coarser and grayer than last summer. His eyes were couched in bags and the flesh of his neck hung loose. He was to take a wife this summer, some arranged marriage with a girl young enough to be his granddaughter. Yet no one spoke of this.

"So he's to remain in Hauger?" Brandr asked. "King Hakon will not change his mind?"

Yngvar shrugged. "We said our farewells to him outside of Hakon's hall."

"He only just came back to us," Bjorn said in a whining note that belied his fearsome appearance. "Ain't fair he has to stay behind."

"He's the only normal one among us," Gyna said. "Who will I talk to now?"

"Hey, you talk to me," Bjorn said. But Gyna flipped her hand at him as if he were a fly to shoo.

Brandr leaned on the table, putting his balled hands beneath his chin.

"Why does he not trust you to return? Where else do you have to go?"

Yngvar shook his head. "He expects I will hide my treasures from him. A king is always hungry for wealth. With Alasdair under his roof, he has leverage against me. He is right to believe I will not risk Alasdair's life for gold. I owe him too much."

"Seems I could be a hostage just as easily," Brandr said. "We're cousins. Unless you're saying you'd let me pay for breaking your oath."

Brandr laughed, but it stuttered out. Birds chirped outside the hall, settling into their nests for the night. Otherwise, no one made a sound.

"Well, that's a warm feeling." Brandr said, now folding his arms.

"Let's talk about what is rather than what might have been," Thorfast said. "We have Hakon's permission to undertake this journey. The crew is excited for it. Hamar knows the way, just keep the coast always on the left and trust the sun and stars. Our ship is supplied and our weapons sharpened. We've everything readied but a sacrifice to the gods. The only blot on this pure white sheet of linen is Alasdair's absence."

"And that Hakon does not trust me," Yngvar said.

"He's right not to trust you," Gyna said, her smile falsely sweet. "You were never planning to give him a full quarter share."

All but Yngvar laughed. He thought of his young companion. Alasdair had accepted his lot, though the pain of being left behind showed in the slouch of his shoulders. Hakon had tried to lift his spirits with talk of the good Alasdair could do in spreading Christianity. A hostage he may be, but his life would be comfortable. Yngvar had attempted to convince him of the dangers they would face, and that he was better off remaining behind. But everyone, including himself, remained unconvinced. Hadn't Alasdair seen the worst dangers the sea road offered? He had survived those dangers without injury.

"There are only two choices," Yngvar said.

His words settled the laughter around the table. They watched him expectantly.

"There's no imagination here," Yngvar said. "We either continue on as we have led everyone to believe we will, or we snatch Alasdair out of Hakon's hall."

"Stealing Alasdair away will make you an outlaw," Brandr said. "You'll break your oath and then I'd be obliged to bring you to justice."

"Hey, Jarl Brandr," Bjorn said, twisting the title with contempt. "We're family, ain't we? It's not like we'd be stealing from the king's treasure pile. This is Alasdair we're after. He's one of us."

"It's not like you're saving his life," Brandr said, rising to Bjorn's hostility. "Alasdair accepted his part as a hostage. He might not have liked it, but that is his fate."

"Peace," Yngvar said, raising his hands. "I'm just listing our choices. Alasdair deserves to go with us on this raid, but Fate has decided otherwise. We cannot disobey Hakon's will in this matter and hope to retain our honor. It is a pity, for I think Alasdair would have liked to see these distant lands."

"He brought us good luck," Bjorn said, the whining returning to his voice. "It will go ill-luck without him, I promise."

"He is a good little thief, too," Thorfast added. "I think we will need a ghost like him to walk through fortress walls as he does. Who knows what we will find in that strange land?"

"You should've argued for him," Gyna said, pointing her thin finger at Yngvar's nose. "You should've stood up to Hakon when he challenged your word."

"You think I accepted these terms like a meek servant? Hakon would not be swayed."

31

Yngvar rubbed his temples. He waited for silence before continuing.

"I will not dishonor our names by stealing Alasdair out of the hall. As much as this pains me, there's nothing for us to do but continue on without him."

The Wolves remained wooden-faced and silent. Yngvar accepted a sympathetic pat on the back from Brandr.

"I was Hakon's hostage, you'll remember, and he treated me well. The worst pain was knowing all of you were facing dangers while I idled my days with conversation and riddles. Just don't be gone long, or Alasdair will grow soft."

Yngvar scrubbed his face in frustration and let out a long sigh. "Of course, you're right. I need to get some air."

He slid off the bench and shuffled across the hall. No one looked at him as he passed. The benches were empty but the tables set. The fat woman at the hearth clapped an iron lid over the pot as Yngvar left. It sounded like a cage slamming shut on him.

Outside, Brandr's hirdmen mingled with his crew. They had occupied their afternoon with various competitions: wrestling, stone throwing, and racing. They had made it a festival day for themselves. He wished he could have shared in his crew's exuberance. This adventure had soured before it started, and he considered returning to Hauger rather than travel on without Alasdair.

He had sailed down the fjord a short distance to Grenner in a mental fog. He had no answer to Hakon's demand. Alasdair had been chosen because he was closest to Yngvar, as close as kin. Though Bjorn was his blood cousin, Hakon was shrewd enough to know no one would sail without Bjorn's mighty strength. He had guessed they would if Alasdair was left behind—and that they did, hurt Yngvar. Alasdair was as important to success as Bjorn was. He did not stand as tall or strike fear into a man at first glance. But he had delivered them victories before and was every bit as instrumental as Bjorn had ever been.

Now he was abandoned.

The hirdmen and Yngvar's crew passed him as they filed into the hall. Their smiles and bravado helped him force his smile. Yet he had to flee them as well and think.

Ancient tree stumps studded the wide field around Grenner's hall. His great-grandfather, Orm the Bellower, might have been the one to clear these. He made for the distant trees where his grandfather Ulfrik had hid from his brother. The land was rich in family history, but he felt no connection to it. He had not been born here, though he had heard the stories of this place from his own father. It seemed less grand to stand in the actual setting. Everything was ordinary, unlike his imaginings.

Would Langbardaland be the same? Would magnificent palaces of the stone called marble become insignificant piles of rock in reality? Would these piles of gold he was promised become a few sacks of old coins unworthy of the long journey?

The night drew down the sun and he approached the dark trees. Elves were said to live in this forest, but they had never bothered his grandfather. Perhaps they would recognize him as kin and leave him alone as well.

"Lord!"

The whispered voice was urgent but unmistakable.

"Alasdair? Where are you?"

"Closer to the trees, lord. I'm right before you."

Yngvar leaned into the gathering darkness. The woods were foreboding and black, though their depths echoed with birdsong as ravens and blackbirds found their nests at day's end.

"I can't see you."

Then Alasdair moved and Yngvar's heart jolted with shock. If Alasdair had been an enemy, he could have run Yngvar through with a spear. His normally smooth and bright face had been smeared with dirt. His coppery hair now hid under a hood of green. In fact, his whole body was enveloped in the green cloak, into which he had set branches and leaves to break up his profile. He seemed more like a bush than a human.

"Gods, that is unnatural," Yngvar said, his heartbeat settling after the surprise. "What are you doing here?"

"Lord, I slipped out of Hakon's hall and raced here with all haste."

"You are a hostage." Yngvar looked about, realizing others would see him speaking to the edge of the trees. He stepped into the dark, tangled woods smelling of rotting underbrush and pine needles.

"Of course you had no choice, lord. But you cannot go so far without me. God has told me I must accompany you."

"God told you?"

Alasdair, still seeming more like plant than a person, stood up from a crouch and squared his shoulders.

"God told me." His words were stern and clipped. Yngvar knew he would not explain more. He had probably stretched some sign to its limit of rationality in order to interpret a message from his god.

"Well, even King Hakon cannot argue with God's will."

"He cannot," Alasdair agreed. "But he will not believe my word alone. God will have to explain this in His own time. For now, King Hakon has sent riders after me. I've lost them in the woods. But there they are, lord."

Yngvar followed Alasdair's pointing finger to the hall. The sharp profiles of five horses and two riders showed against the last rose-colored light of the day. Men greeted them peacefully at the hall doors.

"Three of them must be searching the forest," Alasdair said. "I did not cover my trail well, being rushed. But they won't find me here, lord."

"I didn't see you nearly underfoot. But they will be searching more carefully."

"It is a large woods, lord, and night covers it. The forest spirits will be allies of mine, for I know how to tread their lands with respect. But Hakon's men are warriors of the shield wall. They will become lost or worse."

Hearing Alasdair describe the fate of these men sent a chill along his neck and back. Would the spirits treat him so cruelly as well? He would not find out.

"I must get back to the hall," Yngvar said. "But our situation couldn't be better. No one knows you are here but me. I will keep it secret. You should head to the coast. We will sail away without you and pick you up down the shore. Travel through the night and be ready by midmorning tomorrow. We will sail for Langbardaland together."

Alasdair's smile grew bright enough to defeat his carefully arranged camouflage.

"Until tomorrow, lord."

Yngvar raced back across the fields, weaving among the rotten, moss-covered stumps that remained of the old woods. He had to force the smile from his face, or else reveal his secret.

The gods loved him, for this could not be a better outcome than if he had planned it from the start. Truly they could prove their innocence to Hakon's men. Alasdair would have made himself an enemy of the king. But as long as they all returned with enough riches, Yngvar was certain he could buy Alasdair's forgiveness.

And now he did not need to return if he so desired.

Fate was kind.

The riders' horses were being led away as Yngvar arrived. He crashed through the doors behind the new arrivals.

The hall was now full of men who had only just taken up their seats. The two riders were strong men in wolf-furs and thick leather jerkins. They had respectfully surrendered their weapons, which leaned against the wall to Yngvar's right.

They stood before the high table, where Brandr and Yngvar's Wolves sat looking down in surprise at their guests. The two warriors glanced back at him, their hard eyes widening in recognition.

Brandr stood, extending his arms in welcome.

"My hall is yours," he said. "Be welcomed for our evening meal. I am honored King Hakon sends his finest to visit me at this late hour. What is the cause for such a happy event?"

Brandr's wit had not dulled with age, and his sarcasm was well disguised. The guards did not seem to understand Brandr's displeasure at their intrusion.

One of the two, a bulky man with jet black hair and a voice like broken pottery, gave a slight bow.

"I am Tovi the Black, come from King Hakon's hall on an urgent task. The hostage, Alasdair, has fled. We followed his trail which has led us here."

35

"What?" Brandr's surprise was genuine. "To this hall?"

"Not exactly to the hall," Tovi said, glancing at his companion who was taking hard looks at everyone around him. "We lost his trail west of here. He might have fled into the woods to confuse us."

"I doubt much can confuse you," Brandr said.

Tovi nodded at first, but stiffened when he realized the jab. He stepped closer to the high table. Though the gesture was innocent enough, from a man of his size wearing the battle scars he did, it was as threatening as a drawn sword.

"By the order of King Hakon, whose mark I carry here, I am to search your land and ships for the hostage. The king believes your guests have contrived to steal him away and break faith."

Tovi produced the wood chip with Hakon's rune carved on it. A skilled man could fake such a thing, but the runes and Tovi's word were sufficient verification.

"We've done no such thing," Yngvar said, approaching Tovi and his companion. Both showed him some deference by moving aside. Even Tovi, as proud as he seemed, lowered his gaze.

"Yngvar, I cannot believe you would break your word. But Alasdair has been seen fleeing and we followed him this far. We expect he wishes to join you, even if you have not encouraged him."

"Then search every home and our ships," Yngvar said. "If you find him, I will send him back myself. I will not break my word to the king."

Tovi nodded, then looked to Brandr once more.

"Three men search the woods. We would search the hall and your homes, with your permission and in the company of your own men. We've no desire for troubles with your people."

Brandr gave Yngvar a confused look. Thorfast smiled as if he had figured out the entire ruse, which he likely had. Only Bjorn and Gyna seemed offended, and when Bjorn stood, Yngvar jumped in.

"Search my ship first," he said. "I suspect he would hide among our supplies and reveal himself once we were out to sea."

Tovi nodded to his companion. "Go to the ship and I will begin searching this hall."

Yngvar gave Bjorn a warning look and he sat down. His brow creased as he tried to work out the facts for himself.

King Hakon's men searched his ship, the woods, the shore, and every home in the village. Stars now splattered a soft black sky, lost behind yellow torchlight that Tovi and his fellows had raised in their search. They had gathered before the hall doors along with Brandr and all the others.

"He has slipped us," Tovi said. "You are not hiding him. Of that I am sure."

"You even went through my sea chest," Bjorn said, frowning. "There's things in there no man should see."

"Don't tell me you're still playing with dolls," Thorfast said, jabbing his elbow into Bjorn's side. "Is that why you sit facing the corner and whisper in a high voice?"

Gyna gave an explosive laugh and Bjorn growled with anger.

"Yours was the chest with the thread of finger bones, was it?" Tovi asked. "You need to clean them properly, as there's a scent of rot in there. Turned my stomach."

Bjorn smiled. "I'm making a necklace."

Yngvar and the others stared at him in silence. He could not reconcile his cousin's two faces, one of boyish simplicity and the other of blood-crazed madness.

"I don't know what would have made Alasdair flee," Yngvar said, now warmed to the act of offended, honorable man. "He knows I would not tolerate disloyalty."

"Maybe he wishes to go home again," Thorfast said. His faint smile hinted he recognized the farce. "He has said as much, hasn't he?"

Bjorn scratched his skull. "No, he's—"

"He's probably looping back north," Yngvar said, putting his hand on Tovi's shoulder to gather his attention. "Led you on a fine chase, and now he goes to sail out of Hauger and leave us all behind. He has been anxious to return to his family again."

Tovi made no expression, nodding in agreement.

"Well, this is all we can do. Jarl Brandr, could we beg hospitality tonight? We will take a corner of your hall for our beds."

"Be welcomed," Brandr said. "You will leave tomorrow morning, after you are fed."

"Our thanks," Tovi said, bowing.

"If you hurry tonight, you might catch him." Yngvar smiled, trying to mask his hope that they would disappear forever.

"Horses don't like to travel by dark," Tovi said. "A fine way to break a leg. Alasdair will have to sleep tonight as well. We will take up his trail tomorrow."

"We sail tomorrow," Yngvar said. "You can send us off to be certain Alasdair is not among our number."

"I'm certain he won't be," Tovi said. He squared himself up to Yngvar and smiled. "And I'll be sailing with you to be certain he doesn't join you later."

5

White gulls called overhead as Yngvar's ship rocked on the gentle waves. He scanned the beach. The sandy strand had held scores of ships over the long years, including his grandfather's. The dark line of pine and hazel trees up the slope were familiar and plain. As much as he wanted to drink in this last glimpse of his ancestral home, his mind pulled his vision inward.

Bjorn and Hamar dragged the anchor stone out of the water and thumped it to the deck. The sail remained furled, and the crew sat on their sea chests and fed oars through the tholes. The deck creaked and popped as the ship nosed away from shore.

"Thor keep you safe," Brandr called from the beach, cupping his hand to his mouth. He and four of his hirdmen had escorted them to their ship.

Yngvar raised his hand to his cousin and offered a wan smile.

He had not told Brandr of his plan for Alasdair. Ignorance would protect him from King Hakon's wrath. Besides, Alasdair would not return to Grenner. He would be waiting down-shore to be picked up before Yngvar turned to the open sea.

Tovi had understood this possibility. He now sat with his back against the mast, his dark hair covering his face as he considered his fingernails.

"I assume you've got a plan for Alasdair?"

Thorfast joined Yngvar at the rail and waved to Brandr as well. He spoke under his breath and never looked from the shore.

"You know what is going on?" Yngvar whispered, also watching the shore. "He will be waiting for us south of here."

Thorfast gave a slow nod, his striking pale hair glistening in the morning light.

"Then what of our guest?"

Yngvar sighed, waved to Brandr a final time, then turned to face his crew. None of them knew they aided in an oath-breaking. If uncovered, Yngvar's crime would be theirs as well. Hakon had picked his hostage well, he mused. Alasdair was indispensable, and undertaking a journey of this scale without him diminished its chances of success.

"What of him?" Yngvar answered, folding his arms and leaning against the rail. "If he interferes then I must remove him."

"That smells of murder," Thorfast said. "He's merely doing his duty to the king, who we are defying. We're the villains of this play, I fear."

"A villain I may be, but I am no murderer." Yngvar tugged on his beard as he watched Tovi resting carefree in the shade of the mast. "We will just have to deal with whatever challenges the gods put before us."

Bjorn, who manned an oar, started a song that the crew took up as they found their rhythm.

"He knows, too," Yngvar said. "Otherwise there'd be no end to his complaining."

"Tovi knows," Thorfast said. "This will be an interesting afternoon."

A scattering of high, thin clouds laced the sky, but nonetheless Yngvar felt as if a fat, black raincloud dogged their progress. The oarsmen took long, slow strokes to contain their strength. The crew off-shift sat in quiet conversation. Hamar and Leiknr Bone-Feet, both talented steersmen, also took shifts. Wide-faced Hamar steered them now, angling for a wind that would relieve the rowers.

"Keeping close to the shore," Tovi said. He had stood to stretch then joined Yngvar with a wan smile.

"Of course, we are not ready to catch the open sea, and I assume you are not heading with us to Langbardaland. We will have to set you ashore when we are ready to hit the North Sea."

Tovi held Yngvar's smile a heartbeat longer than was comfortable. The sun caused him to squint, drawing deep lines on his hard face.

"I would not go so far, only just far enough to ensure you meet no unexpected travelers along the way."

"If we do," Yngvar said, "they will be Danes. So pray that we meet no enemies."

They approached the point Yngvar had guessed Alasdair would wait for them. The thick trees grew almost to the shore, where a stunted beach would allow a single ship landing. He could hide among the trees until he judged it safe to emerge.

Yngvar leaned into Hamar as he steered, speaking in a low voice. "Bring us in as if we are about to land, but then steer away. Order the crew to change to their short oars."

Hamar leaned back with a frown. "Why?"

"Just do as I ask. There is a reason you will learn in time."

The ship shifted atop the waves with lithe grace. This was a magnificent ship, a true gift from his king—whom he now defied. The ship was large enough for a full crew of thirty and their gear, yet traded nothing in agility and speed. The sudden change of direction across the waves set men lurching for a grip.

Tovi stood up again, staring toward the shore like a hunting dog certain it had cornered a rabbit it could not see. He had cornered a rabbit. For Yngvar was certain Alasdair watched from the shadow of the trees.

"Short oars!" Hamar yelled. "Shallow waters ahead."

The crew obeyed, pulling up their oars and letting them clatter to the deck. The off-shift crew traded them short oars from the rack. No one protested.

"What's this for?" Tovi asked. "Why are you pulling to shore?"

"We're letting you off here," Yngvar said.

Tovi frowned, then turned back to search the shore. Yngvar's hands burned to throw him overboard as he leaned across the rails. But he intended less violence for poor Tovi.

"You will not catch the current south for some distance." Tovi shielded his eyes against the sun, searching the trees. "I will sail with your faurther."

Yngvar smiled and shrugged. "As you wish. Hamar, take us back out to sea."

Hamar stared at him as if he had gone mad. Thorfast gave a blithe look. Bjorn threw down his short oar.

"What's this, then? You trying to tire me out?"

Gyna hissed at him from across the deck, where she coiled rope that had fallen loose. She gave Bjorn a warning look and he retrieved his oar in silence.

"You heard the order," Hamar shouted. "Get the long oars back in the water."

Tovi stared at Yngvar, suspicion written in the slant of his mouth and lines of his forehead. But he had seen nothing.

Yngvar was certain Alasdair had seen Tovi.

Once they were riding the waves again, Thorfast approached when Tovi looked away.

"You think he saw Tovi?"

Nodding, Yngvar leaned against the rails and searched the horizon as if he were considering his journey ahead.

"We will leave Tovi off at the southernmost spot we can. Alasdair will be smart enough to remain in place, and we will double back to fetch him. Tovi will be unable to walk back in time. The gods love us."

He tried to keep the smile off his face. Tovi had fit perfectly into his plan. So when they did arrive at the southernmost point, he found a spot to let Tovi ashore.

"You've a long walk home," Yngvar said. "But your duty to King Hakon does you great honor. You will tell him we have kept our word, that Alasdair acts alone?"

They stood on the beach, only Yngvar and Tovi plus the two crew who had helped beach the ship. The sun was low in the western sky.

Tovi gave a sharp look at Yngvar. "The sun will set in three or four hours. You've no rush, so why not make camp here?"

Yngvar's hands went cold. Tovi realized he was being deceived but could prove nothing.

"Provisions are enough to keep us at sea. The faster we reach the mainland, the better we will be. I waste no time."

Tovi grunted agreement. "I will find my way north again. I have family nearby, and we will travel together."

Back aboard the ship, Yngvar watched Tovi standing on the shore with hands on his hips.

"The bastard knows where Alasdair is," Thorfast said. "But he can do nothing about it."

"Nothing," Yngvar said, smiling. "Now to fetch him."

Hamar complained about backtracking. The wind favored the direction so the oars were withdrawn, and after the sail was set, the crew stretched out on deck.

"What's all this?" Bjorn asked. "We're sailing like our rudder is stuck."

Yngvar patted his one-eyed cousin's back. "Here, I'll explain things to you and the crew."

He gathered the men as Hamar steered the ship the way they had come. He told all of his meeting with Alasdair and his plans.

The veteran crew, a pitiful handful by now, cried out with joy at the news. The rest looked on either indifferent or angered. Standing at the center of the deck, Yngvar felt as if the sun had suddenly shined only on him and revealed him as a fool.

"King Hakon will not know," Yngvar assured them. "Your honor is not stained. You will all be glad to have Alasdair aboard."

They reached the same thin beach where they had attempted to set Tovi earlier. The ship glided on the rolling waves and Yngvar leapt into the cold water, bare feet sinking into the muck, to aid his fellows in beaching the ship. The light vessel slid onto the beach like a seal on ice.

"Alasdair!" Yngvar called toward the trees. With night falling, they were like dark sentinels overlooking the placid waters of the cold sea. He drew another breath, inhaling the pine scents wafting down from the forest.

No answer came, though he called out thrice more.

"Maybe he has retreated deeper into the woods," Thorfast offered. The crew were leaping off the sides of the ship, sleeping sacks slung over their shoulders. They would camp on this tiny strand.

Yngvar cupped both hands and called Alasdair's name, leaning forward to add strength to his shout.

"He would be waiting for us nearby," Yngvar said. "He must have traveled south, thinking we will catch up with him there."

"But Tovi is to the south," Bjorn said. "He'll run right into him."

"He won't travel so far so fast." Yet Yngvar watched the dark trees waving their branches in the gentle ocean breeze. Perhaps Alasdair had never been here at all or was yet to arrive. He shook his head. "No matter, we will camp here."

They collected firewood, started campfires, and settled into their sleep sacks when the sun set. Guards were set in rotations, but Yngvar sat awake with them throughout the night. He dozed only to awaken when his head slumped forward.

Alasdair would come. Though they had not discussed the location in detail, he would be certain to find this spot as the only logical meeting point. The rest of the coast either would not allow ships to land or else be too exposed to other ships traveling past.

Yet by the chill morning Yngvar had not seen Alasdair slip into their camp, as he had expected.

"Yngvar Hakonsson!"

The voice called out from a tall rise on the south. It broke into the morning birdsong and the thrumming of the ocean. Yngvar had sat by the embers of the fire with his knees tucked beneath his chin. Hearing his name, he shot to his feet. So did everyone else beside him. Only Bjorn and Gyna snored side by side in their weather-beaten sleep sacks.

"You seemed to have missed the open sea."

Tovi the Black sat upon a horse, his massive shape cut out of morning sunlight. Shadow filled a sardonic smile as he gazed down.

"What brings you here?" Yngvar feigned relaxation, but glanced at the dark pine trees. He expected scores of hirdmen to explode out to attack him.

"This horse," Tovi said, laughing. "Borrowed from my cousin's farm. She carried me all night."

He patted the chestnut's neck.

Yngvar hated horses, for they were over-proud and unpredictable.

"I thought horses would not travel at night." Yngvar glanced toward his sword, which lay in the sand beside him. The rest of the crew were gathering closer, even as Bjorn's snores defeated the purr of ocean waves.

"It seems you are not the only liar here," Tovi said, his smile widening. He patted the horse's neck again. The beast was unlike the proud animal he had ridden into Grenner. This was a farmer's nag, and was probably exhausted from pushing throughout the night. Yngvar doubted the horse belonged to Tovi's relatives.

"Well, we are setting out again if you wish to join us once more." He turned his back on Tovi and pulled Thorfast close.

"Wake up Bjorn and Gyna. Get the ship launched and the crew aboard. I've no intention of letting him interfere. We'll have to continue down the coast until we find Alasdair."

He smiled then turned to kick Bjorn's leg. "Up, you lazy dog. Your snoring could shake down a mounting. You too, princess. Stop pretending to sleep."

Tovi sat on his horse, hand on the hilt of his sword. Even mounted he would not dare draw the weapon against such numbers. If anything, he challenged Yngvar to reveal Alasdair's presence that he could report back to King Hakon.

Whoever had been asleep now shambled through the process of breaking camp. Bjorn sat like a bear that had been hit over the head. Some crew were already standing on the deck, tying lines and preparing for launch.

"He's in the trees," Gyna said from behind. Yngvar turned to face her. Her dark eyes were alive with excitement. "I waved to him and he returned it."

"Don't wave at the trees!" Yngvar ducked his head as if he could

45

hide then felt foolish. He wiped his hand across his hair, then led Gyna aside. "You've sharp eyes to see him. Without making it obvious, could you show me where he is?"

"Your cheeks are red," she said, laughing. She then picked up her sleeping sack and shook it out. She snapped it twice toward the woods and looked at him with a raised brow. As she rolled up the sack, Yngvar followed the direction she had indicated.

Alasdair stood plainly among the trees, clear enough that Yngvar gave a worried whistle. He raised a tentative hand and Yngvar gave a short nod. He looked to Tovi next, but he was intent on studying the men gathered at the ship.

"I think Tovi assumes Alasdair is already with us," Yngvar said. "But that's a fair distance to cross without his being caught. We'll have to signal him to go south."

Gyna clucked her tongue as she held her sleeping sack to her chest. "Are you going to waste all our supplies playing games? It's too late to pretend you're not breaking your promise to Hakon. Anyway, have you not seen Alasdair run? Even on a horse, that bastard won't catch him."

Yngvar's eyes widened. "Gyna, you are cleverer than I ever thought."

"What?" She paused in turning to join Bjorn. She looked back at the trees. "Well, whatever you're thinking, if it's good I'll gladly accept credit. If it goes to shit, that's your mess."

He grabbed Thorfast as he directed men to the ship. A queue of men waited to launch once all were aboard. Their camp had been simple enough to break and the crew waited on the command.

"He's in the trees and will make a run for the ship on my signal."

Thorfast leaned away, his fair brows arched. "You've made this plan with him without my seeing?"

"He'll know what to do. For now, go start a fight with Bjorn for being too slow. Make it loud so Tovi doesn't watch me."

He trotted off to where Bjorn sat, then kicked beach sand into his face. "I told you to get up, lazy bastard!"

Bjorn fell back as if he had been sprayed by a geyser rather than beach sand. He cursed and pawed at his face, then stood up.

"What's that about?"

Thorfast shoved him toward the ship.

Yngvar slipped away, watching Tovi's attention flick toward the fight. He snatched up a smooth, heavy stone and tested its cool heft. He rounded behind Tovi's horse.

"A fine target," he said. "Now to hit it square."

He flung the rock and it struck the horse's rump with a meaty whack.

The horse shrieked and jumped. Tovi, who had been absorbed with Thorfast and Bjorn's shoving match, snatched for the horse's mane. The animal was not a cavalryman's mount. This was a farmer's nag and it was not prepared to be struck unexpectedly.

Tovi sloughed to one side as the horse flailed and kicked. The beast twisted as if it had been struck by a spear. Unable to maintain his grip, Tovi rolled to the dirt.

Alasdair ran from the trees.

Yngvar ran.

"Onto the ship!" he yelled at Bjorn and Thorfast as he shot past them.

While Bjorn's anger was honest, Thorfast laughed and followed Yngvar.

"Come back, you white-haired bastard!" Bjorn thundered after him.

"Launch!" Yngvar threw himself against the cold hull and began to push. The other men joined him. Thorfast's white hair was a blur as he leapt aboard. Bjorn chased after him, dumping himself over the railing.

Alasdair's lithe shape slipped aboard like a hawk's shadow.

When the ship caught the waves, Yngvar grasped a crewman's arm and got aboard ship. He thumped to his knees on the deck, where Alasdair lay flat. His face was smeared with dirt and sweat. His coppery hair sprouted twigs and leaves. But his smile was clear and clean.

"A good plan, lord."

Yngvar jumped back to the rails to see Tovi throwing his cloak over his shoulder as his horse fled up the shore. He raised his fist at Yngvar.

"The hostage is aboard your ship," he shouted. "King Hakon will know your treachery."

"Tovi," Yngvar shouted. "Be a practical man and I will reward you when I return."

"You'll never return," Tovi shouted. "The gods curse an oath-breaker."

"He's mad at being outwitted," Yngvar said, turning to his crew. Alasdair now stood, even though Tovi might yet see him. Bjorn's anger converted to astonishment. Thorfast and Gyna both patted Alasdair's back in welcome. Gyna pulled twigs from his hair.

"Got in fight with forest spirits, did you?"

He laughed. His silver cross had fallen out of his shirt and he stuffed it underneath again.

"I am glad to be back. God told me I must follow or your Fate would be terrible."

Yngvar laughed for joy. He could feel Tovi's stare even as the ship rode the waves out of sight.

But beyond the smiling faces of his Wolves, the crew stood with folded armed and grim faces.

Leiknr Bone-Feet was first among them, his face dark and threatening.

"The gods curse oath-breakers."

6

The sail cracked full overhead. The hull slashed across the gentle waves, sending cool spray over the rails to settle across the deck. The boards creaked and groaned and an oar slipped from its rack to clatter on the deck.

But for these sounds, Yngvar stood at the center of utter silence.

Thirty crewmen—some of long-service, the majority new to his ship—drew together in a dark mass of hulking shoulders draped in wolf furs or thick woolen cloaks. The wind set their hair flying and morning light shined through as if setting it ablaze. Their arms were either folded across their thick chests or else set on their hips.

At their fore, Leiknr Bone-Feet stood, an expression of utter disgust on his face. Only the rocking of the ship caused him to move. Thin shadows shaded his hollow face.

Yngvar felt as if he had boarded a different ship. He had forgotten how fast a crew could turn, especially men who were only beginning their first raiding season together. They had yet to form bonds with each other and to Yngvar. The lure of gold and glory had kept them in high spirits. Now that Leiknr had proclaimed Yngvar an enemy of the gods, their mood soured.

"No oaths were broken," Yngvar said. The words were weak even to himself. "Alasdair is here of his own choice."

He cringed at shifting the blame to Alasdair and regretted the words the moment they had fallen out of his mouth. Yet Alasdair took no offense. Instead, he straightened his back and lifted his chin. His youthful voice carried a note of maturity that had only bloomed in him since returning from Scotland.

"I keep a higher oath to God in heaven. I know none of you keep the same faith as I. But God showed me a vision and impressed on me that I must join all of you."

Yngvar wanted to jump to Alasdair's defense, but judged it better he have his own say. In fact, his words softened the stances of a handful of crewmen. While none of them were Christians, none of them doubted the Christian god lived. He was a weak god, captured and killed by men then nailed to a cross. Yet if the White Christ had spoken to Alasdair, could any man deny this was a powerful thing?

"But it is not your god who is offended," Leiknr said, his voice grating. "Odin and Thor, Tyr and Baldr, these gods demand we keep our oaths or become unworthy of their attention."

"I think it is more practical to think of bondsmen and bond-holders rather than gods," Yngvar said. "We should fear the reach of a man's sword more. And look, we are fast sailing away from King Hakon."

"And many of us hoped to return to him." Leiknr's retort drew nods and grunts from some of the newer men.

Was Leiknr seeking to take this ship for his own? The surprise of such a thought hit him like a hammer to the skull. The shore was not even out of sight. Leiknr had always been a dour man and a defeatist. But a traitor?

"You will return," Yngvar said. "Even if you believe to return with me will shame you. Listen, we sail for gold and glory. Are you not sailing with me because you believed I would bring this to you? Now, we've had one small change in plans and you are already dissatisfied."

"You broke your oath to King Hakon that Alasdair would be hostage to your return." Leiknr pulled his bony form up and dared to point at Yngvar's face. "The gods will curse you—and us—for it!"

Bjorn, still flushed with anger from his false fight with Thorfast, stepped forward.

"Hand down, or I'll fucking rip it off your arm." Bjorn's sudden charge forward cowed not only Leiknr, but the rest of the crew. They had all seen Bjorn fight, something one needed witness once to remember forever. He scanned the group, fists balled and ready to pounce.

"Any of you worrying like old ladies, quit it. If you're not feeling good about the trip, then I'll let you off here. We'll see how much the gods love you then. I expect you'll go down to Ran's bed at the bottom of the sea. No better place for crying cowards."

Bjorn glared at the crew. The veterans stifled laughter, for they were true to the Wolves and would not falter. The new men, however, looked aside. Bjorn folded his arms in satisfaction.

"Now, Alasdair's my friend. I wanted him with me from the start. He'll do more good with us than he would sitting with the women in King Hakon's hall."

Seizing the opening, Yngvar moved to Bjorn's side.

"If you are all concerned with my standing in the eyes of the gods, then I will make a sacrifice to them. I will give them my best treasures, and pledge them more should they only allow me the chance to take it."

The crew nodded to each other, but Leiknr remained sullen.

"Do not justify him," he said to the crew. "Or you'll share his shame. He has broken an oath to a king. The gods will not treat it lightly."

"You are eager to oppose me," Yngvar said. "And here I thought you a loyal if sour companion. If we must talk of oaths, then let us talk of yours. Do you still serve me?"

Leiknr put his blue-veined hand over his chest. His eyes widened to where it seemed they would pop from his head.

"I do serve! That is why I am so upset. I will follow you into this shame and bear it because I am your sworn man."

Yngvar held Leiknr's shocked gaze. He judged the steersman to be true. This anger was simply Leiknr being his usual, dour self. Rather than indulge the crew in further worry, he strode to the rails. As he looked over the side, the gray waters reflected sun into his eyes.

He worked off the gold bands on his arms, collecting them all in one palm. The crew watched in silent attention as he held the clinking and sparkling bands overhead.

"Here is the best of my treasures. Rings awarded to me by kings and jarls for heroic deeds. I offer them to Thor, mighty lord of storms, so that he will blow fair winds into our sail. I offer them to Odin the All-Father, that he may set his one eye upon our daring and be pleased enough to grant us his favor. Finally, I put these all into the sea so that Ran, who lies in her bed at the bottom of the ocean, will be distracted by their beauty. May she not see us while we sail, and take none to her bosom."

The gold bands were heavy in his hands. The rocking of the ship set them clicking and chiming against each other as he extended them over the waves. He gave his crew a solemn look. Both Bjorn and Thorfast looked on, their eyes and hard lines of their faces filling with shadow.

While Yngvar took great pride in his armbands, his greatest treasure was the sword he wore at his side. He had carried the weapon back from Ireland. Nothing could match its balance and grip. When he wielded it, the sword became a weightless blade that sewed doom among his foes. The edge was ever keen, and could be sharped with a feather. He prized this sword more than anything. If the gods dug into his heart, they would see he would sooner part with his life than throw the weapon into the sea. To make an honest offering of his greatest treasure, he would have to sacrifice this weapon for one of lesser quality.

He gambled that the gods would not look too deeply into him. The gleaming gold in his hands, quivering above the waves and ready to be sent into their treasure halls, would gather their attention.

"With this sacrifice of gold, let the gods see us worthy and honorable warriors."

Yngvar flung the rings across the waves. The men gasped and the gold slapped into the water with a flash of metal and white spray.

A gull dived out of the sky to chase the shining rings.

"The gods see our sacrifice," Thorfast shouted. He leapt up to the rails, grabbing a rigging line for balance. "This is a good sign!"

The crew cheered. Even Leiknr's expression shifted from disgust to mild repugnance.

"I'd have liked some of that gold," Gyna said, seating herself on the rail. "You could have made me a bracelet of one. Haven't I saved your life enough to earn your gold?"

She gave a wry smile, her dark hair blowing across her face.

"And you claim to guide the winds and keep us safe across the sea."

Her laughter chimed like the gold rings he had just cast into the water. Its sound lifted the hearts of the men, and soon all were set back to their tasks. The sail was adjusted and the crew began their songs.

They had seen the gods satisfied with an offering of gold. Their excitement for the sea road was renewed.

The excitement was not unwarranted.

Days sailed past and the weather remained fair and favorable. Dolphins followed their ship, leaping into the air in joy. The crew saw it as approval from the gods, and no amount of Leiknr's brooding on Alasdair's presence dampened their mood. By the time they had threaded the channel between Wessex and Frankia, even Leiknr had no more complaints. Weather in the channel was unpredictable and petulant. Yet they threaded the channel as if Thor himself held a gleaming shield over their heads.

Merchant ships and their escorts passed without challenge. Raiding ships saw their full deck and steered aside. The cruelest hardship they faced had been a crewman accidentally knocking a shield off the rack into the sea. By the time they were along the coast of Frankia, the men were convinced of impending success. Langbardaland would be laid bare and its marble palaces would bleed gold into their waiting hands.

"Should we visit my father?" Bjorn had asked one morning as they broke camp along the coast of what was now being called Normandy, the land Yngvar's father and grandfather had helped claim from the Franks.

"Not while the skies remain so clear and the winds so favorable," Yngvar said, overseeing his crew boarding the ship for another day at sea. "Besides, what would visiting Uncle Aren avail us? He is sworn to his jarl and neither is a Norseman any longer. Though Frankia might've been our birthplace, it is not where we will build our halls. There is no room for a man to win fame and land there anymore. That was the opportunity of our fathers. Let us leave the past in the past. Let Uncle Aren die in the peaceful bed he has made for himself."

Bjorn's single eye held his. Yngvar felt his face heat.

"I'm sorry for the harsh words, cousin. He is your father, after all. I meant him no disrespect."

"Think nothing of it," Bjorn said, waving his hand. "Just wondering how you felt. I feel the same. Thorfast ain't got nothing there anymore. Neither do you. Just me, and my father wasn't nothing. He showed me last time we visited, didn't he? You're right. Our time in Frankia is gone forever. Nothing there for us, no matter what our fathers thought."

"Hamar says we are a day from the north tip of Spanland," Yngvar said, shifting the topic. "Our supplies run low. We will have to take what we need from the coast. Your ax will be needed."

"My ax will be ready," Bjorn said, clapping Yngvar on the back.

The temperatures grew warmer and the seas choppier as they proceeded south. While Hamar knew the general direction to Langbardaland, he did not know the shorelines with the intimacy he did those of the northlands. So he kept to deeper waters farther from the coast. He would not risk rocks or strange currents in unfamiliar waters.

The northern tip of Spanland was much like Frankia in its tree-shrouded shorelines. Northmen were not uncommon there, and so when they made camp along the shores, they sought out peaceful trade. They were warned that the farther south they went, the more hostile they would find the coast. These people were called Moors, and came from lands more distant than even Langbardaland.

Within another day, they had crossed into this place, though the shoreline showed no visible changes. They had spotted more shipping on the horizon. These were ships with graceful profiles and two triangular sails. Whether they were traders or military ships, no one knew. Yngvar thought it best they avoid the unknown and let these ships fade over the horizon.

On the morning of their next day at sea, Leiknr called toward the land. "A town lies ahead."

Excited for their first sight of these Moorish towns, the crew gathered to the rails and strained to see across the yellow light shining off rolling waves.

A pile of square white buildings seemed to be tumbling down a steep hill to a small bay. Massed as they were, Yngvar could not count their number, but the town might rival Hauger for size. Pleasant smoke lifted above the rooftops, which were not of traditional thatch. He could not tell what they were from so far off, but they were various shades of brown and red.

"A strange gathering of homes," Thorfast said. "And look at the bay traffic."

A half dozen of the same graceful ships with single or double masts bobbed at anchor along the waterfront. Scattered beyond these were what must be fishing vessels from their small size and low profile. These ships had single, triangular sails that were fat with the wind.

"The fishermen will warn the town," Bjorn said. "Guess we better move along."

Yngvar grunted. "We've been moving along for too long. Now we're in need of ale and provisions. Who knows how much longer before we find something else?"

"That's a lot of people," Bjorn said. "We're only thirty men."

"Thirty Norse warriors," Yngvar said. He leaned both hands on the rails and peered harder at the shore. "And our ship shoots like an arrow over the waves. We will be ashore and gone with all we need before they can give chase."

The crew laughed and threatened the unsuspecting townsfolk still at peace in their morning routine. They were restless for action. If these so-called Moors were the conquerors their northern neighbors had warned about, then they would also be rich.

"We could offer trade," Thorfast said.

"Trade what?" Yngvar asked. "The gods took all my gold, and we're not here on a peace mission. The fool who leaves his treasures unguarded soon loses all. There is no wall around this town, not until high up that slope. The waterfront is open to us."

"That's where the riches will be, behind those walls," Bjorn said. "Can't get that far up and out before we're cut off."

"First, we are here to resupply. The real riches are waiting in Langbardaland," Yngvar said. "Second, that wealth must flow toward the sea. If we are lucky, we might catch a part of it while we are ashore."

Bjorn shrugged. "All right. Let's get the killing started."

"No more killing than needed," Yngvar said. "I've no love for these Moors, but I don't want them chasing us down. Kill their sons and soon all those ships at anchor will be after us. We want food and drink, and whatever else Fate puts before us. We land, strike, and flee before their guards organize."

The crew did not need any more encouragement. The sail billowed and the mast creaked, but the men sat on their sea chests and began to row. Hamar steered them toward the southern edge of the bay. Their attack could leap off there, and then allow them escape along their planned route.

The ship rocked and sped, sea spray flying over the sides and into Yngvar's face. The air rushed warm and salty over him and he laughed in delight. Ahead of them, ships began to scatter out of the bay. If only the locals united against him, Yngvar thought, he would be repelled. Yet fear turns a man's heart into itself and only thinks to unite with others when it is too late.

Their speed exhilarated Yngvar. Hamar, however, gritted his teeth and sweat shined on his brow as he directed the ship. But his co-steersman, Leiknr, stood in the prow and watched for rocks, sand-bars, or strange currents. Together they flung the ship like a spear at the nameless Moorish town.

"Oars in and grab your shields," Yngvar called. The wooden thump of oars yanked through the tholes mixed with the clatter of shields pulled off the racks. Yngvar stood ready to jump ashore with

Thorfast and Bjorn beside him. Gyna and Alasdair piled in behind where other crew joined.

Ten men would stay to guard the ship and keep it ready for escape. The other twenty would flood the shoreside stalls and markets and grab whatever they needed.

A horn sounded from the town as their ship glided toward the beach. Hamar turned it hard to slow the approach, splashing white waves into the sea. The moment the hull skimmed land, Yngvar leapt over the rails with shield and sword raised. He wore no mail but his heavy cloak and leather jerkin would protect him. The nose guard of his helmet clipped his vision, but he would never dare battle without it. Warm water filled his boots and mud sucked at his slogging footsteps through the knee-high water.

The people on the shore had either fled or hid at their thunderous arrival. All the crew roared battle cries. Untrained men could not withstand the terror of a score of charging Norsemen.

Yngvar summarized the layout. Back from the beach, roads led into the twisting maze of buildings. Running too far along those paths would end in death. None of the white buildings and their flat red roofs seemed distinct from the other. However, before these buildings were lines of stalls and carts filled with goods.

"There's our take," Yngvar shouted, pointing his sword at the cluster of wagons, bales, and crates. "Add a few casks and two chickens, and I'll be pleased."

"You heard," Bjorn said. "Get to it, boys!"

The horn continued to sound from within the depths of the town. Otherwise, the waterfront was eerily quiet and empty. Perhaps they were raided more often than it seemed.

With that thought, Yngvar looked up from his prizes to a line of three white buildings that jutted out from the rest. The white material that covered them had fallen away in patches to reveal reddish bricks beneath. Black run-off stains marred the walls. Unlike the surrounding buildings, these had flat roofs.

He saw the first heads appear over the edges of the buildings as his crew dashed forward.

"Shields up," he yelled. "Archers!"

7

The first arrow snapped on the packed earth of the waterfront. Yngvar shaded himself from the archers on the flat rooftops to his front and left by holding up his shield. He feared other archers on the lower level, who would be guaranteed an open shot at his belly. The skin there grew cold, expecting a shaft to plunge into his guts at any moment.

Yet his boots slopped seawater as he trudged forward in the company of his crew. Bjorn's shout was loudest, but even so cut short when more arrows rained down on them. They had drawn together out of instinct and could build a shield wall in an instant.

"I see six archers, lord," Alasdair said, peering out from beneath his shield.

"Six?" Thorfast, close to Yngvar's left side, shouted in surprise. "This many arrows for six men?"

"Their bows are small and swift," Alasdair said.

More arrows sprayed them, and bodkins clattered on wood shields. A man behind howled in pain, one of the shafts having slipped between their defense.

"Forget the wagon," Yngvar said. "Get close to the buildings."

He was the first to fall into the shade of these strange buildings. Their walls were hard and cold against his back. They were stone, but covered in a fragile white material that cracked and chipped after he had crashed against it.

"Get into the streets," he shouted. "Grab what you can find. Don't give the archers targets. Alasdair and Thorfast, with me. We'll get rid of those bastards to cover our escape."

Puddles showed on the hard sand where they had run up from the water. A bright splash of blood showed where an arrow had injured someone. As long as they cleaved to the walls, the archers had no angle for a shot.

Bjorn and Gyna both went screaming off into the side streets. Strange scents both sweet and foul emanated from the buildings. Yngvar glimpsed a flashing blue streak darting down the road as he passed, but he was intent on finding the archers. They would rain death upon them during a retreat.

"Lord, the door is barred," Alasdair said, being first to have threaded the shadowed paths that wended to the flat-roofed buildings. Yngvar looked up in time to see a dark face crowned with a blue turban leering down on them. The man lifted a small, curved bow over the wall.

He threw his shield over Alasdair in time to feel the arrow's shaft shudder against it.

Next, he shoved Thorfast back and hauled Alasdair with them.

Water splashed down over the door, splattering where Alasdair had only just stood. A short look up revealed two more men pulling a small iron pot back over the wall.

"Boiling water!" Thorfast shouted. "You saw?"

Yngvar shook his head. He had guessed it, having remembered the horrifying stories his father had told of the Norsemen's assault on Paris. Grandfather Ulfrik had seen boiling water and flaming pitch dumped on his companions as they scaled the walls. It was a logical defense, and this town had endured raids before.

Realizing the change in Moor tactics had created a pause. Yngvar flung himself across the brief distance to ram the door. It bent but did not break.

Thorfast added his shoulder as well. Strangely, not until Alasdair threw his slight form onto the door did it snap inward. Boards collapsed into the darkness beyond and revealed the bolt still in place.

Yngvar lifted out the bolt, working fast and fearful of an ax chopping into his forearm. But the bolt thudded inside and he shoved the door in.

Thorfast shouted, more from shock than pain. Alasdair had slid beneath him to enter first, his small shield out to defend against anyone waiting.

All three were piled inside. Heavy footfalls sounded above, and strange, dark words rushed between the men on the roof. Rough beds and a table and benches filled most of the room. The walls were bare but hung with decorative rugs. His wet feet slipped on rotten straw spread over the floor.

"They've pulled up the ladder," Thorfast said. He kept his shield up and dared to step into the square of pearly light falling through a hole in the ceiling.

The iron pot shot down and Thorfast stepped aside before it shattered his shield.

"Fucking thing's still hot!" He hopped away as the pot rolled over his foot.

"I could stand on the table, lord."

"And give them your head as you went up the hole?" Yngvar pulled Alasdair back toward the door. "I was hoping for steps or something else. Look, there is how we deal with these bastards."

A small hearth glowed with orange embers. A trestle stood where the iron pot had once been. Thorfast was already setting flame to one of the wood coverings.

"Gather the straw and their lice-eaten bedding. A nice smoky fire will chase them off the roof."

Yngvar looked around for whatever he might need. He kicked a small cask and it sloshed only with dregs.

"Fire's on," Thorfast said. "Let's go greet our friends."

The wool blanket he had thrown over the flames shuddered and threw reeking smoke up toward the hole. Yngvar's eyes already stung.

The Moors above started shouting, which seemed clustered toward the rear of their building.

"Around back," Yngvar said, then led his companions back into the alleys.

The water puddled at the door had already gone cold as he stomped through it. He heard screaming and his men whooping from the maze of warm gloom that led into the Moorish town. Pottery shattered somewhere and a woman shrieked.

All signs of success. The town had a militia defense and the real guard had not found them yet. Yngvar smiled.

Storming around the corner, he found the ladder and the men scrabbling down it as he had expected.

Despite the danger, this was his first encounter with Moors and he was curious. They wore baggy, cream colored clothes. Leather cuffs protected their wrists. The men were dark-skinned, even darker than Gyna. Their eyes were black and desperate and flashed as they spotted Yngvar.

In the cramped space, bows and swords were useless. Yngvar sheathed his and drew the short sword at his lap.

He bowled the first man over with his shield, then stabbed his sword into the back of the man descending the ladder above him. He fell screaming atop his comrade.

Alasdair swept in and stabbed both men on the ground.

Two remained on the rooftop. One had apparently escaped already.

"Burn to death," Thorfast shouted, then kicked down the ladder.

Black smoke began rolling out between the roof and walls. The two Moors pulled back out of sight.

"They'll jump down in the front," Yngvar said. "If they are smart, they will flee."

The two corpses at his feet were piled atop each other, and Alasdair frisked the bodies.

"Nothing but poor guards, lord. But see their bows." He picked one up, something like a child's toy.

"That'd never break mail," Yngvar said. "Probably good only for shooting their own townsfolk. Thorfast, sound your horn. We've no time to spare. If the men haven't claimed anything yet, then it is our loss."

Three sharp notes sounded retreat to the ship. Yngvar did not know how much time had passed. His heart raced and sweat poured from beneath his helmet, bringing an itch where the leather lining pinched his hair.

He ventured to the other side of the building to see if his men had gone this far.

They had. One of them lay bleeding face-down on the street. Two others huddled behind their shields while jabbing their longswords at two Moorish men standing on a wagon.

Whatever had drawn the wagon had broken free, leaving it pinned against the blank sidewall of a building. Yngvar's two crewmen hemmed the wagon, barring any escape that would not bring the Moors onto their blades.

One man was naked to his waist, where his dark skin glistened with sweat and blue tattoos writhed across his flesh. He was all snarling white teeth and black beard. Blood shined over half of his face. His turban had been knocked away revealing a cut flap of skin on his forehead. He slashed out with a strangely curved blade that seemed to grow wider toward the end.

The other Moor was much older, garbed in blue robes and a blindingly white turban. Gray hair showed beneath it and his neat beard was iron gray. He clutched something to his chest with one hand, and jabbed at Yngvar's men with a broken spear.

Yngvar ran for his man lying in the path. He groaned when Yngvar crouched beside him.

"Thorfast, Alasdair," he shouted. "Get this one back to the ship."

A glance down the path revealed the bright light of the water-front. Yngvar turned back to his crewmen surrounding the cart.

"We're pulling out," he shouted as he joined them. The fierce Moor with the strange blade, however, swiped at Yngvar. The sword was heavy and clanged against the boss of his shield to send a numbing wave through his forearm.

"The old man's got a fortune," said one of the warriors as he panted. "Not letting that get away."

Whatever the old man clutched to his chest was wrapped in a

soft-looking red cloth. He hissed like a poisonous snake and his broken spear darted like a snake's tongue.

"Then finish this," Yngvar said.

He leapt up to the wagon, drawing even with the bare-chested swordsman. His eyes widened, shocked to find the length of his sword a burden with Yngvar pressing him.

"Get down," Yngvar shouted, then bashed the Moor with his shield. For all the Moor's ferocity, fighting atop a wagon left him disadvantaged. He caught his foot in the crowded space of the wagon bed and he fell forward amid Yngvar's waiting men.

The old man sought to run, but Yngvar battered him with his shield. The old Moor toppled over the edge of the cart, and Yngvar leapt down beside him.

"I hope whatever you hold was worth your life," Yngvar said as he drove his foot onto the Moor's arm to pin him.

A stream of words fell out of the Moor's mouth. Yngvar pulled back his sword to stab, but suddenly the words made sense. The man was speaking Frankish.

"Do you understand this? Please don't kill me!"

The accent was hard and clipped, but Yngvar had no difficulty understanding.

"You speak Frankish? Well, my friend, you've earned yourself a place in my crew."

He raised his foot, and the old man made to slither away. Yngvar put his blade under the Moor's neck.

"Stand and follow," he said in Frankish. "Or you'll join your friends."

The bare-chested Moor had become a bleeding heap of flesh. Yngvar's two warriors were picking through the wagon. Beyond them, Alasdair and Thorfast dragged the injured crewman toward the end of the road.

Hounds began barking, and now bells began ringing in the distance.

He prodded the old Moor, who glared at him. His eyes were ringed with dark circles and fleshy bags. Despite his dark skin and apparent age, his eyes were a striking blue that fixed Yngvar as sure as two arrows.

"Your anger is wasted," he said to the Moor. "Accept your fate and life will be easier. Now move."

The sword point in his back set the Moor down the track. Yngvar's crewmen whooped as they filled their sacks from the wagon bed's contents. Yet as the barking drew closer, they joined Yngvar in retreating to the waterfront.

His men dashed across the sun-drenched waterfront and down to the beach. The ship rocked gently on the water, and the crewmen waiting on deck leaned over the rails as if they sought to grab their brothers from the shore.

The Moor ducked out of Yngvar's blade and sprang away. For an instant, Yngvar considered letting him run. What good was another man to feed? Yet he could speak Frankish and at least his local language. Such a man could be useful, especially as they traveled deeper into strange lands.

For his age, the Moor moved with speed and grace. His blue robe fluttered after him as he sped back toward the maze of buildings. Both arms clamped the object covered in red cloth to his chest. Yngvar charged after him, but his moment of hesitation had bestowed a lead to the Moor.

Alasdair turned toward the shouting, but he and Thorfast were already tramping into the water with the injured crewman between them. The rest of the crew were too distant to aid in pursuit. So Yngvar ran, but the Moor dodged into an alley and out of sight.

He bounced out, sprawling to the hard-packed earth with a shocked scream. His cloth-covered prize remained pressed to his chest as a bloom of brilliant red in the sunlight.

Yngvar bounded up to him and found Gyna sprawled out opposite the Moor as if she had collapsed in a drunken stupor, arms and legs thrown wide and head back. Her deerskin pants were splashed with the blood of her opponents.

The Moor stirred first, sitting up to face Yngvar's sword point.

"Fast for an old man," he said in Frankish. "It'll be a shame to hamstring you. Stand."

The Moor's face shaded even darker in anger. His cold blue eyes flicked behind Yngvar, but he did not take the bait. Instead he poked his sword into the base of the Moor's neck.

"I'm not leaving you behind alive. So make a choice before I can flick my wrist and open your throat."

The Moor collected himself, rising slowly. As the barking hounds drew closer, Yngvar understood the Moor delayed for help to arrive.

He slammed the pommel of his sword into the Moor's head. He staggered back, heavily veined hands covering his face, then toppled. His red cloth bundle thumped to his feet.

Yngvar caught him then swept him over his shoulder. His turban remained fixed in place despite hanging upside down. Yngvar wanted to know how that trick was done. Yet for now, he had deeper worries.

Bjorn pounced out of the small alley. He held Gyna underarm like a child's doll. Yet the moment her feet touched the ground she wrestled free with a curse.

"Cousin!" Bjorn shouted, his single eye bulging white. "Run!"

He then seized Gyna's arm and fled.

Yngvar did not need to know what could frighten Bjorn. He turned with the Moor over his shoulder mumbling in some evil-sounding language.

The crew were throwing casks and sacks over the rails, or handing up crates that had been carried by small groups. They were jubilant, laughing and joking with the crew that had remained behind. As Yngvar reached the surf, however, he noticed two of his crewmen stepping back from the rails and pointing behind. They began to shout for their companions to get aboard.

Yngvar turned back, the Moor groaning with the sudden twist.

Mounted warriors were exiting from the alleyways onto the waterfront. They were the real troops. They wore gray and white robes bulked out with armor beneath. Pointed helmets gleamed over their heads and their dark skin showed only teeth gritted in hatred.

They did not ride down Yngvar, but dismounted with fluid ease and pulled bows from their shoulders.

"Get the ship launched!" Yngvar shouted. "Get us to sea!"

He splashed through the knee-high waves that shoved him back toward the archers lining up their shots.

Arrows plinked around him or clanked against the hull of his ship. These were not the toy bows of the waterfront guards. These were war bows that shot across the deck of his ship, flattening the crew as they avoided the missiles.

"Take this old man," Yngvar shouted as he shoved the Moor to the rails. The old man was thin and weighed less than a sack of grain. Someone pulled him aboard, and Yngvar mounted behind him.

Ten archers had lined up. Now huge, black dogs raced out of the alleys followed by more men carrying spears and colorful, teardrop-shaped shields.

"That's what I ran into," Bjorn said. "The dogs are rabid, I swear it."

The archers were swift to send another volley. Each shot had been chosen. Yngvar could draw a mental line from their shafts to the targets on deck. He grabbed what men he could and fell flat. The others had to be trusted to fate.

One man splashed overboard with a scream. The rest cried out as the arrows sliced past them. Yet the ship rocked and lurched as the sail snapped full and men fed oars into the water.

Yngvar was proud of his ship. King Hakon's gift had been well made as the fairest representation of Norse ship-building skill. Its draught was so shallow it could sit ready to sail in ankle-high water. The rudder could be set to either end for expeditious retreats. All this and the ship sped faster than any he had ever known. He smiled as Hamar shouted encouragement to his oarsmen.

They sped into deeper water and beyond the range of bowshot.

The crew realized this as well, and lusty cheers went up as the longship shuddered across the low waves. The Moors were lined up helplessly at the shore. Yngvar watched the bowmen stow their weapons and the footmen put leashes to their war dogs once more.

He raised his sword over the pile of sacks, casks, and crates thrown around the central mast.

"Praise Odin All-Father! The gods have rewarded our daring!"

Believing themselves free of danger, the rowers paused and joined the entire crew to raise their fists in celebration. Their shouts echoed across the waters as they glided past rocky cliffs that threw a shadow over the deck.

"Lord, on the rocks above," Alasdair said. "What is that?"

Yngvar stopped shouting and followed Alasdair's pointing finger.

What he saw did not make any sense. A half-dozen men seemed to be dancing around some wooden contraption while two other men leaned on hands and knees at the cliff edge to study Yngvar's ship passing below. They shouted back to their companions, gesturing as if to guide the wooden machine's rotation.

Something metallic gleamed as wooden clicking echoed down the cliff.

"Hamar!" Yngvar shouted. "Pull out to sea now!"

8

Yngvar did not know what to call the war machine pointed at his ship. He knew they had only a moment to jink out of its aim. It seemed nothing more than a wooden wall that could be angled in every direction by some mechanism worked by its crew. Alasdair continued to point at it after Yngvar had called Hamar to change direction.

Whatever it was, it could not react as fast as his lithe ship. Yet if whatever it fired struck his hull, he would be grabbing for broken deck to keep himself afloat.

"Turn hard!" Yngvar shouted again.

The celebration stuttered to silence as they followed Yngvar's and Alasdair's gaze. The world fell silent. Yngvar heard or saw nothing but that gleaming object training on his ship's path.

The two Moors leaning over the cliff edge, heads swathed in gray cloth, raised their hands in unison.

"Turn!"

Hamar groaned as he threw his weight on the tiller. Thorfast, who stood near him, jumped on him to add his weight.

The deck creaked and snapped, and the ship shuddered as it skipped across the current.

A hard snap echoed from above and a massive metal shaft

launched down at them. The black iron caught a dull gleam as it streaked down.

The ship tipped hard to the side and anyone not already gripping the rails staggered with the shift.

The massive iron arrow, for Yngvar could call it nothing more, smashed into the rails on the far side. Wood snapped and splintered. Men screamed as the entire ship juddered with the impact.

But the iron arrow plunged into the water and the sea gulped it down.

Hamar let off the tiller and the ship again snapped into its old course. Yngvar staggered the other way, but he felt feather light. The shot had missed and merely blasted apart a section of the rails.

The crew let out a cheer for Hamar.

But Yngvar did not relent. "Whatever that was, it must have a mighty range. Bring us to safety."

They rowed and one man started a song of heroic victory. Another joined and soon the air filled with their raucous voices. Yngvar watched the shadowed cliffs recede. The nameless town remained unperturbed despite the violence they had visited upon it. He had lost a single crewman and one whose injuries seemed likely to lead to Valhalla. He was laid out against the gunwales, having rolled into it when the ship listed, and his blood pooled thick around his back.

Gyna rolled him over while keeping fresh bandages tucked underarm. She stared hard at him and gave the bandages to Alasdair who had gone to help.

Two men traded for a heap of valuables and supplies. Every one of his crew understood the risk. All of them knew death earned them a seat at Odin's feast where battle and celebration carried on until the end of days.

"A fair take," Thorfast said, wiping his brow with the back of his arm. "If those horsemen had arrived earlier, our heads might decorate those high Moorish walls."

"Never thought I'd see horsemen in a city," Yngvar said. "But imagine crashing into them in those narrow streets. Those evil beasts would stamp you into a bloody puddle."

"And their war hounds would lap that up." Thorfast laughed at the gory imagery. Yngvar shared it, though he knew how close to truth it had come. He needed to laugh.

Thorfast crouched before the old Moor, who sat on the deck slumping like a sinking ship. The smoldering fire of his blue eyes had petered out, leaving the bags and dark rings to hide his eyes. His arms were wrapped around his chest, but his red cloth and whatever it had hidden was lost.

"So, you made a friend?" he asked. "Everyone else was sensible enough to grab and run, but you had to mix with the locals."

"He speaks Frankish," Yngvar said, not to Thorfast but to the old Moor. He crouched beside him as well, but the Moor looked through them into a world of ruin and loss.

"You speak my mother's language?" Thorfast asked. "Well, you and I are going to be best of friends."

The Moor spared a shift of his eyes to Thorfast, then looked back into this gloomy world.

"Your mother laid with goats then dropped you from her rotten womb."

"The accent is fair," Thorfast said, smiling. "But I can help you adjust it."

His fist slammed into the Moor's cheek, snapping his head back. Still the white wrap around his head and neck remained in place. But now blood dribbled from the corner of the Moor's mouth to stain the brilliant white cloth under his neck.

"If you keep talking like that, I'll give you more practice," Thorfast said. He drew his dagger and pointed it at the Moor's face. "Maybe if I pry out a few teeth you'll pronounce your words better?"

"Enough," Yngvar said. "I want him to speak for us as we travel south."

Thorfast glared at the Moor, then shifted back to his easy smile. "A slave has many uses. He can bail, and if storms rise against us, we can sacrifice him to Thor."

The threat penetrated the wall of despair ensconcing the Moor, but he merely widened his eyes as his only response.

"He's dead," Alasdair said.

Yngvar stood, ready to call Alasdair blind for not seeing the Moor lived, then realizing Alasdair spoke of his crewman. He turned to find Gyna arranging the man's sword so that it rested over his body with both his pale hands over the hilt.

The singing faded away as the crew realized they had lost their second companion this day. Bjorn stood solemnly behind Gyna. He turned his single eye to the Moor. Yngvar read the anger boiling in his cousin's heart.

He stood between Bjorn and the Moor. "Peace, the Moor is our captive. We need his aid in speaking with the people here."

Bjorn's lip curled and he squared himself to the Moor, who remained staring into nothing.

"We didn't come this far south to talk. And how would you know he's speaking honestly for us? Let me twist his head off and feed it to the sharks."

"He might serve a purpose," Yngvar said. "The gods put him in our path for a reason. If he has no value then we will sell him."

"An old man like that?" Bjorn sneered at the Moor. "He's not worth a hen in trade. Better to throw him over the side now."

Yngvar considered the Moor. Desperation molded his gaunt face. His eyes remained vacant and unfocused. His dark skin was pale even against the whiteness of his head cover. Such a state might lead him to rash decisions, either to attack or to kill himself. Wanting neither outcome, he nodded to one of his crew.

"Tie the Moor to the mast. At least until he regains his senses."

Confident no one pursued, Yngvar ordered the ship to turn south again. The shoreline was a faint strip now, but they needed to hew closer before nightfall. While they could sail throughout the night, it was more restful for the crew to beach each night.

They counted their booty from the raid. Casks were filled both with beer and wine. They had also found casks of fish and eels preserved in salt. They would be fed for days, at least long enough to reach the sea leading to Langbardaland.

Gold and silver had also been looted, and while it could not feed a man's stomach, it amply fed his greed. If this was a sample of what could be pulled from a simple seaside town, then what would the palaces of the old world yield? The crew speculated through the long journey south, each guess becoming more outrageous than the last. Soon they were anticipating mountains of gold and jewels along with beautiful women with silken hair and milk-white skin. All of this would spill out of magical palaces into their eager hands. They shared laughter at their expectations, but Yngvar guessed more than one believed most of their imaginings.

Yet of all the imagined treasures, none were as grandly envisioned as the Moor's lost red cloth. The two who had pinned him to the wagon claimed he held a brick of solid gold. Yngvar knew whatever the Moor carried had been light. It might have been only a treasure to the Moor, and no one else.

The Moor remained lashed to the mast, listless and staring into nothingness. After insulting Thorfast, he remained unresponsive. A crust of blood formed where his lip fattened after Thorfast had battered him. He refused water and conversation.

The crew regarded him with a wary eye. The day they gave their sword-brother a sea burial, they each looked to the Moor as if he should answer for the death. But Yngvar had kept them away, instead heaping praise and glory on the dead man. He had hardly known this crewman, who had joined this summer. He felt guilty for not feeling the man's death harder than he did. He was perhaps no older than twenty, and likely younger.

The journey remained blissfully dull for days after the raid. By afternoon of the third day, Hamar guided the ship to a narrow strait between Spanland and a foreign coast called Blaland. No one knew what Blaland was, but it was home to the Bluemen. He had heard descriptions of these people with blue skin and tightly curled hair. They were tall and fierce warriors, or so he was told. But none were present as they threaded this strait.

The waters here turned startling blue and the air was hotter and more humid than anything he had experienced before. Ahead of them a massive slab of island jutted from the sea. Surely it had been set there by giants at the beginning of the world, and it filled the crew with silent reverence.

"It is a wonder to see," Thorfast mused. "But if my eyes are not wrong, there is a fortress atop it. Where there is a fortress by the sea, there must be warships. Let's stay clear."

"Jebel Tariq."

The Moor spoke his first words since insulting Thorfast's mother. Where the majestic profile of the island had quieted the crew, it seemed to reinvigorate the Moor. As their ship glided atop the clear green water, the Moor began to fight his bonds and shout in a foreign language.

"Thought he spoke Frankish?" Bjorn asked. He and Gyna stood in the prow to get the best view of the mighty island.

"Well, Moor, you have a tongue, it seems," Yngvar said. "Don't struggle against the ropes. I'll let you off if you promise to mind yourself. Come now, you've already pissed your robes. Don't want to shit yourself as well, do you?"

The Moor glared at him, but the days of accepting nothing more than water and wine had hollowed out his face. The bruise-like pouches surrounding his lusterless eyes had sunk into the sockets. His cheekbones stretched his mole-speckled skin.

"That is Mount Tariq," he said. "To see it means you have taken me far from my home. You did not seek to ransom me."

Yngvar raised a brow. "Did you think we were sailing in a circle while waiting on your words? We're headed to Langbardaland. You were just a lucky find along the way."

The Moor frowned, but then bowed his head. "So I am to be your slave?"

Bjorn joined Yngvar's side. "Ain't much choice unless you were thinking of being his wife."

He exploded into laughter, slapping Yngvar's back and looking to the rest of the crew to join him. He had apparently forgotten none of them spoke Frankish. He wiped at his eye with the back of his wrist and let his laughter fade.

"You amuse yourself," Yngvar said. "That is well, but do it elsewhere."

"Hey, it's half-true. You need a woman, more than those whores you lay with between raids." Bjorn paused and smiled at the Moor. "He wears a head cover like a woman. I just thought—"

73

"Go check the hull for barnacles," Yngvar said, shoving Bjorn aside. His cousin seemed confused at the order, then realized the insult. He walked off, grumbling.

The ship rocked and swayed and the sail snapped taut above them. Yngvar locked eyes with the Moor.

"You must have a name and a history. I'll untie these ropes and you'll tell me both. You might be my slave, but I am a good master as long as my will is obeyed."

The rope softly thumped to the deck. Alasdair picked up an end and began to coil it. His bright face looked up at the Moor.

"He's a strange man, lord. I do not trust him."

"Nor do I," Yngvar said. The Moor's knees buckled and he fell forward onto Yngvar. He caught the old man, who was no heavier than an armful of firewood.

"I am Jamil Ibn Asim," the Moor said as he straightened and smoothed his blue robes. Sea salt and sweat stained what had been a fine robe days ago.

"I am Yngvar Hakonsson. You will refer to me as lord, or Lord Yngvar."

"You are not a jarl?" Jamil asked. His voice was warm but rough.

"And you are not a king," Yngvar said. "Yet I do not judge you for it."

"And you know I am not a king?"

"You travel with poor guards for a king."

"Yet one of three of your pitiful warriors died fighting my single guard. The other two could not combine their wits to outsmart a senile ox."

Yngvar laughed. The Moor's estimation was not far from the truth. Yet he accepted crewmen for bravery and strength and not their minds.

"There was gold and wine in your wagon," Yngvar said. "So you are no poor man. Who are you and how have you come to know my language?"

Jamil sighed and his shoulders drooped. "I am a scholar and languages come naturally to me. I learned Frankish from settlers who lived near my birthplace. Traders and travelers have kept it sharp all these years. I learned Arabic, Greek, and Latin at school."

"But you don't understand Norse?" Yngvar wondered if the Moor might feign ignorance of Norse to listen in on plans or to seek advantage. It seemed such a smart man should know the language of the north, but if he did know then he should have used it when begging for his life.

"My teachers did not see any value in learning the babble of savages." Jamil's expression clouded, then he shook his head. "I was not a resident of the place you found me. I was visiting my cousin, who is married to the ruler of that town. The treasures your stole were to be gifts for her and her husband."

"But you carried something of greater value, and we lost that. I've no care to return for it, but I am curious what it was?"

"A book," Jamil said. "From a land too far away for your barbarian mind to know it. Books are rare and precious things. My cousin's husband collects books and scrolls of all sorts. He has a clever mind. I pray that God has seen that gift into his hands. I fear one of his soldiers picked it up and didn't understand what they had found."

"We had thought it a gold brick," Yngvar said. "Glad it was nothing valuable."

"If it had been a gold brick, I'd have smashed your skull with it—Lord Yngvar."

Yngvar laughed, clapping Jamil's shoulder. "You have fight in you. That must be why your back is so straight and your teeth so full despite your age. It keeps a man young. As for books, I suppose some can be held for ransom like a nobleman. But that's a rare thing. For me books are good for starting fires in churches when you need to burn them fast."

"No doubt your people do little more than read animal entrails and signs in the clouds." Jamil sniffed and looked across the sea to the mighty island at the horizon. "Mount Tariq. My people have erected a fortress there. If you think yourself a great warrior, why not test your sword against them?"

"I have taken my blows in battle, but my head has not been hit so many times that I'd be fool enough to attack a fortress with a single ship. Your low estimation of me is insulting." Yngvar faced the island. "We sail beyond this place. Your Mount Tariq is not our goal. The palaces of Langbardaland are what we seek. Palaces built of a stone called marble are filled with ancient treasures. I have seen these myself, sacks of gold coins all of the same design. We go to plunder these halls and return as kings to our own lands."

Jamil gave a wan smile. "Certainly all of you hairy beasts crowded on this strip of wood you call a ship must feel invincible. You row and sweat and sing songs about rape and murder. But do you know the dangers you will meet?"

Yngvar raised a brow. He disliked the smug expression spreading across Jamil's face.

"These palaces you imagine. They exist. But you fool yourself if you imagine they sit empty. Where in the world do rooms of gold hang open for anyone to take?"

"I know the treasure will be guarded," Yngvar said, his playfulness vanishing. "But we are Norsemen. No one stands before us. No one has more valor or strength in battle. We laugh at death and give it freely to our enemies."

"Yes, I saw that while you fled from a few horsemen and archers," Jamil said. He pointed with his sharp chin toward the island on the horizon. "There is treasure on that island, more than this pathetic ship can carry. There are also hundreds of warriors stationed there. No matter your valor, you will be destroyed before you can defeat all of them. You are a fool to believe palaces of gold will be guarded by fewer men than these. You have quite the estimation of your own strength."

Yngvar noted both Bjorn and Thorfast listening in sullen quiet. Alasdair and Gyna showed concern, though neither understood Tariq's speech.

"Are you ready to face the might of the Berber warlord, the Arab warrior, and the Byzantine soldier? You've not even tasted the strength of my own people, the Moors. If you believe you will sail past them with a ship full of gold, then you are even a greater fool than I thought. You'll never make it home."

"Some of our people did," Yngvar said, drawing up to Tariq's face.

Heat spread across his cheeks and he glared into the Moor's unsettling blue eyes. To his surprise, the Moor did not flinch.

"Some out of how many? You are not the first of your people to sail here expecting wealth beyond measure. You will not steal it, not in the quantities you expect. Lord Yngvar, if you hope to survive this journey of yours, I suggest you align yourself to one of the powers in this region. Your people make fine mercenaries. Sell yourself to one of the rulers here. Otherwise, you will be the enemy of all and ally of none. And you and this ship will be sent to the bottom of this beautiful blue sea and rot."

Jamil smiled as if he could sink the ship with his words alone. The crew, seeing but not understanding the confrontation, had paused in their duties to stare at Jamil.

Then Leiknr Bone-Feet let out his shrill warning.

"Sails on the horizon!"

9

The sails on the horizon were bigger than anything Yngvar had ever seen, even from this distance. The ship had three masts of triangular sails and it had the wind in its favor.

Yngvar pointed his own ship in the direction of the wind and let it carry him across the waves. He laughed at the silhouette of the foreign ship as he sped away. They could never be caught.

"This is the bravery you speak of?" Jamil asked. He was now freed of his bonds, and had not yet been assigned work. His salt-stained robes pressed against him, revealing a weak frame withered by days without food.

"It is wisdom," Yngvar said, sitting on the rails and enjoying the cool spray on his face. The weather here was hotter than anything he had ever known. He had stowed his wool cloak, as had the rest of the crew. Even the sea smelled different here, sharper and clearer than the murky waters of the north.

"You will face larger ships than that one," Jamil said. "Reflect on what I have warned. In truth, you are safer to turn back."

"You've not eaten in days," Yngvar said. "Feed yourself so that I can break your back on the oars. Or perhaps I'll tie you to the spar and you can watch for these ships you warn of."

Jamil's eyes widened. Perhaps the old Moor did not understand his position. He was a man of comfort and a master of slaves, not one himself. Yngvar would enjoy teasing that haughtiness out of him. Yet, in truth, Jamil had value for his knowledge and Yngvar would not put him to base use.

The giant warship faded over the horizon. The wide green sea glittered in peace and the sun strafed the deck with heat. He saw no clouds in the rich blue sky.

"It's like a land of dreams," Thorfast said, leaning on the rails beside him. "I've never seen such colors."

The sea hissed beneath the hull, sending white foam flying into the ship's wake. The wind kept the sail full and the crew off the oars. Hamar leaned on the tiller, his strong arm untaxed by the calm water. A warm period of restful silence had fallen over them.

"The heat is a bit much," Yngvar said. "I don't think we have taken the right clothing for this raid."

Thorfast laughed and the both stared at the foamy waves in silence. Bjorn and Gyna joined as well as Alasdair.

"Hamar calls this the Midgard Sea," Alasdair said. "The Moor calls it the Mediterranean Sea."

"You spoke with Jamil?" Yngvar asked. "I thought you would just toss him some food."

"He speaks Latin, lord. I understand bits of it from my time with the priests. I can at least make some of the sounds."

"Medtha-jir-yan-in See." Bjorn struggled with the strange sounds, then shook his head. "Midgardarhaf is much easier."

Gyna poked Yngvar's shoulder. "What did you and the old man talk about? I thought you'd kill him. Be a pity if you did. Finally someone here darker than me."

Yngvar scanned Gyna with fresh eyes. Compared to the Moors he had seen, she could no longer be called dark.

"It's the babbling of a slave," Yngvar said. "He is mad from hunger."

"Actually," Thorfast said. "He spoke the truth."

"Which was?" Gyna poked Yngvar's shoulder again. "You're not going to keep it a secret from me and Alasdair. Never mind the whole crew who knows something has soured your handsome face."

Yngvar started at the compliment. Gyna had so few of them for him. He looked to Bjorn, who squinted with a single eye at an empty horizon.

Thorfast cleared his throat. "The Moor thinks we cannot oppose the enemies we will find in Langbardaland. He said the fortress we avoided is a shadow of what will come, and the ship we fled from this morning is one of many others waiting to oppose us."

Gyna followed Bjorn's gaze out to sea, her smile vanished. As Thorfast had spoken in Norse, the crew nearby perked up their ears.

Yngvar turned toward the mast, where Jamil sat clutching a wood bowl beneath his chin. He sipped from it thoughtfully, his black-ringed eyes lost in another place.

"He said we should sell our swords to one of the powers in the Midgard Sea," Yngvar said. "Otherwise, we will become enemies of all and crushed between them."

Bjorn slapped the rail. "I didn't break an oath to a Norse king to give my oath to some blue man in a dress."

"We would not give an oath of service," Yngvar said. "We would sell our strength to whoever would buy it for the price we name. And we would claim whatever prizes we earn from fighting our employer's foes. It is not the same thing."

"Well, it's not a palace of gold either," Gyna said. "I imagined bathing in a tub of gold coins."

"You'd never get clean that way," Bjorn said. She and Bjorn laughed.

Yngvar wanted to join them, but he continued to stare at the Moor. Damn him for bringing everyone to their senses. He had sobered their expectations and dampened their taste for adventure. Now they were learning caution and might crawl home like beaten dogs before facing a real challenge.

"We will raid this coast," Yngvar said. "Even if it is not Langbardaland, it is an old place and must be full of unclaimed treasures. We need to taste those riches, and then we will renew our spirts. The men will be hungry for more and will dare greater foes to grab it."

The call to glory roused the men around him. Yngvar felt his spirits lift. His Wolves followed along, but Thorfast had been bitten hardest by the Moor's dire predictions. He might have shouted for gold and fame along with the others, but his face betrayed his worries.

Wanting to strike at dawn when everyone would be fresh and their victims yet unaware, he kept the ship at sea. They slept on deck in shifts throughout the night, where the brilliance of stars guided them eastward. They now kept sight of land to the south and knew that following it would lead to their destination. Shipping traffic increased as well, a sure sign of riches laying ahead of them.

By dawn, Yngvar had chosen to follow the distant line of ships to wherever they intended to dock. He asked Jamil for his estimation of where they were, but the Moor had no head for navigation. He shrugged.

"You will find either Berbers or Arabs of the Caliphate. I've never left my homeland."

"Nothing you've said means anything to me," Yngvar said. "Will there be riches here?"

"If those shores are part of the Caliphate, then you can be certain. Berbers can be little better than barbarians at times. I cannot comment on an individual warlord's wealth. I do not care what you find, for once you are defeated, I will at least become a slave of proper Muslims. They will know me for what I am worth."

Yngvar leaned over the rails as he looked toward the coast. The rocky land was dotted with tall, thin trees unlike anything he had seen before. They lacked leaves except for the very tops, where many grew like the fronds of a fern. Beneath these were scrubby bushes and yellow rocks, all obscured by dust kicked up in the wind.

Following the barren shores, he spotted the towers of a walled city.

"There is where we will strike."

Though he spoke in Norse, Jamil understood enough to laugh. Bjorn cuffed him for his insolence. Thorfast sucked his breath. Alasdair peered alongside of Yngvar.

"Lord, I expect those walls will be impossible to scale."

"We will strike into the bay, and raid the ships there. Then we shall speed away with our rewards. Can any of these fat ships match us on the open sea?"

He spoke with willful ignorance. No one knew the capabilities of the enemy they would face. For all he knew, they might have tamed dragons and giants that would pluck his delicate ship out of the sea and smash it to splinters. Yet his crew needed victory and a taste of what lay ahead. Even if all they did was pluck bales of wool from a trading ship, it was proof they could have their way in this strange land.

"Hamar! Guide us to their port and find us a plump trader!"

The crew let out a cry and Hamar shook his head. Leiknr Bone-Feet frowned at Yngvar.

"You test this ship," he said. "If we get hooked into one of those bigger ships, we'll never break free."

Yngvar waved the fear aside. Leiknr, of course, had a legitimate point which Yngvar refused to concede. Nothing about this journey would be rewarded for caution. It was a bold plan. The gods loved a bold plan and would favor him. If he cowered like a boy behind his mother's skirt, then the gods would rightfully crush him for his worthlessness.

Their ship sped as good as the wind. An array of different-sized ships converged on this place. Some were high-sided and others clung to the sea as low as Yngvar's own ship. All had the strange triangular sails, though the number of masts depended on the size of the vessel. Rigging lines cut across their outlines in the early morning light.

A walled city of white stone had grown up beside the port. Round towers brooded over the waters, and oddly curving roofs showed behind these. Yngvar noted a wall section had been built out into the water to form a protective barrier capped with a tower. They would have to snake around it or else be filled with arrows on their flight from this bay. He had never seen such defensive works, but it made good sense in this setting.

"We draw nearer," Leiknr shouted, which no man needed to know. Leiknr wiped sweat from his brow and fidgeted with a rigging line. Worry dogged him, unlike his fellows who had chosen to gulp beer and prepare for the impending fight.

"Shields ready," Yngvar ordered. "I see a ripe ship stacked with treasure."

"Please," Thorfast whispered from beside him. "Don't treat them as children. They're drunk enough to do what you ask."

Yngvar waved off Thorfast, grabbed the rough twine of a rigging line, and jumped up onto the rails. He aimed for drama and pulled his sword from its sheath. The beautiful balance let him produce a graceful flourish as he pointed toward their mark.

"For gold and glory!"

The crew echoed him, raising their shields together.

Then from behind the wall that jutted into the sea, a ship unlike anything Yngvar could imagine lumbered into their path.

The crew's cheers turned to croaks. Shields clunked to the deck.

Yngvar's hand pressed harder into the rigging line, turning white and cold.

"By the gods," Bjorn shouted, a voice for everyone's thoughts. "That is the hugest fucking ship I've ever seen. How does it float?"

The massive vessel moved like a bloated water beetle. It rose at least three man-lengths above the water. Two rows of oars, one atop the other, beat the water in time. These were close to the waves, but still impossibly long. Yngvar could not imagine the size of tree that could yield such lengths of wood. Two masts rose above the deck, but their sails were trimmed back to the spars.

The first waves of its wake slapped Yngvar's hull. The ship rocked and he slipped to the deck. The groaning of the hulking ship's deck was like that of some ancient beast. Within the hull a deep, sonorous beat of drums echoed. Its measured cadence timed the rise and fall of its oars.

Yngvar thought of trained dragons once more, and this ship was not far from it.

"We've got to pull back," Leiknr shouted. "It will clip us if we don't get out of its path."

This was true. Yngvar did not need to shout an order before his crew took their oars to row out of the path of the oncoming giant.

"Lord, more ships," Alasdair shouted. "Three."

Ships as large as his own trailed beside their giant cousin. These had the higher, gracefully curved profiles and dual triangular sails common to this region. Unlike the giant ship, which seemed to move without any visible crew, these ships were full of lively men at their duties.

"They don't seem to be hostile," Thorfast said.

"But they are approaching us," Yngvar said.

He looked to his crew. Each oar had two men, and each man turned a frightened gaze back toward the creaking and moaning giant approaching. Their terror was plain.

If they fled now, they would continue to flee. Their spirits would be broken and they would return home in shame and defeat.

Yngvar ground his teeth and lifted his sword once more toward the giant ship.

"Are we Norsemen? Are we not a match for a hundred of these weaklings? Stop your rowing. Turn and meet glory! We will not slink away like cowards."

If he had been on land, Yngvar would have charged and prayed his men followed. On sea, the best he could do was leap up to hug the prow and point his sword at the oncoming ships.

"If you must row," he shouted. "Row us to Valhalla!"

"Deliver me to their deck," Bjorn shouted. "And I will clear it myself!"

He raised his ax and shouted at the swiftly approaching ships. The crews of these ships wore head covers of every color, all faded from sun and sea. They were naked to their waists with their skin as dark as burnt wood shining in the sun. Some of these crew carried shields and spears. They lined up on the rails of their ships.

"Hamar, guide us to their outside edge."

Yngvar watched the ships pick up speed as more of their sails loosened. The three ships were already run in gout and would swallow them in moments. All the while the enormous ship continued to glide past, throwing out a wake that rocked Yngvar's ship like the start of a gale.

"Hurry! They are moving fast."

But it was too late, and Yngvar's ship was now being caught like a bird in hand. The three ships glided up to them, stopping out of boarding range.

With only a handful of bows among his ranks, he had no answer to the threat surrounding him. Now flight was the only recourse to a battle he would not win. Yet these dark enemies did not launch an attack. Their ships rocked on the same wake spreading behind their giant cousin. Half the crewmen did not even acknowledge danger, but busied themselves with their duties.

"It seems they want to talk," Thorfast said.

"Well, they must recognize our threat."

Yngvar cast his voice for the benefit of his crew. They had been caught. But he had to act like a leader to these men or else lose all respect and possibly lose his right to lead. The situation called for bluster and posturing, but nothing that would lead to violence.

"Lord, a man is hailing us," Alasdair said, pointing to the center ship where a figure in its prow waved them forward.

"Yes," Yngvar said, shamed for not noticing. His vision had been filled with possibilities and not what was before him. He fixed his sight on this man. "Take us closer. This is obviously a parley. Let's make sure we get all that we can out of them."

The crew looked to each other, but Hamar shouted for them to row. They slipped closer, while the giant ship finally passed them for the open sea. With its mammoth shadow gone, the threat of their situation abated.

"Jamil, translate. A false word from you and Bjorn will spit you like firewood."

Bjorn palmed his ax haft with a smile. Jamil blanched and inclined his head.

"I will speak truly," he said. "And accurately. So be careful what you say. These are ships of the Caliphate. They will not tolerate fool-ishness."

Glad none of the crew could understand Frankish, Yngvar smiled in answer. "And remember if you send this ship to the bottom of the sea, you will go with it."

The man in the enemy ship was tall and thin. A cream-colored robe and yellow head cover flapped in the breeze. His face was filled with shadow but a neatly pointed beard caught the light. The man held up a hand for peace.

Yngvar hesitated, as if he were debating whether to end this man's life. But he hailed the man, who he assumed was one of these Arabs that Jamil had mentioned.

A stream of words flowed out in a high, girlish voice. It drew snickers from the crew, and while Yngvar had no heart to laugh, he joined them. Yet the Arab was unconcerned and rattled off words as Jamil dipped his head intermittently.

When he stopped, Jamil shouted something back that sounded like he was clearing his throat of a fish bone. Then he turned to Yngvar.

"He represents the harbor master of Algiers. He asks your business and will collect the harbor fee."

Yngvar raised his brow. "Fee? What is that?"

"You must pay the ruler of Algiers tribute. Does that make better sense to you—Lord Yngvar?"

The deliberate twisting of his title had to go unpunished for now. Yngvar had not expected to pay a man simply for sailing in his water.

"We're not paying a fee," he said. "Tell him we come here to bring ruin to his port. If he pays us, then we will leave him in peace."

Jamil's dark-ringed eyes drooped. "Lord Yngvar, if you say these things for the benefit of your crew, then at least speak it in a language they can understand."

Heat spread on Yngvar's face and he repeated his threat to the crew, who responded with hesitant grunts and growls of approval.

The Arab shouted again and Jamil bowed deeper to the man.

"He's waiting, Lord Yngvar. May I direct your eyes to more of the giant ships that caused you to wet your pants at anchor by the city walls. You have found Algiers. This is no small city and no small navy. You are a gnat threatening a bull."

"I understand," Yngvar said, his voice lowered. "Just get us out of this situation. Tell him whatever he needs to hear."

Jamil's smile flattened. "And you will not hold me to the outcome?"

"A slave does not bargain with his master," Yngvar said, nearly shouting. "Now answer him."

The exchange sounded like two walruses barking at each other. Even the effeminate voice of the Arab could not overcome the impression. Yngvar wanted to grab at Jamil's sleeve and ask for a translation. He knew better than to seem nervous. Instead, he smiled confidently at his crew, meeting as many eyes as dared look up. Most men still looked after the behemoth ship lumbering out to see, its oars keeping a melancholy beat.

At last Jamil finished the exchange with more deferential bowing.

"Lord Yngvar, you must pay the fee for having occupied the time of the harbor guard captain. But you are otherwise free to continue along your journey."

"I am free to continue on?" Yngvar blinked.

"After you pay five dirhams."

"Five deer horns?"

"Five silver coins," Jamil said, rubbing his face. "And be quick. The Arab enjoys watching you worry, but grows bored. Other ships approach that he must tend to."

"Silver coins?" Yngvar repeated. He looked to Thorfast who looked to Bjorn.

"I've got a silver ring," he said. "But Gyna gave it to me."

Gyna leaned on the rails, her face slack with boredom. When eyes turned to her, she spit over the side then shouted in Norse at the Arabs.

"You bastards don't want to fight? Are you afraid of a woman? Come get me, you dress-wearing girls!"

Her threats drew laughter from Yngvar's crew. The Arab guard captain startled at her words, a bemused smile breaking the shadow of his face. The crews across all three ships fluttered into a hum of conversation. Men put down their burdens and regarded Gyna.

"That's right," Gyna said. She drew her sword and pointed it at the Arab. "I would cut out your heart if was worth my time. But yours is probably smaller than an acorn."

"Lord Yngvar," Jamil warned. "Get your woman under control. A woman has no place in this matter, particularly one in pants and carrying a sword."

Using the distraction of Gyna's spectacle, Yngvar brushed up against Bjorn. "Give me the ring so I can pay this fee and get us away."

Bjorn grumbled but the ring slipped off easily and he pressed it into Yngvar's palm.

He clutched the warm and hard ring to his thigh as he then pulled Gyna back from her posturing.

"Enough already," he said. "You're braver than all of us."

"I am," she said, frowning at Yngvar. "You were just going to pose all morning. Leave it to a woman to get any real work done."

Contrary to expectations, the Arabs seemed delighted with the spectacle of a sword-waving woman in pants. Calls and whistles went up from the three ships, and some men clapped. Gyna frowned.

"What the fuck is wrong with them?" she asked. "I'll cut their balls off."

"They don't know it," Yngvar said. Then he waved at Hamar. "Bring us closer so I can deal with their captain."

Hamar relayed the orders to the crew, and a dozen men sat at the oars to row them the short distance. Jamil blathered on in his grating language, and it seemed to appease the Arabs. Once they drew aside the center ship, their crew tossed a rope across to draw them together.

Yngvar faced the Arab captain, who gestured that he should board and to take Jamil. They both crossed the short gap. Yngvar did not fear losing Jamil here, for he was a slave and therefore property. These Arabs must respect at least that much, even if Jamil had not been properly marked a slave as of yet.

"Your woman is bold."

One of the Arab crewmen spoke clipped Norse. Yngvar nearly fell from the rail of the Arab ship in shock. He looked to the captain, who shrugged and held out his palm for payment.

"Lord Yngvar, he does not speak your language, but it is not completely unknown here. Trader crews and your own people have bought it south."

"Yes, I traded with the north." The crewman was shorter than

Yngvar, naked to the waist, and covered in enough black hair to make a bear jealous.

Yngvar slipped the harbor captain the silver ring. The Arab examined it, turning it in the light then weighing it in his palm. At last, he closed his hand over it and gestured Yngvar to leave.

"Friend," Yngvar said to the Norse-speaking trader. "Where can we sell our swords here?"

The sailor shook his head, not understanding, but Jamil translated. The sailor's eyes widened.

"Ah, go to Sicily. Kill Byzantines for the emir."

Yngvar nodded, understanding the gist of what he had been told, then returned to his own ship.

He put his hands on his hips and stood in the prow. "Men, we have been recommended to the emir of Sicily. We go to sell him our might!"

10

The land of Sikiley—or as Yngvar had struggled to pronounce, Sicily—rose as a deep green stripe on the horizon. The wind had turned against them, instead pushing their frail ship away from their destination. The brilliant blue skies had turned angry gray but the stifling heat never abated. The crew sweated at the oars and cursed the heat. Yngvar's back and shoulders burned from his shift of rowing. Jamil was flattened on the deck after a half shift, and his blue robes clung to his scrawny frame with his sweat.

"Not far now," Hamar called. "Leiknr, I'll let you land us. My arms ache."

Yngvar worked with Alasdair to tie off rigging lines then paused to study the distant shore. After their fiasco at Algiers, Yngvar worried for an equally humiliating outcome in Sicily. None of his crew had voiced any discontent. No one could have misunderstood their chances against such adversaries. He guessed most were as pleased as he was to escape having suffered no more pain than derisive laughter.

"Will we be welcomed, lord?" Alasdair asked, leaning on the rails as well. The wind tousled his brassy hair.

"Welcomed or not, we will be respected," Yngvar said. "I think these people believe we are not civilized men. But have our people not built ships to carry us around the circle of the world? Are our swords and mail any less than theirs? I will not be laughed at again."

"Lord, I think most of that laughter was for Gyna."

"Ah, she could be a problem here," Yngvar said. He glanced at her, asleep under a cloak. Bjorn sat beside her, legs crossed, resting his hand on her hip as he stared into the distance.

He envied their relationship. He had no idea how they had come into it. One day they began sleeping together and were now as good as husband and wife. What a pair. Yngvar shook his head at the thought of them having children.

"Lord?" Alasdair asked.

"Sorry, I should not become distracted. Well, we will find this emir and he will pay us well to destroy his foes. We will be doing the same for him as we did for Hakon. But we will be better paid and we will have more than cooking pots as a reward. I can see that even without setting foot on Sikiley. And when we are rich, we will return north."

"When will that be?" Alasdair asked. There was a strange melancholy to the question.

"When we are rich," Yngvar said. "Not before. The gods have set us on this path of gold and glory. We will have our fill of it and return home as heroes. Don't fear never seeing the northlands again. We owe Erik Blood-Axe a horrible death. Bjorn's eye and my back will never be healed. For that, I've sworn to kill Erik, and so I will."

Gulls had joined them now, squawking and diving around the mast looking for scraps to steal. Their ship was so light and fast that Sicily was no longer a stripe, but resolved into a rugged coast of green hills and cliffs. The magnificent blue of the water had grayed with the clouds, but it was still a vision from a dream.

Along with the gulls, shipping traffic had increased. Against these shores triangular sails of all sizes glided along their various routes. Most seemed to keep to the coast, but others headed out to sea. One such vessel approached.

"Leiknr, I want to hail that ship," Yngvar said. He then switched to Frankish to yell at Jamil. "Get off your face and be ready to speak for me."

The old Moor rolled onto his back, his black-ringed eyes staring at the sky. Bjorn, who sat close by, kicked the Moor's side. Jamil sat up, rubbing his shoulders.

The approaching ship was of roughly the same size as Yngvar's, though its sides were higher and belly fatter. The wind favored their course and the triangular sails were full. Yet Yngvar stood in the prow and waved hazel branches that he had carried from Norway.

"Lord Yngvar," Jamil said, having stood again. "What are you waving dead branches for?"

"For peace," he said. "Is that not understood here?"

Jamil frowned. "Wave a white cloth or something bright to get their attention. And for the love of God, tell your men to get back from the rails. They look ready to jump to the other ship. No one will stop for you this way."

Yngvar had not realized his off-shift crew had gathered to the rails. They were sizable and imposing men compared to those they had met so far along the Midgard Sea. So he held them back and waved a white bandage cloth. The approaching ship trimmed sails to slow their approach and soon both ships were aside each other.

"We come seeking the emir," Yngvar shouted. "Where is his hall?"

Jamil shouted words across the water at the other crew. He counted less than twenty men total, all olive skinned with curly hair. They wore dirty linen tunics already dark with sweat. The sounds of Jamil's words shifted until at last he seemed to find a language they shared. They shouted back and forth, and pointed toward the shore.

"Lord Yngvar, they say the emir is on the opposite side of Sicily, in a city called Palermo. But one of his sons rules from the palace at Licata, which is just ahead."

"Do you know these places?" Yngvar asked. Jamil shook his head, adjusting the white head cover that had slipped over his eyes.

"I have read of Palermo. This is an ancient land, and there are too many places to know."

"Thank them for me," Yngvar said, then inclined his head to the native crewmen.

Yngvar had prepared for this arrival to be as dignified as possible. Dreams of sailing up to seaside fortresses and tearing apart their walls until gold spilled out had now been mulled with reality. Blind ferocity would carry all of them to the grave. The armies of the Midgard Sea counted soldiers beyond even what the kings of Frankia could raise. Even more than the massive armies that had clashed in far-off Brunanburh. Moreover, the people of the Midgard Sea had warriors in what they called navies—a concept Yngvar did not understand. A navy, Jamil had explained, were warriors who lived on and fought from ships with other ships only. These ships were like the enormous one that had cowed them in the port of Algiers. Only a navy was comprised of fleets of such ships, and some bigger still than what he had already seen.

Their lone ship would prevail against neither armies nor navies of these Midgard Sea folk.

The port of Licata reminded Yngvar of Algiers, but was greener and somehow more welcoming. Scores of ships either docked or departed under the dark skies. Apparently the local sailors feared no storm from such brooding clouds, or else believed they could outrace one.

A pilot ship hailed them, and Jamil conducted the business of negotiating a berth. Leiknr had only to follow the pilot to where they would dock.

The men rowed, but all were curious to see where they would finally land. This was the start of all they had expected, and animated speculation began to circulate among them. Strangely, treasures was not their first musings. Instead, they spoke of exotic women and what temptations they would offer.

Compared to landing in Hauger, which was a controlled collision with either the beach or a dock where spearmen greeted you with a threat for payment, landing in Licata was an orderly process. Leiknr guided their ship up to a dock where a waiting group of young men helped to tie them off. An officious man in a maroon robe and wearing a yellow head cover waited with three spearmen. Yngvar smiled at them. Some customs remained the same no matter where they traveled in the world.

The robed man, despite his dress, did not look anything like Jamil or the other Arab people he had met. He could have been Yngvar's cousin but for his costume. He carried no weapon other than a curved dagger at his belt. He held up his hand in a sign of peace, then began to ramble in a foreign language. Yngvar had wearied at so much incomprehensible speech. He turned toward his ship and let Jamil speak. Bjorn and Thorfast were organizing the crew, and Gyna and Alasdair had already disembarked.

"Lord Yngvar," Jamil said. "Your attention is needed here. There are fees to settle first. How many days will you be docked?"

"How many days?" Yngvar asked. "How would I know? That depends on the emir's son."

"Lord Yngvar, the prince is not going to see you the first day you arrive. He might not see you at all. You should pay for no more than a week."

"Good, tell him that."

Jamil stared at him, then turned back to the man in the maroon robe. He had a large, triangular nose and hazel eyes that flitted between Jamil and him. For all Yngvar knew, the man could be plotting with Jamil to capture them into slavery. But Yngvar's sword weighed at his side and he feared nothing.

"Three dinar," Jamil said. "Which I know you don't have. So the equal amount in gold. You have prepared at least this much, I pray."

Yngvar smiled, proud of his forethought. "I have. We cut up a gold chain Gyna had. How much is three dinar of gold?"

He offered the dock master two links, which he looked at in confusion until Jamil rushed an explanation. The dock master's laughter angered Yngvar. He wanted to jam the gold links into the greedy bastard's eyes until he went blind. Yet, he endured and smiled. He produced another link from the pouch of gold he carried. The cycle repeated until the harbor master held a half-dozen links that looked to Yngvar to be more than three coin's worth.

Jamil and the harbor crew exchanged words. The dock master handed a slip of paper to Yngvar, which was covered in strange writing.

"This is proof you have paid," Jamil said. "Don't lose it or you will be charged again. You are paid for seven days. He also advised you to get real coins if you don't want to lose all your wealth in one day."

Yngvar stared at the slip in his hand. He was not sure of paper, being something like flimsy cloth. "Where should I keep it?"

Jamil rolled his eyes. "On the ship where you will not lose it and the weather will not ruin it."

With Jamil's help, they had learned where the captain of the guard resided. From his office they could negotiate a meeting with the prince. He was stationed in one of the high square towers that dotted the walls surrounding the city.

Dusky people in robes and head covers of every color and pattern flowed through a tunnel into the city. Stern-faced guards in banded armor and flowing pants watched over the human river, wearing their strange curved swords open in their sashes. Atop the walls, more of the same looked down bored and leaning on their spears. Some sat together in groups and seemed absorbed in some sort of game.

The chaos of language surrounded them. The inane chatter of foreign sounds scratched at Yngvar's patience. As he joined the flow into the main city, people jostled and pressed against them. Their foreign stink and strange dress further irritated him. At last, when a wiry man in a gray robe and white head cover bumped him, Yngvar shoved the man into the crowd with a growl.

The frail man screamed and fell into another woman who carried a covered basket. She in turn collapsed against two other women. In an instant, the crowd flowed around them and the wiry man stood up to begin cursing.

Yngvar, with thirty Norsemen in heavy furs and iron helmets behind him, stood like a boulder parting the current of a brook. The wiry man stared at them, then sped off into the crowd.

"The people here know little respect," Yngvar said after the man. "I will teach them to have a care if they will not learn it themselves."

"Let's find this captain before we meet him as captives," Thorfast said. "If we upset the wrong person, it could go ill for us. For my part, all these people look the same."

"I'll agree to that," Yngvar said, sniffing at the crowd flowing around them. A mule plodded along with a cart and driver. The old man looked down on Yngvar and offered a creased smile. "Let's follow this cart a while. He'll clear the way without trouble."

Fearing Jamil might flee, Yngvar kept Bjorn on him. The slave would have to be marked as such, or else he could slide into this city and forever vanish. Yngvar needed his language skills.

Once they found the tower, the guards outside did not scoff at them as Yngvar had expected. Jamil had explained something and the guards arranged for them to meet their captain after a brief wait.

Only Yngvar, Jamil, his Wolves, and four other crewmen were allowed inside. They had to leave their swords with the rest of their crew. The request was reasonable and Yngvar entered the cool shadows of the guard tower. He was relieved to be away from the heat a moment, though the familiar odors of barracks-life greeted him instead. Sweat and fouler scents filled the square rooms where the guards either rested or chatted with friends. Their dark eyes followed Yngvar and his strange crew.

At the top of the tower they met the captain, who was a mature man with a round head and heavily creased brow. His iron gray hair was short and wavy, pressed to his head from sweat. He was clean-shaved and his smile forthright. He spread out his strong arms on a wide table, behind which three spearmen stood at attention. Yngvar liked the captain. He appeared competent and fair.

Their exchange flowed through Jamil. It seemed the captain and his guards understood Jamil was a slave. He was treated as if he did not exist but for the words he translated.

Yes, Prince Kalim ibn al-Hasan al-Kahbi does employ mercenaries.

Yes, he would be delighted to meet with Norsemen.

Of course this could all be arranged, and fortunately, tonight Prince Kalim is seeing visitors.

It would only cost thirty dinar to ensure all this transpires smoothly.

Yngvar's mouth hung open, and he stared at Jamil.

"Lord Yngvar, if you want respect, act like a man worthy of it," Jamil said, lowering his voice. "Of course you must pay a fee to see the prince."

"Pay to meet their ruler? That is an insult."

"It is the custom here."

"Call it a custom," Yngvar said. "It is still robbery."

The captain's smile did not fade, but the men behind him turned their dark eyes on him. One boyish guard stifled a smirk and Yngvar felt his anger rise.

"So it's a test of wealth," he said. "This prince Kabin—"

"Prince Kalim," Jamil corrected.

"Whatever," Yngvar waved away the correction. "The prince will not hire poor warriors. After all, a poor warrior is either desperate or unsuccessful in his trade. Either way, he should be avoided. But I am not sure if I have enough of these dinar you speak of. I have sacks full of these coins, but I buried them before I sailed south."

"You must satisfy the payment however you can."

So Yngvar presented the bag of chopped up gold. He had nothing to give, but Thorfast offered a ring of silver that had a small red stone set into it. The captain, who never ceased smiling, snapped his fingers. One of his guards produced a scale and the gold was measured to the captain's satisfaction.

"That was probably too much," Yngvar said as the captain swept the gold off the table into a waiting bag.

"Come back tonight and they will all be escorted to the prince's palace."

"Why do I feel like I am being raided?" Yngvar asked, rejoined with this whole crew.

"We'll be poor men if we stay here another day," Thorfast said, rubbing the hand that had lost its silver ring.

Yet they passed the afternoon back at their ship, too timid to explore more of this strange city. The buildings were clean and spacious, all echoing with foreign words and the footfalls of color-fully robed people. Doorways were impractically high and arched. A strange, sweet scent pervaded the air. Jamil had said it came from groves of fruit trees beyond the city. Yngvar counted apples, pears and a handful of berries as fruit and little else. What fruit could make a scent to fill a city?

Evening arrived soon enough and they arrived at the captain's tower, all thirty of them in their mail and shields. Yngvar was intent on displaying his power. To his surprise, not only did the city guards allow them to pass without issue, but the captain greeted them warmly. Yngvar had cynically worried the captain would have stolen their gold, which he would answer by burning the docks and killing every guard he could find. He was glad this gambit did not come to such an unprofitable end. The captain was a man of honor.

Yngvar focused ahead as they wended through streets paved with stone. He did not want to gawk like his companions. The buildings stood higher as they proceeded up a small hill. They were uniform in their design, covered in the same brittle material he had seen in Spanland. Yet as they arrived at the palace, they found buildings that were impossible to believe, even standing before them.

Thin towers shot into the sky so high Yngvar thought they were to defend against dragons. What other enemy could threaten from such a height? The outbuildings before the wall were lined with arched galleries set with tile designs of harmonious colors. Guards patrolled these galleries, watching them from beneath glinting helmets. Beyond the walls, the buildings stood proudly. Some had domed tops covered in gold that gleamed in the rose light of the evening sun.

These drew gasps from the crew, and a chuckle from Jamil. Truly, there were buildings made of gold here. Yngvar had not been deceived. Wealth beyond imagining waited him in these lands, even a small city such as this one. What would the emir's city of Palermo hold? His heart raced with the thoughts of riches ahead.

The captain led them to the gatehouse. Scores of warriors were stationed at the ground level or along the walls or else inside the flanking square towers. The captain spoke to some of these men and shared low laughter. They were waved through.

In the dark of the tunnel, Yngvar imagined himself being trapped here trying to escape. Above him slits in the ceiling showed where boiling water could douse them or else spears struck down on them. It made him shudder.

As they exited, the captain spoke with three more men who regarded Yngvar and his crew with appraising glances. Again they were waved into a large courtyard where yet another wall waited that sealed in the main buildings.

At this wall, the captain again negotiated their passage and began to escort them inside.

Then someone shouted.

The captain was half beneath the archway leading into the palace when he stopped. A wiry man in a gray robe and white head cover was shouting at him and pointing at Yngvar.

"That's the bastard I pushed over at the docks," he said.

"And he's claiming you tried to kill him," Jamil said. "This is not going to end well."

11

The shouting of the wiry man in gray robes echoed through the archway. His rapid speech sounded like hail falling on a hard rooftop. The captain stood before him, his round head swiveling between the wiry man and Yngvar. The shadow of the archway hid his face, but Yngvar read the posture of desperation. The wiry man could not win a fight with the strength of his arms, but his verbal punch had seemed to knock the captain senseless.

"What's he saying?" Yngvar asked of Jamil, pulling him closer.

"He claims you knocked him down while on official palace business and that you threatened him with your sword. He has seven witnesses who can back up his claim. He wants you arrested and thrown in the prisons beneath the palace."

Jamil rattled off the translation as fast as the wiry man could shout his demands and punctuate each word with a jab of his finger at Yngvar. Guards that had been content to walk away into the surrounding courtyard now returned to the commotion.

"He lies," Yngvar said. "I have thirty witnesses who will say as much. Thirty to seven, should be enough to convince any lord of my innocence."

The captain now raised his hands for peace, gently pleading with the wiry man. This only incensed the liar more, and he stepped up to Yngvar, who still stood bewildered outside the gate.

He was a reed of a man, thin of body but fat with self-importance. His eyelashes were too thick and long to be masculine. Yngvar thought without his black beard he might make a fine woman, if a bit too thin for his liking. His dark face was flushed darker still as he glared at Yngvar.

Apparently emboldened by the lack of aggression, the liar straightened and pointed his finger up Yngvar's nose. He inhaled to spew more of his foreign invective, but the bastard had used up his luck.

Swift as a striking snake, he grabbed the liar's finger and bent it back. The effeminate liar shrieked and collapsed as if Yngvar had torn his arm from its socket. Between his wailing, he blubbered more foreign speech.

"Lord Yngvar," Jamil said calmly. "He's citing this as an example of your abuses. You should let him go."

"Can't a man defend himself?" His question was full of false innocence. He looked not to Jamil but to the captain.

The captain grimaced as if Yngvar had been bending his finger. This little man kneeling on the dirt before him was apparently of some importance, otherwise the captain would have swept him aside.

Yngvar released the man's finger and snarled at him now sitting on his rump.

"Jamil, tell all of them that if I am falsely accused then I demand a trial by combat with this little fool. I will not accept a champion in his place, either. The gods must judge which one of us is true."

"It's not a wise idea—"

Bjorn struck Jamil across the back with the butt of his ax. "Tell them before I lose my patience and start killing. You'll be the first to drop, seeing you're in my way."

Jamil rattled off a series of statements that no one could verify. The wiry man sat like a chastened child. The captain nodded as if confused, then looked to Yngvar and shook his head. More gibberish ensued, with the wiry man finally standing and dusting off his clean gray robe. Compared to Jamil's sweat and sea-stained robes, he seemed like a prince himself.

The debate ended in a flurry of hand-waving between the captain and the wiry man. The captain began to wave them through the gate once more.

"What happened?" Yngvar asked Jamil.

"There is no time for petty complaints. Tonight you are guests of Prince Kalim and should be afforded courtesy. He can file his formal complaint tomorrow and bring his witnesses."

"What is this fool's name?"

"He named himself Saleet al-Sattar, a clerk in Prince Kalim's court."

Yngvar stepped up to Saleet, meeting his thickly lashed eyes.

"Saleet, I don't know what a clerk is. But I expect it's not more than a pile of dog shit. Cause me any more trouble and you will find yourself on the point of my sword."

He growled the words, and though Saleet did not speak Norse, he seemed to grasp the meaning. He backed up to the wall then shook his head and clutched both hands to his chest.

Jamil leaned in and spoke softly to Saleet, apparently to translate. But Yngvar was impatient to meet their employer and had wasted enough time on this fool. He grabbed Jamil away and pulled him after the captain, who was already waiting at the tunnel exit.

As they proceeded through the tunnel, Saleet remained against the stone wall. Once Yngvar cleared to the opposite side, the wiry man's indignant shouting renewed.

"Persistent little shit, ain't he?" Bjorn said as they emerged from the gate tunnel.

"He is a worry for tomorrow," Yngvar said. "If he wants to complain about us, then we will deal with it later."

The short courtyard led to steps of white stone that spread up to a magnificent archway. Everywhere were tall towers, golden domes glaring with the last light of day, and pristine white buildings. The guards were dressed as richly as jarls in leather jerkins and billowing pants, their fingers each banded with gold rings. They were broad-shouldered and flinty-eyed. Their spears were topped with wide blades like short swords.

The captain stopped and gestured to Yngvar's weapons. He understood they were to surrender them before entering the palace, which was expected. He would not let armed men in his own hall. He set his sword against the wall and followed as well.

They entered in the company of more guards. Despite leading a column of thirty armored Norsemen, Yngvar cringed to enter this palace. Its vastness threatened to swallow him like the Midgard Serpent, Jormungandr. The interior was alive with servants and guards, all padding soundlessly across polished stone floors. Bright tiles formed complex mosaics on the walls that dizzied his vision.

"It is too much," Thorfast said in a whisper.

"Truly, a palace of gold," Bjorn said.

"I can replace my gold chain with a hundred more from this palace," Gyna said.

"Lord, it may offend God to say so, but this is what I imagine the palaces of heaven to be like." Alasdair held the silver cross beneath his shirt as he admired the columns and rooms they passed.

Dark eyes watched them as they proceeded into the heart of the palace. Their boots clacked and their chain armor jangled, amplified by the hard stone. Compared to the graceful silence of the natives, Yngvar felt like the wild man these Arabs accused him of being. He plodded after the captain like a dwarf in iron boots.

Jamil chuckled. "If you were at Córdoba, then you would see the true glory. This is a mere barn in comparison."

"If this is a barn," Thorfast said, "then the hens must lay eggs of gold and the cows give milk as sweet as mead."

The crewmen trailing were less circumspect in their admiration. They pointed, gasped, laughed, and sometimes shouted at everything they passed. Nothing was too minor to amaze them, and their racket disturbed the dignity of the palace. Yngvar had no love of these Arab folk, but standing amid these impossible achievements of construction, his admiration bloomed. How had the stone floor been made like ice on a still pond? How did they make bowls to top their buildings? Without witnessing these achievements himself, he could never believe them possible.

At last, they came to giant doors stained deep red and bound in iron. These were set into an elaborately decorated archway where eight of the fearsome guardsmen stood at rigid attention. They regarded the queue of armored Norsemen with no more concern than having spotted a line of ducks crossing the road.

Jamil and the captain exchanged words. Yngvar was to wait to be presented, which he understood. What he did not understand was the duration of the wait. He expected to be ushered in after a moment, yet now he stood until his feet grew sore.

"Why does it take so long?" Yngvar asked Jamil, who shrugged.

The old Moor had lost his regal bearing. His blue robes were ruined with white stains, his head cover hung lopsided, and the dark rings around his eyes were now like giant bruises. As far as slaves went, Jamil had been treated well. Yet even the small tasks given him seemed to have broken his spirt. Yngvar wondered how long Jamil would be useful, and what he should do with him. Thus far, his service had been fair. Perhaps on returning to Norway he would also return the Moor to where he had been captured.

The squeal of iron hinges broke into Yngvar's thoughts. The double doors to Prince Kalim's chambers now flowed open. The captain stood beyond, framed in a gauzy light, and beckoned them inside. Tendrils of smoke curled behind him and a sweet, cloying scent grabbed at Yngvar's nose.

Thorfast snorted. "Gods, it smells like a hundred flowers being pushed into my face."

Jamil inhaled and sighed. "I am renewed."

Yngvar steeled himself against hesitation. He had to present a strong face to his potential employer. Even without a sword weighing at his hip, he would carry himself as if he bore one. No foreign king would intimidate him with sweet smoke and arched ceilings of stone set impossibly high.

The chamber was expansive and dimly light with brass braziers and lanterns. Ornately decorated columns of stone punctuated the room, leaving no clear line of sight in any direction. Yngvar wondered if it was a defensive measure. Rather than a high table, at the far end was a raised platform, also of white stone, and a grand chair so floridly decorated that he could not fix his eyes on it. Heavy smoke flowed out of a silver bowl at the foot of this stage, and obscured the figures seated in and around the chair.

"Prince Kalim ibn al-Hasan al-Kahbi welcomes you. Come forward and prostrate yourself before him."

The voice echoed in accented Frankish, but was clear and commanding. It came from the stage where figures moved in smoky gloom. A thin silhouette in a gray robe seemed to be the source.

"What does that mean? Bow?" Yngvar whispered to Jamil.

"Kneel on both knees then touch your head to the floor, and keep your hands forward and palms up."

"He might as well piss on our heads," Bjorn said.

"Enough, let's do as he asks," Yngvar said. "Though we're in mail armor. We might end up falling on our faces."

Yngvar translated the procedure to his crew, each one staring at different points in this grand hall. Their mouths hung open like fishes in baskets.

He touched his head to the cold, smooth stone of the floor and extended his hands as Jamil had instructed. The mail shirt pressed on his back as if to force his face into the ground as punishment for debasing himself like this. But he was in the wolf's teeth here, and to struggle would only bring him more injury. He kept his head lowered, peeking to the sides to see Alasdair and Jamil in the same posture.

A light voice spoke in the flowing, hard tongue of the Arabs. Yngvar was fast learning to distinguish the sounds of the various languages of the Midgard Sea. This tinkling voice was followed by the clipped Frankish translation.

"You may stand."

In battle, fear lent a man strength enough to leap to his feet wearing mail armor even if he had been flat on his back. Now was not such a moment. The mail bent his shoulders and pressed against his neck. Without his cloak as a buffer, strands of his hair caught in the links and would have to be cut free later. He struggled up, not as dignified as he had hoped. Setting his feet wide, he now faced the people on the stone dais.

Prince Kalim could not be more than twenty. He was dressed in silk robes of purple and wore a white head cover. This was held tight against his narrow head by a thin band of gold. His beard was thin and thoughtfully trimmed. His teeth shined bright in a youthful, angular face. He sat with one bare foot up on his plush seat, slender arm hooked over his knee as if he lounged on the walls of a captured fortress.

A dozen guards stood behind him. Their arms were folded across broad chests and gleamed with a glaze of oil. None of them bestowed a glance to Yngvar and his crew, but stared into the distance. That was more disturbing than if they had drawn their oddly curved blades.

The thin man standing beside the lounging prince did not look like the other Arabs. His eyes were green and his complexion paler. He wore the same gray robe and white head cover that the wiry Saleet had worn. Perhaps this man was also a clerk.

"The prince is glad for your company this evening," the translator said. "He is eager for stories from your distant land."

Yngvar inclined his head and began to speak when the prince started to jabber again. Jamil grabbed Yngvar's arm, which he took as a warning not to interrupt. Royalty everywhere was the same in this regard. They loved the sound of their own voices and their every thought was of the most profound importance.

"Prince Kalim wishes to know if you sacrifice babies to your gods and drink the blood of your enemies while on the battlefield."

Jamil tucked his head down to hold his laughter. Yngvar arched his brows at Thorfast.

"Tell him we sacrifice our enemies and drink the blood of babies."

Yngvar flashed Thorfast a smile, then bowed to the prince.

"I've never heard of babies sacrificed. But our enemies are certainly crushed before our swords. If we drink their blood it is only because so much of it is spilled that we are fairly drowning in it."

Thorfast whispered a Norse translation to the crew, and this drew proud murmurs. Yngvar waved behind his back for their silence.

The prince listened to the translation then clapped his hands and laughed. It was boyish but honest. His black eyes sparkled as he leaned forward on his chair, examining Yngvar from foot to crown. He pointed and jabbered more of his strange speech.

"The prince wonders if it is true that your women accompany you to battle."

"Gyna," Yngvar said, turning behind. "Remove your helmet and come forward."

She frowned but pulled off her helmet. The face and cheek guards had thus far obscured her gender, and a chain shirt rendered everybody the same shape. Yet now that she shook out her hair and turned up her sharp chin at the prince, she was unmistakably revealed as a woman.

The prince fell back with his eyes wide and his mouth caught open between a laugh and gasp. The long fingers of his left hand covered his mouth and he pointed with the other.

The piles of blankets stirred his chair. Yngvar had not noticed the women in embroidered robes resting at the prince's feet. They wore head covers like their men, but their faces were also hidden except for wide eyes that now stared out in shock. Even the unmoving guards behind the dais looked on.

Prince Kalim looked to his interpreter and seemed to ask if he could believe his own eyes. He stood and pointed, excited babbles falling like a waterfall.

"If that whelp is laughing at me," Gyna said, her hand flexing for a dagger she kept hidden in her tall boots.

"You're a sight even among our own folk," Yngvar said, never turning from the prince. "Just bear with this. It is not disrespect but surprise."

"Ah, fair-minded Yngvar," she said. Still she narrowed her eyes at the prince and curled her lip.

Rather than being threatened, the prince clapped harder and fell back into his chair. His voice rose higher than a child's as he fought through delirious laughter to speak to his interpreter.

"The prince is greatly pleased with this."

"Can I put my helmet back on?" Gyna asked under her breath. Yngvar waved her off and she slunk back into the rest of the crew.

"Prince Kalim," Yngvar said, projecting his voice above the laughter. "We have heard of your generosity. So we have come to you in hopes we might deal profitably."

He let the interpreter feed his words to the prince, who regained his composure and seated himself more elegantly upon his chair. He now rested both hands on his knees and moved to the edge of his seat. Yngvar held the prince's gaze as he continued.

"We are mighty warriors from the north. We come for gold and glory. You have enemies, my prince, and we will crush them in your name. For a price. We hear you want Byzantine heads. We will fill this hall with them, if that is your desire."

The translation echoed into the now still silence of the spacious chamber. The prince's face shifted from interest to evil delight.

He leaned forward on his knees, his answer given in a growling whisper. The boyish prince was gone and now staring down at Yngvar was a bird of prey about to swoop on its kill.

The Frankish interpreter's words were bright in the stark silence.

"The prince has a task for you."

12

The ship rocked on the peaceful tide rolling through Licata's bay. Yngvar wrapped his hand into a rigging line, its roughness tickling his palm. The crew gathered to him in the prow, their eyes alight with anticipation of the battle awaiting them down the coast. Even Leiknr Bone-Feet smiled. Spirts were as fair as the salty breeze that flowed across the deck.

Yngvar methodically looked to every man, showing his own resolve and testing theirs. Prince Kalim's promises seemed preposterous. Yet he lived in a magical stone palace topped with golden domes, and Jamil said this was a mere barn. So he and his men chose to believe the offered rewards. No eye flinched from Yngvar's gaze. No one would shrink from the fortune offered them.

Shoremen called to docking ships and merchants chattered over the slapping of waves on hulls, all echoing across the wide bay. Yet on Yngvar's deck, every warrior held a reverential silence. No one dared break the dream they had been living in since hearing Prince Kalim's offer.

Satisfied no one held any doubt, Yngvar released his grip on the rigging line and clapped his hands.

"Your swords are sharp and your armor scoured," he said. "Your strength is unmatched and your fury is legend. We came to find gold. We have found it. Now, we earn it with glorious battle."

Bjorn raised his ax and shouted. The crew followed and soon their battle cries shook the decks of every ship in the bay. Merchants and their crews paused to stare at them. Yngvar only offered them a defiant roar. He and his men were invincible.

Soon, they would be richer than any of them had imagined.

Even Jamil did not believe the offered price, granted without any negotiation. The prince knew the valor of the Norsemen. He knew they were fearsome warriors capable of fighting on when other soldiers fell. He wanted their strength and would pay generously for it.

Each man would be paid one hundred gold dinar—a full pound of gold! Not even the prince's household warriors were paid as much.

"Your task in words is simple," the Frankish translator had said. "But know you would not be paid so richly if it were easy in execution. Down the coast, where freshwater springs flow, is a Byzantine outpost called Pozzallo. A small fleet rests in its bay and Byzantine soldiers man the walls of its fortress. Destroy the fleet and you will be paid one hundred dinar each. That is three thousand coins of gold in total."

Before the translator could finish, Prince Kalim began raving. His words were rough and guttural, punctuated with stabs in the air by the prince's delicate finger. When he at last flopped back into his chair, the translator explained his master's hysteria.

"Prince Kalim will pay twice as much—another two hundred dinar—to whoever brings him the head of the wall guard captain, Basil Gregoras. He captured and tortured the prince's favorite champion and hung his corpse from Pozzallo's walls. Take revenge for Prince Kalim, and you shall be doubly rewarded."

After accepting the terms and swearing to burn every ship at anchor in Pozzallo, Yngvar and his men were treated to a feast of strange foods served by women that smelled like flowers but remained hidden in robes. They drank wine as well, a treat Yngvar had not tasted since his youth in Frankia. But he ordered his men to stay sober for the next day's fighting.

Now he stood with them on the deck of his ship, casting off from Licata and heading southeast along the coast.

"Lord, what is the plan for the Byzantine ships?" Alasdair fixed his cloak over his shoulder. Though the humidity smothered them, all his men wore their woolen cloaks. A heavy cloak served as a second shield in battle.

"I don't know what we will face," Yngvar said. "You were with me when we spoke to the captain. There could be anything from a scant few to a score of ships. It depends on the Byzantines' plans. We will first study their numbers before attacking."

"Seven ships, at last report," Thorfast added, joining their conversation. Their own ship leapt over the waves as the crew rowed them out to sea. From there they could catch the wind and rest their arms.

"A good number," Yngvar said. "We can deal with seven."

Thorfast laughed. "Only you would think that a good number. Our ship might be as nimble as a dolphin at play, but a hit from one of those big hulls or giant iron arrows and we will be smashed to splinters."

"We will not be hit," Yngvar said. "These Byzantines, they are old people. Isn't that right, Alasdair?"

"It is, lord. They used to rule the world once when they were Romans."

"I don't understand any of that," Yngvar said, waving his hand in the air. He turned to the rails and watched the port of Licata falling away. "Old people are arrogant people. They will underestimate us and learn a bloody lesson in return. Prince Kalim has heard rumors of the Norsemen's strength. But I believe he promises so much gold because he expects us to fail. He sends us to harass his foes, sink some of their ships, then oblige him by dying."

Crew nearby glared at Yngvar's statement. He laughed.

"You men know it, too. The rewards are great, the risk is greater, and the prince does not expect to pay. But we will surprise him when we return to claim our gold."

Thorfast leaned closer and whispered. "And he'll try to kill us before we sail off with it."

"He might," Yngvar agreed. "But he might also have use for men so cunning and strong. No matter, we will guard against treachery."

He looked across the deck where Jamil sat on an oar by the tiller. The old Moor's face had paled and his eyes stared into nothing. He gritted his teeth as he struggled to keep the easy pace. Jamil's language skills might not be needed on this journey, but he could not remain behind in Licata. He would flee before his usefulness was done.

"Lord, how can we prove that we sank the Byzantines' ships?" Alasdair now pushed sea chests toward the center of the deck as he spoke.

"The prince's spies will verify our claims," Yngvar said. "And I will gift him the head of this Captain Basil Gregoras. I'll drizzle the Byzantines' blood all over Prince Kalim's palace floor."

The claim silenced more conversation. Yngvar thrummed the rails, harboring his own doubts about the challenges ahead. The Byzantines would be dismissive of his small ship. They would swat at him and his crew as if they were no more than black flies. Yet the Byzantines would learn they are not flies but a swarm of hornets.

And they would learn this too late.

Stacked around the mast were the casks of oil granted by the prince. Two dozen were lashed together and covered with a dirty linen tarp, likely an old sail. A stack of oil-soaked brands lay in a box beside these. Alasdair shored up the stack of casks by butting unused sea chests against them. The tide was mild, but if the waves rose, Yngvar wanted to prevent any chance of these casks rolling overboard.

Their journey was a half-day's sailing. They beached and rested close to where they estimated the Byzantine border began. Given their task, they would be best served striking in darkness.

According to what Yngvar had learned from Jamil, the Byzantines once ruled all of Sicily but now clung to its eastern coast. Terrible battles were fought between the emir and the Byzantines. Prince Kalim set his palace close to the border but off the main axis of attack. His position, it seemed to Yngvar, was to serve as a distraction to the Byzantines and hold them in place. If they pulled up and marched inland, the prince's warriors could sweep in behind them. So a stalemate had formed with neither side committed to settling this section of the border.

Yngvar's unexpected appearance in Licata meant Byzantine spies had no time to pass the news of an attack back to their masters. Their spies might not have had time to learn of Yngvar at all. The prince had hired and dispatched them within a day, keeping them at dock only long enough to load the oil and brands onto the ship. Captain Basil and the ships he overlooked from his fortress walls would not be alerted to an attack.

After an afternoon of dozing and resting, they took in their sail to reduce their profile and set short oars through the tholes so they could work close to ship and shore. It made for slow rowing, but they had to proceed slowly. Neither Hamar nor Leiknr knew these waters, so they took shifts watching for sandbars and hidden rocks. To run aground or breach the hull in these waters would be their doom.

The dark cliff faces and hilly shores of the Sicilian coast led unerringly to Pozzallo. They sailed east and then curved south until they rounded a small cape. Pozzallo, he was told, sat at the edge of the calm waters just east of that position. With only starlight to guide them, they would have to be certain of their path home. It meant following the coast back, but with the gods' favor there would be no Byzantine ships to give chase.

"Only four ships," Hamar called back as he leaned across the prow to study the docks ahead. "And a fifth one is beached."

Though only an hour after sunset, the sky was deep blue and countless stars glimmered white. Lanterns winked aboard the ships anchored in the bay. Behind them, a stone tower sat just back of the beach. It had been raised higher with a new building of unpainted wood that glowed white in the gloom. Stone walls spread from each side of the tower and formed the boundaries of the Byzantine fort.

"Well, it's a sight less grand than the prince's palace," Thorfast said, nodding toward the Byzantine walls.

"It serves them well enough," Yngvar said. "To draw near their ships, we must pray archers do not rush to those walls. Otherwise, our ship will sink from the weight of their arrows alone."

"We've got shields against arrows," Bjorn said, joining their study of the enemy positions. "And we're fast. Burn and row, that's all we need."

Yngvar raised his fist to signal the crew to cease rowing. They had kept a languid pace so as to preserve their strength. Also, if they moved too fast they would be readily spotted. Approaching from the west with the small cape behind them, Yngvar believed his ship's low profile hid them from easy sight. Thus far it had proven true.

"I want Captain Basil's head," Yngvar said. "Besides the reward, we need the reputation it will bring us. Think on the jobs we will be hired for if we succeed. A pound of gold for every man will be too little for such a crew."

His crew murmured agreement, and Bjorn dipped his head as well.

They drifted with the current while men slipped on mail coats and helmets. They wrapped themselves in their cloaks both for added protection but also to cover the gleam of iron. They pulled hoods over helms and threaded their arms through the straps of shields. The battle was not far now.

While the men prepared, Yngvar sketched the plan in his mind. He considered the pattern of ships in the water. Their spacing allowed Yngvar's ship to glide between two so that flaming casks could be thrown from either side of his ship. The next two would be alerted. Yngvar expected arrows from these. Let the gods shield them. Once flaming oil broke over their bows, they would have to stop the fire or lose their vessel.

A second pass with more flaming oil would ensure the ships would burn long into the night. Perhaps not all the ships would be beyond repair, but all would be crippled.

Yngvar gathered the crew into a huddle, removing the dirty tarp from the casks as he described the approach. It was a daring plan, but it played to the strength of his ship and the weakness of the Byzantines. They could never get under way in time to catch their fleeing ship.

The iron tinder box was now lit with touchwood and a striking steel. Thorfast covered its glow with his shield, while Alasdair blew the small glow into life. He then sat back and raised his brow at Yngvar.

"Lord, what of the Byzantine captain? What you described seems as though our ship will never cease moving. How then do we take his head?"

Yngvar smiled and turned back to face the Byzantine fortress. Though shrouded in indigo gloom only punctuated with orange flames on the walls, he saw enough silver outline to determine the wall construction.

"You will set me ashore," he said, turning back to the crew. "Just ahead of our attack. Two men will accompany me. There will be no space on those walls for more. We need one of the spare long oars. We will set it against the wall once we see the first burst of fire. It will aid us in scaling, but to mount the top we will have easy handholds on the walls. They are of undressed stone, easy to scale when the enemy is looking elsewhere. It is a poor design, though a simple one to build. The captain will regret it tonight."

The crew stared at him, a few looked to each other. Alasdair stood up.

"Lord, you mean to scale the wall, find the captain among the chaos, kill him in the middle of his warriors, then flee?"

"A fine summary," Yngvar said, smiling.

"That's madness," Gyna said.

"I'll go with you," Thorfast said.

"Me too," Bjorn said. Gyna slapped him across his gut.

"You're too big of a target," she said. "You'll go mad and fall off the wall."

"It's true," Yngvar said. "Your strength is welcomed, but on that wall I fear you cannot bring it to bear. And Thorfast, I need you to direct the attack on the ships. I've described it simply, but I trust only you to respond if the plan starts to fall apart."

His cousin and best friend exchanged glances. Both knew not to dissuade him.

"Lord, I am an obvious choice to accompany you," Alasdair said.

Conversely, Yngvar knew not to dissuade Alasdair. He nodded to him, then looked to his crew.

"One more. Who will share in the glory and the reward?"

Every man raised his hand, even sour-faced Leiknr who could taste the finest mead and call it goat piss. Yngvar's chest swelled with the show of daring.

"Lord, if I may," Alasdair said, raising his hand. "I think it will be better if only two of us dare the walls. One more man will not add much and might be more than the top of the walls will allow. Two are easier to look after than three, and we cut out chances of being spotted by a third. If any man believes I am motivated by greed, I am prepared to share my gold equally with all."

"We will share the prize for Captain Basil's head equally. For all of us share the risks of his bounty." Yngvar folded his arms as if he had settled any dispute. Less experienced men frowned but abided his decision. The veterans let their breaths out, relieved to have a chance at a bonus without taking the risk.

"Alasdair and I will flee west along the shore. If you've done your jobs well, the Byzantines will not be chasing you. If they are, then we will meet you at the cape. You will lose them eventually and we can easily find the turn in the coastline from the land. It is the closest landmark we can all agree upon."

With their plans confirmed, Yngvar gave his last order. "Tie the slave to the mast. He will neither fight nor row, but I will not learn if he can swim for shore. Do not abuse him. He must speak for us longer still."

Jamil did not understand Norse, but huddled against the gunwales, he understood the threat of the heads turning toward him. The whites of his eyes were clear in the dark.

They drew as near to the Byzantine ships as they dared. Yngvar and Alasdair both eschewed armor, taking only their weapons and a shield. They dared not wear helmets for fear of a gleam betraying them on the wall. Yngvar felt naked without its weight clamped to his crown, but Alasdair insisted they were safer without it. They slipped off the rails into warm water up to their knees. The waves nudged them to the shore where danger waited. Yngvar carried the oar under arm.

He waved at Thorfast and the others, shadows barely lit by a faint orange stain from the concealed tinder box. His ship could sit on water only knee deep and turn away into the tide once more. His crew lowered oars into the water to shove them back into the tide.

They slogged to shore, watching for shore patrols or anything that might give them away. Once on land, they emptied their boots and let the night breeze cool their skin.

Then they scrambled, bent low to the ground, toward the shadows of the stone fort. They encountered no one. A row of small boats leaned on the beach. They seemed like fishing boats left in the safety of the walls. Waves broke on the shore in a hypnotic thrum. Yngvar watched the walls for guards, spotting one staring out to sea with his head resting in the palm of his hand.

Yngvar settled down against the walls, testing the rough stone and finding handholds to facilitate scaling. He loosened his sword in the sheath, nodding to Alasdair to do the same. His small friend was nearly invisible in the shadows though he was less than an arm's length distant. They both waited, watching the giant Byzantine ships. Their lanterns cast long wavering reflections into the water.

Then a burst of fire exploded across one of the decks.

Another brilliant plume of fire followed on the next.

Yngvar set the oar against the wall, driving it into the ground with his heel. He looked at Alasdair.

"Time to collect a head."

13

Yngvar shimmed up the pole, delivering him a third of the distance up the walls. He clung to the heavy oak oar while he tested the wall with his foot for purchase. His shield dragged him backward as he shifted off the pole. He clenched a dagger between his teeth, needing a weapon at the ready if he were to mount the wall into a waiting enemy. Once he steadied himself, he shifted off the pole then began to climb.

He made sure of each step and dug his fingers into the rough cracks between stones. Above him a deep purple sky shined with milky starlight. Behind him, distant shouts of alarmed crewmen echoed across the waters. Ship bells began to clang in response to the attack.

Unable to shift his head to see, he imagined his lithe ship slipping away as his warriors threw their last kegs and flaming brands onto the unsuspecting decks. By the time the Byzantines spotted them, they would already be falling on the next ship. Though his teeth bit down on hard, bitter iron, he still managed a smile at the thought.

Glancing down, Alasdair was already crawling up the wall. The sight of him in his hooded cloak leaping up the wall gave him a chill. It was as if he walked where Yngvar crawled. Alasdair was already drawing parallel to him. Yngvar grunted and redoubled his effort. He would not be beaten to the top.

They arrived together. Yngvar hauled over the edge and slid into the side of the stone wall. Alasdair flowed over the side next to him. Beneath his feet was a wooden ledge wide enough for a single man to stretch out comfortably. Two men abreast would cause one to topple.

"I was right, lord," Alasdair said. "These are ramparts for single guards only. There is one now."

The guard wore a heavily padded gambeson that stretched to mid-thigh. His black-plumed helmet sat back on his head, as if he had pushed it out of his eyes. He stretched forward, both hands gripping the stone edge of the wall that came up to his stomach. Following the guard's line of sight, Yngvar saw two Byzantine ships engulfed in swirling flames that had already sped up rigging lines and into the masts. He glimpsed shadows of the frantic crew dashing between the flames.

Yngvar took the dagger from his mouth and sheathed it. Instead, he drew the short sword kept at his lap and flipped his shield onto his left arm. He crouched low and crawled toward the stunned guard.

Alarm bells began to ring from the main fortress tower. Yngvar's target, however, remained fixated on the brilliant fire illuminating the night. As distant as the flames were, they still stained the guard's face with orange light.

He turned too late to find Yngvar's shield pressing him back onto the wall. The guard struggled to draw a weapon, but the shield pinned him to the stone. Yngvar shoved his short sword under his shield and into the guard's gut. He groaned as it slid into his belly.

Alasdair grabbed the guard's feet and lifted him over the side of the wall. He went backwards and head first, guaranteeing his death upon landing. His scream died in with a soft thud as he hit the earth.

Ringing bells and shouting guards had masked the commotion. Yngvar's heart raced as he looked left to right for other enemies. None were on the ramparts with him—yet. Lights flared in the main tower, and on its top figures appeared. Down in the main fortress, Yngvar saw a large courtyard that led to the main structure. A forge sat dark and quiet to the right of the main barracks. Guards streamed out of the building and headed for wooden stairs leading to the ramparts on both sides.

"We have no time to find the captain," Alasdair said. "Even if we do, we have no escape, lord."

"We will cut ourselves a path," Yngvar said. "They can only fight one at a time on these ramparts."

"The captain will be in the tower, lord. There will be plenty of men to fight us there."

"Speak no more of it," Yngvar said, wicking the blood from his short sword. "These men fight in formations and according to orders. They won't know how to deal with us. Let's go."

"I have taken a rope, lord. Here is a leather patch to grip it with. You could slide down the walls with it."

Yngvar felt Alasdair pressing something into his side, but he did not turn. Instead he watched men rushing to the wooden building set atop the stone tower. The captain would be there directing the defenses. Once Yngvar had his head, then he could fight his way out.

He laughed. This was a fool's gambit. Yet what could please the gods more? He would gift them the blood of heroes, and perhaps he would find his seat on the benches of Valhalla this night. If he succeeded, his name would be immortal. He was a fool, he decided. But he was brave and strong and the enemy worthy. To die here would bring him no shame.

The tower door gave way against his shoulder. No bar was set to it, for none would expect anyone other than a friend to enter. The hearth light momentarily blinded him, though it was small and set in a blackened brass bowl that smoked into a chimney. Still, a haze of smoke spilled into the square room, which had bunks three high set along each wall. A ladder in the center of the room led to the roof.

A set of bare legs disappeared into the square hole above. Three men in red cloaks stared out the windows, chattering to each other at the spectacle unfolding on the water.

He and Alasdair spread out so that each would take a man on either side, leaving one in the center for both of their blades. Alasdair, cowl still hiding his bright face, nodded silently with his shield and short sword poised for a strike.

Yngvar padded across the wooden floor. It squeaked but the men did not turn. They must have believed it was only more of their number filling behind them.

The guard before Yngvar pointed out the narrow window and expressed amazement. Whatever language he spoke, his shock was obvious.

In time with Alasdair, Yngvar slammed his shield against the back of the guard's skull and stabbed his kidney. The padded gambeson was good for deflecting an errant strike or arrow. It availed nothing against a direct puncture from a strong blade. The guard arched his back and screamed.

Alasdair's target made no noise, but fell back into the room holding his neck as bright blood spluttered between his fingers.

The guard in the middle looked to Yngvar, who smiled and pulled his shield up. The guard's amazement paused him long enough for Alasdair to reach from behind and carve his throat open.

The guard toppled, gagging and coughing. He crumbled to his knees as if he were prostrating himself to his god. Alasdair finished him with a stab into his side.

"Vicious work," Yngvar said. "But their brothers are swift behind us. Don their helmets and cloaks. Let's get to the top."

Yngvar picked a helmet that teetered on his head. It only needed to disguise him as he climbed up the stairs. He swept the light red cloak over his own. Above him men shouted and footfalls mingled with heavier thuds. He heard metallic clicking.

"Lord, please, take the leather." Alasdair now wore an oversized helmet and red cloak that flowed onto the floor. He held out a square of yellow leather. "We can glide down to safety with the rope."

Yngvar accepted it and tucked it into his baldric. He expected to lose it in the upcoming battle. He had no care for how he would escape. The walls were easy enough to scale. He could not guess how it would go with the captain's head in the empty sack he had taken.

"I'll enter first," Yngvar said. "See if you can tie off the rope while I guess at which one is the captain. We will have a few heartbeats before the men up there realize we are not one of them."

Slinging his shield onto his back, he began to climb. His heart slammed against the base of his throat as he put hand over hand on the smooth rungs. Each one brought him closer to the strange orders and responses shouted back and forth. Just beneath the entrance, he heard an iron click and a heavy snap.

The Byzantines shouted in joy, but it died with a strangled moan.

Yngvar poked his head up to the floor. His eyes were level with a dozen bare feet of men roused from sleep to their posts. Some wore red cloaks, others did not, but all were crowded around a huge machine that sat on a wooden platform. At a glance it seemed a giant crossbow mounted to a swiveling wood platform. Two were working furiously at a hand crank, while two more hefted an iron bolt between them and waited to load it on the bow. Two more men in red cloaks leaned over the walls and shouted directions to the crew. One broke away to rotate the platform with another crank.

A hand reached down to him. One of his erstwhile companions offered to haul him up, and he accepted. Yngvar pulled up level to a man a full head shorter than himself. He wore a red cloak and black-plumed helmet. His friendly smile lent his dark face a boyish cast. He spoke in his odd language, pointing toward the glow lighting the sky where the others crewed their giant bow.

Yngvar swept into the man, carrying him straight to the wood wall enclosing this new level. The Byzantine gave a short gasp of surprise, but his full scream did not come until he was over the wall and falling to his doom.

The rest of the crew of six were intent on lining up their next shot. Alasdair slipped onto the roof like a living shadow that flowed to Yngvar's side.

Two iron lanterns hung from black iron hangers that swayed with the shuddering of the plank floor. Yngvar dared a moment to look over the walls. Archers lined the ramparts. They were firing flaming arrows into the ground to light up the areas by the walls.

"Odin's balls," Yngvar said under his breath. "They'll turn night into day before long."

Alasdair had already tied his rope to the corner post and fed it down the side.

The six crew worked furiously. One glanced back at Yngvar but did not recognize the threat and continued to crank the bow.

"We can't let that fire again," Yngvar said. "It'll sink my ship."

"Lord?" Alasdair looked up innocently despite the proof of murder sprayed across him face and hands.

Yngvar smiled and sloughed his shield onto his arm. These men crewed a war machine and armed themselves with mere daggers.

Truly, it was a night for murder. He drew his sword once more.

"Basil Gregoras!"

None of the crew responded. Each one concentrated on his task.

Yngvar pointed his sword at the crew.

"Basil Gregoras! Face me!"

His forceful shout gained him more attention, but the men tracking his ship continued to look over the walls.

"Basil Gregoras!" His shout cracked with frustration. Bows on the walls beneath thrummed. Time was running out.

The two crewmen carrying the iron bolt set it into its slot then stepped back. Freed of their duty for the moment, one man with curly golden hair shot him an irritated look and shouted at him in his twisting, hissing language. He pointed angrily at the ramparts behind him.

"He's not here, lord," Alasdair said. "We have to escape now."

"He's on the ramparts," Yngvar said. "And I will not leave without my prize."

The curly haired man jumped when the bolt fired again, the cord snapping with force enough to shake the entire floor. In the same instance, his companion straightened up from fetching another bolt. He stared at Yngvar's shield.

"Kill them," Yngvar said. Then rushed the two men.

He and Alasdair fell upon the bolt-thrower crew. The curly haired man was first to die, followed by his companion. The spotters tracking his ship were shouting frantically, but not in response to Yngvar's attack. They jumped in place like two men holding their piss. Yngvar nearly laughed. They pointed out to sea. A glance over the wall and Yngvar saw his ship silhouetted against the fires of two huge ships. They sailed directly into the path of the bolt-thrower.

Alasdair killed both men on the cranks. Now the two spotters realized their danger. They drew daggers and shouted defiance as they charged. Yngvar smiled as he caught a dagger on his shield and forced it aside. He easily slashed the unarmored man's belly. The other landed a blow to Yngvar's ribs, which shocked him but did not cut.

The fool had dropped his dagger and hit Yngvar with an empty hand.

He did not dull his blade on the spotter's flesh. If the fool could not hold a weapon, he was unworthy of it. Instead, Yngvar slammed the rim of his shield into the spotter's face until he was crumpled against the wall then threw him over the side.

But rather than fall to the ground, he crashed to the wood ramparts below. His body thudded, and the men lined up there shouted in surprise.

Yngvar looked over, and a long line of dark faces stared back at him.

"Well, they know we're up here now," he said. "Alasdair, drop the door on that hole please."

"I can bar it with one of these iron hangers, but I doubt it will hold long."

Yngvar did not care. He hefted a bolt by himself and dropped it into the slot.

"It doesn't take two men to lift these bolts," Yngvar said as he kicked away a corpse draped over a crank. "I bet it won't take six men to work this. Let's the two of us give it a go. Rotate this platform toward that rampart."

"Lord? I think the enemy will be here soon. We must escape."

"We will escape," Yngvar said. Though his pulse throbbed across his entire body, he was filled with battle joy. An entire fortress of enemies waited for him. He would pluck glory from their midst and become a legend.

"Lord, they're in the room below."

Yngvar cranked the rope back as Alasdair cranked the platform around. Clearly, he heard the horrified shouts from below. Alasdair had spiked the trapdoor shut with one of the iron hangers. In his craftiness, he set the lantern at the door's edge so that it would fall on anyone climbing onto the roof.

"Lord? What are you aiming at?"

"This is cranked as tight as I can get it. See if you can figure how to launch it. Wait for my command."

Yngvar leaned against the wall where the curly haired Byzantine had pointed. The ramparts were full of bowmen, and these turned toward him. Though he had lost his helmet, he still wore the red cloak. So the archers wavered.

"Basil Gregoras!"

Yngvar's shout sent a ripple along the line. The men were two body-lengths below him, but their wide eyes were clear beneath the rims of their iron helmets. Each turned down the line like one rock knocking over one behind it. They settled on an unassuming man in a black-plumed helmet.

Yngvar shouted the name once more, confident he had found the captain. He waved him closer.

The Byzantines were still uncertain of his identity, so they pressed close to the walls as their captain squeezed past them.

Stealing the moment to look toward the sea, he found three of the four ships blazing beyond hope and the fourth one with guttering patches of flame twisting along its rails and rigging. His own ship was already vanished into the darkness, only the wild calls of victory from his crew betraying their presence.

Captain Basil Gregoras had shoved through crowd to draw close, possibly assuming Yngvar had some report to make. He was younger and less physically imposing than Yngvar had expected. This man had killed Prince Kalim's champion. Having seen the Arab warriors in person, he doubted this slight man beneath him could have handled a champion.

Captain Gregoras tucked his helmet under his arm and shouted up to Yngvar. His voice was strong and clear, but the words were gibberish.

"Alasdair, release the bolt!"

14

Yngvar jumped aside from the wall. Beneath him, Captain Gregoras shouted in his bright and powerful voice. But now Yngvar landed on his rump and saw nothing but Alasdair pull a lever that released the bolt that they had loaded onto the war machine.

The rope snapped taut with a crack. Alasdair had intuited he should aim the bolt down. Though the machine could not angle as steep as Yngvar would have liked, it was sufficient for the random damage he intended.

The iron bolt shattered the wall, sending wood and splinters into the air. Yngvar leapt up in time to hear the sound of shattering wood and wailing from below. He rushed to the remnants of the wall and examined the results of his plan.

The rampart was destroyed and dumped a dozen archers to the ground. Others clung to both sides of the breach, hanging like hares over a cooking pot. Captain Gregoras had been close enough to the tower to avoid the shot. Also, the bolt had not struck with enough force to demolish the entire wooden platform.

The captain had fallen flat and clung to the remains of the ramparts. Two other archers curled up as if to protect their heads.

Across the breach, a dangling section fell away with the man clinging to it.

"Good shot!" Yngvar shouted, drawing back from the wall. "We're about to get raked with arrows. So time to go, Alasdair."

"Lord, I think we have more to fear."

He had forgotten the enemies below. He was breathless with excitement and his pulse thundered in his ears. Turning his attention to the trapdoor, he saw it shaking and leaping as something heavy battered from beneath it.

"Go to the rope," Yngvar said. "You've served me well here. But I finish this alone. Watch for me at the bottom of the wall."

"Lord? What is this?"

Alasdair pulled back his hood as if he could not hear from beneath it. His blood-splattered face twisted with confusion and fear.

The iron hanger wedged into the trapdoor popped up then clanked to the wood.

"We've both got to go," Yngvar said. "I will see you soon."

He turned from Alasdair and ran to the breach the iron bolt had shot through the wood wall. Keeping his shield out against arrows, he tightened his hand on his sword and smiled.

"See me, Odin. Guide my sword."

He leapt down to the shattered rampart below.

The Byzantine beneath him flopped out of the way and rolled off the platform into the darkness. Yngvar landed on both feet and crumpled down to ease the force of his drop. The boards beneath him cracked but held. Before Captain Gregoras could stand, Yngvar leapt up from his crouch.

Yet being the only one standing made him a target. An arrow hissed across the gap and slammed into the top of his shield. The shaft vibrated as the bodkin exploded through the wood to blow splinters into his face. He stepped back with the force of the shot just as another arrow swished past his cheek to break on the stone wall behind him.

The other archer on the rampart scrabbled to his feet. He wielded his bow staff with two hands, sweeping low at Yngvar's legs. It was a fine strike, aimed at the side of the knee. But Yngvar knocked it aside with his shield and thrust with his short sword.

It sank into the archer's neck. The Byzantine screamed and yanked back, taking the sword with him. He clamped his hand over the blade as dark blood bubbled into the well of his collarbone. Yngvar could not risk being pulled off balance and falling into the courtyard below. So he released the blade and his enemy plummeted backward into the gloom below.

A dozen more arrows screamed across the gap. The captain remained prone, which Yngvar had not expected of him, and left his archers a perfect target. With his shield lowered, Yngvar's unarmored body faced the volley.

One razor edge cut through his shoulder with burning force. It spun him so that another shaft grazed his neck on the opposite side. It might have taken him down had he not been hit. He felt the air ripple with the other arrows speeding past.

"Gregoras! Face me!"

The captain, now alone, stared up in shock, but had presence enough to reach for his dagger.

Behind Yngvar, a door slammed open. He had not seen it, but of course it must have always been there. Arrows still quivered in its planks. Ranks of Byzantines filled the room beyond, their iron helmets gleaming with the hearth fire in the guard room. Above him, more Byzantines peered cautiously through the shattered wall.

Yngvar did not know where to face his shield. His long sword remained strapped to his side and to reach for it invited attack.

Captain Gregoras lumbered to his feet, now confident Yngvar had been captured. He pointed with his dagger and barked some command in a foreign language.

Yngvar turned back to the doorway. A strong man with a red cape marked with a white hem now stood in the doorway. Crude stitches held his left cheek together, pulling his mouth into an artificial snarl. His hands were covered in white scars and one gripped a short sword with an oddly shaped blade. He growled another command at Yngvar.

"Captain Basil Gregoras," Yngvar said, turning back to the

captain. "My thanks for standing up. You make this much easier. I'm not leaving without your head."

The captain cocked his head at Yngvar's words, but had lowered his dagger out of disdain. After all, he was one man on a rampart surrounded by enemies and unarmed.

But Yngvar had his heavy, leather-rimmed shield.

He snapped his shield arm back, releasing the grip so it flew of his arm and struck the Byzantine with the stitched face across his nose. He fell back in shock, roaring.

Yngvar leapt for Gregoras. He seized the captain at the shoulders with both hands and wrenched him to the wall.

"Time to leave!" Yngvar shouted.

He shoved the captain and jumped with him over the wall. The captain screamed in panic, but Yngvar laughed. He would land in Odin's hand, he was certain.

They fell together in what felt like an impossibly slow speed. Yngvar rode the captain down like a sled, holding him tight to his own body.

The impact sent a white flash across Yngvar's vision. His jaw snapped shut and he bounced away like leather ball. He flopped on his side and rolled to a stop in short grass.

He stared up at the stars, unsure of what had happened. His body throbbed but he felt no pain. He curled his legs and realized he had survived the jump. He must have fallen thirty feet or more. From the ground, the top of the fortress walls seemed to reach to the roof of the sky.

Top of the fortress.

He scrambled away, out of the thin light of burning arrows that speckled the landscape. Thrusting directly to the wall, he held his breath. Men above him called to each other and shadowy heads craned to see where he had landed.

His shoulder ached and the blood flowed readily to his hand. The impact had jarred it such that to raise his shield arm halfway filled him with bright shocks of pain.

Captain Gregoras lay face down as a still heap, his red cloak flipped up over his head.

Yngvar panicked, fearing he had broken his magnificent sword in the reckless jump. But he found it still at his side and drew it. The blade slipped free of its scabbard and hummed. Stars reflected from its polished edge. He stalked over to the prone captain. His knees hurt, but within a few strides he found his gait once more.

He flipped off the red cloak from the captain's head. His blank eyes stared off to the side.

"You saved my life," Yngvar said. "And made me rich. I will repay you in Valhalla, my friend."

Voices from the wall shouted. An arrow fell far ahead of him, thumping the earth.

With a single stroke, Yngvar lopped the head from Captain Gregoras's shoulders. A rush of blood and fluid spilled out, and Yngvar fished the head from the mess.

Arrows began falling around him, and would soon strike their mark if he remained. Holding the head by its short hair, he limped off toward the darkness.

"Lord!" Alasdair hissed. His slight form detached from the dark earth. "That was madness!"

"I don't think I can run, but I can trot. Let's hurry before they open their gates to seek us."

The fortress gates were not along this wall, affording them a lead. They loped along the shoreline, passing the row of fishing boats left as if no one could touch them. The shores were now lined with crewmen that had swam or otherwise found their way to the beach. But they huddled together to watch their giant ships shudder and groan with the fire consuming them.

"We did it, lord." Alasdair's excited whisper felt like a shout in the darkness. But the crewmen were too despondent to notice or care for their passing.

"Three ships burned and one hobbled, it seems," Yngvar said as he skulked past the lines of Byzantine survivors. "And one bloody head, as promised. The gods love us."

"They do, lord!"

Though Yngvar's shoulder and knees pained him, he was light with joy. He had achieved what no one before him had done.

Granted, he had to only face four unsuspecting ships. In other circumstances he would have had to retreat. But was that not the gods working in his favor?

Alasdair led and soon sighted their ship off the coast. He boldly called out across the water. But why fear now? Everyone on the shore would be drawn to the bright fires down the coast. Here they were free to hail their ship and wade back across the warm water.

It was soothing to Yngvar's ankles and knees. He realized he had probably hurt both jumping not from the walls but from the tower to the rampart. Zeal had carried him thus far without reporting his injuries. But now as Bjorn and Thorfast both hauled him on deck, that excitement ebbed and the myriad pains of his foolishness seeped into his bones.

"You're bleeding," Thorfast said. He pulled Yngvar to his feet.

Gyna pushed between them to examine his shoulder. She sniffed.

"A gash. Nothing to worry for. Two stitches will keep it from tearing more."

"Never mind that," Yngvar said, fumbling with the leather sack. Blood had stained the bottom of it. He fished around, feeling for the wet, gore-soaked hair. He wrapped his fingers into it and tore it from the sack.

"Captain Basil Gregoras!"

The crew cheered, heedless of any danger haunting the darkness beyond their sight. For had they not just felled a giant? What fear did they own?

Only Jamil fell aside, landing on hands and knees. He heaved as if to vomit. This set the crew laughing harder.

"Hey, do you need a better look?" Bjorn grabbed the severed head from Yngvar and held it over Jamil's body. All the blood had rushed from it earlier, but it still drizzled dark drops across Jamil's ruined robes. The old Moor scrambled aside as if acid had fallen on him.

"Don't lose that head," Gyna screamed at him. "It's worth its weight in gold."

Bjorn swayed the head in his hand, flecking blood all around. "You're right. He must've had a lot of brains, this one. That's a heavy head."

Yngvar collected the head back into the sack. "He had more brains than muscle. He was barely a grown man, to be honest."

His crew surrounded him, clapping his back and whooping in celebration. Once they had calmed, they took the oars once more and rowed along the coast to find a safe place to camp.

They set watches of seven men each, rotating through the night to keep every man fresh. If they were pursued by some means, then Yngvar wanted to flee with their spoils.

He slept with the captain's head close to his own. The scent of blood and sweat was poor comfort. Yet he was so exhausted from his exertions that he fell asleep the moment his eyes closed.

They were away with the dawn. Yngvar caught the wind and his ship fairly flew back to Licata. Any chance of Byzantine pursuit had been ruined.

By early evening, he and his crew were standing before the astonished Prince Kalim once more.

They had been told to bathe before meeting the prince, which every man welcomed. Instead of being sent to a pond or stream, they were taken into a building of stone where hot water waited for them in a pool. The marvelous room defied their most outlandish dreams. Some of the crew wished for daggers to pry out the tiles lining the walls. Even if these were worthless, who back in Norway would believe their stories without proof? But they had no weapons or armor, which were being cleaned and sharpened by the prince's own blacksmiths.

They had lost no one in the battle. The Byzantines had been roundly surprised, and the horror of burning oil and pitch had stolen all their fight. Yngvar had suffered the worst injury of any.

Now Prince Kalim sat at the edge of his chair with his impassive guards lined behind him. Though even these hardened, rugged men leaned forward to hear the interpretation of Yngvar's exploits. The prince's women were conspicuously absent, to his regret.

"At last I come to the best part of my tale," Yngvar said, standing before his men. Their armor had yet to be returned so they wore their salt-stained, patched clothes. Though their hair and beards were neatly combed and their cheeks still apple red from a refreshing bath, they remained the shabbiest sight amidst the grandeur of the audience chamber.

Jamil stood beside Yngvar. As a slave, he had been denied a bath. He smelled of blood. More telling, he stooped over as if he had suffered a hundred lashes. That wildmen from the north had been allowed a bath while his civilized self had been forced to wait outside injured him worse than lashes.

Now Jamil held a wooden box in both hands. Yngvar gestured him toward.

The old Moor, already stooped, lowered his head as he took a tentative step toward the prince. His white head cover was now dotted with brown stains, compliments of Bjorn's teasing. He held the box up.

The prince clapped, and from out the darkness beside his ornate chair a young boy appeared. He was dressed in fine clothes made from light cloth, brightly colored in blue and yellow. His hair was completely shaved, marking him as a slave. He accepted the box from Jamil, not daring to meet the Moor's eyes. Jamil faded back to Yngvar's side.

The prince stood now, a lusty glare shining from his eyes. He spoke quickly to the slave, who placed the box on the dais beneath him.

Yngvar straightened his back and smiled.

"I bring you the head of Captain Basil Gregoras."

Though the translator rendered the name into the prince's language, Prince Kalim had no need of it. He lunged down to the box, standing over it and cursing. He stabbed a finger at the boy slave, his words spilling out in a jumble.

The slave opened the box, and with both small hands carried out the head of the dead captain. It was coated in dried blood. Despite having placed it in a box, a scattering of flies leapt off it.

The vile odor of death spread into the light perfume of the room. But Yngvar welcomed the more natural scent. Whatever the source of this sweet smoke, Yngvar found it impossible to tolerate for long. He was no beggar, but he would have rather spent a night in a barn than breathing this scent.

The prince screamed like a girl just gifted a puppy. He leapt up to his dais and clasped his hands together toward the sky. His words were thick with pleasure and he streamed what must be praises to his god.

"The prince praises Allah for his many blessings," the interpreter said. "Prince Kalim is greatly pleased."

Yngvar nodded. He glanced across his shoulder to Thorfast and Bjorn, who smiled like two uncles who had just gifted their niece a puppy. Only poor Captain Basil was unhappy with this moment. His severed head remained eternally frozen with his broken mouth shaped into a scream.

The prince stopped dancing, drew a deep breath, then ordered the head returned to the box. The slave carried it away to whatever humiliating fate awaited the remains of the Byzantine.

He again clapped his hands then smoothed his clothes as he regained his composure. He waited, standing as still as a hunting crane. After a moment, he gave a shallow but satisfied nod and began to rattle off a series of pronouncements in his rough language.

The interpreter began in Frankish.

"You have done a great service to me and my father. These Byzantines have not learned their place in this new world. They cling to the past like rats to the deck of a sinking ship. I have your word on the destroyed fleet, but I shall soon confirm it for myself. That you have delivered me the head of a hated enemy is proof of your valor."

The prince paused, and Yngvar did not know what else to do but bow in recognition of the achievement. To his mind, there should be more shouting and praising than this. A good song would have to be composed from his daring raid. But these Arabs could not be expected to understand. Prince Kalim accepted Yngvar's nod with one of his own.

"I freely admit I thought to send you to death. Are you surprised? I am. I had hopes you would wound the Byzantines and prick them into attacking me. My father holds my arm back from them. But if they attack, then I may go to war. But you have done more than I dared dream. Their ships are ruined and their leaders shaken.

"Let no one say Prince Kalim does not honor his word. Your

payment has been prepared and the bounty for Basil Gregoras to you who have delivered his head. You Norsemen are mightier and craftier than any I had expected. I am honored to have you in my service. And it is my pleasure to bestow these gifts upon you."

The prince raised his hand and flicked it. Two guards lifted each end of a large chest of battered wood. They lugged it to the foot of the dais and set it down, pulling open the lid.

Gold coins shifted and glittered beneath it. Yngvar and his men leaned forward and gasped.

"Three thousand gold dinars," said Prince Kalim. "And more to come for the head of the Byzantine. You become rich men this day."

15

"Wealth beyond measure," Bjorn shouted.

"You can measure it," Thorfast shouted back. "A pound of gold for each man!"

The table erupted with laughter that echoed off the polished stone walls of the dining chamber.

Yngvar sat with Alasdair at his right and Jamil at his left. They sat upon chairs, which he found constraining and awkward. But such was the custom in Prince Kalim's palace that men wore no shoes in certain rooms and used chairs whenever they must sit.

Across a table piled with spicy meats and vegetables with flavors that defied anything Yngvar understood, Gyna swilled wine from a silver cup while Bjorn threw his arm around Thorfast and laughed. All down the length of the table his crew laughed and grew drunk of bitter wine the color of old blood. But it gifted them with a warm glow, and no man denied it was a fine drink.

"Lord, if I were to eat another feast, I believe my stomach will burst." Alasdair sat back in his chair and rested his hands across his gut. "Truly, now I understand why gluttony is a sin. I will not eat again."

"And lying is a sin to you Christians, is it not?" Yngvar picked up a rib bone and began to gnaw the marrow from it. "Only yesterday you swore you would not eat again."

"Leave him alone," Gyna said. "If he eats more maybe he will grow."

Everyone laughed, even Alasdair. Only sour-faced Jamil sat and stared at his food. Yngvar had hoped that including him in the celebration and allowing him a seat by his side would cheer the old Moor. But the honor did not shake his despondency. He had hardly eaten, and when Bjorn had reminded him that by rights he should be sitting on the floor with a shaved head, Jamil gave a wan smile.

Yngvar wondered if the Moor would die from the shame of his predicament. Yet he could not be freed, for no one could speak for him. Jamil had proven too useful to let go. His eyes darted from side to side, as if looking for something to appear and sweep him to freedom.

"If he's going to sulk," Thorfast said, noticing Yngvar's attention to the Moor, "then shove him under the table so I don't have my mood spoiled."

Jamil blinked and straightened himself, yet the false smile did not last more than a heartbeat before it crumbled.

"Forget him," Yngvar said. "If two days of feasting will not rouse his spirits, then he has already died."

Prince Kalim had feasted them the night of their return. The prince had gathered his court to recount Yngvar's tales. Important men in colorful robes and wearing gold and silver attended the feast. Dozens of these so-called clerks in gray robes and white head covers listened in rapt attention, applauding in time with their betters. Even the vicious little rat called Saleet who had tried to frame Yngvar listened attentively. He clapped the loudest and his facile smile was worse than Jamil's own ravaged attempts. In fact, Yngvar had sent Jamil to deliver his message to Saleet.

"Tell the little shit that he may dine with us heroes and I will forgive his insults if he apologizes."

Yngvar laughed once the message had been delivered and Saleet's dark face turned purple. The reedy man fled from the hall rather than endure more shame.

After a day of rest, they had been invited back to the palace. Yngvar had spent a morning discussing possible attacks he could lead against the Byzantines now that they were hobbled. Nothing had been formally decided, but another raid was in the offering. They were invited to feast again that night, alone this time but for servants and guards.

Yngvar of course feared the trap he and Thorfast had discussed earlier. The prince did not hesitate when he asked for his weapons to be returned. He warned that any drunken violence would not be forgiven and that more guards roamed the palace than Yngvar knew. But he had no compunctions in granting them leave to carry weapons.

Yngvar had been feeling relieved until Thorfast mentioned poison. Yet Jamil had sampled the food and lived. Perhaps that is why the old Moor's humor was low. Yet who should taste for poison if not a slave?

Now that the food was done and his men emptied the carafes of wine as fast as they were replaced, a gray-robed clerk entered. He wore no head cover, which Yngvar took as strange for these Arabs. Though in truth the clerk was a handsome lad with sharp features and intelligent face. He should not hide it under cloth, Yngvar thought.

The clerk came directly to Jamil, who jerked upright as if he had been hauled by his collar. The clerk jabbered in his reedy voice, bowing and smiling. Jamil answered in single words. This exchange ended the merriment around the table, and the men leaned in for the anticipated translation. First Jamil would speak Frankish and Thorfast would relay it in Norse.

"Lord Yngvar," Jamil began. "Prince Kalim hopes your food has been agreeable. He feels it is unbecoming of his newest heroes to sleep on the deck of a ship like common dogs. He bids you to make residence in his palace."

Yngvar looked to Thorfast as he completed his translation. The men grumbled agreement. Leaving the ship meant surrendering the freedom of the sea, but the palace and its serving women were a rare opportunity.

"Tell him we would be gladdened to sleep here," Yngvar said. "But our weapons and armor are ours at all times, except as courtesy demands."

Jamil rattled off the rough translation. Yngvar would have to learn this language himself if he were to deal with these Arabs successfully. The gibberish was already starting to tune itself to his ears and actual words broke through.

"The prince will arrange for a barracks suitable for heroes. But in the meantime, he invites you to end your night with deeper pleasures that only his greatest heroes may earn."

Jamil gave Yngvar a tired look, but Yngvar's own eyes widened with understanding. As Thorfast completed the Norse translation, someone at the far end of the table shouted.

"We'll get our hands on his girls?"

The crew laughed. Gyna groaned and lowered her forehead to the table.

Jamil leaned in closer. "Not the prince's harem, lord. No man may touch his women and live. But he has other beauties, I am certain."

"I like how this prince thinks," Bjorn shouted, having listened in on the exchange. "Kills the bastard that touches his women and has plenty to spare for his friends."

Gyna lifted her head and glared at him. "Did you lose your brains along with your eye? You belong to me."

Bjorn slapped the table and laughed. "Of course I do! But you ain't going to keep me from having a spot of fun! Follow along if you're worried."

Yngvar left Bjorn and Gyna to their complications, and pulled Jamil by the shoulder to draw even closer.

"We'd never decline the prince's hospitality, but how safe is this? Drinking and eating is fine, but as soon as women are added to this mix, well, they're usually the spark to the fire that burns down the hall."

"A fair question, lord." Jamil winced as if in pain. "In truth, I would not go weaponless. Nor would I throw all caution away. Prince Kalim probably thinks this is what you barb—er, Norsemen —require to feel satisfied. But I believe the prince is a religious man and over-doing tonight would lower your reputation in his eyes."

"But he's offering?" Yngvar asked. He was as excited as his crew to see these dusky beauties up close. Their flowery scents as they passed through the palace were driving him mad with lust. "We've all spent a long time at sea, and returning from battle stokes a man's loins even more. It would go a long way toward peace if the crew enjoyed the attentions of beautiful women."

Jamil smiled, seemingly genuine. "Lord Yngvar, I am but your slave, as I hate to admit. Heed me in this, though. This offer is full of peril. The prince will not countenance such base revels in his palace. You will be taken to a brothel in town. So I beg you to bear your weapons as caution to those who might think a foreigner is an easy target for quick profit. Yet at the same time, those weapons must never be drawn. But your men are already drunk, and if they argue about women, I cannot imagine the outcome."

Yngvar released Jamil's shoulder. "You have never heard of peace straps? Here, see mine? These straps hold my sword in its sheath so that I do not draw it in haste. A man must be deliberate about it. By the time a drunk man gets the straps free, everyone is alerted to his intent. I will stay above the celebration tonight and you will attend me. If any of my crew act imprudently, I will deal with them."

"As you will, Lord Yngvar." Jamil bowed his head and spoke rapidly with the handsome clerk who had waited patiently with hands folded behind his back.

The clerk accepted everything with frequent nods. Jamil at last seemed animated and alive. Perhaps he had been unemployed too long, Yngvar thought. A man of learning such as Jamil needed to use his mind more than Yngvar had called upon it.

Servants cleared the tables while his crew assembled, belching and back-slapping each other in anticipation.

Gyna stretched into an exaggerated yawn. She then looked to Yngvar. "I'm not spending a night with a crew of aroused berserkers. Tell the prince he can send that handsome clerk back to the ship as reward."

"That thin boy?" Bjorn asked. "That'd be like beating a cave with a hazel branch."

Gyna slapped him, and the meaty crack stopped both Jamil and the clerk. Everyone else was accustomed to these outbursts. She kept her hand poised to slap Bjorn again as he cowered, laughing and holding his cheek.

"Be sure Jamil explains to the local women what you're doing, or they might not know why you're bouncing atop them. Now, I'll be at the ship, sleeping."

"We'll find a reward for you," Yngvar said. "But if you'll be at the ship, then see to our gold before you do. It should have arrived with the tower captain by now. Be sure he has it. Here's the prince's sign."

Yngvar handed the instructions written on paper he received from the prince's hands directly. Their gold was to be kept safe in the tower by the dock where they had met the watch captain. Yngvar had insisted the gold be kept safe but close at hand. The tower was his idea, which again the prince agreed to. After all, the captain was his man and it made no difference where the gold was held. Licata and all within it belonged to the prince and his father, the emir.

With the crew assembled and Gyna following a brown-skinned girl servant out of the chamber, Yngvar nodded to Jamil that they were ready to depart. The old Moor's dark-ringed eyes were wide and staring. Perhaps he was not so old and anticipated the women as well. He would be disappointed when Yngvar kept him away. He was needed for translation still.

They followed the handsome clerk through the halls, occasionally halting as some guards passed. This seemed strange to Yngvar, but after a quick exchange, Jamil translated the rationale.

"These guards have long served Prince Kalim yet they have no gold nor women as you do. It makes for peace to keep your rewards secret."

Yngvar smiled at the thought of these Arabs envying him. He supposed the thought of foreign men laying with their women might enrage them. So he agreed they should take the circumspect route out of the palace. They passed through empty halls and out of a rear exit onto the street. The guards at that exit had little to say and waved the clerk and all of them through the archway. The two flanking the tunnel offered only a quick glance as if they were no more than cattle passing to the slaughter.

The night was dark, with clouds obscuring the sky. A puddle in the street paved with stones caught reflections of yellow light flowing out of shuttered windows. They were motioned to silence as they slipped along the pavement. The clerk was not overtly hiding them, but he paused at intersections to check for oncomers. Yet like cities everywhere, when the sun set, the majority of folk were abed.

At last they came to a grand building with domed roofs and a single high tower. Jamil paused and muttered something to himself that sounded like a prayer.

"What is wrong?" Yngvar asked, hushed as if he feared to alert a guard.

Jamil shook his head, and wiped his face. "Nothing, Lord Yngvar. I have never seen such a brothel. Look at its magnificence."

"Looks like it ain't got no business," Bjorn said, scratching his head. "Where're the girls?"

"Prince Kalim has bought the brothel for the night," Jamil said. "I assume the girls are inside, lord."

The clerk did not approach the front, but instead slipped into the alley before beckoning them to follow. Yngvar noticed several of his crew balk and lower their hands to their sword hilts.

"Come now," Yngvar said. "There are thirty of us here. Does an army lie in ambush down that narrow passage? Fear nothing."

To show his confidence, Yngvar left both his hands hanging freely by his side as he followed the clerk into the alley. It was narrow and fastidiously clean. The clerk led him to a wider area in the rear, where buildings formed something of an arena. The buildings were equally magnificent to the brothel, with windows two floors up that were covered in latticework. These Arabs had a taste for the gaudy, Yngvar thought. Even their alleys were decorated.

The clerk waited by a small wood door set into an arched frame. He smiled patiently as Jamil and the rest of the Norsemen gathered into the cleared area.

Not even a speck of trash could be found here. No animal bones, no waste, not even a weed sprouting from the pounded dirt.

Despite numbering thirty drunken men, they remained reverentially silent. The cleanliness of the place was as oppressing as the high walls leaning over them. Silence seemed the only appropriate response.

The clerk knocked on the door three times, his small fist gently rapping the bright wood. It cracked open and the clerk leaned in to speak. Words were exchanged. The clerk passed something inside that seemed like a pouch. Likely the prince's payment for use of the brothel. More words fluttered back and forth.

Yngvar elbowed Jamil. His face glistened with sweat.

"Sorry, Lord Yngvar, he's making payment and discussing the girls available. It seems there's some confusion over which women were to be present tonight."

"But there are women?" Yngvar asked.

"Yes, lord. There may not be enough for thirty men."

Yngvar chuckled but said nothing more. Even one woman would be enough if the men could be patient. At last, the clerk spoke to Jamil and waved him forward. The clerk spoke in a swift-flowing stream of words. To Yngvar's ears their speech made no sense, though now he was beginning to pick full words out of the babble. The clerk gave the impression of haste and impatience. But at last, he waved Yngvar forward.

Jamil wiped his brow and smiled. "There are four women only. The prince expected five times as many, and has paid as much."

"What kind of brothel has only four women?" Bjorn shoved to the front, frowning at Jamil.

"The women are often sent to their customers," Jamil said. "It seems you are not the only men wanting celebrating this night."

"I expect the little clerk is going to be in trouble," Yngvar said. But he noticed the clerk had already vanished inside. Jamil just shrugged.

"Let's waste no more time, Lord Yngvar."

Inside was dark. He did not trust a blackened room. But in the same instant he was put at ease by the strong scent of flowery smoke and the giggles of young women.

"Please, enter the main room," Jamil said. Sweat beads caught the light as he stood outside, and he blinked frantically.

Yngvar clapped his shoulder. "Easy, old man. You're not laying with these women tonight."

He offered a weak smile and dipped his head.

The rest of Yngvar's crew piled inside. Bjorn thundered through the door and roared.

"Show me these fetching beauties without all that cloth hiding them!"

While the crew had all been armed, Bjorn had left his ax at the palace. It was too unwieldy to carry, and in truth, Bjorn did not need a weapon to be intimidating. His massive bulk darkened the entrance as he plowed deeper into the room.

Once they had been taken to the main chamber, they were met not by the clerk but by an Arab naked to the waist but for a brown vest too small for his muscular frame. His eyes were narrow and cheekbones high. A red scar showed at his throat. Behind him, four women in dark blue robes covered their mouths and laughed. They wore the clothes of common women that hung loose about their bodies and covered their heads. They were nothing like the beauties that clung to Prince Kalim's feet. Of course, the prince would keep the best women for his own.

"Hey, that's all there is?" Bjorn asked. "No drink? No one else in this whole place?"

Candles lit around the walls expelled the darkness from most of the chamber. It was large enough to accommodate hundreds. The four women and their lone keeper were minnows in the ocean of this chamber's grandeur. The floor was of polished stone that amplified the weak candlelight. Pillows were collected into a pile off the center of the room. Archways led off to darkness. The handsome clerk had vanished.

"Lord, this place is too beautiful for prostitutes," Alasdair said. He whispered, but his voice echoed around the room.

The women moved toward the gathered pillows of red and blue. One sat on her side and beckoned to Yngvar's crew.

"But those are whores without doubt," Yngvar said. "What does a brothel look like here? Sicily is a strange enough land that we cannot say what anything should be like."

Bjorn was the most enthusiastic. He charged forward to the women, who spread out to allow him a place to sit. He threw down on the cushions, a bear among fawns, and laughed.

"I'll have all four if none of you will join!"

His laughter boomed around the hall and relieved any hesitation from the others. They surged forward and the women squealed with delight. Even if there was no room on the cushions, they sat on the shining stone floor. Thorfast hovered at their edge, seemingly unsure of what to do. Only Alasdair remained uncommitted.

"Lord Yngvar," Jamil said, blinking as if he had sand in his eyes. "Will you not join them as well?"

"Did we not just discuss this? I will stay above the activities, in case any of my men step too far."

"Of course," Jamil wiped his brow once more and began searching the darkness. Alasdair stared up at the old Moor with a frown.

"It's not so hot that sweat should pour from his face," Alasdair said. The Moor did not understand Norse, so made no answer.

"He's nervous," Yngvar said. "Maybe he is embarrassed to witness this. Aren't all you Christian people afraid of a good lay?"

"I am not," Alasdair said. "Careless acts of random sex outside of marriage offends God's command. And Jamil is not a Christian."

Yngvar ignored the sharp edge of insult in Alasdair's voice. Instead, his eyes were drawn to the women disrobing for the entertainment of his crew. While they could have lifted their dresses off, they instead indulged the men in their fantasies by inviting them to tear it from their bodies. Bjorn had no hesitation in this, ripping one woman's dress open to reveal the light flesh of her breasts.

"Lord, where does that Arab go?"

Alasdair pulled Yngvar away from the spectacle of women rubbing their exposed bodies over his crewmen. The Arab man hurried for one of the dark archways.

He whirled on Jamil, who looked away into the darkness.

"Where does he go?"

145

"Perhaps to fetch wine," Jamil said.

Yngvar peered after the Arab, who vanished into the dark archway. The shouting of his crew and the titillated screams of the women echoed around the chamber.

"I'm going to see what he's about," Yngvar said.

"I will go with you, Lord."

Leaving the candlelight swept them into heavy gloom. Thin yellow light sketched faint edges on objects and walls that lay beyond sight. Truly there was not another person in this brothel. The cloying scent of flowery smoke wafted through the darkness. The laughter and squealing from the main chamber trailed behind them.

Alasdair gasped and stopped short of bumping into something.

"What is it?" Yngvar asked, his voice dropping. He reached for his sword.

Alasdair stood before a wide pillar that rose up to his chest. A ceramic bowl of water rippled with the points of candlelight still reaching into this room.

He began shaking his head. "Lord, I am no Muslim, but if I'm not mistaken, this must be holy water. This is no brothel. It is a Muslim temple."

Yngvar hands went cold. "We've been deceived."

16

Yngvar stared at the points of candlelight dancing on the rippling water in the bowl before Alasdair. Faint light drew the edges of his horrified stare in the heavy gloom. He kept shaking his head, hands held back as if to deny he had ever bumped the column that held the bowl.

Bjorn's hoots of delight echoed from the chamber behind him. It galvanized Yngvar. He snatched Alasdair from before the water bowl.

"Forget the Arab. We have to get the men out of here."

They both dashed back across the floor, their boots clapping to the polished stone. They slid into the candlelight.

The four whores were disrobed, their dark blue clothing torn and scattered. Yngvar could see bare legs and feet protruding from the press of men surrounding them. Some had pulled down their pants and their white buttocks were glaring in the dark.

"They defile the temple or whatever Muslim's call this place," Yngvar said.

Though Alasdair was not a Muslim, through some confused history Yngvar had no patience to learn, he shared a common god with them. Seeing the whores being ravished inside what must be the main hall of this temple caused Alasdair to turn aside and make the sign of the cross.

"It's a trap!"

Yngvar's voice boomed out as if he were shouting across a battle-field. To his dismay, only Thorfast stood up from the press of men. At least he was still clothed. His pale hair glowed in the low light.

"Where's Jamil?" Alasdair asked.

The old Moor had vanished along with Arab. Before Yngvar could curse, however, from the darkened front the slam of doors opening into the stone walls echoed. He turned to face the darkness, and saw a warm globe of light spill beyond the archway.

Arab voices shouted.

"Get the men!" Yngvar ran to his crew and began to pull them back. "Flee! We are trapped!"

The crew were sodden with lust and drink, and while they staggered away, many ran back to the throng.

"Thorfast, get out of here!"

Arab guardsmen poured into the chamber. They wore chain shirts and heavy belts that cinched off billowing pants. The points of their spears and the iron of their small round shields gleamed with the light.

The whore, who had just been moaning with pleasure, now began to scream and cry out. The crew remained unaware of the threat, except for those that Yngvar had pulled free.

A half-dozen Arabs flowed into the room, spears lowered, but stopped in shock. Their shouting turned to hisses and their spears dipped.

Yngvar shoved Alasdair toward the rear door. "Flee to the ship!"

But from the rear, more guards flowed in. The same armored men charged from the darkness to also pull up in horror.

A sharp wail from the women, splitting the lusty laughter of the men pressing over them, launched the guards forward.

"Don't fight!" Yngvar shouted.

A guard stuck his spear into Yngvar's gut, but held it back from a full thrust. His black eyes burned with hatred hotter than the furnaces of Muspelheim. He roared at Yngvar and prodded him against the wall with the blade of his spear. Yngvar raised both hands and obeyed.

Alasdair dutifully surrendered and joined Yngvar against the wall with his hands raised. Their captor shouted at them and gestured they should drop their weapons.

"Follow his command," Yngvar said. "We are caught and bloodshed will only worsen our crimes."

Yngvar's magnificent sword, carried from distant Ireland, clattered to the stone floor. Alasdair's short sword thumped atop it.

The Arabs had recovered from their shock and now reset their spears against the crew. More guards continued to flow into the room, each new arrival pausing in shock at the scene in the center of the chamber.

They used their spear-butts to break up the clot of bodies like chipping ice from the hull of a ship. Those on the outside fell aside, still not understanding what happened.

When the Arabs broke to the center, Bjorn's naked backside showed. It took only one enraged Arab to prick his exposed back to draw Bjorn's rage.

He stood and found himself surrounded by enemies.

"Stand down, Bjorn!"

Yngvar might as well have called him to battle. Bjorn glared at the spear leveled at him and frowned in disgust.

His size often led opponents to believe he was slow and ungainly, capable only of battering a path straight head. Yet Bjorn was bred to battle, and once enraged he moved with speed and flexibility more like a lynx than the bear he appeared to be.

He snatched the spear away and slammed the Arab across the head with its haft. More than knocking the Arab flat, it shattered the wood and likely killed the hapless guard. He whirled on the next man, slamming his elbow into the Arab's face and shattering his cheek.

The women shrieked and scrambled away, their naked bodies shining with sweat. Some men were so drunk they crawled after them despite the chaos erupting over their heads.

Yet those who saw Bjorn fighting drew their weapons. What better entertainment for a drunken Norseman than glorious battle?

Swords rang from sheaths. Yet peace straps did their work, and a dozen men struggled against their hilts too drunk to remember these were set. The Arabs seized their confusion to knock the Norsemen flat and disarm them.

A flood of Arabs in chain shirts trudged into the room. Yngvar kept his hands raised, even when his guard looked to the new arrivals. Whatever trap had been set, had been set well. The entire city guard was alerted. Thirty Norsemen were no trifle, and these Arabs had been warned of it.

Bjorn was drunk and aroused and not in his best form. Yet he now held the broken spear and a shield from another guard. Three men lay on the floor around him, two holding their faces. The rest of his crew fumbled and tripped with their weapons. The large space allowed the Arabs to separate them from their companions, leaving each Norseman surrounded.

"End this, Bjorn!" Yngvar shouted. But his cousin could not hear him.

"They will kill him, lord," Alasdair said.

Bjorn rammed the broken spear through a guard's neck. He collapsed with a gurgled scream that was echoed by every Arab in the chamber. It was as if all had been struck. The guard crashed to his knees and pulled the shaft from his neck. A gout of blood flooded the floor.

That proved Bjorn's undoing.

He roared a battle cry, naked and painted with gore, and leapt for another Arab only to skid on the fallen guard's blood. He crashed back and four men leapt atop him. These were brawny guards in heavy mail. Even Bjorn's tremendous strength did not prevail, and soon the struggle ceased.

Seeing Bjorn overwhelmed, the more sensible of his men also surrendered.

Yngvar smelled the sour smoke of the burning torches before he realized a number of guards had carried these into the hall. There had to be at least thirty of them in armor, all dark faced and scowling. Some had tears streaking their cheeks.

"We're in trouble," Yngvar said. "Perhaps we should have fought."

"There is no way out of this," Alasdair said. "The prince set the trap well."

Despite the general surrender, both Norsemen and Arabs continued to shout and scuffle. The Arabs were reluctant for more violence in their sacred place, and so subdued Yngvar's crew by force of numbers.

Thorfast was eventually shoved against the wall beside Yngvar, his guard barking something at him then pointing at his face before turning back to the fray.

"I'd hoped you got away," Yngvar said, watching the churning confusion as swords were gathered and thrown aside from nude, red-faced crewmen.

"I had to turn back from the door when the others arrived," Thorfast said. "Alasdair, now would be a fine time to walk through walls as you so often do."

"I wish it were so," Alasdair said. "But we are herrings pickled in a cask."

Both Thorfast and Yngvar nodded at the assessment.

At last, Bjorn emerged with his face swollen and bloody. Yet the guards had not killed him. Yngvar realized Bjorn had allowed his capture. Perhaps he had heard Yngvar's pleas. The Arabs seemed to realize this too. For unlike the others who had surrendered and were shoved summarily aside, three guards kept their spears pressed into Bjorn's flesh.

"I hope they throw him a cloak," Thorfast said. "I don't want his hairy ass to be the last thing I see before the Arabs cut off my head."

The thought of execution chilled Yngvar's guts. What other fate could await them?

"We should have fought," Yngvar said, lowering his head. "We will not gain entrance to Valhalla like this. I have shamed us."

"After all I've done in this life," Thorfast said. "I will beat down the doors of Valhalla with a Valkyrie's head if I must. I will not go onto Freya's hall."

Yngvar laughed. It was cold and out of place, and every Arab within hearing snarled at him. His guard pushed the spear blade back into his gut and spit out a warning. He sucked in his stomach to relieve the pressure of the edge cutting through his shirt.

More guards arrived and lamps were lit. At last Yngvar's guard shoved him toward the front exit. An army of Arabs had assembled, all waiting outside with torches aloft and judging eyes cast in shadow. Their hatred was unmistakable. With a shove from behind, Yngvar crashed among them. The Arabs recoiled as if he were filth flung at their faces.

The civilians of Licata had been aroused as well. Yngvar heard their inquisitive chatter beyond the circle of stern guardsmen. These carried curving swords and long knives, which they held at the ready. One anxious guard's brown hand was turning white at the knuckles. He just needed a reason to cut into Yngvar and his men.

Some guards bought iron chains and manacles through the crowd. Yngvar blinked at these bonds. The seriousness of his situation was summed up in those irons. Once they were clasped to his wrists, his doom was secured.

"Wait, we were deceived," he started to explain. "A small man, a clerk, he took us here. He said Prince Kalim—"

A spear butt slammed into his back and again he collapsed to his knees. Warm, rough hands wrangled him up. A blur of dark, angry faces swirled about him. Foreign curses hailed down. Beyond this, angry fists reached into the air and commoners called for bloodshed.

"We were deceived," he said again, aware of his cracking voice.

One guard gripped his arms and another held out the manacles. Yngvar pulled back, but a sharp point on his kidney warned he might meet an accidental death if he struggled. The iron cuffs slammed cold and abrasive over his wrists.

He was pushed ahead. He turned behind, but the Arab there shoved him by his head. The rest of his crew shouted and struggled, but they would meet the same fate. They were lost in a sea of enemies. A stone sailed out of the darkness and struck his shoulder. The pain was numb and dull. Guards shouted at the civilians and shoved them aside.

Yngvar led the column of prisoners. The streets were no longer dark but lit with torches and lamps carried by spectators come to witness the capture of the wild Norsemen, who only hours ago were lauded as heroes.

A staggering march to the palace ended in the familiar tunnels where he had first met that weasel Saleet. The memory sparked the connection in Yngvar's mind. Was this some plan between Saleet and Jamil? Could they have plotted all this in their brief exchanges? He thought of their whispered exchange in this same tunnel while their captain guide waited on the other side. Had a bargain been struck then? Jamil's freedom for his aid in Yngvar's downfall?

It seemed too trivial a thing for such a staggering outcome. No, this was the prince's ploy to recover his gold. It had to be.

Emerging from the opposite end of the tunnel, he met the same captain he had just been recalling. But this time he had no smile, but a disgusted snarl. When Yngvar met his eyes, the captain spit into Yngvar's face. The warm spittle trickled down the side of his nose as he was shoved into the grandeur of the palace again.

This time in irons and chain.

Rather than be led into the flowery scents of the prince's chambers, they instead turned down a side corridor that led toward one of the palace towers. Oil lamps set at intervals down the walls shed a flickering light. Yngvar had the strange thought of a palace slave running through these halls lighting and extinguishing lamps and refilling oil. His odd rumination ended with the hallway, when his guards opened the heavy door into the brighter light beyond.

In this circular room, more guards waited. They confiscated his short sword and daggers, the silver amulet of Thor's hammer at his neck, and anything else but his clothes. Even his boots were taken.

He was then forced through another door to winding stone stairs that descended into darkness. A fat guard with a pug nose showed the way with a torch held overhead. All pretense of beauty was gone here. Nothing but cold stone walls surrounded him. The reek of waste and fouler scents reached out of the darkness fleeing before him. Behind, his crew argued with their guards.

The pug-nosed Arab stepped into a short corridor, but stopped beside a heavy door with a small, square window filled with bars.

Yngvar raised his hands, hoping the manacles would be removed.

153

Pug-nose laughed and pulled him forward into the room. He staggered into darkness that smelled of shit and rot. Something wet and cold squished beneath his feet. In the pool of light slipping inside, he glimpsed the glistening stones of the floor.

Alasdair and Thorfast followed him inside. A half-dozen more of his crew were tossed inside. He was soon pressed against the back wall, the coldness of the room fading with the heat of the bodies crammed into the space. The heavy door boomed shut onto darkness. It rattled and something metal clicked beyond. A wood shutter was drawn over the small rectangular opening and darkness fell complete.

The commotion of the rest of his men being shoved into their own rooms was faint outside the door. It was heavy enough to bar most sound. Within, no one spoke a word. Yngvar, his back pressed to the rough stone, slid to the floor. A wet coldness spread beneath him. He did not know what manner of filth he squatted on. It did not matter now.

Once they had all been imprisoned, the weight of their drunkenness pulled them into slumber. Even Yngvar nodded off.

He awoke some time later, unsure of the time passed or the hour of the day. Others stirred with him, but no one spoke. Even Thorfast, as talkative as he was, remained in silence. The darkness was so complete Yngvar could not see his hand before his nose.

As hours passed, or what he thought were hours, he felt hunger and thirst overtake him. Some of his men had urinated, and the stench was intense. One man growled at another for staining him. But their shoving ended in sullen silence. Only the rattling of their chains made any sound and only when they moved.

Bjorn was screaming somewhere beyond help. Yngvar worried that his cousin was being tormented for his violence of the night before. With Bjorn one could not tell his roars of pain from the roars of anger. He prayed to the gods for mercy on his cousin.

At last the door rattled and swung open. The orange torchlight was like a blinding sun. Yngvar cringed and turned aside, folding his arm over his eyes.

The guards shouted and spears poked through the door to

threaten them. Yngvar stood and faced them. His men lay on the ground, like dead fish washed ashore in a storm. Alasdair was at his side, and struggled to regain his footing. Thorfast was already standing in a corner.

He thought of strangling the guards with his chains, then seizing their weapons to make a last stand. But he had not yet been judged. Perhaps he could make his plea to the prince and he would know they had been deceived. If he fought now, then he would certainly doom all of them.

They were all led back the way they had come. The chains on Yngvar's wrists chaffed his skin, and he discovered a thousand itches on his body that his hands could no longer reach. But he trudged along, his bare feet slapping the cold and smooth floor as his guards led him and the others like dogs.

Thorfast began to speak from behind, but it was cut off by a heavy whack. He cursed but held his tongue. Yngvar did not dare turn about. He did not fear being struck himself. He feared worsening their plight with misbehavior. If their situation was due to the plots of Jamil and that rat, Saleet, then he might have a chance to plead for mercy. He would not risk anything until he knew more.

Once assembled in the prince's chamber, Yngvar dared a review of his crew. Like him, they were stripped to their clothes. A mere night in the dungeon had reduced their proud glory to shame. Some had stained themselves with urine, others with vomit. Their hair was disheveled, beards tangled, and faces reddened. Some bore the swelling cheeks or split lips of the beating they had taken in resisting capture.

Bjorn stood tall above them all, yet at the rear. He could not study his cousin overlong. He stared ahead with his single eye, head tipped back in defiance. He had no wounds, which relieved Yngvar. A plain gray robe covered in ancient stains had been thrown over his naked body.

Yngvar enjoyed breathing the fresh air and flowery scents. The impassive guard lining the back walls had drawn their swords and the dozen of them were ready to attack. The guards that had escorted them to the prince now lined both walls with spears and shields in hands.

Despite everything, he felt a strange pride at the heavy guard. These Arabs recognized that even in chains Norsemen were to be feared.

They stood in silence, each man holding himself straight with as much dignity as his chains and condition allowed. Their drunken minds had cleared in the stinking darkness of their prisons. As Yngvar knew, so did every other man know that their only shield now was pride. No matter how their accusers might belittle them, they would not be diminished in spirit.

At last Prince Kamil arrived. He swept into the room from a rear door with a dozen attendants and a dozen guards surrounding him. Clerks in gray robes and white head covers hovered around him.

His boyish cast was gone now. The prince seemed to have darkened to near black upon seating himself on his throne. His guards stood behind him, staring ahead with spears set to the floor.

The interpreter stood to the prince's left, looking at Yngvar with hooded eyes.

Prince Kamil sighed and shook his head. A mirthless smile stretched across his thin lips.

For a heartbeat Yngvar thought he would laugh off their crimes as the unfortunate bumbling of ill-bred foreigners.

Then Prince Kamil burst into his tirade.

He flew off his chair, screaming and wheeling his arms. He shouted at Yngvar. Shouted at the crew. Shouted at the columns of his spacious chamber. His voice broke as he emphasized his words by pounding his fist into his palm. He kicked his chair. He shrieked at the ceiling. He gnashed his teeth, pounded his chest.

He jumped down from his dais and stood on Yngvar's toes. He was like a boy in expensive clothing. But he glared up with black eyes full of a grown man's wrath.

The slap cracked across Yngvar's face. The pain sparkled sharp through his cheek. The prince hissed and drew his hand back, holding it as if he had burned himself.

He did not need Jamil to translate. Nothing Prince Kalim shouted would be worth hearing. The court interpreter had remained stationary throughout the raving. When Prince Kalim flopped back into his chair in exhaustion, he waved a hand for the translation.

"The prince is greatly displeased."

Yngvar choked back a laugh. Was he now?

The interpreter paused and raised his brow but continued to look out across the gathering.

"He will decorate the walls of his palace with your heads."

17

Yngvar blinked.

Nothing changed.

He blinked again.

Still the dark-faced prince seethed on his throne, heaving as if he had carried an anvil up a mountain. His imperious Frankish interpreter looked down his long nose at Yngvar. His words still echoed through the chamber.

This could not be right, Yngvar thought. He had just been handed a death sentence without a fair hearing. He shook his head this time and blinked harder.

Behind him, Thorfast cleared his throat and dared a whisper.

"Do I translate that for the others?"

Yngvar shook his head, then squared his shoulders and met the prince's scowl.

"What manner of trial is this? Do we not get an equal say? You call for our heads and will not hear the truth? In my land, a jarl hears both sides and weighs the stories of witnesses. I've got thirty men here who can tell you we were made drunk and then deceived into believing your holy place was—something else."

The interpreter stared at Yngvar as if he could taste the bitterness of the words. But when he did not translate, Prince Kalim clapped his hands. Their curt exchange could not have been a translation of all Yngvar had said. It drew a derisive snort from the prince. He waved his hand at the clerks and guards assembled. He prattled on, often raising eyes to the sky. Yngvar was learning the word Allah, which seemed to be the Arab word for heaven. The prince looked up every time he said it.

After a silence, the interpreter summarized the long speech.

"Prince Kalim has all the witnesses he needs to judge the crime. You were found in the mosque where you defiled it with filth and sin offensive to God. The four women you raped have condemned you for your crimes. They have sworn before the prince and God Himself that you forced them into the mosque to have you way with them—so drunk were all of you. Death is the only reward for such acts."

"Raped?" Yngvar's shout echoed off the ceiling. The guards behind the prince leaned forward. "We were told the prince wanted to entertain us with whores but not within his palace walls. One of your damned clerks led us to those women. You tell your little boy prince that, and don't leave out any of my words. I demand our story be heard."

The interpreter smirked. He spoke to the prince at length. Kalim leaned on his knees and listened. He nodded, smiled without mirth, rubbed his face twice, flopped back and forth on his chair like a child bored with his tutor, and finally shot to his feet when the interpreter had finished.

Yngvar swallowed hard.

Prince Kalim began ranting again. He pulled out all the clerks from his entourage, all slight men who stared in pale-faced horror at the sudden attention directed to them.

"The prince wishes you to identify which one came to you last night. These are all who were present."

"None of them," Yngvar said, after staring at each one. "But the guards at the walls saw us, didn't they? They'll know who led us."

"The guards have been questioned," the interpreter said. "They were found relieved of their weapons, tied and gagged at the walls. Seems you were all in a mood to see the city, despite the prince's express wishes you should be not be allowed to roam free while drunk."

Yngvar's mouth fell open.

"Your prince is a fucking liar," Bjorn shouted from the rear. "I'll tear out his black tongue."

As Yngvar turned behind, he saw his men wide-eyed and pale. The crew, who did not understand the Frankish being spoken, understood the outrage in both the prince's ravings and Bjorn's outburst enough to be frightened. Rendered helpless in chains, each must know an ignoble death awaited them unless Yngvar could persuade the prince.

"We should have fought, cousin!" Bjorn shouted over the heads. He spoke in Norse, so that his fellows could understand. "We'll have no justice here. Strike now before we are carried off to the headsman."

The crew murmured. Some stirred, looking at the short chains holding their hands to their laps. Balled fists against shields, spears, and mail coats would avail nothing. They would still die weaponless.

But they would die fighting.

The Norse outburst brought the guards from the walls. They herded Bjorn, three spears against him in chain, out the rear doors. Yngvar closed his eyes, expecting his cousin to fight and thereby die.

Yet he vanished beyond the door, which closed over his fate and left Yngvar and the others staring after him. The prince spit out more invective. His interpreter let a small smile curl his lip.

"The prince has indulged your lies beyond his patience. You will be executed three days hence."

The prince stood, raking the Norsemen with his haughty glare.

Yngvar threw himself on his knees. "Spare my crew. I am responsible for them. Kill me but let them live."

"All have committed the crime," the interpreter said. "All must suffer the sentence."

The prince had not even spoken. Yngvar raised his head to see young Prince Kalim assembling his guards and entourage. He acted as if Yngvar's pleas still did not echo across the spacious chamber.

He thought to leap at the little traitor and strangle him with these chains. In fact, the muscles in his legs flexed and he anticipated looping his chain over the prince's head.

Then a shape rushed out of the hidden corners of the chamber. He was a reedy man in the gray robes and white head cover of the prince's staff. His bare feet swished across the polished stone as he skidded before the dais and prostrated himself before Prince Kalim.

Yngvar could only see the clerk's prostrate back as he spoke in a rushed burst. The prince had stopped, half turned away. As the clerk rattled on, the prince's brows raised. As the clerk spoke, Prince Kalim faced him fully. He asked a question of his own. The prostrate clerk nodded and touched his head to the stone floor.

Prince Kalim gave a satisfied smile and clapped his hands together. He then spoke to his interpreter.

"The prince has revised his sentence," the interpreter said. His face crinkled with disgust, clearly dissatisfied with this change. "Rather than beheading you, he will let God choose the worthy among your number. Three days hence, you will all be lashed one hundred times. Those who die under the whip are forgiven in God's eyes. Those who live are damned and will be sold as slaves."

Yngvar gasped. "What mercy is this?"

The interpreter smiled. "It is God's mercy. Pray that he chooses to forgive you. As a slave, you will soon wish for death. You have my word upon it."

Prince Kalim nodded and whirled away with his guards, servants, and the interpreter. The spearmen that had escorted them from the dungeon now converged on them again.

The prostrate clerk remained with his head down until Prince Kalim left by the rear door. Spearmen interposed themselves between the clerk and Yngvar. When the reedy man stood, he turned to offer his wicked smile.

"Saleet!" Yngvar lurched forward, but a spear point jabbed his ribs. He shoved past it, letting it score his flesh and draw hot blood.

The guards shouted in answer. Yngvar's men, who still had not learned their fate, responded with their own shouts. But Yngvar focused only on the reedy clerk, seeing him through a halo of red.

The smug expression on Saleet's face fell and he backed up to trip over the dais.

Yngvar roared as he leapt upon the prone clerk. Pulling his chains taut, he pressed them across Saleet's thin neck. His hands pinned each side so that the frail Arab began to choke and gag.

Then Yngvar went blind.

In the moment of confusion, he slackened the make-shift garrote across Saleet's neck. Something soft covered his face. As hands grabbed him back, sprawling him on the hard floor, he realized a sack had been thrown over his head.

He kicked out, but spear butts battered him on every side. One struck the side of his temple, dazing him.

The fight drained from him. He lay still, panting, feeling a half-dozen cold iron points set across his torso. What would death achieve now? If he lived, he might yet find a way to save his men.

The shouting and struggle of the crew filled the chamber. Arabs shouted them down, and he heard men crying out in pain and rage. Thorfast shouted for them to be still. No one appeared to hear him.

Yngvar's feet were bound, and two men carried him out of the chamber before the chaos had died. He hung like a trophy boar on a spear. The blood from the cut on his ribs pooled on his stomach and slid around his back. His Arab handlers cursed and muttered as they jostled him into a better grip. He could see nothing, but flowery scents gave way to the pungent fumes of waste and rot. His body dipped as they hauled him down the winding steps until he was again hurled into a room. He landed on his side on rough stone, the cut on his rib burning as it tore wider.

They unbound his feet, then ripped the cover from his head. Fetid air cooled his sweaty face. He was again in darkness. By the time he got his bearing, he had only a moment to see a rectangular gray light flash before the heavy wood door slammed shut.

There was heat from another person with him. He lay still, then groaned.

"We should've fought," Bjorn said. His voice was a low rumble. "It's never wrong to fight."

"I don't know about that," Yngvar said, curling upright. He held his hand over his cut to stop the leak of blood. "I had hoped for some mercy."

"No mercy from these Arab bastards. Traitorous lot."

"The prince will have us each lashed a hundred times. If we die, then his god forgives us. If we live, we will be sold as slaves. Seems we are worth more to him as slaves than wall decorations."

"Fuck him."

The simple response struck Yngvar as funny. He began to laugh. It hurt the cut on his ribs, but he could not stop. Soon he was leaning back in laugher, heedless of the bleeding.

"Ain't nothing funny about this."

"No," Yngvar agreed. "But the gods are laughing, are they not? They spared us for their entertainment. It will be grand sport for them. Why not enjoy the jest as well?"

"You've gone mad, cousin."

"Gyna is out there," Yngvar said. "And she might yet own a good portion of our gold. We have three days before we are lashed. Perhaps she might devise a way out for us."

"The prince arranged this trap to steal back the gold he gave us."

"No," Yngvar said. "There is no sense in that. If he had no wish to pay us, he could have done so far more simply. Nor would he defile his holy place. No, this was the work of Saleet and Jamil."

"Who is Saleet?"

"You remember the little bastard I knocked over when we first arrived? He accused me of trying to kill him. He was ignored and it must have riled him. He contrived this plan to ensure our downfall and enlisted Jamil to help. We obliged them, being too ignorant of the customs of this place to smell shit from daisies."

Bjorn grunted. "The list of people I must kill grows every day."

"I'll agree to that." Yngvar felt the cut on his side. The blood had begun to clot. "What do you think Gyna will do? They have not caught her, else she would be with us."

"She's crazy, ain't she? No normal woman fights in the shield wall like she does. Wearing pants and all. If she's got our gold, she'll probably just buy passage back to her people. The Old Saxons'll accept her, especially if she brings them gold. No, Gyna ain't rescuing us."

Yngvar agreed but said nothing. Even if she could return, women had no standing among the Arabs. Besides, who was to say she had not been captured and added to the prince's collection of female slaves. Yngvar would have to count on his own wits to escape this situation. The iron manacles scraping his wrists reminded him how firmly he had been caught. Even if he could slip away, where would he run? He knew nothing of the land or language. Everywhere would be enemies. His ship was their only hope, and by now he imagined the prince had confiscated that as well.

As he ruminated on his options, he heard the rest of his crew and their captors shouting and struggling beyond the door. Rough voices barked orders and Norsemen offered curses in exchange. But slowly those Norse voices were smothered and lost behind the slamming of iron-bound wooden doors.

The door to his own cell opened again. More bodies were shoved inside. In the brief moment of thin torchlight, Thorfast's white hair shined clear. He could not tell who else had been crammed into the cell, but he guessed four more. The heavy door slammed hard in the frame, blowing the foul air across Yngvar's face.

"Who else is in here?" Thorfast asked into the darkness.

"Bjorn and I are here," Yngvar said.

"Lord, God has set us all together again." Alasdair's voice was filled with hope. "Truly it is a miracle."

"Miracle?" The ragged, angry voice of Leiknr Bone-Feet filled the room. "This is what your White Christ offers as a miracle? We're stuffed into this cesspit to await our executions. Some fucking miracle."

"I don't want to hear your moaning." The other voice was Grith Audunsson, a crewman who had been with Yngvar since Ireland. "If it's our time to die, then we die. If it is not, then Fate will weave what strands they will."

"I agree," Yngvar said. "We must wait to see what opportunities the gods offer us. They test our wits and resolve. But until my last breath, I will seek the path out of this trap."

They were packed tightly enough that he felt the roughness of Bjorn's hairy arms against his own and Alasdair's smooth skin against his leg. Their heavy chains chimed and scraped against stone as they shifted to find a patch of the cell to claim as their own.

"We'll be pissing and shitting on each other soon enough," Leiknr said. "How long is three days?"

Thorfast laughed and Leiknr growled. "I mean, do you think we won't kill each other before the three days are passed?"

"I'll kill you now if you don't shut up," Bjorn said. "That'll make some room for the rest of us."

Leiknr fell silent.

They sat in silence. Soon the complete blackness made Yngvar wonder if anyone was still alive. Yet the clink of chain or the occasional snort of breath reminded him. Bjorn had begun to snore, drawing a moan from Leiknr.

Time became meaningless. Yngvar counted the hours by the way his wound healed. Once it had formed a scab, that marked half a day. By the time the flesh began to stitch together again would be the day of their lashing. Yet in the end, he could count the days by the arrival of food.

The Arabs shoved two buckets into the room, one of water and one of brownish slop. With chained hands, they struggled to eat and drink. Leiknr was always first to the bucket, but someone would pull him off. Unlike Leiknr's gloomy predictions, they did not try to kill each other. Certainly the cell stunk of waste and sweat and this could not help but stain a man's rags. But amongst themselves they acted with kindness.

This was not so for other cells. Even behind the doors he could hear the muffled raging of fights. Men could not endure such deprivations without conflict. They were not a brotherhood like Yngvar and his Wolves. Their caring for one another spread to both Grith and Leiknr, even if they were surly among themselves. But in other cells, men tore at each other by the end of the second day. Their Arab jailers alternately shouted them to silence or laughed at their brawls.

After three meals, Yngvar had counted three days. They had been using the food buckets to empty their bowels. He wondered how well these were cleaned before being reused. No one had grown sick after three meals. So when he heard the rattling at the door, he expected an end to the food buckets. The guards would drag them out of their cell to the courtyard for their lashing. Instead they shoved food buckets inside, retrieved the old buckets, then slammed the door.

They had not closed the small barred window, allowing gray light to fall across Yngvar's leg in a bright rectangle. He had dried blood on his shin barely distinguishable from the filth clinging to his leg.

He scrabbled up to the window and banged on the door. The hallway was filled with murky light flickering from the end of the hall. Otherwise, he could only see the door across the hall, which also had its barred window opened.

"Has it not been three days?"

When his calls in Frankish drew no response, he tried again in Norse. The Arabs either did not hear or did not care. Yet across the short hall a set of wide, blood-shot eyes appeared in the window.

"You led us to this!" the crewman shouted. Yngvar could not recognize the voice, and eyes alone were not enough to determine who spoke. "You broke your oath. The gods hate an oath-breaker!"

"It's true!" Another voice, muffled through the door, came from farther down the hall. "We should not have broken faith with a king."

"Kings are closer to the gods then we," said the man across the hall. "To deceive one is to deceive the gods."

Yngvar stepped back, his face burning. More voices added to those shouting in the hall. Dozens of muffled protests echoed beyond the door. At last he welcomed the darkness for covering his humiliation. No one else in the cell spoke, but he sensed their eyes on him. The heat of their bodies brushed his skin. The rattle of their chains as they shifted rang in his ears. The silent accusation was louder than if they had shouted into his ears.

"It is true what they say," Yngvar said to the darkness. "Even my sacrifice of gold was insincere. The best part of my treasure was my sword, and I withheld it. The gods know this, and so gave it to the Arabs as punishment for my arrogance."

"That is not true, lord." Alasdair said. His voice was dry and weak, but as always close to Yngvar's side.

"That is empty comfort," he said. "You cannot know what was in my heart. I did not believe I did wrong. I was too arrogant to obey my king's wishes. I was too greedy to give the gods the best part of my treasures. I brought us shame and so earned the gods' ire. You suffer because I was a fool."

The shouting echoed behind him. His crew began to kick the doors and cry for blood. Their voices were rough and indistinct, but their hatred flowed together into a spear that could pierce the walls and lodge in Yngvar's heart.

"I will kill you myself if ever we are set free!" The voice from across the hall was the only point of clarity in the angry shouting.

Yngvar bowed his head, expecting more from Leiknr and Grith. Yet neither man stuck their word-daggers into his heart. Their clinking chains were their answer. They were rotting in a prison beneath their anticipated palace of marble filled with gold. The wealth and glory they sought were buried in their filth. Now open sky and clean air would be worth more than a mountain of treasure.

The noise drew the Arabs back at last. They shouted and banged on doors. Their threats went unheeded. The window across Yngvar's cell clacked shut. But he heard Arab mumbling beyond as the crewmen continued to protest. He heard a door in the hallway creak, a splash of liquid, then men scream.

Yngvar pressed his eyes shut and covered his ears. The unlucky cellmates howled in agony and the Arabs shouted more threats into the hall. A door slammed and further protest ended. All that remained was the sobbing and screaming of the victims.

"Boiling water, probably," Thorfast said from his corner. "Their wounds will rot in this filth, and they will surely die."

"No more," Yngvar said. "I cannot bear more."

The lashing never arrived. Yngvar counted seven more buckets. Grith no longer moved after the fifth day. His flesh had grown cold as stone. Yngvar set his corpse against the door so the guards would carry him out. By the seventh day, Leiknr coughed out blood and died with a curse.

"Rot in Niflheim, Yngvar Hakonsson."

These deaths meant the rest ate more. The Arabs did not adjust the slop or water according to the count of cellmates. Bjorn had also caught a rat biting his leg and ate it raw. Yngvar's guts churned and boiled. He was weak and tired, and now any light hurt his eyes. With more space, he was able to lie flat. But still his flesh ached from sitting on cold, hard stone.

Two more buckets were exchanged before the doors opened to a different scene.

The torchlight dazzled like lightning. Yngvar threw both his hands across his face. The blood-red light shined into his eyes nonetheless. The Arabs shouted and swept into the room.

Yngvar opened his eyes to a spear prodding his leg.

The pug-nosed guard who seemed to run this prison stood with folded arms. He spoke in his strange language and gestured Yngvar should stand. More guards waited in the hall beyond.

He struggled to his feet. The effort of it shocked him. Once he could spring to both feet with a chain shirt pressing down on his shoulders. Now, his rags were heavier than three layers of mail.

He was in a cell with three other strangers. He blinked at these filthy, pale men with wild hair and ragged beards. They too covered their eyes and moaned as if in pain. Their hands were chained as were his, and the flesh there was red and scabbed.

Were these his Wolves? Not these frail things, surely.

A rough hand pulled him into the hall. He cursed and bumped between irritated Arab jailers. One shoved him down the hall where he tripped and fell onto the stone floor. He saw feet in cloth shoes before him. He looked up into the light of the room, but the shape was a shadow.

"What is happening?"

He asked in Norse, and to his shock, he received an answer in simple, accented Norse.

"You have been sold. Your owner must decide who lives or dies."

"What? No lashes?"

"No lashes," the shadow said. "Broken backs no good for rowing ships, yes? Up, slave. There are more of you to gather."

18

The winding stairs seemed to grab at Yngvar's bare feet. He crashed to his knees every third step, driving painful bolts into his legs. Yet he had not walked for two weeks or more. Despite a lifetime of this simple motion, in such a brief span it seemed all but forgotten to him. His guards cursed and hauled him up until he stumbled into the upper room.

Cool and fruity air greeted him and he drew in a deep breath. The Arabs rushed him through this room into the hall, but his sensitive nose caught the scent of meat and broth, beer and wine. Saliva flooded his mouth, but he kept his eyes ahead. From behind he heard Bjorn muttering protests, but otherwise everyone else followed in silence. All the sound came from the impatient curses of their Arab escorts and the clatter of the crew's manacles.

The stone was smooth and cold under Yngvar's bare feet. He crossed the hall, led by two men in chain shirts and bearing curving swords. Servants bolted out of their path, some holding their noses as they fled. Yngvar still squinted against the brightness, but the lamps here were not lit. Instead, shafts of pleasant sunlight slanted in from high, narrow windows.

At last they were led into the courtyard. The sun dazzled him, but he forced himself to look skyward. He might not see sky again for a long time to come. It was deep blue and clouds like raw wool drifted through it. Gulls circled, teasing Yngvar with their limitless freedom. He inhaled the salty scent of the sea, not far downhill from Prince Kalim's magnificent palace.

Harsh voices drew him back to earth. On the hard-packed dirt of the courtyard, scores of palace guards lined up. Yngvar smirked at this. Even starved and in chains, the Arabs would not underestimate the Norsemen. It was not much comfort, but the draught of pride that the Arabs' caution offered warmed his chest. If he could grab a sword, withered as he was, he would kill a dozen of these men alone.

Yet the manacles remained tight over his wrists. Their rust-encrusted edges had worn red sores into his wrists. His shoulders ached from not being able to lower his hands to his sides. The chain was barely wide enough to allow anything more than folding his palms over his lap.

The rest of his crew were made to rank up as if they were forming a shield wall. Yngvar was ignored and used the freedom to examine his men. About a fourth of his crew were missing, probably dead. The rest were in various stages of death. Bjorn and Thorfast seemed the healthiest. Alasdair had not fared as well. His eyes were sunken and cheeks hollow. Sores formed around the edges of his lips and his back was stooped. The rest of his crew glared at him, if they could focus at all. Some had raking scabs across their gaunt faces, particularly near the eyes. Remnants of fighting for extra slop and water, most likely. Could two weeks in darkness do this to a man? They looked like souls escaped from Niflheim.

I should accustom myself to this appearance, he thought. I will spend my death in the mist-world until Ragnarok comes.

Once all had been assembled, the Norse-speaking man addressed the group.

"You are property of Shaahir al-Salameh." The Arab was short and round, as if he had stuffed a barrel under his fine clothes to enlarge himself. He wore a sash of brilliant red across his protruding belly. His white head cover revealed a face of full cheeks that jiggled as he spoke.

"He is gladdened to purchase strong Northmen for such a

generous price." The Arab paused and scanned the group. "Though you are sick, yes? Hungry? My master must feed you to see who will live or die. So today, you eat. Tomorrow you eat. After, you live or die. Then you will row my master's ship. Maybe fight for my master. You are Northmen, yes? You like to fight?"

The Arab gave a yellow smile that was met with nothing more than hopeless stares. He waited, then clapped his hands and laughed.

"I know Norsemen," he said. "Good traders. Good fighters. Now, be good slaves. You will live. Maybe fight. Go to see God in Valhel."

"Valhalla, you stupid fucking walrus," Bjorn shouted. Even after being starved for two weeks, Bjorn's muscles still stood out from his flesh. They were diminished now, his voice weaker as well, but only a fool would consider him weak.

The Arab clapped again, laughing at the curse. "Yes, Odin and Valhalla. Yes, yes, but you would do better to seek Allah. Your Odin does not see you now."

Spearmen rounded them up and marched them toward the palace exit into the streets of Licata. Like people in every country, the common folk were always eager for the spectacle of punishment and humiliation. Crowds must have been warned the Norsemen would be released today. They gathered at the sides of the stone-covered streets. Old and young faces alike, all covered in cloths of every color, scowled at their emergence from the dark tunnel leading from the palace. Women in black dresses that revealed only their eyes wailed in their horrid language. One woman fell back into the crowd as if she had passed out at seeing Yngvar.

He snorted at the display. Fucking whores, the lot of them, he thought. They'd defile their holy places for a few coins and then come out in the daylight to pretend piety. May the Fates see their rotten crotches torn out.

Just as when they had been dragged into the palace, as they were herded out of it, the crowd flung rotten vegetables and stones. Yngvar tried to stoop to snatch a heavy, rotted cabbage that had bounced off his shoulder. The guard at his side kicked it away and shouted at him. He continued to stumble forward.

He scanned the crowd, believing Gyna would be hiding among

them with a hundred hired mercenaries. She would spring the trap, cut down the Arab guards and scatter the crowd, then lead them to his waiting ship. In days this would all become naught but a vague nightmare as his agile ship delivered him and his crew to safety.

But Gyna was not in the crowd. No savior would burst from the ranks of hateful faces. He cursed his helplessness. Never in his days would he have daydreamed of another coming to his rescue. Such dreams were fantasies of the weak and ignoble. A warrior saved himself or else died in the effort. Yet the chains remained fast about his wrists. He could avail nothing.

Yet.

Three dozen strides from the palace exit, Yngvar saw them in the rear of the crowd. Saleet's thin face grinned with hatred. Behind him, swathed in a clean, white head cover, stood Jamil. His dark-circled eyes were brighter now. He stared dispassionate and unflinching.

Yngvar wanted to curse them. His hands itched to take each of their necks in his grip and crush the life from them. Yet he trudged forward, letting the eyes of the two slide off him to gaze upon their other victims.

He marked them in his memory. Neither Saleet nor Jamil would live their full lives. When the gods had completed their punishment of his arrogance, Yngvar would return for them. They would hang by their feet as their headless bodies drained blood into a silver bowl. He and his Wolves would drink from it and burn their flesh to the glory of the gods.

That day would come. He swore it in grim silence, plodding on beneath the pelting rocks and garbage.

The crowd thinned as they approached the docks. Yngvar searched for his ship among the dozens either at dock or else navigating the bay. He saw only an enormous ship like they had encountered in the port of Algiers. Perhaps it was the same one, for how could he tell one behemoth from another? The massive ship sat at anchor in the deeper water, unable to approach the land due to its size.

Their guard led them to a long, low building like a barracks. A man in shabby clothes opened the door and stood aside. Yngvar's guards shoved him inside.

Other Arabs waited inside. These were also guardsmen, but not the prince's. These were harder men with lean faces and untrusting eyes. They wore no mail, but carried their curved swords openly. A score of them sat around the empty place. At the far end, an anvil waited with several boxes stacked beside it. One of the men took up a hammer that rested atop the anvil.

The prince's guards exchanged words with these new Arabs. Yngvar wandered into the center where two men grabbed him by his chains without a word. They led him to the anvil where the man placed his manacles atop it. He held a chisel to the bolts that kept his manacles closed and hammered it free.

The manacles clanked to the dirt floor. Yngvar lifted his hands in surprise, as if they might float to the rafters above. The dark room was lit only with the light of the open doors. But it was enough to see the Arabs smiling.

Was he being spared? Hope bloomed in his heart.

The Arab at the anvil smiled and nodded Yngvar to the side. He waited patiently while the remainder of his men got the same treatment. Their manacles were collected in wood box and the broken bolts were tossed into a barrel. Each plink of a bolt against the barrel bottom lifted Yngvar's spirits.

When all were set free, they were given water and bread. The Norse-speaking Arab addressed them.

"Eat now. But not much, or you will be sick. Tomorrow you eat more. Then we see who is fit, yes? Do not seek escape. Outside the doors, your death is assured."

The words rang in Yngvar's ears, but he did not truly hear. No water tasted as fresh and pure. No bread was ever better baked. Weeks before he might have spit it out as nothing better than flour built up with crushed straw. Today, it was a feast.

They slept that night in the spacious hall. Each man stayed as far from each other as they could. Yngvar reveled in spreading arms and legs wide. The air was sour and thick, but the note of sea salt comforted him. The sounds of sailors docking and disembarking was far better than the wailing of tormented prisoners. Every man was stunned by this small luxury, and no one dared speak lest they awaken to discover freedom was a dream.

The next day passed in tedium, but they ate four times. Each feeding they ate more bread, and by the last they were fed dried fish. Some men vomited. One man died. No one mourned him. Yngvar could not even recognize him. The Arabs carried him away without a word.

Yngvar and his Wolves huddled together away from the rest of the crew. The food had strengthened them. Yet their eyes were staring and fearful. Alasdair's back straightened but the sores on his mouth seemed to cause him pain when he ate or spoke. Neither Thorfast nor Bjorn had much to speculate on their circumstances.

"I have both hands and feet free," Thorfast said. "I never thought I would celebrate such a thing."

"I miss Gyna," Bjorn said. "I hope she's going back to her folk. Away from this cursed place forever."

Besides this, a long day of rest and eating passed. As promised, on the third day, the Norse-speaking Arab returned to determine who had lived or died. He arrived in the morning. He brought a dozen new guards with him. Their light, sun-faded clothing hung open to the sashes around their waists where curved daggers hung. Their skin was as brown as roasted hazelnut. They smelled of smoke and the sea.

"As strong as ever!" The Arab clapped his hands. "A joy that only one has gone on to Valhel, yes? Now, you shall row to meet your master. Then maybe fight? Maybe row more? The master decides."

Their guards shouted at them to stand. Yngvar did not understand the words but understood the gestures. They rose to their feet, slowly and with groans and curses. The sailors who had accompanied the Arab now filed into the hall. They drew their knives then pulled aside men one at a time.

"Relax," the Arab said. "We shave your heads and beards. Proper slaves you will be. Do not struggle or you will know deep regret."

Tension flowed from Yngvar's shoulders. Bare iron blades flashed in the dim light. It was a call to battle born from long instinct. But the men were weak and obedience came readily. One man tipped his head back to expose his throat.

"Cut my beard or cut my throat," he said. "It is no matter to me."

With such a simple surrender to Fate, the shaving proceeded peacefully. When Yngvar's turn arrived, he too offered his throat with the same sentiment.

His shorn hair fell about his feet. Cool air rushed across his scalp which ached from the scraping of the blade. His beard too was deftly whisked from his chin and neck. He endured nicks that drew blood. The sailor's hands were dry and rough, twisting his face side to side as he worked.

When all were done, their hair was collected by one of the smaller Arabs. It could be spun into rope by a skillful craftsman. Yngvar looked at Bjorn. His one eye was wide in shock.

"The bear is shorn," Thorfast said. "If they were to scrape the hair from your back, they could weave a sail from it."

"Feels unnatural," Bjorn said, running his hand along his bald head. Yngvar had never noticed how round his cousin's skull was.

"You look like another man," Yngvar said, pointing to Thorfast. "No more white hair to mark you in a crowd."

Thorfast rubbed his own crown. "My head is lumpy. I never knew."

Alasdair looked up to Yngvar. "Lord, only your eyes look the same."

"Well, a man does not look himself without hair. You had no beard to speak of, but without your copper hair you are a different man. In fact, you seem older somehow."

"No, lord, I mean your eyes are not as empty as the others. You are not defeated, are you? You believe we have hope."

The words drew looks from everyone in hearing. Bjorn and Thorfast and half a dozen of the crew snapped their eyes to his, their faces brightened. Yngvar swallowed, feeling his cheeks heat.

"As long as the gods have not killed us, then we have hope. We have been brought low. But even a man on the ground might kill his enemy as he passes overhead. Let these Arabs shave our heads and mock us. We shall see who laughs before summer arrives again."

Speaking the words forced Yngvar to believe them. He was not sure what the gods intended for them or if anyone would be alive a year hence. But they all needed to believe this, or else death was a certainty.

The Arab clapped for their attention. He smiled patiently as if explaining some adult secret to a small child.

"Norsemen are proud, yes? Chains make them weep. But you must wear chains or you might flee. Each will be chained to a brother by the foot. Do not resist. My master's punishments are harsh. You will not die, but will wish you had. Now, because I like Norsemen, pick a friend for your leg. Hurry now."

"I think he means we should partner with someone," Yngvar said. He looked at Alasdair, who stared at him with his lips pressed tight. "Alasdair and I should pair. Bjorn and Thorfast?"

"Of course," Thorfast said. "Bjorn will have the best chance of breaking the chains. I want to pair with him."

Bjorn grunted. "Who else'll have you, anyway?"

So men selected their pairs and the sailors brought new shackles with longer chains. These were clasped cold and rough around Yngvar's bare ankles. The sailors hammered bolts to clamp them shut. The entire procedure was as amicable as old friends being fitted for new boots. The fight was beaten from the crew. For Yngvar's part he looked forward to sea spray and the cries of gulls. Nothing could be worse than unending, fetid darkness.

His last glimpse of Licata and its impossibly domed buildings came atop the deck of the huge Arab ship he had seen two days ago. Dozens more slaves were taken aboard as well, and they were all assembled on the upper deck. The crew were of the same cloth as the sailors who had shaved their heads and bound their feet. They paid the horde of slaves no attention, and instead attended their duties.

"I will return to burn this place to ash," Yngvar said. "The gods grant me but a dagger, and I will make it so."

Some of his crewmen hissed at his oath. In truth, they were his crewmen no more. They were all made equal under slavery. The Norse-speaking Arab was the last aboard the ship. The rowboats that had ferried them from shore were now hauled aboard and stowed on racks. Sailors called to each other across the decks. One small man with a face like a withered apple began shouting at them and gesturing to a hatch on the deck.

A whip cracked over Yngvar's head. Painful memories of the lashes Erik Blood-Axe had given him echoed in its snap and he cringed. Some of his former crew sniggered. But when the lash cracked again, and the gigantic Arab wielding it closed on them, their smirks vanished.

They were herded below decks. They descended past one deck where rope-thin men sat at oars. Rows of benches at the very bottom of the ship were lined up to the tholes. The long oars were stowed now, sitting across the unseated benches. Yngvar, his crew, and the other slaves were shoved at the benches. Sailors came along to set their leg chains to iron loops in the floor. They hammered these closed over the chains.

"They mean for us to sit here the entire journey," Alasdair said in surprise.

"It can't be a long journey then," Yngvar said. He meant to comfort Alasdair, who nodded in agreement. Yet he had no idea what the Arabs intended.

Bjorn and Thorfast had been seated a dozen benches ahead. They looked back and confirmed Yngvar's location. The rest of his crew, at least those he could recognize now that they were hairless and starved, were interspersed with the new slaves.

At last the giant with the whip threw it down and took up a drum at the fore. He shouted at them, and the new slaves took their oars. Yngvar found his crew by watching for those who did not react to the foreign speech. They followed the other slaves, each setting their grip on a mighty oar.

The drum sounded one beat, and they fed their oar into the water. Above them, the same note echoed and more oars slipped down into the water. Two more beats and men braced to row.

Then the huge Arab began to strike his drum. A slow and steady beat that controlled the stroke of the oars. Despite the huge size of these oars and Yngvar's weakness, he felt less strain on these than he did on his own ship. They glided easily and smoothly.

The monotonous beat continued and Yngvar fell into a trance. The crowded deck and chains allowed no possibility of escape. Therefore, he would not waste the strength of his mind on it. He rowed. Push forward and lean back. Alasdair beside him did as well. Two men on each oar, perhaps thirty oars. The room—Yngvar could not call this a deck. What deck had rafters above?—soon smelled of sweat. He knew it would soon stink of worse odors as men worked past their limits vomited or loosed their bladders. He could not imagine these Arabs would allow them shifts. He had to hope for good winds for relief.

Long past the time Yngvar's shoulders burned, the Arab struck three quick beats on his drum. The new slaves, who must have been experienced from other ships, pulled in their oars.

"At last, the sails will carry this beast," Yngvar said, falling over his oar.

Sailors walked down the row with buckets of water, pausing at each bench to ladle it into cupped hands. At Yngvar's turn, he gratefully slurped the water. The Arab allowed him three handfuls before bestowing the same amount to Alasdair.

"Where do we go, lord?"

"I don't know. And do not call me lord any longer. I am a slave as you are."

Yngvar brushed his hand along the length of the smooth oar resting across his lap. Sweat had soaked through his shirt and dripped onto his legs. The naked back of the man seated to his front shined with sweat. The heat of the small room pressed on his face.

Alasdair stared at his feet.

They remained in silence as they rested. The winds carried them through the remainder of the day until sunlight fled the sea and candles were lit beneath the decks. The hard bench delivered aches to Yngvar's hips, but there was nothing more to do than slump on the oar and wait. The experienced slaves fell asleep over their oars.

Then shouts came from above. Yngvar recognized the fear in those distant, muffled voices. Calls repeated down the decks, growing clearer like the crunch of mail from of an enemy warband.

The huge Arab drummer, who had seated himself on the floor,

now leaped up to his drum. He gathered his whip and cracked it over the heads of the slaves. The Norsemen quailed but the experienced slaves merely sat straighter.

His words spilled out fearful. His fat face was taut with urgent lines.

The slaves rushed their oars back into the water as the Arab continued to blabber and crack his whip. Yngvar could not distinguish any of the words but one, and it set his hands to ice.

Byzantines.

19

Byzantines.

It was the only word from the Arab drummer's ravings Yngvar understood. He repeated it with the same rhythm that he struck his drum. Fast and relentless.

"Lord, are we being chased?"

They both pushed and pulled on their oars in unison. Yngvar's palms were already hot from rubbing the smooth wood.

"Do you hear the word, Byzantines?"

Alasdair shook his head. He and Yngvar could barely keep pace with the beating drum.

"Well, it would seem Prince Kalim is getting his war. He sent us to beat the bee's nest and so the bees come to deliver their sting."

"But we have been at sea all day." Exasperation filled Alasdair's voice. "We must be far from the Byzantines by now."

"Depends on what direction we sailed," Yngvar said between gasps. "Maybe this is a chance meeting at sea. But I doubt it."

"Why?"

Yngvar could not answer as the drummer's pace increased again. The slaves groaned at the effort. Above decks, the Arab crewmen shouted to each other. Their voices were muffled and distant, but the urgency remained clear.

He imagined ships as huge as this one prowling silently under sail, oars shipped, every light extinguished and every patch of iron blackened. Each crewman holding his breath. Every loose pin or board held fast against noise. Dark predators gliding against the night's black shroud, tracking a giant overconfident in its own size. Then, when the predators drew within striking distance, their oars slid into the waves and their crews cried for blood. Revealing themselves as mere black forms pressing with threatening speed for the giant's hull.

"This is an ambush," Yngvar said. "The Byzantines come to avenge their brothers. See the pace set? Our enemies struck out of the darkness, nearly atop us. That is not chance at work. It's a shipmaster's plot to send us to Ran's bed at the bottom of the sea."

"Does Ran even dwell in these warm waters?" Alasdair asked.

More Arab sailors scurried down the near vertical stairs. Four of them. They cursed the drummer, whose fat face now poured as much sweat as the slaves on the benches. These new sailors carried long switches. They spread down the two aisles between oar banks, shouting at the slaves they passed.

Whenever they found a slave lagging, they whipped him across his back and exhorted him to greater effort.

"Row," Yngvar said. "I've no wish to feel the lash again."

He had not realized how much he feared whipping until this moment. He had not been lashed since Erik Blood-Axe stripped the flesh from his back years ago. The scars left behind were not just across his spine. Those lashes had also cut to his heart.

The drumbeat reached the limit of the rowers' capacity. Yet the Arabs believed they could whip a man beyond his own strength. Yngvar's right foot was bound to Alasdair's left, and their mutual chain was hooked permanently to the floor. But his hands remained free.

If he were lashed, he would strangle the fool with his own switch.

But no whipping came for him. The Arab walking his row was white-faced with fear. His eyes looked through Yngvar, through the hull, and at the sea where he doubtlessly believed he would soon be drowning. He slid past Yngvar, lashing no one and shouting rote commands.

"Can you see anything through the tholes?" Yngvar sat on the inside of the bench, and Alasdair had a better view of the sea than he.

"It is nothing but darkness."

Yngvar listened for the crews above. Yet the drumming, groaning, and shouting masked any other sound. He experienced the desperation without any of the reasons for it. He was blind and did not like this.

Sweat burned his eyes. His shoulders were inflamed with agony. His back rippled with tingling pain.

"My palms will catch fire, lord!"

Yngvar nodded. He blew his breath out and sweat speckled the back of the man before him. Over their heads, he saw Thorfast and Bjorn rowing as well. Even without their hair, he knew the shapes of his oldest and dearest companions.

He hoped to protect them, to keep them from whatever fate the Arabs so feared. But what could he do chained to the deck as he was?

A bell sounded above, dim and frantic ringing. The Arabs looked to each other, then threw down their switches. The drummer abandoned his post. They all scrabbled up the steep stairs, shoving each other to get ahead.

The slaves all stood, shouting and screaming. They pulled on their chains.

"Lord?" Alasdair's bright face had dulled to ash. He made the sign of the cross. "It is not too late to ask God for forgiveness. Join me in heaven, lord! Give yourself to Christ now!"

Yngvar scowled. "He kills you as well as me. He is worthless."

The screaming set his ears throbbing. Every slave yanked at his chains. But Yngvar saw no outward sign of danger. Had the Byzantines boarded?

"Look outside," he said to Alasdair. "Do you see a hull?"

He peeked through the thole, setting both hands aside it.

"I see nothing. Not even stars reflected in the water."

Yngvar looked across the benches, over the panicking slaves. Thorfast and Bjorn stood unflustered, resolute with jaws set. No words could cross the barrier of hopeless screaming. No words needed to.

Yngvar and his Wolves did not fear death. Let it come.

They had dared to live as warriors. They had dared to pluck riches from the world's stinting grip. They had trodden across the backs of dead foemen, driving the weak and worthless before them.

They had lived for gold and glory.

Let death come.

"Stand straight," Yngvar said to Alasdair. "Do not cry out as these fools do."

Alasdair did as commanded.

And death arrived.

An enormous ram head of iron crashed through the hull between Yngvar and his Wolves. The shattering of strakes and frame was like the crack of thunder. The iron beast crushed benches and bodies. Sea water exploded into the breach as the ram head drove deeper.

The rush of water and force of the collision sent Yngvar sprawling atop the man behind him. Screams drowned beneath the roar of water and shattering wood. He pressed his hands over his face to shield against the water forcing into his nostrils. But such was the blast strength that his hands were shoved down to his sides.

The ram head continued to push in, its horrible charge incomplete. Yngvar rolled off the man he had landed on, and found the deck rising beneath him. He instinctively sought to claw up, but his leg pulled sharp against his chain.

The iron ram head had now cleared to the center of the deck. Candles extinguished, casting them into hellish black filled with the wailing of doomed men and the gush of sea water.

Then the ship broke.

Like a dried branch bent too sharply, the hull opposite of the impact burst open and expelled slaves still chained to the deck.

Yngvar grabbed at his chain. Water was already up to his waist. Across from him, he could see only the long timber of the ram and foamy water rushing around it. Bjorn and Thorfast were lost to him. As was nearly everyone else.

Rafters and decking collapsed. Sailors fell through, their shrieking brutally silenced as they plunged into the water.

"Lord, the deck is shattered!"

"So I see," Yngvar shouted. His eyes stung and now water had risen to his chest. It pulled him toward the opposite breach to the patch of gray in the gloom of the flooding deck.

"I mean we are freed."

Alasdair's head barely held above the water. In the darkness, he was no more than a glistening hump buffeted with the current. Yet he forced up a hand with a broken length of chain.

"The gods let us die as free men." He could see it as no other sign.

Then the gargantuan Arab ship could withstand no more. With a shriek of wood, it broke into two pieces. What had been the fore of the ship now set its nose toward the sea floor. Its shattered edge rose above the water revealing the stack of decks where slaves still remained chained. The section where Yngvar had found himself slid out from under him as it rolled to its side. Debris and men toppled out of the decks above as Yngvar glimpsed the last of the world above the waves. He was tipped out of the ship like a pebble shaken from an old boot.

The force of the water sucked him out into the open sea. It pulled him under and shoved him down. In the cool, swirling world beneath the waves, the splinter and crack of timber echoed like thunder through the blackness. Roiling bubbles growled in his ears. The spirits of the drowned grabbed his feet, eager for a new companion in the sea grave.

It would shame him to die without a struggle. Yet his weary body wanted to drift down to Ran's bed and meet the sea-whore goddess who was never sated no matter how many sailors she claimed.

His breath caught fire in his chest. He could hold it no longer, and soon he would gasp the ocean into his lungs. Bright lights flashed behind his closed eyes.

But in the churning chaos of a sinking ship and its drowning crew, he heard the call of the gods.

Swim. You have learned this skill. Swim and be saved.

He pulled up, and his body rose. He kicked and pulled as Alasdair had taught him. And he rose again.

The shackle on his leg was a weight he could not escape. But the gods were lending him strength.

Swim. The voice was clear, powerful, omnipresent.

His head breached the surface. He gasped and thrashed out with both hands, searching in blindness.

Though the night was not so dark. Yellow light skimmed across the churning waves. Acrid smoke rolled atop the water. Men wailed in terror while others shouted in triumph.

Yngvar kicked and struggled to keep his head up in the madness.

"Gods, if you mean to save me then send me aid."

"God does, lord!"

Alasdair grabbed at the collar of his shirt. It peeled away and Yngvar sank back down so water rushed into his mouth.

"Lord! Remember to kick!" Alasdair's hands slipped over his naked shoulder, pulling him near.

Yngvar flopped around to see a giant fire dancing on the surface. But limned in front of it was Alasdair, one arm thrown across a section of deck. He laughed, his youthful voice bright with cheer.

"God saves us! My chain got wrapped in this decking, or else I would have surely drowned!"

The burning ship was smaller than the one Yngvar had just escaped. It had sunk nearly to the deck, its masts now flying sails of flame. It must have been the escort for their own ship.

Yngvar felt a sudden pull back toward the water.

"The spirits of the drowned seize me."

"Lord, it is the drag of our own ship as it slips beneath the waves. Grab here. We must paddle ourselves away or we will be taken down with it."

Together they paddled while holding on to the wreckage. Yngvar's mouth was full of sea salt and blood. He and Alasdair kicked away from the water sucking them back. Screams filled the air. Burning masts ahead of them groaned then crashed into the water. Steam hissed up into the air. Behind, a sound like a giant guzzling from his bowl filled the night. Yngvar felt the spectral hands of the drowned sweep along his leg and hold to his feet.

But he pulled free. He and Alasdair lurched forward and let themselves float.

"Hold fast to this," Yngvar said. "At least the water is warm. We shall not freeze."

"There are sharks here," Alasdair said. "There must be with so much blood in the water."

They bobbed along the dark water, slumped over the beams and the planks nailed to them. Yngvar remained submerged below the armpits. Something bumped his foot and it tingled with anticipation of pain. But perhaps it was merely debris or a corpse, not the shark Alasdair had fixed in his mind.

With both the massive Arab slave ship destroyed and its escort on fire, the Byzantines howled victory into the night. Through blurry eyes, Yngvar saw the balls of lights from their lanterns. Two giant shapes loomed out of the water. From the level of the waves, each seemed as tall as mountains. One had a massive ram fixed to its prow, and it floated among the destroyed wood of what had been the Arab slave ship. The other ranged a short distance away, so that both crews could shout congratulations between them.

Throughout this, hundreds of voices cried out to the night. Despite the complete destruction of both ships, enough of the crews had endured to cling to the flotsam as he and Alasdair had.

The words were not Norse. He spared a thought for his crew, for Thorfast and Bjorn. He could be certain most had died. Thorfast and Bjorn had been nearly in front of the ram as it breached the hull. They must certainly be dead. Yet he listened to the blaze-brightened night for familiar voices.

He heard pleas to Allah. He knew this word, and after this horrid night, he would never forget it.

"What do we do, lord?"

Yngvar shook his head. "What can a man do? To call out is to invite ourselves to slavery once more. Yet if the morning comes and we are near land, then we might have freedom again. The current could take us to a shore."

Too many questions floated alongside them on the waves. The only right answer was that Fate had woven this thread and so had a design for the rest of their lives, however long those might be. Perhaps they would feed a hungry shark before the dawn arrived. Perhaps they would come ashore and be named Kings of Langbarda-land. Only witches could drive the Fates' plans, and then often without any specificity. They would float and see what the gods delivered them.

He did not know how long he floated in the water. Yet soon he realized the screams and cries to Allah diminished. The behemoth ships drifted over them, their crews now silent and mysterious. They remained as massive-shouldered giants brooding over the pitiful remains of their rage.

Yngvar and Alasdair both raised their heads together at the same sound.

Water splashed gently, and foreign voices whispered. A weak globe of light shined over them. A small rowboat with five shadowy men wrapped in cloaks approached. One man worked the oars while the others leaned over the sides and searched the water. One scooped something out, examined it, then flung it back into the waves with a splash.

He and Alasdair exchanged glances. Whether Byzantines or Arabs, they were enemies. Either faction would enslave them.

"Slavery is better than drowning," Alasdair whispered.

"That is a Christian idea," Yngvar muttered in return. "Better that I pull myself aboard their ship and die with my enemy's throat crushed in my hands."

A sharp cry turned both their heads back to the rowboat.

Two of the cloaked figures stood. They both had thrust spears into the water and together hauled out a body.

The victim was naked but for tattered pants clinging to his waist. The spears had driven into his neck and his side. The spearmen hauled him out of the water like a fish, while the others pulled the victim onto their small vessel.

It rocked with the violence. But this was sport to the cloaked figures. The rest of the crew drew daggers that flashed with orange light. Each man stabbed the victim in his face and throat. Then they shoved the corpse back into the water with wicked laughter.

"Revenge is cruel," Yngvar whispered. "It is not enough to see us killed, but each must draw blood before they are satisfied."

The oars dipped back into the water and the boat slipped toward them.

"Quick, get below this decking." Yngvar sucked in a breath then slipped under the waves.

He felt Alasdair kick beside him. He held underwater until he could stand it no more. When he surfaced, his head bumped the wood floating above him. He struggled to control his gasp. It sounded like a spouting whale to his ears.

The boat of cloaked Byzantines still lingered close to them. Alasdair surfaced, close as a lover in bed. But he made no sound as he broke the water. He blinked hard and looked about until he found the boat.

Were there so many survivors near to him, Yngvar wondered. They had speared another Arab, and each man cursed violently as they raked their daggers over their victim.

Yngvar laced his fingers through the deck above him like the bars of a prison cell. The rocking waves caused it to thump his head repeatedly. It seemed as if the Byzantines had already examined their position. But with that very thought, one grabbed the lantern from the hook on which it swayed and sent its light after them.

Alasdair vanished like a frog into a murky pond. Yngvar was not as swift.

One shadowy Byzantine leaned forward, grabbing the side of his boat to steady himself.

Yngvar realized he had been transfixed. He sucked his breath and ducked into the waves. The world of water was full of sounds unheard in the air. Bubbles created gurgling noises. Wood and debris bumped each other to thuds three times louder than those on land. No one above the waves could hear this, but to Yngvar, he feared even his racing heart sounded loud enough to alert the Byzantines.

His racing heart depleted his breath faster. He could hold no longer, and forced himself to the surface.

The rowboat was alongside the lattice-like section of broken deck. The light of the lantern was bright in his eyes, turning the world to golden brilliance. His bald head must gleam beneath it. The Byzantines would see him. Yet they prodded the debris with their spears, touching edges and poking into empty spaces.

Yngvar wanted to dive again, but to draw breath now would reveal himself.

Then he realized the difference between himself and the other survivors. He and Alasdair could swim. Only one in a hundred men knew this skill, even if they spent their lives on the sea.

Alasdair surfaced, and despite the gentleness of his arrival, one of the Byzantines spoke up and pointed with his spear.

"Get under their hull," Yngvar said, then sucked his breath before ducking under the water.

He opened his eyes and the sea water burned and blurred his vision. But the brilliance of the lantern was clear enough. He saw the shadow of the rowboat's hull and swam up to it.

The boat rocked and lifted, and the Byzantines searching for him over the sides fell headlong into the water. He heard their splash and their liquid screams.

Alasdair was with him now, and together they shoved up against the hull. Another man fell into the water.

Now Yngvar grabbed the edge of the rowboat and hauled himself up. The sole Byzantine not flailing in the water, dragged down by the weight of their cloaks, had fallen on his backside amid the short benches. Yngvar slithered onto the deck and atop the man.

The Byzantine reached for his dagger, and Yngvar expected this. So he followed his enemy's hand to the sheath and arrested it there. Now the two wrestled, but this sailor was neither as fierce as Yngvar nor as desperate.

Yngvar smashed his head down on the Byzantine's face. His nose flattened and crunched and the sailor wailed. He also loosened his grip out of reflex, and Yngvar snatched the long, straight dagger out of the sailor's belt.

He plunged it up into the sailor's neck. His face was a ruin of blood as the Byzantine convulsed and choked. Before his throes were done, Yngvar slashed across his neck and ended the sailor's life. He flipped him overboard.

In the water, the last sailor vanished as Alasdair rose above him.

"Get into the ship with me," Yngvar said, holding out his arm.

"I can't. My chain is wrapped into the decking."

Yngvar pulled Alasdair up, and found he could leave the water. The ruined deck, however, bumped into the side of the boat.

"They lost the oars," Yngvar noticed. "Let's douse this lantern."

He stuffed it beneath the rippling waves and it hissed, casting them back into darkness. They lay crouched so only their eyes were above the rails. Yngvar studied the circle of darkness they floated through.

A dozen globes of light bobbed and rocked all across the water as Byzantines searched for survivors. Perhaps not all would be slain, but some taken as slaves. Even these bloody-minded sailors must desire some profit from their exertions this night. As a small blessing, none of the light globes were close to Yngvar's rowboat.

"If the gods favor us, the Byzantines will forget these sailors and this boat," Yngvar said, tugging at Alasdair's chain. "But for this chain, we might actually get somewhere."

"If we are alive by morning, I can probably untangle myself."

Yngvar and Alasdair fell silent, huddling against the bottom of the boat where blood and sea water churned.

No Byzantine came for them, but soon they heard thrashing from the water. Something thumped against the hull, jolting them with fear. A sound like tearing sails met Yngvar's ears. He dared a look over the edge to see the fins of sharks flop above the water as they feasted only an arm's length distant. The water foamed red with their frenzy.

"The gods have turned away from us," Yngvar said. "How well do you suppose we can defend against blood-crazed sharks?"

"Not very well, lord. Not well at all."

20

The morning sun brushed Yngvar's face and prickled his skin. His eyes opened to a clear field of azure light. For the space of one breath, his chest filled with joy at the brilliance. Then his body began to throb and ache. He had slept with feeding sharks close enough to touch and bloody water sloshing around his ears. Alasdair was wedged beside him. For a moment, Yngvar though he had died. But his naked torso was warm and his sides rose and fell.

Yngvar blinked, feeling as if each eye had been filled with sand. Tears slid from the corners. His mouth was pasty and filled with stale blood and ocean water. The only sound was the slap of the waves against their drifting boat and the intermittent bump of the ruined decking striking against the hull.

Alasdair's naked leg rested atop the side. The shackle pulled tight with the chain that had wrapped into the broken deck. It had saved their lives, but would only burden them now.

A gull cried overhead, wheeling through the sky and swooping out of Yngvar's vision.

"Land," he said hoarsely. "A gull means land is nearby."

Alasdair had not been as deeply asleep as Yngvar had supposed. He shimmied away from Yngvar and yawned.

"My foot has gone numb," he said. "The chain pulls at me so often that I cannot sleep. I will go mad if I cannot be freed of it."

Yngvar put one hand on the cold wooden side and carefully pulled himself upright. The rowboat floated in a wide circle of blue water and sky. Clouds swam through the air like scattered whale pods. But for a smattering of debris bobbing on the rolling waves, no sign of last night's disaster remained. All had been taken to the bottom or else washed away.

"The sea leaves no trace. None have survived but us," he said. The gull above cried out and headed off to the west. "There is land where that gull flies."

Alasdair sat up, rubbing the bloody stains of the water from his naked arms.

"Perhaps we have drifted from where the ships sank. We are on a boat, lord. We might drift farther than any man clinging to wreckage."

"Don't call me lord any longer," Yngvar said. "Fate has joined us as equals to share an equal destiny."

Alasdair lowered his head and rubbed the back of his leg that rested atop the side.

"I should try to disentangle this chain."

Yngvar found the knife he had stolen from his Byzantine victim. It sat in water at the bottom of the ship. Orange rust already gathered around the simple hilt.

"That bolt is loose," he said. "I think I can pry it completely off with this."

"Be careful, lord. The blade may be ruined, but it is yet sharp."

"I am no lord, Alasdair. Now, trust my hands while I still have strength to do this."

The Arabs had been careless in securing the shackles. They knew Yngvar and his crew would be trapped deep in the belly of a slave galley. The shackles had been mere deterrents. The violence of the prior night had nearly popped the shackle free. He tucked Alasdair's leg under his arm and held his ankle straight. With his other hand he tucked the dagger between the shackle section and levered out the bolt.

It snapped away, one section still holding the bolt. Alasdair groaned with immediate relief and pulled his leg to his chest. The shackles and chain plunked into the water and vanished.

"May I never endure such torment again," he said. "Praise God for this generosity."

"Praise any god that will hear us out in this barren sea." Yngvar set the straight dagger to his own shackle. The thin chain that had bound him had snapped at the connecting loop. So his shackle had not endured the same strain as Alasdair's and was more firmly set.

"I cannot get the right leverage on this," Yngvar said after trying the gap in his shackles. "See what you can do."

He handed Alasdair the long, straight knife. It tapered to a thin point crafted for stabbing and piercing. Alasdair stared at it as if it was the greatest gift he ever received.

"It is a fine weapon," he said. "It is the only thing we own now."

"Well, I own this shackle," Yngvar said. "But I'd be glad to rid myself of it. Not every possession is worth holding. Come, get this off me. If I must swim again, I'll not fight with it. I am poor enough at swimming without a pound of iron on my ankle."

Iron scratched against iron. The water lapped at the hull as the boat rocked with Alasdair's struggle. He had hooked his arm over Yngvar's leg and wrested with the bolt. At first the sections separated with ease. It seemed as if Yngvar could pull his foot through. Then the bolt stuck before it released.

"I cannot move it more," Alasdair said, sitting back on the small bench. "It is stuck."

Yngvar growled and snatched away the dagger. He set it into the widened gap and levered until he thought the bolt moved again. "It's coming free!"

He worked harder, and in the same instant the dagger snapped along with the shackle. Iron splashed into the bloody water sloshing in the boat. The skin beneath the iron was red and scabbed over. Yngvar held the stub of the blade.

"It can still kill a man," he said, looking at the jagged break. "I will keep this."

Alasdair fished out the shackles and cast them into the water. A gull dove after it, swooping up once realizing it was not edible.

"Another bird," he said. "We must be near land."

"That is well," Yngvar said. "For starvation in this sinking tub is not what I hoped the gods planned for us."

Alasdair looked again to the dagger in Yngvar's hands. With sudden understanding, his eyes widened and he held up the blade for peace.

"I would never use this against you," he said. "I owe you my life too many times over. Do not fear violence from me."

"Of course not, lord." Alasdair said.

He prepared to correct his old companion, but then realized as long as he held the only weapon, he was still lord. Even in this desperate situation he had grabbed power. Only now did he recognize Alasdair's frightened expression when he had violently plucked the dagger from his hand.

"Here, you should carry the dagger."

Alasdair stared at it, then turned aside. "I trust you, lord. I do not trust myself."

Yngvar laughed. "We're not even one night at sea. Do not imagine we will be eating each other when night comes again. Besides, there is land over the western horizon. Take this dagger."

Alasdair turned to the west instead and shaded his eyes to scan the horizon.

Yngvar lowered his hand, still holding the broken weapon.

"Curse Jamil for luring us to these worries. I will force him and Saleet to eat each other's livers. I swear it."

"Be gladdened we can still curse them, lord. Our brothers' mouths are filled with brine at the bottom of the ocean."

Yngvar frown, unwilling to summon his last memory of Bjorn and Thorfast. He did not want to remember them as slaves but as the heroes they were. Surely the gods had not let them drown. Yet he could not deny his eyes. He and Alasdair drifted alone in a massive circle of empty blue.

His Wolves were dead.

"Let's paddle west while the wind and sea are calm. Thor has granted us peaceful winds. We should not waste the chance."

They used their arms to scoop the warm water, guiding their ship away from the wreckage that had saved them from the death that had visited every other slave. Yngvar looked more into the water than to his course. Indistinct objects floated just beneath the rippling waves. Flashes of reflected sunlight barred him from seeing anything other than what passed in the shadow of their boat. He dreaded discovering a familiar face staring up from the waves. Of course, dead bodies would have sunk by now. Yet the irrational fear of Bjorn or Thorfast accusing him with vacant stares from beneath the water followed him along their wandering course.

"A current is here," Yngvar said. "And there is land ahead."

They had paddled until both moaned from the aches in their shoulders. Yngvar's elbows burned and his hands were pruned and red. His eyes throbbed from squinting.

"None too soon," Alasdair said. "This boat is sinking."

"So it is." Yngvar sat up, noticing how much more sea water had seeped into the rowboat. It was not meant for long use. It was likely a ferry boat the Byzantines used to board their warships. The blood in the water had diluted with the flooding.

"Perhaps we will still need to swim," Yngvar said. "The current will lead us to the shore without doubt, but let's hasten. I want to land by daylight and have a look at our surrounding."

"Do you know where we are, lord?"

"No more than you. But that strip of land is an island and not the coast of Sicily. I only pray there is fresh water there. My thirst is fierce."

By the time the sun had reached the zenith of the sky, their boat had struck a sandbar. Yngvar and Alasdair waded ashore. They had plodded through the muck of the sea floor to collapse up the slope of the beach. The tide was gentle and pleasant, yet to Yngvar he felt as if he had fought the god of storms. They both spread out in scraggly grass that hid sharp rocks.

Yngvar's parched throat burned. He had last taken water during a break in rowing, and now regretted not drinking more. He lay silently with Alasdair beside him. Both had lost their clothing but for shreds of their pants which had turned gray from salt water and sun. Yngvar still had a belt, and he tucked the broken dagger into it. For now it would serve. In another day it would rust beyond usefulness. Today, he could still kill a man if he needed.

The precaution was not unwarranted. Though the shore was barren of anything but flotsam, seaweed, and stones, the land uphill was a mystery. While Yngvar lay on his back, recovering his strength, Alasdair had gone scouting. He now scurried back, his feet swishing through the grass.

"Lord! Men approach. More than a dozen!"

Yngvar closed his eyes. "Of course men approach. Would the gods not laugh all the harder to see us in chains once more? Let me guess, a horde of Arabs in bright head covers come with their curving swords?"

"No, lord."

"Then Byzantines in shining mail and helmets more pretty than useful?"

"No, lord. These men are much less grand. Fate has granted them not much more than us. Though they carry swords and spears."

"That is all they must carry to be greater than us," Yngvar said. "Gather as many of these sharp rocks as you can. Keep one in hand to defend yourself. Hurl the rest at their heads."

"We can't defeat a dozen men with rocks."

"We cannot. But we can die as warriors. I'm not running or begging mercy anymore. Flee if you will. Every man in these cursed lands is my enemy. I will not bend before any of them, even if my only weapon is a rusted, shattered dagger."

Yngvar pried edged stones out of the sand, not bothering to watch for the approaching enemy. They had likely seen their rowboat earlier and now came to investigate. They would have their sport, but Yngvar determined not all of them would live to brag about it over their beers.

"Fourteen men," Alasdair said. He crouched low to the slope ridge. A pile of half a dozen rocks was at his right hand.

"No sense wasting our strength until they are close enough to break skulls. Throw true and strong, and we might only face ten men."

"That seems optimistic, lord."

"Why not? The gods have preserved us so far. When they crush out my life for their entertainment, it will be far more humiliating than this. We court a hero's death today."

"As you say, lord."

Alasdair made the sign of the cross. Yngvar did not begrudge him his beliefs. Though he had no wish to believe as Alasdair did. He felt a pinch of irritation remembering how Alasdair had tried to convert him before what seemed certain death. He would have to clear up his wishes with Alasdair.

Yngvar mounted the crest, carrying his armful of rocks. The fourteen men were nothing more than bandits. Even a foreigner such as himself could tell with glance. They strode across the grass which faded off to tree-covered hills. Their faces were dull and cut with sharp shadows of the noonday sun.

They were led by a giant—of course—who wore a sea blue head cover and a white shirt open to the waist. His ballooning pants fluttered in the wind that flattened out a long black mustache like the Old Saxons wore. He might have passed for one had his skin not been so brown. His companions were smaller versions of himself, with faded colors and patches over their garments. The majority gripped curving swords in strong hands, though at least two carried spears.

"A fine group," Yngvar said. "The leader probably has the thickest head. So aim for the others."

He winged his first rock at a small man on the outside of the approaching group. The force of his throw caused him to spill most of the rocks gathered in the crook of his arm. It struck the unsuspecting bandit square in the forehead. The soft crack it made filled Yngvar with joy.

"The gods love me!" His heart raced. At last, a battle was at hand.

The bandit stupidly dropped his sword and put both hands over his face before collapsing to his knees then falling to his side.

Alasdair's stone skimmed across another bandit's shoulder. He cried out, for the sharp edge had cut through his loose shirt and drew blood.

Yngvar pitched another stone, and again he caught the next man in line. This time the stone thumped heavily into the man's collarbone. He shouted with shock and stepped back. But he would live.

The remainder of Yngvar's stones had tumbled to his feet. He stooped to grab them up while Alasdair flung his next rock.

He heard a thud and a shout from the bandits, which were now a dozen yards away. He giggled as he snatched up another rock. Such a way to die. His father and grandfather waited for him in Valhalla. They would clap his back and toast him for standing his ground with nothing but rocks and a broken dagger.

Now the bandits were at last aware of the fight they had joined. The leader bellowed something in one of the angry, guttural languages of this hateful place.

Yngvar stood up and blinked at the gift sailing across the gap between himself and the bandits.

One bandit had thrown his spear. He was a lighter-skinned man with clear eyes and white teeth bared in rage. Blood flowed down his temple, likely drawn by one of Alasdair's stones.

The leaf-shaped blade glittered with the light. Though it wobbled and spun toward Yngvar's heart, the gods had slowed the world down so that he might admire their gift to him. It was a long spear, thin enough to throw but sturdy enough to hold up to thrusting combat.

He stepped out of its flight. The spear arced into the ground beside him. It would have missed him nonetheless, but now its haft pointed up as if to invite Yngvar's grip.

Alasdair stared at it, arm cocked to loose another rock.

"Strong but stupid," Yngvar said as he snatched the spear out of the ground. "And they didn't remove the locking pin, either."

The spear snapped around to his front and the blade remained fixed. When he or his warriors threw spears like this, they were careful to remove the pin first so the shaft and blade would separate and deny the enemy a new weapon. This bandit had thrown away his spear in rage, and now armed Yngvar.

The bandit leader knew this too. His dark face turned purple and he rounded on the fool who had cast his spear. Yngvar did not need to understand the language to feel the withering curses the fool endured.

"Don't give them a moment," Yngvar shouted to Alasdair. "Hit them!"

The next rock struck the leader on the back of his shoulder. While it thudded heavily, the stone only succeeded in ending his blast of invectives. He turned slowly to Alasdair. All of his men had paused with him.

"If you'll throw me a shield," Yngvar shouted at them, "I'll show you how a Norseman fights. But don't think I can't spear your balls with this. Come closer and I mark half of you dead already. The other half will be missing eyes and fingers. But come. I need to kill someone!"

"I'm out of rocks, lord."

"Protect my right side," Yngvar said.

The bandits stood stupefied by Yngvar's belligerence. He doubted they ever expected unarmed men to make a stand against seven to one odds. Their leader scanned Yngvar's stance. As a warrior, he should recognize Yngvar's competence. That recognition showed in a flickering smile across his dark face. He stroked his big mustache, then stepped forward.

His words were gibberish. Yngvar shook his head at every statement, shouting back in both Norse and Frankish.

"I don't understand nonsense. If you want a fight, here I am. But I'll not surrender."

No language he understood made any difference. At last the leader turned aside in frustration. He grabbed a spear from his fellow bandit and then pointed it at Yngvar. He gestured to the ground between them.

"You want to fight? The two of us?" Yngvar pointed at the same spot with his spear. Then he pointed at the other bandits. "And they're going to stay out of it?"

He repeated the gesture until the leader nodded his understanding. He repeated Yngvar's gesture, facing his palm across all his men as if to force them back.

"And if I win, we'll go free?" Yngvar pointed to himself and Alasdair, then used his fingers to imitate them both walking away. Again the giant smiled and nodded.

Yngvar handed his broken dagger to Alasdair. "When I kill their leader, we're probably still going to die. Use this to take out as many as you can. We'll not be slaves again."

Alasdair took the broken weapon wordlessly. He held it in both hands and stared as if he did not understand what to do.

Taking his place in the grass, he set his feet wide and readied his spear. He was tired and hungry from a long ordeal. Yet the offering of battle filled him with strength impossible without the blessing of the gods behind him.

The giant leader weighed his spear and smiled. He stepped toward Yngvar, and without warning exploded forward with a roar.

21

The vast-shouldered bandit's black eyes were wide as he screamed. He charged forward with his spear leveled for the center of Yngvar's torso. His black mustache flowed back with the speed of his strike. Yet for all of his uncoiling strength and fury, it was the strike of an untrained farmer.

Yngvar held his spear level, facing the bandit chief. When his spear darted in, Yngvar batted it down from his body then flicked up to stab the chief's chest. It hit him high in the thick pad of muscle connecting to his shoulder. It was not fatal, not even serious, but a warning to the chief that he did not battle with a fool. Blood flowed easily and the chief shouted with surprise. He bounced back as swiftly as he had charged.

His men shouted now, raising their swords and calling out what must be the chief's name.

"Taahir! Taahir!"

"Well, Taahir, you'll soon regret taking a spear to me, seeing how you don't know how to handle one." Yngvar smiled and waited with his spear pointed at the giant Taahir. The chief seemed startled at the use of his name. Yet he gave a wicked smirk at the cut to his chest.

"That's right," Yngvar continued. "I'll bleed you out. You're a faithless Arab bastard, aren't you? Your word is worth less than week-old dog shit. What shall I cut from you next? How about an ear?"

Yngvar struck, never intending the blow to land. Yet Taahir defended and backed off the strike aimed at his face. As distraught as Yngvar was, he knew he could tire out the chief first. The explosive strike he had led off with had already brought sweat to his brow. The wound on his chest must pain him, and his reflexive block both wasted his energy and belied his actual confidence.

"He's going to crumble soon," Yngvar said to Alasdair, never taking his eyes from Taahir. "Then his men will swarm us. You might flee and live. But I will die here."

"As will I, lord."

Yngvar shook his head. Such loyalty and bravery was admirable. He wished the Christian god valued those qualities enough to seat Alasdair at the high table of whatever mead hall Christ ruled from.

Taahir roared and sent another thrust at Yngvar. It was a feint which the bandit revealed in his stance and gaze. He spent his energy like a rich drunk spends his gold. Yngvar kept his guard and batted the real strike aside. Again, he struck with swiftness that caught Taahir's unguarded flesh. This time he gashed the chief's shoulder and skimmed across his chin.

"Your eye is next, you oaf," Yngvar said. "If this is how you fight, then I might take all of you alone."

Yngvar shifted right, careful not to turn his back to Taahir's gang. This was a restriction on his motion that the bandit did not seem to recognize. Half the field was denied Yngvar, for the other bandits could brain him the moment he set his back to them. Yet Taahir never pressed this advantage. Instead, he snarled and blinked the sweat from his eyes.

The chief followed Yngvar as he circled closer to Alasdair. When he finished this fool, he wanted to link with him to face the wave of traitorous bandits who would seek revenge for their chief. Though his arms began to tremble from holding his spear, it was from the strain of his recent ordeal. In better times he could toy with the bandit for hours.

Yngvar determined where to strike when Taahir made his next

attempt. He would drive close and slash up to plant his blade in the chief's neck. He did not want to impale the torso and risk losing or bending his blade. The edge would slide through the thin flesh of the chief's neck and kill him, allowing Yngvar to face his spear at the first fool to charge him.

They both paused. The stifling humidity drew sweat to Yngvar's brow. With no hair to protect his scalp, it felt as if it shriveled from the noonday sun.

Taahir's feet shifted. His grip tightened on his spear. Yngvar read the intent and waited for the strike. Neither seemed prepared to make the first move.

Impatience finally broke Yngvar's discipline. He struck with a quick feint to the body that Taahir did not believe. Already committed to the attack, Yngvar slashed up toward the chief's neck.

But now it was his spear knocked aside.

And Taahir's explosive lurch sent him colliding with Yngvar.

He crashed back as Taahir roared in victory. Weakened and thin from imprisonment, Yngvar collapsed like a dead tree. The sun stabbed into his eyes, and he soon expected a stab through his guts.

Instead, Taahir settled the point over the base of Yngvar's neck. He flicked his wrist and the blade slashed up to score Yngvar's cheek. It burned, but it was a symbolic wound. Taahir smiled and waited for Yngvar to acknowledge defeat.

"So you toyed with me?" he said. "Still, you didn't expect to get cut, you dog-shit. Go ahead. I hold this spear and am ready to greet my kin in the hall of heroes."

Taahir recited something that sounded more pedantic than vengeful.

"Do it, you bastard!"

The bandit chief laughed. His companions laughed as well. Yngvar could see only the massive shadow of the chief blotting the sun.

"Lord, I think he means to spare us."

Taahir stepped back, but did not disarm Yngvar. Instead he extended his arm in the universal sign for peace.

Yngvar crawled to his knees, then used his spear to lever himself upright. The battle had extracted more of his strength than he had expected. Sweat rolled into the cut on his cheek and stung him. Taahir stood, letting his blood seep freely into his heavy beard, and kept his thick arm extended.

"What do I do here?" Yngvar asked. He planted his spear in the ground, unwilling to let it go. His other hand itched to grab Taahir's. He needed an ally, even a lowly bandit, if he was to survive. He had a duty to honor his life, granted him by the gods and envied by his fallen companions.

"Accept his peace," Alasdair said. "God has sent him to us for a purpose. Even if it is only to deliver us to fresh water."

Yngvar grabbed Taahir's strong, rough arm and shook. The bandit chief seemed perplexed at the gesture, but soon realized what it meant. He began to laugh and prattle on in his harsh language. He gestured to his men, talking to them as if he had just found a long-lost cousin rather than a broken man who had cut and stabbed him.

The bandits nodded. The man Yngvar had laid out now sat in the grass, holding his broken nose. The bandit who had cast his spear pointed to Yngvar, and Taahir shouted him down. It seemed after a round of negotiations, he and Alasdair were to be accepted. At last Taahir pointed to his chest and named himself. Then he pointed to Yngvar.

"I am Yngvar Hakonsson," he said. "And this is Alasdair. We are Norsemen."

Taahir's smile weakened and his flowing mustache wiggled as he tried to work out the words. After a time he shook his head and made noises that sounded like "Wain-zar" and then "Al-Ja-Hair."

He nodded to Yngvar's spear and spoke in a low voice. Whatever he said, the threat was clear enough. If he attempted to fight he would be swarmed. Yngvar held it forward and offered it to Taahir. He glanced at it then shook his head. More words, less threatening now, followed and "Wain-Zar" seemed to be one of them.

"I guess this is mine," he said, giving Alasdair a bemused look. "We're going to become Arab bandits now."

"Not far from what we came here as," Alasdair said. "God is strange."

Taahir and his bandits turned toward the hills. The injured gave them dark looks, and the one whose nose Yngvar had broken had to be carried on another's back. Yngvar held close to Taahir as they traveled across the grassy plain.

They followed a path that led up to hilltop ruins of the old people. Crumbled stone towers presided over fallen stone walls. Green vines and bushes had invaded the old fort. The gatehouse remained though its gate had vanished along with the original builders. Three bowmen kept watch from the top of the gatehouse.

Taahir introduced the heap of moldering stone with grandiose sweeps of his hands and explanation rich with pride. Yngvar thought it sounded as if Taahir were claiming to have broken these walls himself. Yet it seemed that had been the labor of time and trees, for strangely shaped trees sprouted between gaps and grew their roots over ancient stones. The lookouts on the gatehouse waved to them. Yngvar turned back to see the glittering ocean through the tops of trees.

"They can see to the end of the world from here," he said. "No wonder they saw our rowboat."

"Sharp eyes, too," Alasdair said. "Such vigilance tells me they fear enemies from the sea."

"Bandits fear everything. But let us sort our worries into smaller parts. For now, I want water, then food, then a place to sleep through the rain. That is enough."

They passed under the gatehouse. A stone eagle was carved above the archway. Its wings were spread as if they could hold the entire world between them. The Franks knew such craftsmanship with stone, but nothing like this. Even after countless years, it was majestic and inspiring, and yet only a mere decoration. What other glories of the old people did this place hold, he wondered.

Behind the crumbled walls, Yngvar met a scene far more familiar to him. Here was the bandit camp, and it looked the name. Wood additions were constructed over the remains of old stonework to complete a dozen buildings. Smoke puffed from a half-dozen points, marking ramshackle homes and their decrepit hearths. A forge glowed across the wide courtyard, probably in place since the time of the old people. A thin, gray-haired and shirtless man worked the bellows. The coals breathed with golden light.

Ugly, boxy women in plain robes of gray or black stared out behind their face covers. Their eyes were piercing and dark. Yngvar felt their prick like skewers as he filed inside. One woman ran to the man whose face Yngvar had flattened. Others gathered young children to them as if uncertain of their safety.

Taahir spread his arms wide as if in welcome. His tone was like a jarl in a mighty mead hall as he introduced a famous skald. Yngvar noticed a well and pointed for it. The bandit chief smiled and nodded, waving both him and Alasdair to it.

They wasted no time, but ran across the grounds. A chicken fluttered out of his path and a shirtless boy reclined on the remains of a stone wall nearby, watching with dispassionate eyes. He and Alasdair dropped the bucket in, rejoiced at the splash, and pulled up fresh water. Such a crisp mineral taste had never been so welcomed. They guzzled from it, neither wasting a drop.

By that night, they had been fed a soup of strange vegetables and bits of meat that tasted like fish. In truth, salt overwhelmed all flavor. But compared to the slop he had eaten from shit buckets in Prince Kalim's dungeon, this was a godly feast.

He and Alasdair stayed close that night. They were allowed to find their own sleeping quarters. Alasdair found them a corner where no one could approach them unseen. He was like a cat in this regard, instinctively finding the best spot to watch for all threats. The air that night filled with the scent of rain, but none came. If they were to sleep here for any duration, they would have to construct a better roof. For now, they had broken walls on three sides and a pile of rubble to their front. They had cleared spiderwebs and old animal droppings from the ruin. They sketched out a place to sleep, and found it easily enough.

Yngvar slept wrapped around his spear like a lover.

The next morning they awakened to their leisure. The rain had been a simple dusting that left the stone walls of their enclosure darker at the top. A dog barked and a child laughed.

They wandered around the camp, watching people at their work just like any village. Yngvar kept his spear, but it threatened no one. Men walked about without their weapons ready, though all carried curving daggers in their belts.

"Twenty men," Yngvar said. "Maybe fifteen women and half as many children. That's a lot to support year-round."

"But their winters can't be too harsh," Alasdair said. "If they're not farming, they're trading or stealing everything they need."

"I'd expect they must fish," Yngvar said. "What do you suppose they will do with us? How are we going to learn to talk to them?"

Taahir met them at last. He introduced various men with scarred faces and searching eyes. They tried different languages, but Yngvar recognized none. At last, Taahir shook his head and roared laughter. The others seemed to enjoy the joke. Taahir grabbed Yngvar and Alasdair. He only glanced at Yngvar's spear.

He led them across the yard to the gatehouse. A rickety ladder was set to it, which he pointed to. They climbed it. Yngvar had to tuck his spear underarm and nearly dropped it twice. But a weapon was his guarantee of a good death if it ever came to battle again. He would not surrender it.

Atop the gatehouse, Taahir shouted at the three men. They studied Yngvar and Alasdair. Their gray head covers shaded their dark faces, but he could feel their judgment in their shifting stance. One seemed upset and turned back to the edge of the gatehouse. The other two laughed and scooted down the ladder.

"Looks like we've got a new job," Yngvar said.

Taahir pointed to the sea, then used his hand to demonstrate the rise and fall of waves. He pointed at his eyes, then out to sea, then made the wave gesture again. At last, he mimicked raising a horn to his lips and blowing. The guard sitting with his legs hanging over the gatehouse ledge did not turn but held up a huge shell to demonstrate that this was the horn.

"What in God's name is that?" Alasdair said. "Is it natural?"

"I've seen them at market," Yngvar said. "A shell of sorts. I suppose it must be their warning horn. So, we are to be lookouts. Not a bad job, seeing how no one can talk to us."

Taahir clapped them on their backs, shoving them forward, then left down the ladder. The remaining Arab ignored them, tossing pebbles off the roof. Yngvar and Alasdair approached to sit beside him, but the Arab gave a sudden shout. He laid out a string of commands, gesturing that they should stand.

"I guess we can't really see over the trees if we sit." Yngvar stood up again, resting on his spear. Alasdair scratched his shaved head in answer.

So day after day passed. Yngvar kept watch with Alasdair from sunrise to sunset. Water was delivered to them by one of the children whenever someone remembered them. They took one meal a day at evening, though they could fill their bowls as often as they liked. The women cooked, and as the days became weeks, Yngvar developed a preference for one woman's cooking over another's.

The work of a lookout was tedious at best. On the second day, a three-masted ship sailed past, and Yngvar was excited to sound the conch. Yet his Arab superior had batted it from his lips. The ship was just passing and not headed for their island. The Arab, while never friendly, made the best of their situation by introducing him and Alasdair to dice games. No one had anything of value to wager, so the fun diminished.

The only relief to this tedium was one day they were taken to the shore to help with a large catch of fish. Otherwise, they idled their days on the rooftop of the gatehouse and regained their strength.

Both he and Alasdair were taking well to their restful schedule. Yngvar's muscles fattened. The sores around Alasdair's mouth had receded and he stood straight. Both of their eyes brightened. At last Yngvar felt his old self, and with renewed strength came plans to escape.

While Taahir had been fair, even generous, he was still Yngvar's master. He accepted none as a lord, especially one he could not understand, so he and Alasdair talked about various methods of escape. They had little else to do when their Arab overseer had no mood for dice.

Then, one day while they fell into idle silence staring at the unchanging horizon, masts appeared. A single ship rode the wind toward them. The Arab stood and squinted, and when the three triangular sails resolved from the blue haze, he pointed to the conch Yngvar had set down.

"At last, we fulfill our purpose!" He grabbed the rough shell and put it to his lips. It took power to create the straining, stuttering note he sounded. The Arab laughed, and Yngvar tried anew, yet to no avail.

"This takes some skill," he said, then handed it to the Arab who blew three clear notes.

The bandit camp responded, but it was not panic. Women collected their children and ducked into their homes. The men went to fetch their weapons with no more urgency than preparing for a routine meeting. Taahir appeared from his shack, fixing his head cover and blinking sleepily.

"It's a Byzantine ship," Alasdair said. "It looks like the same ships from Pozzallo."

Yngvar stared after the ship, and his stomach tightened. It was high sided and bulkier than the Arab vessels. The Byzantines built everything with a grandeur that reflected their ancient pride. The sails were full and the ship rode the waves with purpose. Their helmsman aimed for the cove where Taahir kept his lone ship. Yngvar had only learned of it from his lookout post.

The Arab with them quipped, gesturing everyone to take the ladder down. They joined with Taahir and his men, who had retrieved their swords and spears. No one was excited, except for Taahir whose voice boomed off the crumbled walls. When he saw Yngvar, he beckoned him close.

Taahir slapped his back and grabbed Yngvar's spear. He shook it playfully then rubbed his hands over the stubble regrowing on Yngvar's head. They all marched to the shore, taking a branch in the path that led to the cove.

The Byzantines had dropped their anchor stone out to sea, and now a white rowboat lurched over the rolling waves. About fifteen heads bobbed with their rocking ship, all wearing black-plumed helms that gleamed yellow in the sun.

Yngvar watched the scene unfold. The Byzantines wore heavy cuirasses reinforced with plates. It seemed impossible that a man could move in this gear. Yet Yngvar watched in admiration as they waded ashore and aided their leader in disembarking. Their leader appeared as the others, though his pride was apparent in the lift of his chin and the squareness of his shoulders. Taahir was the only one of the bandits to step forward and greet the Byzantine.

They had a friendly exchange, both sides gesturing back and forth to their respective bases. Taahir kept pointing towards his men. Yngvar felt he was actually singled out among the group. None of the Arabs said anything, waiting with arms folded. One dug his finger into his nose and examined the result.

"Not an urgent matter," Yngvar said.

"I wonder what these Byzantines want with Arab bandits." Alasdair itched the brown stubble regrowing on his head.

"My guess is they're in the Byzantine's pay. Probably use them for things those fine soldiers aren't allowed to do themselves. Look, if I'm not wrong."

The Byzantine leader had raised his hand and two crewmen retrieved a small but heavy chest from the rowboat. Each held an iron ring as they carried it to the sand. It sank into the soft beach as they set it down just beyond the surf. The rolling waves made the only sound while both Taahir and the Byzantine stared at the chest.

They exchanged more words and finally he pointed at Yngvar.

"Wain-zar," he shouted, then waved him forward.

Yngvar looked to Alasdair, who shrugged. The other bandits stared on at the chest, but again no one seemed alert to danger. One turned his finger back to his nostril for a second probe.

"Let's see what this is about." Yngvar picked up his spear and approached Taahir.

He stood while the Byzantine looked him over and Taahir carried on at length. He made spear-fighting gestures and pressed Yngvar's muscles.

The Byzantine was a young man with a close-trimmed, brown beard. His eyebrows arched so that he looked as if he were in a continual state of contrition. Yet a fierce pride framed his body and he stood as if he presided over all his countrymen rather than a shabby gathering of bandits.

At last the Byzantine nodded. The two soldiers beside the chest unlatched it and lifted the lid. Inside was a leather bag, and the soldiers pulled out a cross of silver and a circlet of gold. The Byzantine snapped his fingers and chirped a few angry words. The gold circlet went back into the bag, and the silver cross was handed to the leader.

The Byzantine showed the cross to Taahir, who frowned as if he had been shown a dead fish. The leader shoved it at him and again barked a few hard words. Taahir smiled and accepted it with both hands.

One of the Byzantine soldiers grabbed Yngvar's arm and led him away from Taahir to where they stood.

Taahir smiled and waved, speaking what must be the only Norse he knew.

"Far-vel, Wain-zar!"

22

Understanding bolted through Yngvar's mind. He had just been sold to the Byzantines for a silver cross. Taahir admired it, laying it against his palm and angling it to catch the afternoon sun. The Byzantine commander continued his droning discourse, oblivious to Yngvar even though he held a spear.

Yet in his bewilderment, he had allowed the Byzantine guard to lead him by his spear arm. Now that soldier held a sweaty hand over his forearm. Yngvar snapped his head toward him, and the soldier gave him a suffering expression. He also voiced what sounded as a quiet warning.

Rage coiled up through Yngvar's arms, but he did not act. He could achieve nothing as a dead man. More infuriating than anything, he had let his guard down. Long, boring days in the wet heat of this island had bound his mind as firmly as Prince Kalim's manacles had bound his hands. He had grown witless and lazy. Now he paid for it.

In truth, serving the Byzantines might be preferable to Taahir and his lot. Yet the Byzantines would be more organized and less likely to provide him a chance to escape. He could run nowhere on this island, which he knew nothing more of than what he had spied from his post.

He had to go with the Byzantines. Fate had woven this thread into his life. It could not be changed.

Across the beach, the Arabs continued to stare dispassionately. The one fool digging at his nose continued exploring his nostril.

Alasdair stared at Yngvar in confusion.

He's not being sold, Yngvar realized. They think him too small or weak. Taahir sold me off as a spearman to these Byzantines. But all he knows of Alasdair is he can throw a rock.

He had lost all his companions. Thorfast and Bjorn were drowned. All his crew had either died in an Arab prison or else went to the sea bottom. Gyna had disappeared, perhaps escaped but more likely captured into an unknown fate.

Now he was being pulled from Alasdair.

"No," Yngvar said. No one but his guard watched him. The Byzantine clamped his hand over Yngvar's spear and the other reached to take it from him.

"Alasdair goes with me," he shouted at Taahir. He pointed across the beach.

Taahir looked up from his silver cross, brows furrowed.

"Al-Ja-Hair? No far-vel."

Being underestimated, Yngvar was dismissed with this simple statement. Being underestimated, no one noticed the fury engulf Yngvar's head in a burst of red anger.

He shoved his spear into the two guards who sought to wrestle it from him. He used their strength against them, pushing them as they pulled away. Both stumbled back into the surf, and one fell on his rump.

The Byzantine commander was still absorbed in his self-important speech. His dagger sat loose in its sheath that hung from his belt. These Byzantines did not know peace straps.

He jumped forward, snatching the dagger from the leader's hip. He did not even react until Yngvar was gliding past him. Then, he only lurched and shrieked in surprise.

Taahir fumbled with his cross, caught between wanting to secure it and wanting to draw his sword. The instant of hesitation yielded all advantage to Yngvar. He rammed his elbow into Taahir's diaphragm, then slid around his doubled over body. His stolen dagger, a long tapered blade like the one he had taken from the sailor, dug into Taahir's neck. The thick vein pulsed beneath the tip.

"You Byzantines don't know how to secure your weapons," Yngvar said to the bewildered leader. His two guards jumbled over themselves attempting to stand. The other soldiers stood in amazement, only now drawing their blades.

The Arabs began to shout behind him. Yngvar heard footfalls across the sand.

Alasdair arrived beside him.

"Lord, I'm sorry I did not realize sooner."

"Think nothing of it," Yngvar said. Then he poked the knife into Taahir's neck. The chief spluttered protest, his long mustache fluttering like two black flags. But Yngvar wrenched him to silence.

For the moment, neither Arab nor Byzantine moved.

"Alasdair is coming with me," he said to the Byzantine leader. "That silver cross pays for both of us. Get him on your ship first. I'll follow."

Yngvar used his chin to indicate Alasdair and the distant Byzantine ship. Taahir laughed and pawed at that dagger at his neck. He did not struggle to free himself, but stood bent at the waist while the dagger pricked his skin.

The Byzantine leader and Taahir exchanged words, then one of the soldiers took Alasdair by the arm.

"I'm going with you, lord!"

"Excellent," he said. "Don't call me lord again, especially not now."

Alasdair had no time to reply, but was dragged off to the rowboat. Once confident of the exchange, Yngvar released Taahir but kept his dagger level to the Arab's gut.

Taahir fixed his head cover, laughing. He fetched the silver cross he had dropped during the attack. He simply waved Yngvar off as if he no longer mattered. He had eyes only for his prize of silver.

The Byzantine leader snapped something at Yngvar. He stared at the dagger in his hand. For a moment, Yngvar considered sticking it in his own belt. Yet this bastard was thick with pride. He flipped the blade around and offered the hilt to the Byzantine, who received it with a glare. Once he slid it to its sheath, his glare faded to a wan smile.

Then he backhanded Yngvar across the face.

The shattering pain streaked through his cheek, into his eyes, and around his head. The leader wore a heavy silver ring that had gouged his skin. But Yngvar understood he had deserved the strike. Once he cleared his head, he met his new leader's eyes with as much dignity as he could summon through the pain.

The leader nodded for him to join Alasdair in the boat.

"That sounded painful," he said.

"It was. Well, we're slaves again, it would seem."

"No, lor—I mean, if we were to be slaves, Taahir wouldn't have fed us and rested us as he did. He intended to sell you as a warrior from the day he accepted us. He wanted us rested and healthy to ensure the Byzantines would be interested."

"We are still slaves," Yngvar said. "Silver was exchanged for us. I doubt he bought our freedom."

The Byzantine commander remained ashore, but six men took Yngvar and Alasdair to the main ship. Of course, they were ordered to row while the Byzantine's folded their arms and frowned at them through the shadows thrown from their pompous helmets.

Once beside the giant Byzantine ship, he was made to scale a rope ladder and gain the deck. He expected rougher treatment from his new masters, but the guards merely herded him away from the rails. Together with Alasdair, they joined crewmen who offloaded cargo stacked on the deck. They were positioned by the rails to lower crates into the rowboat. None of them were heavy. One open box contained sheaves of arrows fletched with white feathers.

"So they supply Taahir's band," Yngvar said. "They must be in the Byzantine's pay to harry the Arabs. That means we are not far from where our slave ship went down."

Alasdair nodded. "Do you think the others survived? I think Bjorn might've been struck by the ram when it breached the hull. Even he could not survive that."

"It is my hope," Yngvar said as he worked with Alasdair to lift a long and narrow crate over the side. The soldier below snapped impatiently while they lowered it via ropes. "But it is not my belief. I only wonder at my ship, and Gyna's fate. I have little hope for her, though."

"She is more cunning than you think, lord."

"Don't call me lord." Yngvar let the rope slide from his hands to deliver the crate to the soldiers in the rowboat. "We are made equal in our slavery. And worse, if these Byzantines think I am above my station, it could create trouble. I don't need that while I'm trying to plan how we'll get home."

"Do you really think we'll get home?"

Yngvar considered this while accepting another long crate from the crewmen who formed a line back to the pile of goods.

"We will get home," he said at last. "But I see no easy road back. Nor do I see a swift one. I have no other goal while I live. You and I will return to the north, so that the stories of our companions can be told and remembered. It is my duty to see this done."

"It is a noble answer," Alasdair said. "Perhaps God will favor this purpose."

"As I've often said, any god who listens is worth praying to. So pray to your god and I will pray to mine. We will find a way through this."

The Byzantines delivered their goods, and Yngvar and Alasdair found themselves questioned by several men speaking different languages. Norse had not traveled so far south, it seemed, for none recognized his speech. Frankish at least seemed to spark recognition, but no one spoke it.

When the Byzantine leader, the captain of this ship, returned, his crew also brought their treasure chest. Yngvar watched it pass beneath decks, where he eventually expected to be sent. Yet they were soon under sail again, and Yngvar and Alasdair were ignored. A boy with dark skin and sad eyes offered them wood cups of water. Otherwise, they passed their voyage as guests rather than slaves.

"The beat of that drum will forever bring me unease," Yngvar said, sitting by the rails as he listened to the rowers' drum beneath the deck.

"It would seem they have other plans for us," Alasdair said. "But I wonder if our fate will be kinder or worse. There are stories of the old people, how they made sport of human life. Christian saints were fed to lions. Perhaps that is what they spare us for? To fight in an arena or feed some ferocious beast."

"I'd like to see a lion," Yngvar said. "If they feed me to one, then I shall teach it not all its food dies without giving pain with equal measure."

"You believe you could fight a lion?"

"Where there are lion fangs, lion eyes must be near. I will tear them out before I am slain."

The day-long journey revealed nothing of the Byzantine's plans. Yngvar passed the idle times describing increasingly absurd ways he could slay a lion with his bare hands before a horrified crowd. By the time they grew bored with the fantasy, he imagined himself hurling lightning bolts handed to him by Thor, not only slaying lions but destroying the Byzantine's city and every enemy between them and home. Alasdair laughed.

It was the first true laughter they had shared in long memory. Yngvar's chest warmed to it.

Their ship anchored in a harbor of a long, dark shore. Night shrouded most of this coast, but it was typically rugged and dotted with trees. The same oppressive heat smothered this coast, relieved only by a light wind that rippled and cracked in the above. In the darkness, the outline of a great walled city spread out into the dark. It crawled up a hillside with lazy, snaking walls thrown around it. Each building seemed to be toppling onto the building beneath it.

A square fortress stood above all at the heart of this city. It was well lit with torches along its roofs and walls. Yngvar recognized the roof-top defenses as those iron-bolt throwers. Their crews leaned on their weapons, staring indifferently at their ship preparing to disembark its crew.

"Enemies must never dare scale these walls," Yngvar said as he and Alasdair waited for direction. "Everywhere it seems their defense is built to sink ships rather than repulse ladders."

"It is a sea-side fortress, lor—" Alasdair rubbed his face. "It only makes sense to defend from the sea."

"What fool army would try to attack directly from their ships? Men should line up in a shield wall and let Fate sort them into the living and dead."

"I don't think they fight that way here."

They loaded onto the last rowboat, just when Yngvar guessed they might never be made to enter the city. But their guards fetched them, this time with more care. These men were not friends, nor were they enemies. They simply performed their tasks. One even attempted a few words of smiling conversation, but his peers taunted him into silence. Yngvar did not understand, but inclined his head in gratitude.

This fortress town was unlike Licata in every way. The docks were ordered and guarded. Their walls were full of vigilant men who had crossbows carefully trained on them as they approached. A password was demanded by the guards at the gate leading into the city, even when other groups had passed already. To Yngvar's surprise, his companions—for they did not crowd him like guards; they were more like acquaintances guiding them through a new town—answered before proceeding.

They were led through dark but ordered streets. The townsfolk were abed and only a curious few came to their doors to watch the crew pass. The city lacked the beauty and culture of the Arabs, but it emanated cold order and law. Yngvar would welcome that over the duplicity and arrogance of Prince Kalim's lot.

At last they were shown to a barracks and pointed at bunk beds where ratty, gray blankets awaited them. Wood slats were the mattress.

"After a prison cell, this is as good as a jarl's bed." Yngvar slipped into the lower bunk, and Alasdair climbed to the top one. Lice crawled in the blanket, but Yngvar accepted this without care. So many bodies in one place guaranteed lice and rats. He would endure the itches and bites in trade for his own bed no matter how pathetic.

Sleep overtook him before he could count how many others shared this room with him. From the snoring and body heat alone, he guessed at least a score of others. His dreams were filled with ocean waves and cold winds. This minor gesture of a bed and house to sleep in had filled him with hope. So his dreams took him to his homeland, which now seemed impossibly distant. He might yet walk there again.

He awoke to shouts and someone pulling his foot. A Byzantine man dressed only in plain white robes shouted at him. His face was clean-shaven and wide-jawed. His expression was stern and impatient, but not threatening.

"Lord, I have never slept so well." Alasdair dropped from his bunk onto the wooden floor. He vigorously scratched both hands through the dark red stubble on his scalp.

"Today we learn if we will fight lions or something worse," Yngvar said. Their companions were already about strapping belts around their waists or else staring into polished plates to comb their hair and beards.

His wonder at the others was jerked aside by their guide's snapping command. He rattled on in his language, which sounded much softer and flowing than the Arab's. It was still unintelligible. Yet he guessed enough to follow the man.

They were led out of the barracks house into a courtyard of pounded earth. Men drilled there, some lined up in ranks before a leader, others practicing swordplay with wooden swords. Clanging came from a forge out of sight. It was the familiar hum of a fortress, and even this far south the cadence of life here was the same as the north.

They passed into the main building which was dark and smelled of onions. Curious faces of different shapes and skin colors regarded them as they passed through narrow stone corridors. This was nothing so grand as Prince Kalim's palace. If anything, Yngvar drew comfort from the precision and simplicity of the design. This was a defensive structure, meant to ward off enemies and prevent them from running straight through this building.

Upstairs, their guide led them into a large room where double doors bound in iron hung open. Inside, a tall but thin man dressed in white robes edged with colorful stripes stood with his arms folded behind his back. He stood over a table where a large cloth had been spread out. Two other men, both dressed in mail and their helmets placed on the desk to hold down the cloth, stood with him. All had eagle-like bearings, as if they could swoop down on Yngvar and carry him to their mountain aeries. All three paused in their conversation as Yngvar and Alasdair stood inside the door.

Their guide put his fist to his chest, standing straight and proud. The tall man nodded and their guide began to speak at length. Throughout, all three men glanced to Yngvar and Alasdair. Their guide gestured to them a half-dozen times, until the thin man closed his eyes and nodded as if agreeing to something.

He snapped his fingers. Servants who had remained unseen in the corners stepped out of the shadows. Yngvar had to control his impulse to jump. He had been so intent on trying to decipher the exchange that he had missed even the most basic details of this room. Alasdair, however, seemed to have known of the servants' presence. He did not stir when they emerged.

A young girl, perhaps no more than sixteen, trotted up to the tall man. He was the obvious commander, and even without understanding a word, his speech was full of authority. The girl wore a plain blue-gray dress. Her hair was full and golden, held in a long braid that stretched to the small of her back. Her round head bobbed as she periodically acknowledged the commander's words.

When he finished, the girl approached Yngvar and Alasdair.

"You are Yngvar?" she asked.

His speech failed, for he had not seen such beauty in all his wide travels. Her heart-shaped face was clear and bright. Her eyes were cloudy blue and wet. Her voice was more pleasing than the chime of silver.

"She speaks Norse!" Alasdair clapped his hands together. "God is with us!"

The girl's brief smile plumped her round cheeks. Yngvar adored the curve of her neck as she tilted her head to Alasdair.

"And who are you?"

"Alasdair, my lady. Are you the commander's wife?"

Such laughter! Her delicate hand covered her mouth. Traces of blue veins showed beneath flawless skin.

"I am his slave. Would the commander's wife dress in sackcloth?"

"Ah, well, your bearing is like a noblewoman," Alasdair said. Again the girl covered her mouth and laughed.

Yngvar blinked, realizing he had not answered to his own name. Heat spread across his cheeks. The girl's smile faded, but left a golden glow surrounding her.

"I am Valgerd Grettirdottir," she said. "I am from Trondheim, though I sailed with my father to Frankia. And after the gods had mocked him and his fortunes, I was sold as a slave maybe seven years ago. Now I am here. I will teach you to speak Greek, so that you may serve your purpose."

Yngvar still had no words. He had not thought to set eyes upon such a beauty.

Alasdair gave him a sidelong glance. "What is this purpose, my lady?"

Valgerd giggled again. "You are too polite, Alasdair. But surely you must realize why you have been purchased?"

She stared between them, and her smile vanished. Her hesitation roused Yngvar from his infatuation. Now he focused intently on her light brows stitching together.

"But it is obvious. You are to fight and die for our Emperor Constantine the Seventh. You are slave-warriors."

23

Yngvar stood at attention in the parade ground. Alasdair stood beside him. Three dozen other slave-warriors clustered around him. The sky remained dark after the prior night's rain. The ground was cold and muddy with puddles reflecting the gray clouds. Birds sang their morning songs perched on the walls or the square fortress roofs. Yngvar glanced at their black forms winging free from tower to wall and then to freedom.

He had not left the fortress in more than a month. He knew his barracks, the parade ground where he practiced fighting, and the latrine.

The commander, Ambrosius Staurakius, stood before his hundred regular troops. As a slave, Yngvar and the rest were relegated to the rear of the ordered ranks. The regular Byzantines were dressed in their armor and stood like stones before Commander Staurakius. Each had a heavy spear and shield, as well as short sword.

Yngvar had a plain spear, a round wood shield, and dagger. The shield could barely hide a man's crotch, and Yngvar doubted he would ever use it in combat. But his leader demanded it of all the slaves. They were to have some basic protection when the Byzantines fed them to the enemy.

"Valgerd is a skilled teacher, isn't she?" Alasdair said in a low whisper. "A month ago I could not speak Commander Staurakius's name let alone understand some of this."

"What do you understand?" Yngvar asked in an equally low voice. "You spend all your time staring into Valgerd's eyes."

A rod struck bright pain across Yngvar's shoulder. His leader, who had a title Yngvar could never remember, hissed at him to pay attention. One day he would plunge that rod into that toad's gullet and strike off his head. For now, he straightened his back and strained to hear Staurakius speaking from the front of his troops.

He could not understand everything. Valgerd's teachings had centered on the basics of what he must know to follow commands. Yet he had discovered a facility with languages he had not expected. He learned faster than Alasdair, and discovered he enjoyed acquiring knowledge. His fascination with Valgerd's beauty had faded and he was more interested in what she could teach him. Conversely, Alasdair seemed to grow fonder of her each day. For her part, she welcomed them as Norse kin but had other duties that kept her distant.

So Yngvar had wheedled more from his fellow slaves, who were not all Byzantine but spoke Greek to varying degrees. Some were even Arabs, though they did not look as the ones he had encountered thus far. All of them were equal in slavery, but yet they did not all find camaraderie in their plight. Some had been fighting against other Byzantines and had survived these battles. These veterans expected their lives would be spent easily and counted every sunrise a gift they might not receive the next day.

Yet why would the commander invest time into teaching him and Alasdair Greek? This meant he intended to gain a reward for his efforts. No language skills were needed to shove a slave onto enemy spears.

As Commander Staurakius carried on about whatever had excited him to gather all his men, Yngvar stared off to the sides while pretending to listen. He thought it odd that carts and ponies were being assembled and bags and crates were prepared for loading. Civilians had arrived as well, apparently to aid in some undertaking.

Perhaps he should listen more carefully.

"This is a great posting for all of us," he said. "Pozzallo is right atop the Arabs. Prince Kalim has earned his punishment!"

The regular troops raised fists and shouted.

Yngvar's mouth opened and he turned to Alasdair.

"Lord, it sounded like he said Prince Kalim?"

"He did." Yngvar was breathless with excitement. The assembly, the carts, the long speech. They were being sent to Pozzallo from wherever they were now. And to give punishment to Prince Kalim!

Yngvar raised his spear and shouted along with the regular soldiers. He was the only one among the slaves to exhibit any excitement. His leader bounced his rod on his palm, narrowing his eyes but not discouraging the excitement.

He could not suppress his joy, and his words flowed out in Norse. "I claim Prince Kalim's head for my own! I will burn his palace to ash. I will find the bones of Saleet and Jamil and pound them to dust. I will ravage his whores and hang their corpses on trees. I will be avenged!"

His outburst drew laughter from the other slaves. None would understand him, but the joy of vengeance filled him. Only Alasdair looked on, astonished.

"Is it true, lord? We will fight Prince Kalim?"

"Look about you," he said. "We are preparing for a voyage. I heard the name spoken. The commander goes to punish the Arabs."

Alasdair lowered his eyes and nodded.

"And I know you cannot get it in your mind, but you must not call me lord. I am a slave as well as you."

The commander continued to speak once the rally cries had ended. He gave more orders and it sounded as if another force would occupy this fort and while they reinforced Pozzallo. The details of why they had to go remained unclear. But he had no doubt of their orders.

Leaders walked their ranks and shouted orders. The tall and royal figure of Commander Ambrosius Staurakius turned with his retinue of guards and attendants and vanished into the main fortress.

Yngvar's leader slashed his rod through the air for attention.

"Get whatever shit you've collected besides lice and form up by the gate. We're sailing before noon."

The slave-warriors broke up and drifted either toward the gate or their barracks. Yngvar owned nothing but what was on his back. Alasdair had been granted a small wooden cross by Valgerd, which he hid in his bed. He dared not risk it being swiped away by their leader, who rejoiced at every opportunity to humiliate and hurt his men.

"Ah, to be on the sea again," Yngvar said. "And to be headed into battle against my enemy! The gods love us."

Alasdair nodded, and his melancholy at last penetrated into Yngvar's awareness. He softened his stance and pulled Alasdair aside by the shoulder.

"Valgerd? She is a beauty. I had almost fallen for her the moment we met. Yet the gods protect me from the foolishness of love. Not so with you, eh?"

Alasdair sighed. "I have enjoyed being with her. But it is best I forget this feeling. It seems sinful to find even such small happiness when my friends have suffered and died only a month ago."

"She is the commander's slave. She will go with us. And as for sin, neither Thorfast nor Bjorn would deny you happiness even if you were to find it on the day of their deaths. So do not fret over this. But I would say, you endanger us if you toy with the commander's property."

"I will correct myself, lor—"

Yngvar smiled. "Call me lord if it is your wish. I cannot train it from you, anyway. But now think on what this means beyond revenge. Do you see it?"

Alasdair frowned. They both walked toward the gates where the other slaves assembled.

"It means a chance for escape," Yngvar said. "I know these Byzantines fight as ordered ranks, but our lot is to rush ahead and kill what we can before falling back. Every battle will be a chance to run."

"I think they will expect it, lord."

"Of course they will. But they will not expect a Norseman, will they? We will slay whoever blocks our path. The best of these Byzantines cannot stand against us. And we will pick up real weapons and shields from the fallen. Let them chase us, and they will yield ground to the enemy."

"It seems risky."

"Were you expecting an invitation to escape? If you want to tarry with Valgerd, then by all means let these Byzantines use you until a lucky enemy spear takes your life. But I intend to be away from here as swiftly as I can."

Alasdair's ears reddened and he looked away.

"I am sorry for that. Of course you would never act so recklessly. Now, go collect your cross and be ready to sail to our fate."

They journeyed a slow day at sea. The wind was never in their favor and the slaves rowed through the night until Pozzallo emerged on the coastline with the morning light. They had been on the mainland, it seemed.

"So we made it to Langbardaland after all," Yngvar said once he realized where they had sailed from. "Not quite what we planned, was it?"

The fortress at Pozzallo was as he remembered, though in comparison to what he had left behind it now seemed much smaller. He admitted the walls here were higher. Four ships remained at anchor and the arrival of their ship reset the Byzantines to their strength before Yngvar's raid.

"Will they recognize us?" Alasdair asked as they were herded through the front gates with the new troops.

"Among all of these men?" Yngvar shook his head. "Besides, we are bald now. We are safe here. Look, there is fresh wood on the ramparts we destroyed. All the danger we endured, it was for nothing."

"Yet you are not saddened, lord?"

"I am alive, which is greater than any treasure I might have earned that night. While I live, I can still bring honor to the memories of our friends. I can aid the families of the crewmen who died because of my foolishness. It will be scant help, but even if I carry a splinter of gold back, I will share my wealth. Best of all, I can soak myself in bloody vengeance. After that, I can go on to Valhalla and be satisfied."

True to Yngvar's predictions, they remained unrecognized. He and Alasdair were faces of throw-away soldiers. The real fighting men would walk across their backs to engage the Arabs. As such, they were given lodging in an old barn that was still musky with animal spoor and rotten hay.

"We bought our own lice," Yngvar said, as he fixed his cloak into a bed. The other slaves staked out positions close to their own friends. No one owned much more than their war gear, though the veterans owned combs and polished metal plates to admire their pox-scarred faces.

"I did not see Valgerd," Alasdair said. He would have said more, but turned aside.

"Well, we didn't see the commander either. We're shit on his heel, remember? Now that we can point our spears where we're told, I doubt Valgerd will continue to teach us."

"Lord, if we escape, well, she is a slave too. Is there a way to gain her freedom as well?"

"Certainly, give her a spear and have her march with us. We can all run together." He put his hand on Alasdair's shoulder. "Look, it's hard enough to get the both of us free at the same time. I can't imagine how we'd take her from under the commander's nose."

"Of course," Alasdair said, fixing his own cloak into a bed. "But if there is a way, I want to try."

After settling into their new lodging, their leader appeared in the door. He staggered back and wrinkled his nose.

Yngvar had not learned much Greek, but he knew swearing when he heard it. At last, the leader waved in another man with a sack. The slaves all seemed to understand a procedure was taking place. They formed a line before the leader.

"You two," the leader said, noticing he and Alasdair stared after the others. "Form a line for your pay, unless you're giving it to me."

"Pay?" Yngvar was not certain he understood the word. Still not wanting to miss any advantage, he stood in line with the rest. By the time he got to the front, his leader was fishing through the bag his assistant held out.

"There's still something in here for you two," he said. "Here's your month's pay."

He pulled out six silver bits and counted three each into their palms.

"We are slaves?" Yngvar stared at the bits as if he had been awarded a kingdom.

"Fighting slaves," the leader said. "You should be paid something so you don't point those spears at me. Keep saving these bits. Kill some Arabs and collect more pay. If you're good, you can buy yourself freedom. But you're ours forever, Norseman."

Yngvar nodded, clasping his fist over the silver. The leader smiled and drew closer.

"You're eager to fight. That's good. You will fight soon enough. We will watch you, though. If you take a step that does not go straight to the enemy, I'll put a javelin through your back."

"I hate Kalim," Yngvar said in his rudimentary Greek. Hate was one of the first words he had learned. He had no interest in learning words for peace or love.

The leader nodded with a smile, then left them to settle their quarters. The slave-warriors were not expected to survive, at least not in large numbers. Therefore, Yngvar surmised, they were shoved into barns until their number whittled down enough to join the main barracks.

The days passed with extensive drills for the regular troops. Yngvar and his fellows were to run at a mad charge and pray for survival. No training was needed for suicide tactics. He passed his time honing his Greek. The language skill would be needed once he escaped.

Alasdair spent less time with him and more time trying to discover Valgerd's whereabouts. He managed to pass himself off as the commander's household slave and reported back on the third day with breathless excitement.

"Lord, she is here!"

The barracks was a hum of activity as bored men rolled dice or argued among themselves. Yngvar had just finished tiring out a Byzantine named Lucas, quizzing him on words and pronunciation.

Now he sat at the edge of his bed staring at Alasdair's flushed cheeks.

"And how is the fair maiden?"

"Lord, she told me that we will go to battle tomorrow. Prince Kalim has been baiting this fortress for weeks, burning surrounding farms and threatening ships."

"That is welcomed news," Yngvar said. "Did she tell you anything more?"

"We had scant time together, lord." Alasdair's ears reddened and his eyes glanced aside.

"Scant time? Tell me, did you fuck on the commander's bed? Such a waste of a good plan. You could've stolen something of use besides Valgerd's honor."

"Lord!" Alasdair clasped his hands over his chest. "There was no time for that, I swear it. My ruse could not last long. It's only because the commander is new here that I could bluff my way into his rooms. My heart throbbed in my throat the whole time."

"Ah, but that was not all that throbbed, I'm sure." Yngvar laughed at his own jest. He was not given to such foolishness, but the desperation of his lot begged for relief. Besides, he enjoyed watching Alasdair's flustered protests.

"Please, lord, I made best use of the time. Valgerd showed me the cloth Commander Staurakius was studying. It's a map and he placed wood markers to show where Kalim's men were last seen and where he planned to strike. We will be just north of this shore. Remember the fishing boats left there when we raided this place?"

Yngvar sat up straight. "We could reach those ships if we could get away. We'd have to contend with the Byzantine warships at anchor, but would they even be concerned with a fisherman's boat?"

"Well, the fishermen might still be at sea if the battle is early enough. But we can hide until they do come to shore."

Yngvar nodded, then cocked his eye at Alasdair. "And what of Valgerd in this plan?"

Alasdair lowered his head. "She does not wish to escape. She will aid us and keep our secret. But the commander treats her well, better than many other masters."

"Of course," Yngvar said, scratching at the short whiskers of his regrown beard. "Her life could actually be more miserable in freedom. Throwing in with us is no sure success. If we are recaptured again it could be Arabs this time. I hate to think of what happens to women in their clutches."

"I don't think the Byzantines are better," Alasdair said, still staring at the floor. "It is Commander Staurakius that she is devoted to."

"Well," Yngvar said, slapping the frame of his bed. "We've too many of our own worries to think more of her. Though, I do wish she could've taught me more Greek. So you made your farewell?"

"I did," he said, his voice far away. "Though not as well I had would have liked."

They sat in companionable silence while a group behind them shouted over some gambler's improbable luck. Then Alasdair shook his head and patted his shirt.

"Oh, I did find something of use to us, lord."

He pulled up his shirt to reveal the hilts to two long daggers hidden under his rope belt and tucked into his pants. Yngvar sucked his breath.

"These are better than the javelins we'll get," Alasdair said as he drew his shirt back down. "I will share one with you when the others are asleep. We'll have real protection. They're fine blades, right from the commander's chamber."

Yngvar rubbed his hands together. "Excellent, though what if he notices they are gone?"

"He won't, lord. I had stolen some poor daggers from other guards. I replaced the commander's weapons with these. The hilts are mostly the same, though the iron and edges are far different."

They slept that night, no one knowing of the battle to come the next day besides Yngvar and Alasdair. When Yngvar awakened to shouts in the predawn darkness, a hard iron blade was carefully tucked into his rope belt and hidden under his pants.

The leader banged his iron shield with a sword.

"Get up, you dogs! Today we kill Arabs!"

24

The air smelled of rain, though none fell. Yngvar marched with Alasdair on his right and the Byzantine Lucas on his left. The rest of his slave companions were spread out in a rough group that maintained a brisk pace across the rolling grass fields. Pockets of sunlight dappled the green expanse.

The land was beautiful in the morning light. With battle just over the next rise, Yngvar's heart beat with anticipation. It sharpened the landscape, since it might be his last sight of the world. The horizon was all lush hills that led to blue mountains obscured with haze. The fortress and shore lay behind him. Turning to glance at this new angle of the fortress, he admired its functional strength. It was a square peg brooding over the sea, daring the foolish to climb its walls. He had been so foolish once.

Today he would draw upon the same recklessness.

Commander Staurakius rode at the head of his column. He led close to two hundred men, nearly the entire fortress. The slaves were sandwiched between the armored warriors. Yngvar admitted these Byzantines were awesome to see on the march. They were disciplined, crisp, and mighty. Having stepped out from their walls, they now displayed their true strength.

"I would not be surprised if this is a ploy to siege the fortress while we are all gone," Yngvar said. "It would be bad for Staurakius, but such chaos would guarantee our escape."

Alasdair shuddered and said nothing. Of course, he must worry for Valgerd. Yngvar counted it a good thing they were leaving her behind. He needed Alasdair's attention focused, and he seemed to only be thinking of his beloved slave-girl.

"So remember our plan?"

"I do, lord. After we throw our javelins, we fall back with the rest. But then we return to battle when the lines close. We fight into the ranks and lose ourselves. Then we will slip south to the shore."

"Good. It is a fool's plan, to be sure. But running back to our own lines means we will only be made slaves once more. If this plan fails, at least we die as warriors. Besides, if Prince Kalim is there, then I'll enjoy carving his neck before we flee."

The Byzantine Lucas grunted next to him. "What are you two saying?"

"We were talking about killing Arabs. Do you hate Arabs?"

Lucas nodded. "I do now. I hate whatever I'm told to hate. Stay with me. You will live."

"Teach me all your secrets," Yngvar said.

"Lord, you have learned so much so fast." Alasdair scratched his chin. Despite the time that had passed, not much more than red stubble showed.

They were called to a halt just behind the ridge. The commander's scouts scurried back with their reports and all the leaders gathered. His own unit's leader, however, stood leaning on his spear and peering sour-faced over his slaves.

"I hate not being in on the plans," Yngvar said. "They're probably overthinking everything."

"That was always your struggle, lord."

Yngvar tucked his chin down and frowned. "How so? I always won, didn't I?"

The discussion seemed overlong to Yngvar. By now what advantage could they gain in surprise? Yet after what felt an hour's time, units were summoned and ranks formed.

"Gods, do they have a ceremony for surprise attacks?" Yngvar gathered his javelins and small wood shield. He checked the dagger hidden at his side. He would exchange this blade for a real sword, and then both Arab and Byzantine would fear him.

"Get up the ridge," the slave-leader yelled. "When I say run, run. Then throw your javelins and get back here to let better men do the real work. You've got three javelins each. Save one in case you get in a fight. Or throw it if you think you can stick another enemy. A full dirham for each man who kills with all three of his javelins. I've got to see it, though. I'm watching all you bastards. So do well."

"Seems more likely a we'd die long before we collected enough silver to buy our freedom," Yngvar muttered as he arranged his javelins.

"I believe that's their intent, lord."

"We've got weapons and enemies to kill. Let's get to this ridge and see what Prince Kalim is about."

He lined up with the other slaves, and at the bottom of this rise Prince Kalim's men were lined up in ranks of sparkling chain armor and billowing pants. Their spearheads glinted in the spotty light. Yngvar estimated more than a hundred warriors.

"It's a trap," he said. "Does the commander realize this? That's not an army that terrorizes the countryside. That's bait. They're not just sitting down there for the slaughter."

"Perhaps he knows this, but does not care." Alasdair sniffed and readied his first javelin. "I say it matters nothing to us, lord."

Opponents shouted threats across the distance. Yngvar snorted in disdain, for both sides were too far apart to be understood. These cowards dared nothing. He scratched his head while watching both sides draw nearer.

"Yielding the high ground is stupid," Yngvar said. "They can't possibly order us down."

"Run!" The cry of their leader was clear and strong. "Run! Kill those Arabs!"

The slaves raised their javelins and roared a battle cry.

"Now I know why the old people vanished," Yngvar said. "This is madness."

He smiled at Alasdair who returned the same knowing grin. They raised their javelins and joined the charging slaves.

The slope carried them fast. Yngvar felt each stride as if he flew across the earth. The slaves formed a long skirmish line so no man linked to another. This open formation made sense, but it led Yngvar to feel as if he were charging an Arab army on his own.

The Arabs sensibly pulled up their large, brightly painted shields. They were round, like a Norseman's. Yngvar wished for one of those rather than the tiny buckler in his hand.

He and Alasdair skidded to a halt farther away than the rest of the slaves. To draw too close now was an invitation to death. The less experienced, who did not trust their throw, nearly ran atop the Arab line.

Yngvar let his javelin sail. He aimed well, but in the end every cast was guided by the Fates. He did not pause to see if he struck anyone. He was not interested in dirhams to fill his deflated purse. Together with Alasdair, they retreated out of the expected counter-volley.

A few who had charged too close were taken out by Arabs who broke rank to seize the opportunity. The skirmishers were speared and dragged to the ground, where others chopped into them with their curving swords. Their screams mixed with the few Arabs that Fate had claimed.

Yngvar spun back to see a thin volley of javelins flying toward him. These were launched from the rear of the Arab line, tossed blindly in high arcs in hopes of catching skirmishers who had tarried in the kill zone. They wobbled and hissed like white vipers, slanting down into the ground. Yngvar remained out of their reach, but two other skirmishers were caught in the back and fell.

The Arabs howled with laughter, taunting a second volley.

"Let's give it to them," Yngvar said. He began running back, past others who were still falling back.

Lucas the Byzantine watched him running. "Too soon!"

"How fast can they throw?" Yngvar shouted, realizing he was speaking Norse.

Yet he found himself standing with Alasdair and a dozen more of the inexperienced slaves.

The answer to his own question came as the second volley of enemy javelins wailed overhead.

Instinctively he drew his buckler across his body, only to realize this was not his accustomed round shield. All but his chest remained exposed.

White wood shafts slammed into the grass around him like killing sleet. Alasdair batted one aside with his buckler. Yngvar froze in place. The shafts had missed him and left the grass clear around him like a shadow in a field of spent javelins.

He barked a laugh, sharing a stunned glance with Alasdair who was likewise unhurt. Of the dozen other fools who had charged with him, half were on their backs in the grass with white javelins shaking in their torsos.

The rest of the skirmishers were charging for their second pass. Behind them, Commander Staurakius had raised his black and gold standard and began marching his men down the slope. Yngvar had no time for details, but it seemed Staurakius had dispatched his archers to set a line and goad the stubborn Arabs. The skirmishers had screened this maneuver.

"Throw your javelin," Yngvar shouted to Alasdair. "But the battle starts here. The Arab's will charge and spring their trap."

He let his javelin rip across the gap to lodge in an Arab's thigh. He retreated, drawing his long dagger. He had not yet seen the weapon. Alasdair had done well to steal it. The long, tapered dagger gleamed with fresh oil. The edges were honed to frosty white and the point could pluck a fly's heart.

The Arabs weathered the hail of javelins and the skirmishers fled. With arrows arrayed against them, they charged behind their dazzlingly colored shields.

"There's going to be a flanking force," Yngvar shouted to Alasdair over the shouting. "That is where Prince Kalim will be."

"If he fights," Alasdair shouted back.

Unlike the other skirmishers, he and Alasdair raised their daggers and bucklers and screamed their own war cry.

The battle fury was on him now. Every Arab that had crossed him, every enemy that had shamed or injured him, every Byzantine that had brought ruin to his kin and crew—were all assembled in the line charging him. He would warm his face with enemy blood. Taste the copper of it and feel the spray of it. Their dying screams would fill his ears as a sacred song.

He thundered across the gap, unencumbered with only plain cloth weighing on his shoulders. His bare-foot stride carried him in three great bounds.

The first Arab raised his shield to block his charge.

Yngvar leapt atop of it, driving the Arab back. Like a wildcat, he launched himself overhead.

He hovered over the press of dark faces and gleaming iron. It was as if the gods suspended him before his enemies so that they might all witness the vicious hand of their doom. Yngvar screamed.

He landed feet first on the man behind the front rank. Despite his heavy mail and shield, the crushing force of a body slamming into his chest drove the Arab onto his back. Bone cracked and blood burst from the victim's open mouth.

Yngvar stumbled forward, landing on the shields of the third rank, which had not expected battle so soon. He folded himself onto the shield and stabbed down with his dagger. The point of it slashed out the eyes of his shocked enemy.

He rode the Arab down to the ground. For Yngvar, time stretched on such that he could count the bloody teeth of his victims. Yet to his enemies his pounce would seem like a blink. Their charge continued, but now they stumbled upon the unexpected lump of dead in their midst. Men tried to avoid the tangle, jostling their brothers and distrusting the charge.

Yngvar stood, dagger slick with blood. His small buckler was nothing against swords, but in this knot of enemies it was another weapon. He bashed the next Arab in the face and stabbed him through his ribs. The chain shirt was nothing against such a pointed and sharp blade.

Yet it stuck and the enemy fell aside, taking the weapon with it.

He cursed, realizing too late that he should have only slashed and never stabbed for this reason.

The thrum of bows pounded behind him and Arabs screamed to

their mysterious god. The Byzantine archers had loosed their shafts and now Yngvar was no longer amid the Arabs. He was again in the front rank.

The Arabs broke around him, realizing he was no threat if avoided. Their true enemy lay ahead as the archers let loose a second volley.

He flopped to the ground astride the men he had already killed. Byzantine arrows raked the charging Arabs and more fell screaming.

Then the distant horn sounded.

"The trap," Yngvar said to himself. Legs in billowing pants of every color flowed past him as the heavily armored Arabs plowed toward the waiting Byzantines. They shouted with joy at the sounding horn.

He grabbed a shield and propped himself up with it.

A thin Arab with a beard that flowed to his chest ran at him with a javelin. He was the last straggler behind this charge, likely one of the Arab's skirmishers. He held the javelin like a spear.

Yngvar braced with his shield as if to absorb the charge.

Then he stepped aside to let the Arab fly past him. He followed behind, swinging the heavy shield with two hands. He slammed it over the enemy's head, bending his neck with a crack. The skirmisher fell and curled in the grass.

He seized the moment to assess the development. The Arabs had charged through him and now blundered up slope to face Staurakius's heavy troops. To the north the prince had brought his main block of troops to strike the Byzantines in the flank. The commander seemed to have anticipated this, for he had another block of his own men marching to engage the Arabs on their flank. It was a mess that would soon clear once one side decided they could not prevail.

"Alasdair!" he called out over the carpet of dead bodies. A dozen or more Arabs lay in bloody ruin, some pawing at the arrow shafts buried in their flesh.

His small companion emerged from a body pile, struggling to slough the corpses that had covered him. Once extracted, he dashed to Yngvar's side.

"You were glorious to see, lord!" Alasdair's own dagger remained unbloodied. "When the Byzantines shot their arrows, I thought it best I hide until the threat was done."

"Let's flee," he said. "The commander is busy with the main foe."

They both turned south and their shoulders slumped in unison.

Their skirmisher companions were reformed and being led to the rear of the Arab's block. This took them directly into Yngvar's planned route.

"We can't rejoin them. They're herding us into the main battle." Yngvar had only a moment to decide what to do. He shouldered the shield and looked to the fallen. "Fetch me that sword. We will hack through the main block and out the other side. Fate grant that Prince Kalim be there and I will take his head with us."

Alasdair pulled a long, curving sword from beneath a dead Arab. Yngvar accepted the hilt. It was heavy and unwieldy in his hand. He had learned the word *saif* to describe these blades.

"At least grab yourself a shield," he said. "And prepare to get blood on your clean face."

Yngvar jogged behind the battle line with Alasdair beside him. Conserving strength for the battle and subsequent escape was paramount. The crash and thunder of battle washed down the slope to flow over him like a tide of suffering. Iron clanged, wooden shields battered each other, the wounded shrieked, and the dying moaned. Orders were shouted along with death curses. The Byzantines gleamed in their proud helmets and ordered ranks. The Arabs emanated hot fury as they hacked into their foes.

"It's butchery," Yngvar said. "But there's the heart of battle. If the prince is here, he will be protected by his best men. Go to Staurakius's standard. He will fight against the best of the Arabs."

"Lord, should we not cling to the edge of battle?"

"Let no man say Yngvar Hakonsson slinks around the edge of a battle! Besides, when this mess breaks, it will be from the heart of the fight. We can more easily flee under such confusion. Now follow!"

The Arabs pressing up the slope spared only a glance to Yngvar at their rear. They knew the Byzantines were hemmed and unable to lap their troops. So when they saw two Arab shields rushing toward them, no man turned to face them.

He pulled back the first man he could seize. When he fell on his back, Yngvar stabbed him in the throat. Stepping over the next body, he did the same. He had shoved into a gap, shoulder to shoulder with Arabs that did not recognize his threat.

"Alasdair, up here with your dagger. Clear these scum away."

His Norse drew looks from the man aside him. Yet before he could call a warning, his eyes rolled back and Alasdair drew him aside.

"Fools are all trying to reach the front," he said only loud enough for Alasdair to hear. "Your short blade will clear the path."

"There must be four more ranks, lord!"

"Kill as many as you can. This sword is worthless in this press."

Arabs cursed and shouted alongside him. Their companions howled and crumbled as Alasdair punched his dagger through their backs. Not until he had nearly pushed to the first rank did anyone realize these fallen were not from spears from the front.

A dark hand grabbed Yngvar's arm and shouted. He raised his curved sword overhead and slammed it down on the arm of the man hindering him.

"Byzantium!" he cried. He could now see Staurakius's men and their heavy spears slamming into men who swarmed them. He did not want to be mistaken for an enemy.

The Arabs did not fight in a shield wall. But fear and practicality drew men together in battle, where two swords always prevailed over one. This was a far looser formation, and Yngvar muscled his way to the front even as the Arabs tried to claw him from behind.

"A slave!" White eyes stared out at him from the shadow of a Byzantine helmet. The soldier was ready to ram his spear into Yngvar's shield.

"I am a friend!" he shouted.

The Byzantine skirted Yngvar and lunged at the enemy to his rear. Without hesitation, Yngvar and Alasdair slipped into the line. Soldiers greeting him leveled their spears, but again Yngvar shouted for peace. Despite the Arab shield and bloody *saif* in hand, the Byzantines allowed him into their ranks. He pushed through the second rank and grabbed a man jostling for position.

"Prince Kalim? Is he here?"

The Byzantine shook his head. "His dog leads this fight. See him there?"

Over the black plumed helmets waving like an iron sea, he saw Commander Staurakius's standard shaking. The fight was thickest around him, where Arabs in mail coats swarmed the standard.

"We'll take the fight to his dog, then," he shouted to Alasdair.

"Lord, this is not our fight. Let's move to the rear."

Though Yngvar heard the admonition, he had no mind to heed it. These Arabs had ruined his life. As long as he had a sword in hand and Arabs to his front, the will to battle would never leave him. He must be slathered in their blood before his thirst could even begin to retreat.

He shoved along the Byzantine line, drawing angered shouts and protests from men struggling to meet the forward attack. Yet behind them, Yngvar glimpsed the flash of helmets that were already fleeing up the slope.

"Our line is breaking," he shouted to Alasdair, who could not possibly see over the throng of men. "We have only a moment to slash out a bit of revenge before we flee."

Alasdair shouted something lost to ringing metal and screaming combatants.

Ahead, Commander Staurakius hacked into the enemies surrounding him. His chosen guards staggered under the weight of the heavy Arab troops. The Byzantines were outnumbered and had either defiantly stepped into a trap or else were woefully uninformed of the enemy's strength.

A clutch of Byzantines to the rear turned and fled. The new rear rank looked between their broken companions and the enemies before them.

It was all any soldier needed to see to trigger a route. One fleeing group encouraged another, and soon the route was in full force.

The Byzantines called out for retreat and began fleeing up the slope. The Arabs lumbered after them in their heavy mail, faces shining with sweat.

"We go now, lord!" Alasdair pulled at his shirt. "It is all confusion."

Warriors scurried everywhere, tripping over the tidemark of corpses marking their former lines. Blood slicked the grass. White, bloodless limbs dotted the green. A Byzantine sat up, weeping as he held his guts into a gaping stomach wound. An Arab sat a sword length away from him and pressed both hands over one eye as blood streamed down his cheek into his beard.

Where Arab and Byzantine met, isolated clashes ensued with each man seeking to a swift finish to their engagement.

"Now, lord! Before we are overrun ourselves!"

They were poor targets, being ragged men with a single shield between them. Like warriors everywhere, the Arabs sought fatter prizes than two poor slaves. They were best left for the stragglers to pick up.

The thought led him back to Commander Staurakius. He had not fled. The last of his chosen warriors died with an Arab spear through his chest. The commander held his standard aloft and faced a ring of six heavy Arab warriors. Their mail was sprayed with Byzantine blood and their faces were bright with killing lust. Curving swords glimmered as they readied them for a strike.

"To hell with you heathens!" Staurakius yelled. He raised his ornate shield, now battered out of shape and sagging on his arm. He held his sword to the side, then cried out as he leapt at his foes.

Yngvar too raised his shield and charged toward his commander.

25

Yngvar bounded across the blood-drenched grass. Alasdair shouted behind him, his voice lost amid the clangor. Arabs raced after Byzantines who sought the safety of higher ground. Some caught their targets and both tumbled aside in a tangle of flashing iron. Yngvar ran past all this toward his commander's valiant stand.

No matter that Yngvar was a slave who stood below Commander Staurakius's recognition. He fought with honor and bravery against six Arabs intent on slaughter. Yngvar could not flee such a glorious fight. More practically, if he failed to escape, then aiding the commander could not be a wrong choice.

His charge slammed shield-first into an Arab striking from the commander's left flank. Yngvar hit a tree. The Arab roared his irritation, but with heavy mail and his thick legs planted wide, he did not crumble as Yngvar hoped.

This cursed Arab sword in his hand was not the light, close fighting blade he was accustomed to. His technique was wrong for the weapon, which demanded he stay back and leverage the blades heavy slashing and chopping strength.

Instead he slashed out to the side and caught the next Arab across his back. The mail prevented the blow, but he was already off balance for his strike.

Alasdair swept in; with his dagger and short height, he was better placed to hobble Arab assailants. Now, with three to six men, Commander Staurakius roared his defiance.

"Dogs, all of you! Die!"

They spun into a tangle of crossing iron and clanging shields. Yngvar fell back from his foe. If one was too strong, then find one weaker. He led the Arab away from the commander, which created space for their weapons.

The Arab was not taller or wider than Yngvar, but his strength was formidable. Each strike of his curved sword shuddered through his shield to numb his arm. But Yngvar was content to let him expend his fury. He stepped back with care, watching for bodies or debris that could trip him. His foot rolled over a loose stone, which he kicked into the Arab's path.

When he stepped on it, his ankle rolled and Yngvar charged.

Fortunes reversed and the Arab was knocked flat. Alasdair was right atop him, drawing his long dagger into the Arab's neck.

Staurakius had backed away from his standard, but now faced three enemies rather than six.

One Arab feinted at him, which he accepted as a true threat. He stepped out of position and the Arab on his other flank shoved him over with his shield.

Staurakius was surrounded by three men, their bloody swords dripping over his prone body.

Yngvar screamed and flung his shield.

An Arab turned in time for the heavy shield to strike him in the teeth. He folded, dropping his sword as he slumped to the grass.

Alasdair flew alongside Yngvar, both sweeping into the two remaining Arabs.

Yngvar's curved sword rammed through one's knee, just below the hem of his chain shirt. Alasdair failed to strike, warded off by the Arab's shield.

But now Commander Staurakius regained his feet. He had lost

his sword, only a shield strapped to his arm. He brought this down on Alasdair's enemy, battering the Arab to the side.

At last, more Byzantines returned to their standard. Four men cried Staurakius's name. They had lost their own shields, but carried long spears in both hands.

The Arabs around the standard fled into the confusion.

The commander stared at Yngvar and then Alasdair. His regal face was covered with blood and his eyes were bright with the resolve of a man who had seen his death. He raised his sword to them, then grabbed his standard.

"Sound the retreat!" he shouted to the men joining him.

Yngvar laughed, seeing how the ordered blocks had dissolved into a milling flood of killers and victims.

"Lord," Alasdair pulled at his sleeve again. "Before we are joined with the commander. We must flee."

They sped toward the general retreat, following the path up the slope and over the ridge. Arabs chased after them, yet they were still nothing but poor slaves. Arabs wanted greater men to ransom or kill than slaves who were as valued as rotten straw. For once Yngvar was glad his arms were clear of gold bands and his clothing not better than rags.

They ran with the Byzantines until he determined they should diverge to the south.

"I can smell the sea," Yngvar said. "Look, no one pursues us. We are going to make it!"

"I pray for us," Alasdair said. In one hand he gripped his gore-caked dagger and in the other he held a small wooden cross.

They sped down the slope, letting the chaos of battle fade behind them. Someone called after them, but they did not turn back. The green field had shaded to blue with heavy clouds forming overhead. The smell of rain now washed out the horrid odors of slaughter.

They ran until Yngvar's side stitched and he had to pause.

"Look, the fortress," he said through his panting.

The fortress stood heavy and black against the gray sky. Masts of great warships poked up from behind the slope of the land.

"It was not a trap for the fortress," Alasdair said. "God be thanked."

Alasdair kissed his cross, no doubt for Valgerd's sake.

They gained the shore after jogging the final distance. Again, Alasdair praised his god. The fishing ships were beached and only three figures worked around them. Two ships and three men, though as they closed Yngvar noted one was just a boy.

Their bloody and weary appearance did not shock the fishermen. They put down their tasks and lined up before their ship.

Yngvar had wiped his hands on his pants, leaving bloody prints behind. He raised his palm for peace, but gore had dried in the folds of his skin.

"Friends," he said in Greek. "We need the boat."

He extended his open hand to the other boat, hoping it was not theirs.

The oldest fisherman was dark with eyebrows as thick as a man's thumb and gray, wavy hair to his shoulders. He was wiry and strong for his age, bare-chested and dark-skinned. He shook his head.

Yngvar smiled and shook his head as well.

"Boat or your life? Which one?"

"These boats are our lives," he said. "You can have neither."

Yngvar fished the deflated pouch from his hip which contained his month's pay. He threw it on the beach. Alasdair did the same.

"We buy your boat. Now, stand back. I will not ask again."

The fishermen sneered at the pouches. The boy and other men, both with the same heavy brows as the older fisherman, drew spears from their small ship.

"You don't know how to fight," Yngvar said. "I will have your ship."

"I was in the army," the old fisherman said, smiling as he accepted the offered spear.

"I will kill your boy," Yngvar said. "He was not in the army."

The fisherman stared at him. His eye flickered a moment to look behind Yngvar.

Speaking in Norse, he told Alasdair, "They're delaying for help. Someone approaches behind. Leave the father to me. Kill the sons if they will not surrender."

He knew his order bucked against Christian ideals. Yet somehow Alasdair had justified years of raiding and killing along the Danish coast. Now was not the time to find conscience. His god would forgive him if he asked sincerely before he died, or so Alasdair had claimed.

Yngvar sprung for the father. Despite his gray hair, he leapt back and parried the stroke with his spear, attempting to maintain his reach. If Yngvar had not exhausted himself fighting and running, this fisherman would have died with his first strike. Yet Yngvar felt the weariness in his shoulders and the quivering in his legs. The ungainly, heavy Arab sword did not respond as expected.

The old fisherman was hardened from life at sea, no simple man to shove aside. He stabbed back at Yngvar, narrowly missing his eye.

But the fisherman was destined to fail.

"I've got your son," Alasdair shouted in Greek. The words were thick and mangled, even to Yngvar's untrained ears. But they were sufficient to stop the fighting.

The older son lay on the beach clutching the back of his thigh where dark blood flowed between his fingers. The young boy had lost his spear and struggled with Alasdair's dagger point against his neck.

The father dropped his spear and raised both hands. He streamed foreign words to his boy, obvious warning to cease struggling.

Yngvar turned to spot a half-dozen men rushing across the beach. These were fishermen as well, but had gone unseen until this moment.

"We take your boat," Yngvar said, keeping his sword leveled. He crouched down and scooped the spear in hand. "Your son goes with us. Can he....?"

He had not learned the Greek word for swimming. In frustration he growled at Alasdair.

"Get the boy in the boat, and I'll shove us off. We'll find out if he can swim once we're away."

The father had both hands on his head. His friends staggered to a halt beside him and watched Yngvar shove the small fishing vessel into the sea. He threw off nets and anything that looked valuable. These were simple folk that did not deserve complete ruin. Stealing

246

their ship was harsh enough, and possibly killing the son was the highest punishment.

Once they rolled over the waves and the figures on the beach faded to indistinct shapes, Yngvar regarded his captive. He glared with dark hatred but remained as limp as if his back had been broken. The dagger at his neck pinned him.

"Do you think he can swim?" he asked.

"I don't know, lord. He is young. He can learn."

Yngvar set the single triangular sail on the mast. While not the same as a Norse ship, differences were minimal enough to complete the task. They caught the wind and Yngvar laughed. He looked for something to offer the boy as a float. Buckets were all he could find, and these would be needed for bailing and catching rainwater.

"Over the side with him," Yngvar said. "If his gods love him, they will save him. If not, then here is the manner of his death. Fate rules all."

Alasdair raised the boy to his feet. He seemed to understand the intent and began to struggle. Once released, he shoved Alasdair back with unexpected strength and shouted a curse. He grabbed a bucket for a weapon.

Yngvar kicked him overboard.

The boy cried and splashed in the water. He was small enough to hug the bucket, which buoyed him. But if the gods ignored them, then it would tip and sink with him.

"There's a sail on the horizon." Alasdair said. "His father, I expect."

"He'll not pursue us," Yngvar said. "Besides, we've a new fear."

They looked skyward. Black clouds crowded the horizon ahead. Rain clouds that had teased the battlefield had broken from a mass farther out to sea.

"We will sail towards Licata, which is the only way I know," Yngvar said. "And pull ashore ahead of this storm. I expect no one will be on the water in bad weather."

Yngvar and Alasdair were crew enough to manage the small vessel. A third man would have been best. But Yngvar was confident they could make good their escape and still beat the threatening storm. They had only a sail for steering. They left the boy clinging to the bucket, bobbing on the sea to Fate's whim.

The rising wind and oncoming storm created choppy water, and though they were not as far from the fortress at Pozzallo as Yngvar would have liked, he decided they had to make landfall.

Then wind gusted into the sail like Thor's hammer.

They had not grasped the rigging scheme of this foreign boat, though it seemed simple enough. In his eagerness to escape the Byzantines, Yngvar had attempted to carry too much sail for the strength of the wind. When this gust from the approaching storm hit, the rigging parted and snapped away.

His stomach clenched. The ship lurched with the gust, and for an instant he feared it would capsize. With no rigging to control the sail, the mast bent and groaned.

Alasdair was already struggling to find a backup to the parted rigging. Yngvar searched for something to mitigate the damage. Yet this was not his ship and even a moment of hesitation cost him.

The next gust hit and the mast cracked. It did not snap off, but now its integrity was ruined.

"Hurry with that rigging," Yngvar shouted, though he was mostly pawing uselessly through the fisherman's gear. "We need to make shore."

Though it was a strip on the horizon, the storm moved faster than he could imagine. Black clouds drove the sun away like a vanquished foe. The water churned white and the ship rocked and spun as the sail filled beyond its strength.

"The sail will tear, lord!"

The backstay snapped next, and Yngvar felt as if Loki himself were cutting each line to taunt them.

"Tie yourself off instead," Yngvar shouted over the rising wind. Cold specks struck his face as the first of the rain hit him. "We will not count on the gods to send us a float a second time."

They each tied short ropes around their waists as the ship careened along the waves. The mast continued to snap and groan and would soon break along with the sail. The wind strengthened.

Each checked the other's knot and made certain they were tied off to the rails. They would not be thrown overboard. Yngvar wished he had a dagger in case he had to cut himself free, but he had foolishly lost it in battle. Now he lay down in the hull and covered his head with his hands. Alasdair did the same. The storm would buffet them, and without control of their sail they could do no more than beg Thor once more for mercy.

The storm rushed over them with unexpected fury. The gales spun and tipped the boat. Waves soaked them and rain lashed them. The mast snapped and tumbled into the sea with sail and rigging in trail.

Yngvar held to deck, eyes closed against the sea water and fear that washed over him in equal measure. His ears throbbed with the howl of the wind. His mind rocked with the violence of the sea.

The storm was endless, black, and angry. It was the gods, not content to allow Yngvar an end to his torments. He heard their laughter between the flashes of lightning. He felt their derision in the clawing wind. He had broken his oath to them, had withheld the best part of his treasures from them. Their anger was not yet assuaged.

Yet the gods did not capsize their boat. They left it a wreck filled with seawater and shattered strakes. But the storm passed after what seemed a year in the tempest. Black clouds gave way to black skies. Stars winked as if mocking him between gaps in the clouds. Gentle winds caressed him like a father who regretted beating his child. It was all false consolation, for the wind had betrayed him before and would again.

When the sun broke again, the sky was full of cheer and fat clouds. He and Alasdair lay against the rails, their clothes soaked. Orange blooms appeared on Yngvar's sword, which sat in a bath of sea water.

Neither of them spoke. Yngvar would not look at Alasdair, but instead looked to the endless circle around him. It was all blue water and blue sky. There could be no color more foul to his taste.

With no means to steer their ship, they drifted. An entire day they drifted, hearing nothing but the maddening slap of water against the hull. Seeing nothing but endless blue. Tasting nothing but the sea salt dried on their tongues.

The night offered only a reprieve from the slashing rays of sunlight. Yngvar felt the heat radiate off his face and chest into the cool night air.

The next morning, Alasdair broke the heavy silence. His voice was a hoarse croak.

"Pray with me," he said. "Let us ask God to deliver us. It is our only hope."

Yngvar rolled his head back. "I do not look to weakness to find strength. You worship a dead man nailed to old boards."

Alasdair held out his small wooden cross. Yngvar stared at in amazement, expecting it to have been lost in the storm.

"Put your hand on this cross and ask God to forgive you. Ask Him to show us to safety."

"I would put my hand on Thor's hammer first."

Alasdair shot to his feet. The boat rocked and he stumbled to hold his balance. His face, already burned red, flushed to purple.

"Would you? Thor? He threw his hammer upon your head more than once, and you still grovel to him? Your gods are old and false. Can't you see? They have forsaken you!"

Alasdair held his cross forward, bringing it a finger's breadth from Yngvar's face.

"There is one God! He will not forsake you, not if you accept His blessing. He is the one true power. Beg forgiveness, and it will be granted. Beg your gods and your pleas will be heard only by the creatures of the sea."

Sweat poured out of Alasdair's bright, smooth face. The flush reached up into his scalp, still visible through the stubble. He stood panting, brandishing his tiny cross. Yngvar backed against the rails.

Then he noticed something over Alasdair's shoulder. A black shape.

He sat up, looking past Alasdair. The shape was a lump on the horizon.

"Land," he said. "And gulls."

They had drifted aimlessly, now catching a tide that pulled them toward a rocky island. White gulls sailed high overhead, heading for the lump that grew ever clearer, as if escorting them to shore.

Alasdair blinked, then followed Yngvar's gaze. He collapsed to his knees, splashing into the water puddled in the hull of their boat.

"It is true," he said, still breathless. "Gulls mean water and food. We are saved."

Yngvar smiled. He had strength for little more. He closed his eyes, the sun still a bright red spot behind his lids.

"Yes, Alasdair, we are saved. I care not which god spared us. It seems we will live a while longer yet."

26

Alasdair threw the last of the dried wood he had recovered from the bushes that thrived along the rocky island. Yngvar had dragged the boat ashore, hoping to use it as a lean-to. The sun had scorched his exposed skin. He yearned for shade, which seemed impossible here. The trees were tall, with strange leaves that grew like massive fans only at the top. These trees stinted on shade.

"We might kindle a fire from this," Alasdair said. "When the stars show tonight, perhaps we can figure where we are."

Yngvar had lined up a number of rocks he thought might make useful tools. Sharp stones for cutting, stones for hammering, other stones to serve as work surfaces. It was all he had strength to do. Alasdair had more energy and so had to bear more of the load.

"More than where we are," Yngvar said, "I want to know where freshwater is. We lost all our buckets to the storm."

He thought of the boy clinging to his bucket in the gray sea. It would be a fine jest if they were to die of thirst for want of a bucket to catch rainwater. The thought generated a mirthless grin.

"The gulls might show us where to find water," Alasdair said, looking skyward and shielding his eyes against the glare.

"Curse this endless blue," Yngvar said, throwing a small stone out to sea. "I long for the brown and green of home."

"It is more cold and gray," Alasdair said. He picked a rock from Yngvar's pile then started digging a pit in the beach sand for their fire.

"Cold and gray," Yngvar said wistfully. "I yearn for that. All this heat and blue sky sits ill with my Norse heart."

No matter how he wished, Yngvar still felt the prickly heat crawl across his back, still tasted the bitter sea water on his tongue, and smelled nothing but salt. He had flung himself to the bottom of the world and nothing here was the same as home.

They built their fire and watched it smolder into the evening. They set their clothes on makeshift racks. Nothing dried in this humidity, despite the heat. When night fell, the stars revealed nothing to Yngvar that he did not already know.

"If Hamar or Leiknr were here, they might see some differences in the stars. But I am not one who knows the way, like they were."

Leiknr's dying curse echoed in his mind, and he decided to speak no more of stars or his old crew. Renewing those pains would not help him survive. For one night at least, he just wanted rest. He had robbed a bird's nest of three eggs and cooked them on flat stones over the fire. He and Alasdair ate in silence.

With the next morning, he and Alasdair still had little to say. Perhaps Alasdair was still angered from his outburst on the rowboat. Yngvar was not sure. The island was large enough for birds and small game. But it was unknown to man. They would be each other's company, perhaps until they died.

"Everything you said on that boat," Yngvar said as he stared the ashes of the dead fire. "It was true. My gods have left me. If it pleases you, I will pray to your god as well as mine."

Alasdair had been sitting with his knees drawn to his chin, staring at the steep hill that formed the heart of this island. He did not react to Yngvar's words.

"It is not easy for me to believe any god sees us on this island. Yet one must have sent us to it. Perhaps it was the Christian god after all. You were holding that cross when I saw this island."

Alasdair remained staring at the hill.

Flustered, Yngvar shoved the stick into the remains of the camp-fire and stood. His clothes were dry now, and he covered his nakedness with the tatters of his shirt and pants. The Arab saif was now only rusted iron, but even corroded the weapon might have a use. He looked at it sitting against a rock beside their overturned boat.

"Lord, there is something strange about that hill," Alasdair said at last. He pointed to it. "There seems a path leading into it. If there are truly no people here, then why would there be a path?"

Following Alasdair's direction, he saw what did seem a thin, wandering line that led into the piles of browns and gray rocks.

"This island is not large enough for more than a dozen people. By now, we would be discovered."

"But what if there are people like us here?"

Yngvar tilted his head, staring harder at the white path.

"If we were wrecked here, then others might have been wrecked before us. This Midgard Sea is not so big that this island could go unseen by sailors. Besides, a current took us here. Currents guide ships."

They stared at each other, then Alasdair stood.

"We should discover where that leads," Yngvar said. "My sword is so rusted it is more of a danger to us than an enemy."

"Do you think someone lives there?"

Yngvar shook his head. "A man would've attacked in the night or else stole something he thought valuable. But an animal might fear us and hide. That hill must be full of bolt holes."

"My dagger is also rusted," Alasdair said. "But it is all we have."

They climbed into the rough stones and sought the thread through rocks and boulders that seemed to have been scattered by a giant hand. Yngvar carried his sword and Alasdair his dagger. They could fashion spears from the straight wood of the ship, but had not yet done so. Weapons gave them bravery.

"Lord, this is a path," Alasdair said, crouching to rub the earth with his palm. "The ground here is clear of big stones and smooth.

Weeds and bushes spouted wildly amid the stones. Lichen splattered milky green on boulders streaked with dried gull droppings. Ants swarmed a dead beetle by Yngvar's foot. A lizard that had remained frozen on a rock burst suddenly into a crevice and vanished.

"This land is full of life," he said. "Lizards and bugs alone might support a small man. We should go with caution."

They picked over rocks, slipped between boulders and climbed higher into this huge pile. They path grew clearer the higher they went. The debris that obscured it at the foot seemed to have slid down the sides over long years.

"A cave!" Alasdair had climbed to the top of a tall boulder and now stared up the path. The way forward was blocked with similar stones, masking the top from sight.

Yngvar tightened his grip on the sword. They were now careful to make as little noise as they could. Alasdair moved like a ghost, but Yngvar knocked stones free to slide down the path and thump against other boulders. He may as well have shouted rowing songs all the way up.

Once close to the summit of this hill, they both drew up short in front of the hill's inhabitant.

A white skull, ribs, pelvis, and two long thigh bones marked where the person had died. The jawbone was several feet away from the body, and white flakes of shattered bones were scattered everywhere.

"His skull was broken," Yngvar said, pointing to the crack leading out of the empty eye socket. "He was either struck or fell."

High rocks surrounded the bones. They leaned like the deformed teeth of a stone giant.

"Lord, these stones seem arranged. And they are before the cave."

Yngvar still did not see the cave. He kept his sword forward in both hands and approached the bones. Once he stood over them, unafraid of any dead spirit that might haunt them still, he found both shadow and the cave mouth.

The cave was more of a wide crack. It was filled with bricks that had been knocked aside. Either the dead man or the work of nature had collapsed a section of it. Beyond was pure blackness.

Yngvar's stomach turned cold. Evil lurked underground, where dwarfs and trolls made their lairs. Such utter blackness chilled him.

"This man meant to get inside, I think," Alasdair said.

"And was killed for it," Yngvar said. "Whatever is beyond must be evil. We should rebuild that wall."

"Lord, do you not see what this place is? Look at the arrangement of stones here. Look at this pile before us. This is no hill, at least not the summit. This is a burial mound. Probably from the time of the old people or before."

They stared at each other. The wind rushed over the stones and across their faces as if leading them to the black opening.

"Lord, there could be something useful inside."

"True." He stared at the yawning black. Trolls and dwarfs. Elves and spirits. Did these things exist so far south? Even if they did, what evil could they visit upon him? Would they take him to their caves and torment him? Was that worse than dying of thirst while the sun burned the skin from his face?

"I will break down this wall," he said. "You go back and make a torch of what wood is dry enough."

While he excavated the entrance, he thought only of water. He knew this labor was nonsensical. Sweat poured out of his body, creating a thirst that would slay him if ignored. But with every crumbling stone that he broke free, he felt inescapably drawn into the black.

Spirits did dwell here.

They demanded he enter the darkness to hear whispers held for centuries.

Alasdair returned with a broken plank that burned on one end. He cupped his hand around the small flame.

The entrance now yawned open. Yngvar accepted the brand in his left hand and stuck his sword into the darkness beyond. The yellow light shined upon man-made walls that reminded Yngvar of Prince Kalim's prison. A steep slope descended into darkness. Spiderwebs hung across the entrance, and he cut these down before pushing deeper.

"Lord, perhaps it is too dangerous?"

Alasdair stood in the entrance, the blue light behind him framing him crisply against the sky. He seemed to have shrunk. He huddled over his small cross as if it were a fire in a winter storm.

"This is wide enough for only one at a time," Yngvar said. "And barely tall enough for me to stand. But I shall go. It is wisest that you remain outside in case something happens. I might disturb this place and bring it down on me. It seems ancient."

"As you say, lord."

"So quick to agree?" Yngvar laughed, for if he did not, he might tremble as Alasdair did before the velvety blackness.

The plank barely held its flame, but it revealed a natural path that swooped down until earthen steps were carved into the ground. He descended these sideways, carefully placing one foot on a step and testing it before he set his full weight. If one should collapse and pitch him into the blackness—the thought of it made ice out of his blood.

His nose was full of musty and earthen smells. Water had seeped through here, and roots hung above. One touched his shoulder and he nearly fainted. He waited on the steps until he was certain nothing more would disturb him.

At last these stairs flowed down to a chamber.

It was wide and rectangular, built by men who had vanished long ago. The faint light failed to reveal how far back this chamber reached. But a thin, milky ray of light spilled from above. From the same spot above, water dripped with an audible splash.

Beneath that ray, like a finger of the gods directing his sight, sat a stone coffin. It was of plain black stone and covered with debris that had fallen from the ceiling. Yngvar held the plank higher, and metal glinted back at him. He drew closer, keeping his rusted sword forward as if something might rush him from the gloom.

Gold. Silver. Bronze.

Coins had burst from old leather sacks. Plates and mugs of silver and bronze had tumbled beside these. All around the coffin were bags and chests, covered in dust and cobwebs.

Along one wall, his pitiful torchlight traced outlines of shields and spears, a great bow missing its string, bronze helmets too small and impractical for his own head.

He stepped closer and realized the helmets contained skulls that glared at him with empty sockets. In other circumstances he would have screamed. But he was already a man doomed. He flinched back but steadied himself. At last, he inclined his head to the row of skulls.

"You guard your lord in death as you did in life. You were men of great honor. I come not to steal the wealth of your lord, but only to accept what he might offer me in aid. For I am here not of my own choice. If you could but yield to me such tools as would aid me in survival, I would sing praise to your lord in every mead hall of the northlands. I beg this of you."

The spirts might not understand his Norse, he thought, but they must understand his intent. For how long had they stood guard in darkness, forgotten and moldering? Perhaps the spirits would be mad after centuries in isolation. But he did not feel threat here. He had entered into a place that ages had forgotten and promised the spirits a place in the memories of men once again. Relief more than threat filled this musty darkness.

He studied the spears. Their blades were made from bronze, and despite the tarnish, their edges were still keen. The shafts, however, were rotten. He reached a hand to touch the spearhead, curious how sharp the blade remained.

The row of ten spears suddenly collapsed, one upon the other, sweeping along the wall. He leapt back with a surprised shout.

The helmeted skulls set on narrow ledges were also caught by the spear tips. These turned and fell. Skulls rolled out, breaking and collapsing from their ancient fragility. Only one remained on the wall, and it had turned to face the direction of the falling spears.

Yngvar stared wide-eyed at the collapse.

"You are freed now," he said. "You have guarded all these long years, but no more. Your lord sends you onto your gods at last."

The spears and the remaining skull pointed to the ray of light.

"Lord?"

Alasdair's voice was distant and echoing from the top of the shaft.

"Are you hurt?"

Yngvar did not answer. He stepped around the black stone coffin, setting each foot carefully amid the debris.

At the head of the coffin where the light flowed in from above, a bronze bowl caught water that dripped steadily from the ceiling. The water was clear, though dirt and other scum floated on the surface. Each new drop splashed ripples through the filled bowl.

Yngvar dropped to his knees and his rusted sword clanked to the dirt. He scooped the water into his mouth. It was gritty and metallic, but it was fresh rain. He began to laugh.

"Lord?" Alasdair's voice was closer, as if he had entered the shaft.

"We are saved," Yngvar shouted back. "We have water!"

Yngvar slurped again from his cupped hand, careful not to lose a drop. He sat back on his knees, then bowed to the coffin.

"Whatever king lies here was a great and generous lord. Thank you for your wealth, my king. I will learn your name and praise it for all my days."

"Lord, I cannot see in the darkness. I cannot reach you."

"Hold, I will come to you."

Yngvar, filled with strength, bounded up the steps. Some crumbled under his foot. Roots dragged through his hair. But rather than feeling like ghostly fingers, this felt more like joyous friends clapping him as he passed. He discovered Alasdair just beyond the limit of the outside light, clutching his cross in white-knuckled hands.

Though Yngvar laughed, Alasdair tentatively followed back into the chamber. He did not share Yngvar's joy, though he did not hesitate to drink from the water.

"Do you see?" Yngvar said, spreading his arms wide. "This king has offered us all his wealth if we would but carry his name back to the lips of living men. He has sent his guards away. He set us a feast such as he could manage with only cobwebs and dust. The water!"

"It is refreshing," Alasdair said. "But it will hardly keep us alive beyond a few days."

"You still do not understand," Yngvar said.

Alasdair stood up from the bronze bowl. The torch flame burned low and smoke spun out of it like cobwebs that surrounded them. His smooth face gleamed with sweat in the wan light.

"Lord, we have found some water. But we will need a spring or stream to sustain us."

"We will survive," Yngvar said, nearly breathless. "The gods have guaranteed it to me."

"Lord?"

"This! This treasure. The gods have granted me the gold we came seeking. Here it is at our feet. The gods challenge us. If we can match their challenge, then all this treasure will be ours. They will not slay us with thirst or hunger, not unless we choose to lie down in defeat. If we fight, the gods will dare us to return here and claim these spoils. Don't you see it?"

Alasdair stared at him. The expression was one Yngvar had never seen on his young friend's face. Perhaps it was shadow thrown by the uncertain light, but Alasdair seemed doubting and afraid.

"Lord?"

Yngvar blinked. "You cannot see this is true? Look at the gold here. It is more than any Norse king gathers under his hall. I swear that is fact."

"Lord, while you went under this hill, I climbed to the top of it. It is the highest point on the island. This place is not big and it is not inhabited. And there is no stream or pond here. This is all the water we have. I am sorry, lord, but the gods are not challenging you. They are mocking you."

27

From the top of the king's mountain, as Yngvar had accustomed himself to calling the burial mound on the island's highest point, he angled the bronze shield toward the sun. Alasdair had shimmied up the trunk of the strange, branchless trees that dotted this island. He clung to it with one arm and shielded his eyes with the other.

"Three masts," Alasdair announced after staring into the afternoon sun. "Triangular."

"Do they see our signal?" Yngvar twisted the shield so that the flashing might catch a vigilant sailor's eye.

"I cannot tell. The ship does not head straight for us, but it draws nearer."

Yngvar smiled. "That is better than the last two that passed us."

He continued to rotate the shield, which he had dragged from the riches of the ancient king's tomb. Time had tarnished it and the earth had dented it. But Yngvar scrubbed it with sand and polished it with oil he had found in sealed vases amid the king's possessions. This oil did not burn and smelled foul. But it still imparted a rich gleam to the shield, which now reflected the sun at passing ships.

"We've no other choice but to try to gain attention," Alasdair said.

"We've spotted five ships in two weeks. We are not far from people, but they do not draw near to our island."

"I'm certain sailors believe this island is cursed," Yngvar said. "We're standing atop treasure that would make any man a king. Yet no one has claimed it all these long years. Sailors do not come here of their own will."

Alasdair hung from the tree, continuing to peer into the distance. Yngvar hoped he would announce the ship's approach, but at last he said no more and shimmed to the ground.

Both of them had suffered the weeks of poor food. They caught lizards, scavenged bird eggs, and ate insects. They had fashioned a fishing pole and hook but no fish would bite. They had tried to trap birds but their snares were ignored. Neither of them recognized the plants here, and their attempts to guess which might be edible led them to sickness.

Yet they lived.

The gods sent rain every third day. Sometimes it was mere showers, other times it was powerful squalls. But shields and the bronze bowl collected the rain water. They were often thirsty, but they did not lack for water. Both understood when Thor withheld his storms, they would whither from thirst.

They attended their small camp, improved with improvised tools from the king's tomb. While the rain had been a blessing, it ravaged their meager fire-wood supplies. Yngvar had found a bronze ax head and planned to use it in felling trees to build a better shelter for both themselves and their firewood.

As he sat watching the white line of the gurgling surf, something at the edge his vision caught his sight.

"Three masts," he said under his breath. A large ship with long oars churned through the water on the horizon, headed directly for them.

Alasdair, who had stretched himself out beside the wet ashes of the night's fire, shot to his feet.

"It's the same ship," he said. "They are coming to us, lord! We are saved."

Yngvar's first thought was for the treasure hidden in the mountain. He looked around at the half-dozen shields and bronze basin.

"They'll discover the treasure," Yngvar said.

"What?" Alasdair had rushed to the water's edge, waving his hands overhead. Now he turned to Yngvar, his mouth open. "We are saved and you care about the treasure?"

"It is my treasure," Yngvar said. "The king gave it to me!"

He stabbed his chest with his thumb, heat drawing to his face. Alasdair blinked at him. Behind, the large ship's oars paddled through the sea as if it were thick mud. Yet it headed straight toward the island.

"Dump this water," Yngvar said. "We need to hide these shields and this basin. Get rid of your bronze spearhead. We cannot hint of any treasure."

"Lord, until we know their intent, we cannot dump the water."

Yet Yngvar dumped the water collected in a shield. Alasdair screamed.

He picked up the shield and moved to overturn the next one.

Alasdair collided with him as he bent over. He crashed face-first into the dirt, pushing the salty earth into his nose and mouth.

"This is madness," Alasdair screamed. "Stop it."

Even in his weakened state, he was stronger than Alasdair. He bucked him from his back, then scrabbled to his feet. Alasdair landed in the puddle of water spilled out of the shield. Yngvar glanced at him, but turned to the approaching ship.

"They draw ever closer," he said. "We must hide these treasures or they will ransack this island. I will not have it. Not after all I've suffered for this reward!"

"Reward?" Alasdair said, tears beginning to flow. "This is a reward? We are mad with hunger and thirst. We have no hope of living another week. Yet you would dump our only water to save dusty gold coins?"

Yngvar upturned two more shields, and hurried toward bushes where he could hide them. He heard Alasdair, but the words meant nothing. Let him pray to his dead god and beg for a place in his heaven.

The Norse gods shower their heroes with gold if they are but daring enough to reach for it. Here was gold by the buckets full. He would not let some Arab or Byzantine set his hands to it, not without a fight.

He pressed the shields into the ground, then heaped sand over them. He arranged the bushes to appear undisturbed.

"Two more shields and the basin," he said, patting his hands over the remnants of his pants. "Alasdair, help me with—"

He turned and found Alasdair before the basin of rainwater. In his trembling hands the sharp bronze spearhead quivered. Its keen edge shined at Yngvar.

"You can't do this," Alasdair said. "You don't know that ship will land here."

"It's heading straight for us," Yngvar said, raising his hands. He took a careful step toward Alasdair.

His usually bright face was ashen and eyes sunken into black circles. His beard was thin and scruffy. Combined with his thin frame he seemed more a starved dog than a Norse warrior. Yngvar knew he looked no better. But Alasdair had a gleam of madness in his eyes whereas he never felt clearer.

"You don't know when it will rain again," Alasdair said. "There's no flowing water on this island. Neither of us are skilled enough to find water in the earth. You cannot dump our only supply."

"If we leave things as they are, the sailors will know we found treasure here," Yngvar said. He took another step closer, both hands out for peace.

"What does it matter?" Tears streamed down Alasdair's face. "Even if they don't find it, how will we find it again?"

"I have marked the stars carefully in my mind," Yngvar said. Again, he stepped closer only to cause Alasdair to threaten the spear point at his chest. "I will find this place once more."

"And what crew will help you carry this all away? What loyal friends will let you claim all of this for yourself? You will need a crew. Men you haven't yet met. Men who will be corrupted by the gold as you are now. They will kill you and kill each other to steal such vast treasures for themselves."

"You speak foolishness," Yngvar said, remaining in place.

The ship was no longer on the horizon, but now clear in the distance. It was black with white, triangular sails, and crew scurried along the rails and through the rigging. Time was running out.

"It is not foolishness," he said through his cracking voice. "It is why this treasure has remained here so long. It is too much of a temptation for any man. It is evil and brings evil even to the noble-hearted. That skeleton up there by the entrance. He did not fall. He was murdered, hit across the back of his head so that another could gain the treasure alone."

"But there was only one skeleton," Yngvar said. He began to slide closer again, holding Alasdair's fear-bright eyes so that he would not see Yngvar's feet positioning. "Where did the other man go?"

"He probably starved to death on a pile of gold somewhere on this cursed island." Alasdair raised the spearhead. "You cannot overturn this water. Not until we know if we will be rescued. We need it to last until the next storm."

"See for yourself," Yngvar said, pointing to the sea. "The ship has dropped its anchor stone and they lower boats into the water. At the least, we will be carried away as slaves. We are saved from this island."

Long years of conditioning to Yngvar's commands turned Alasdair's head. He glanced toward the water.

Yngvar leapt for the spear blade.

He seized Alasdair's thin wrist, twisting so that he would drop the blade.

Yet he held on, and cried out in anger and shock.

Alasdair pushed back, throwing his body against Yngvar and relieving the pressure on his arm.

"Let go of the weapon," Yngvar said, his face next to Alasdair's.

"Let go of my arm first!"

Yet Yngvar did not trust the mad gleam in Alasdair's eye. He was possessed with fear of thirst to the point he would kill for a basin of water.

He shoved forward.

His foot caught on one of the rocks he had gathered as tools.

He collapsed atop Alasdair, who howled with pain.

Hot blood flowed between Yngvar's and Alasdair's torsos. He scrabbled off Alasdair, shouting his name.

The spearhead had driven into Alasdair's side. Blood flowed readily across his stomach to pool in his navel. His already pale face now turned white and his eyes stared up at the sky.

"Alasdair, no!" Yngvar tore away the remnants of his shirt and pressed it against the wound. The drab cloth drank the blood and bloomed deep red. "Can you hear me?"

But Alasdair stared into the next world. Yngvar had seen this look on too many faces on too many battlefields. He pressed harder, but the cloth had absorbed all it could.

"I need to bind this," he said, casting about for anything to staunch the blood flow. All he had was bronze treasure taken from the king's tomb. What could all that treasure avail him now?

His eyes blurred with tears. He pressed harder against the cold bronze dagger, fearing to draw it out and unstopper the wound.

Alasdair shivered and his breath became ragged. His eyelids fluttered.

"Gods," Yngvar said through his sobs. "Put your hand on a weapon. You will go to Valhalla. You've earned your place."

He grabbed Alasdair's hand and pulled it to the spear blade sticking out of his side. Tears dripped across Alasdair's white flesh.

Yngvar could not see any more. He crushed down on the wound, but the remains of his shirt simply squeezed more hot blood between his fingers.

"Greet my father and grandfather for me," he said, leaning close to Alasdair's ear. "I will fall to Niflheim, as I deserve."

The hand at his back did not shock him. He thought nothing when it tightened over his shoulder and peeled him away.

Shadows spread across him, and deep voices mumbled behind him.

Greek. They spoke Greek.

Yngvar fell back, but would not release his hand from Alasdair's wound.

"Let me see him," said a voice from behind. The hand pulled more forcefully at his shoulder. "He is not dead yet. I can help."

The promise of help stirred Yngvar from his grief. He twisted about, blinking away tears, to see a wiry man with wild black hair and a beard thick and deep as night. A friendly smile dug heavy lines into the man's cheek.

"You can save him?" Yngvar asked. "I'll grant you my fortune if you can."

The man laughed. "Your fortune? Well, step aside and I will see what may be done."

Yngvar stood back and the man knelt beside Alasdair. He tossed aside the bloody rag and produced his own bandage to slip into its place. He whistled at the wound and shook his head.

"It is not wide but deep," he said. "You have cut something inside, for sure. Pray to God that he can survive it."

Another man joined, bringing a longer wrap that looked like a gray cloak. Yngvar now saw the rowboat and four other men armed with swords or spears. These men were examining the shields on the beach.

Yngvar's heart leapt. He scrabbled over to these men. "These treasures and more are yours if you but save my friend."

Two of the men, hazel-eyed and hook-nosed, shared a smile. One flipped the shield and held it up to examination.

"How about we take these treasures, and if your friend lives you can find a way to thank us."

The two other men stared toward the king's mountain. Yngvar's hands turned to ice. He should promise to lead these men to the gold if they would save Alasdair's life. Yet two of them were bent over Alasdair binding his wound while another man looked on.

The two staring at the mountain each shook their heads then made the sign of the cross.

"Let's be gone from this place," said one. "We've found what was signaling us. The flashes were from these old shields."

The Byzantine kicked a shield back toward the grass and shook his head.

"Help me get this one into the boat," said the Byzantine aiding Alasdair. "Our surgeon might save him, but he's beyond my skill."

Yngvar dropped beside Alasdair, whose eyes had closed. Yet

despite his paleness and the dark rings about his eyes, his chest rose and fell.

"Hold on," he whispered. "I will beg the gods save you. They can take my life for yours."

The sailors loaded Alasdair on their rowboat. Yngvar helped shove them off and jumped into the boat with the rest. He saw the shields and basin left on the shore.

"You will return for the treasures?"

The Byzantine with the night-dark beard laughed. "Every six months or so we find sailors like you wrecked on that island. If we find survivors there is only one. All the others are dead by that survivor's hands. No, we're not going back and you'll find no one else willing to go either. We came because of the flashes, which we knew meant someone was wrecked here. Our captain is a good Christian, and so are the crew."

"Not all of us are as good as you, sir," said one of the crew. They all laughed, but for Yngvar who stared at Alasdair laying between the rowers like a wrapped corpse.

"Well, I won't argue that," said the Byzantine. "But it is our Christian duty to aid those who need it, no matter if it is one of our own or Caliphate sailors. We fight the evil that is on that island. But we will never take anything from it. A demon rules that place and it drives men to murder and madness. I would not spread its evil to the world."

Yngvar nodded. "I know. I have seen the demon with my own eyes."

28

Yngvar awakened suddenly. The world swayed and rolled as if he were still at sea. But over his head were the slats of a bunk. Beside him, other slave-soldiers were rousing with the new day. A rooster crowed and a dog barked. The gloom of the barracks broke when the front door burst open and an officer started shouting at men to awaken. He charged down the row of bunks while carrying a thin switch. If any bare foot dared to show itself to him, he whipped it.

When the officer reached him, he stopped. His anger threatened to explode in a burst of swearing and spittle. But he simply gripped the thin switch in both hands and sneered.

"Good morning," he asked in a mockingly polite voice. "I trust you found this bed to your liking?"

"It was good," Yngvar said.

"Excellent," the officer said. His dark face shaded purple. "Well, you are a special man, aren't you? Delivered here by the commander himself. I pray you will speak well of me to our dear Commander Staurakius?"

Yngvar blinked. Sleep, desperate and fitful while aboard the Byzantine ship, had overwhelmed him last night in a proper bed. It had been deep enough to nearly destroy all his memory of where he was.

"I will," he said.

"Ah yes," said the officer. "And while you are speaking…"

The officer leaned closer and dug the switch under Yngvar's chin.

"You will always address me as sir, or I will take this switch and lash your face until your nose falls off. Understood?"

"Yes, sir." Yngvar blinked again. Was he really back at Pozzallo? Was he dreaming?

The officer struck the side post of his bed with the switch, its blistering crack leading Yngvar to believe he was truly awake.

"Get into your new clothes. They're ready for you here." The officer flicked his switch to his attendant, who threw clean black pants and a white shirt onto his bunk. "Then go to the infirmary. You and your boy-lover have an audience with the commander this morning."

The officer swept down the row, cursing at the men whom he no longer had an excuse to lash.

The man next to his bunk laughed. Yngvar glared at him, but paused. He recognized this man. He was olive skinned with honey-colored eyes and wore an expression of constant surprise.

"Lucas the Byzantine," Yngvar said.

"Norseman," he said. His voice was rough but fair, like a favorite uncle's. "You and the other deserter came back. And you were carried in here like heroes. If they found me after I ran from battle, only my head would return. As a warning to other deserters."

Yngvar scratched his scalp, then pulled the clothes to him. They were plain clothes made for men whose lives meant nothing. Yet the fresh, soft touch of the cloth compared to the filthy rags he had worn for so long felt like he had been awarded the robes of a king.

"What did you do to be treated so well?"

"I saved the commander's life," Yngvar said. "He was surrounded by Arabs. Alasdair and I drove them back."

Lucas stared, his sly smile fading.

"Is that true?"

"If it wasn't, wouldn't just my head have been delivered last night?"

Lucas shrugged. "You've been gone close to a month. What happened?"

Yngvar relived the storm and their arrival on the island, their desperation for water, and their terrible fight at the end. He shuddered.

"Many things happened," he said. "But the gods sent a ship. Alasdair had been hurt, accidentally stuck with a knife when I fell on him. The ship's captain had a good surgeon, and he sewed Alasdair's side and helped him heal."

"You told them you were Staurakius's slaves?" Lucas laughed. "You could've said anything else."

"I know nothing else," Yngvar said. "I know no other name. I have no other friend. I prayed that the commander would remember what we did for him on the battlefield. He is a good man. He remembered and so took us even when the gates were closed for the night."

"That was a terrible battle," Lucas said. "The Arabs were ready for us. And I heard they had a cyclops fighting for them!"

Yngvar tilted his head at the strange word. "Cyclops?"

Lucas laughed. "Well, not a real cyclops. But as good as one, as I heard. A cyclops is a one-eyed giant. You don't know Odysseus, do you? I guessed not. Anyway, the Arab's giant, one-eyed warrior broke our lines. He was mad like a stuck boar. Heard he was shouting in some strange language and killed men even from his own side. When our brave soldiers saw that coming for them, they ran."

Yngvar stared at Lucas and his body went stiff.

"You saw this man? What did he look like?"

"Of course I didn't see him. I was in the back where you should've been. I don't know more than what I told you. It's the story that went around until the commander squashed it. Are you all right? You've lost your color."

"Yes," Yngvar said, waving off the concern. "It's nothing. I was thinking of someone I used to know."

Lucas slapped his knees then stood. "Well, you'll have stories to tell me yet. You've not forgotten the Greek I've taught you. But you've more to learn. Now, go to the infirmary."

"What is an infirmary?" Yngvar asked.

"It's where the injured go to die. Better see to your friend before he is gone."

Yngvar dressed and ran into the early morning light drenching Pozzallo's fort. Regular soldiers were forming up for their drills, their officers screaming as if they had been robbed of all their wealth. He was not certain about this place called the infirmary. He asked directions which led him to a building that looked much like any other barracks.

A guard inside stopped him with an outstretched arm. After Yngvar identified himself he was allowed into the cool darkness where rows of low beds lined both walls. In the dozen beds only one small body lay beneath gray sheets.

Alasdair sat with his head raised on a fat pillow. With his face cleaned of dirt and his coppery hair washed, he again glowed with youthful strength.

He gave a faint smile.

"We are to see the commander," Yngvar said, approaching the bed. "Is there anyone to help you stand?"

"The healer said the commander will come here. I don't know where he has gone now. Perhaps to fetch him."

Yngvar lowered his head, then sat on the bed beside his friend. He clasped his hands together.

"Are you still pissing blood?"

Alasdair smiled. "The healer said that will continue. I will be weak a long while yet. But he feeds me a foul, thin broth three times a day. He says it will help me heal and rebuild my strength. I am allowed a strange-flavored bread and something called rice. Have you heard of rice, lord?"

Yngvar shook his head, and looked aside. "You mustn't call me lord. I am no longer worthy of the title."

Alasdair sighed. "Please do not apologize again. If you would please me, then remain my lord. I cannot have purpose in this life if I cannot serve."

"Your service is worth more than what I have given in return for it. I nearly killed you."

"It was an accident, lord. I threatened you first. When I was a boy, my father warned whenever I drew a blade, I should be prepared to either kill with it or find it in my own belly. Otherwise, keep it sheathed. Now I know all too well what he warned me of."

"I cannot forgive myself," Yngvar said, feeling his cheeks grow hot. "I was mad with gold-lust."

"But I have forgiven you," Alasdair said, smiling. "God sees your repentance and forgives you as well. And your gods do not care. You should suffer this guilt no more. If you must repay me, then I command you cast off your sadness and turn your thoughts to getting us back to the north. This heat will kill me sooner than a spearhead through the ribs. And they say this is autumn. Can you believe it, lord? Such a strange land."

Yngvar's eyes stung, and he wiped at them with the back of his wrist. He nodded, sniffing.

"As you will," he said. They sat in silence until Yngvar recalled Lucas the Byzantine's story. He leaned forward, putting his hand of Alasdair's thin arm.

"I have news. I think Bjorn survived the wreck."

Alasdair's face brightened.

"Could it be true?"

He described the story of the cyclops, and Alasdair sat forward until pain caused him to wince back onto his pillow.

"Lord, killing everyone around him sounds like something Bjorn would do."

"He must have gained the shore and Prince Kalim caught him once more. He probably thought to throw his life away against the Byzantines and became overcome with battle-madness."

Yngvar and Alasdair shared a long smile. Scenes of Bjorn's fury filled Yngvar's mind.

"You don't know what happened to this one-eyed warrior after the battle?"

"Lucas did not know more, but I shall learn as much as I can. The commander is not fond of the story, so we must be careful where we ask. But if Bjorn is alive, then I will find him."

The doors at the front of the infirmary creaked open. Commander Staurakius swept inside. Two guards accompanied him along with one balding old man in the short white robes Byzantines seemed to favor. Yellow light spilled inside as they approached.

"This is the deserter," the old man said, extending his hand to Alasdair. "This other one must be his companion."

Commander Staurakius looked less impressive without his war gear. Yet he was tall and proud. His aura of command enveloped Yngvar and demanded respect. His short robes and high-laced sandals would have set Norsemen laughing, but Yngvar knew better. He had seen the commander in battle and judged him a worthy lord.

Staurakius said nothing, letting his shadow hover over Alasdair's bed. Then he licked his lips and spoke in his noble voice.

"You asked to be returned to me," he said. "Be glad it was Captain Honorius who found you, else you'd be on the slave market if you had lived at all. Honorius is a good man, and a good friend."

Yngvar and Alasdair both bowed their heads in respect. Yngvar had not even learned his savior's name. He would have to reward Honorius when he claimed his fortune one day.

"Now, the matter of your desertion." The commander clasped his wrist behind his back as he spoke. "By law you should be executed. But I am the final judge of law in this fort. You ran, but so did all my soldiers. You just ran farther than the rest."

He paused to study them. Yngvar dared no words of his own, and held his breath against his hopes.

"Nor did you abandon me and my standard. Without your aid, I would have died. Without your bravery to shame my best soldiers, no one would have returned to my side. So I am indebted to your actions on that day. This leaves me in a strange position. Most men would have been wise enough to seek me after the battle and claim their rewards. But you two are Norsemen, valorous in battle and fearsome with a sword. But distinctly lacking sense."

Yngvar gave a sheepish smile. He wanted to correct the commander. What he considered a lack of sense was his own underestimation of the value of freedom. Norsemen did not serve by coercion, no matter how worthy their lord might be.

Staurakius smiled, bouncing on the balls of his feet as if he were about to bestow a clever gift.

"In light of this, I am granting you freedom of a sorts. You are too good to serve as skirmishers. I am promoting you to a regular unit. I've not fully decided where you belong, but it should be up front with me. I need strength and bravery in my front line. And you are a keen enemy of Prince Kalim, as I understand it."

Yngvar realized the pause in the commander's speech was his prompt to express gratitude. He bowed to the commander.

"Thank you, sir. I do hate Kalim. I want to give you his head, if I can resist chopping it in half."

The commander nodded. "I would accept that snake's head in any condition you can deliver it. But he does not leave his city. One day, I will tear those walls down and burn his palace around him. You will be there for the celebration."

"It will be a happy day, sir."

Alasdair had tried to sit up, but the pain kept him flat. He coughed and expressed his own thanks.

"Now, the injured one must heal before he is any use. But you, you are ready for duty. Before midday, you will have your new unit assigned. Both of you have learned Greek well enough, but if you are to fight by my side, you must learn more. So Valgerd will continue to teach you."

The commander gave a wry smile. "Alasdair, she was most interested in your condition. When she is free of her other duties, I may send her here. That would not trouble you?"

"No, sir," Alasdair said. His face shined bright enough to light the room. Yngvar had to suppress his laughter.

"Very well, that is all for now. Rest, grow strong, and be ready to fight when I call upon you. It won't be long."

The healer lingered to give Alasdair a cursory inspection. He paused at Yngvar, examining the numerous cuts that scored his body. He shook his head when he saw the scars on his back from the whipping Erik Blood-Axe had given him.

"You are a living scar. I've heard stories of Norsemen, never thought I'd meet one, much less two. Both of you are hardier than any other I've treated."

The healer left them, laughing to himself as he stepped outside. Yngvar grinned at Alasdair.

"Valgerd will tend to you. I'm certain you will now take twice as long to heal."

Alasdair's face flushed red. "I'm hardly in a state to enjoy her company. But I will try."

Yngvar rubbed his hands together. The way ahead was clear to him.

"Our brothers are out there, Alasdair. I know it. The gods have shown me my treasure." He held up his hand to prevent protest. "I know Captain Honorius said that island and its treasures are cursed. But that is because the gods hold it in good faith to our great deeds. I will find the rest of the Wolves—Thorfast, Bjorn, even Gyna. The gods have put us with Commander Staurakius so we may take revenge on Jamil and Saleet as well as Prince Kalim. Then when all our kin are gathered and all our enemies are slain, we will sail north again as rich as kings."

Alasdair remained silent. Yngvar stared off imaging the reunion and the deck of his old ship heaped with gold coins.

"Lord?"

Yngvar turned from his vision. He expected Alasdair to dissuade him from this fantasy. Instead, his young friend smiled.

"Lord, it will be as you say. All of it. Knowing this, I have the strength to heal and fight at your side once more."

"Good." Yngvar turned back to his vision of days to come. "There will be gold and glory for us. But there will be blood first."

29

Thorfast opened his eyes. The world blurred brown and blue. His pulse throbbed in his neck and head, each beat like a hammer to an anvil. His mouth was full of coppery blood, salty water, and grit. Something roared behind him, pulling at his legs. Earthen and fishy odors filled his nose.

Where was he? Not Valhalla. No Valkyrie had carried him up from—

From where?

He closed his eyes again. They granted him nothing but smears of color, and the touch of air delivered a sting to them. Confusion upon confusion.

His hands clenched by his head. Sand gathered between his fingers. Again something pulled at his legs in time with the roaring.

Water. He was on a beach. The waves still lapped his legs, tugging at him as if eager to draw him back to his place in the sea grave. The spirits of the drowned had prepared his bed at the bottom of the ocean. Now they were jealous to find him beyond their watery grasp.

He opened his eyes again, this time not looking upon the world as it was. Instead, he looked upon the world of the night before.

Yngvar had never appeared so frail. Thorfast had refused to believe his best friend—no his true brother—had fallen so ill. But in the belly of that ship and across the rows of slaves, he and Alasdair stood as two skeletons. Their flesh had turned ashen. Their eyes were wide and haunted, set deep in shadowed sockets. Their shaved heads imparted the visage of death to their wasted bodies.

Only moments before that iron monster crashed through the hull did Yngvar show any sign of his old defiance and pride. It was as if he had recognized the moment of his death and wanted to meet it with dignity.

Now he remembered. His fists closed tighter, crushing the dirt into his palms. He gnashed his teeth and moaned deep in his throat.

They had all drowned. Yngvar and Alasdair had been shattered by the iron-headed ram. It was his last sight of them, both flung into the air only to vanish into gushing water.

Bjorn had tried to grab him, whether to save himself or to save Thorfast mattered not. The thunderous crash and force of the impact had sent them both reeling. Their chains had snapped. The deck beneath Thorfast's feet crumbled into splinters and the cold sea sucked him down.

Yet he had learned to swim, if only as a dog does. Bjorn, who had mocked him for learning the useless skill, had surely drowned with the rest. But Thorfast paddled, and though the sodden spirts of the drowned clung to the remnants of his chain, he gained the surface.

Fire and smoke surrounded him. Wood planks floated everywhere and he had flopped himself over one, exhausted. A ship burned and he drifted toward it. At first it seemed he had escaped drowning only to die in flaming wreckage. For the masts collapsed and splashed into the sea with massive gouts of steam hissing behind them. The waves slewing off the collapsing ship nearly sank him.

But the same waves drove him away from the carnage of the Arabs' defeat.

He drifted in the night, listening to the terrified screams of survivors. The night echoed with hundreds of horrified pleas.

Soon these fell to scores.

Then to dozens.

Then to handfuls.

Finally to nothing.

The gods had spared him alone. They sent him a current. His legs were like iron weights. His will was like a broken egg. In truth, if he had been brave enough, he would have slid from the floating plank and drowned.

But he feared such an ignoble death. Valhalla awaited him, and he would not lose his seat on its glorious benches for a moment of weakness.

So he floated with the current the Fates had set for him.

Sometime in the night, he caught waves driving him to the shore. Soon his feet dragged through muck, and he found himself able to stand. He staggered out of the waves until he was certain he had gone beyond their reach. Then he pitched forward in the black and closed his eyes.

Now he had awakened.

What good was survival when all he loved and all he valued had been sent to Ran's bed at the bottom of the ocean? Was his life a jest to the gods? Were they laughing at him now?

Let them laugh.

If he had been granted life, then it was for a purpose. His hour of death was set for another day. So he would stand once more. When he did, he would not fill his hands with sand. He would take up sword and shield. He would kill those who had killed his world. He would have revenge. He would have blood.

But for now, he let the waves pull at his feet and the sand run from his hands.

Then, as he lay as still as the dead with his face to the beach, a shadow slid across him.

Author's Note

~

Vikings are typically associated with the northern regions of the European world and sometimes accorded status as early colonizers of North America. However, the Vikings traveled everywhere their long-boats could carry them. They were a bold and adventurous people. The Mediterranean might not be the first place one would consider a Norseman to go a-viking. However, there is evidence of Vikings in Frankia traveling to Iberia and then to Italy as early as the 860s. There are rune stones in Sweden commemorating warriors who died in distant Langbardaland—which was the Viking name for the countries that comprised modern Italy.

Varangian mercenaries are perhaps best known as bodyguards for the Byzantine Emperor. However, more commonly these Varangian troops were Norse mercenaries who fought for Byzantium against the Arabs. Records of such Varangians go back to 936, which is several years earlier than Yngvar and his Wolves arriving in Sicily.

Sicily was an emirate at this time, ruled by the Shiite Fatimids based in Egypt. The Byzantines had ruled Sicily prior and still clung to the eastern coast, fighting Arab domination through war and fomenting revolt. The Arabs made their capitol in Palermo, which became one of the most populous cities in Europe after Constantinople and Cordoba. The Arabs also introduced rice, lemons, oranges, and sugarcane along with fantastic architecture and engineering. They left an indelible mark on the country.

Prince Kalim and his palace at Licata and Commander Staurakius and his fort at Pozzallo are both fictional. However, Prince Kalim's father ruling in Palermo was a real emir, al-Hasan ibn Ali al-Kalbi. He was the first emir of Sicily, appointed after serving the Fatimids as governor of Tunisia. He fought several decisive battles with the Byzantines and would eventually leave the emirate to his son, Ahmad. However, many more years would pass before the Byzantines were fully ejected from Sicily.

Yngvar traveled south expecting a land overflowing with wealth. Certainly, this region of the world was filled with riches. But it was also an ancient land where powerful cultures clashed for supremacy. Even a dozen Viking longboats under his command would fail against the galley ships of the Arabs and Byzantines. Here were also professional armies using technology and techniques honed throughout the centuries. A Viking raider who dreamed of razing Mediterranean cities and carrying away fortunes would have to lock shields with these forces—which were nothing like the levied armies of the frozen north.

The gods have set Yngvar on a shadowed path. He must find his way out, navigating foreign cultures and dangers. He has been granted hints at the fates of his fellow Wolves. He has been shown his reward.

Now he has to reach forward into darkness and grasp his destiny or else perish.

～

If you would like to know when my next book is released, please sign up for my new release newsletter. You can do this at my website:

http://jerryautieri.wordpress.com/

If you have enjoyed this book and would like to show your support for my writing, consider leaving a review where you purchased this book or on Goodreads, LibraryThing, and other reader sites. I need help from readers like you to get the word out about my books. If you have a moment, please share your thoughts with other readers. I appreciate it!

ALSO BY JERRY AUTIERI

Ulfrik Ormsson's Saga

Historical adventure stories set in 9th Century Europe and brimming with heroic combat. Witness the birth of a unified Norway, travel to the remote Faeroe Islands, then follow the Vikings on a siege of Paris and beyond. Walk in the footsteps of the Vikings and witness history through the eyes of Ulfrik Ormsson.

Fate's Needle

Islands in the Fog

Banners of the Northmen

Shield of Lies

The Storm God's Gift

Return of the Ravens

Sword Brothers

Grimwold and Lethos Trilogy

A sword and sorcery fantasy trilogy with a decidedly Norse flavor.

Deadman's Tide

Children of Urdis

Age of Blood

Printed in Great Britain
by Amazon